MW00720221

DEAD ENDS

DEAD ENDS

A Jack Taggart Mystery

Don Easton

DUNDURN
TORONTO

Copyright © Don Easton, 2011

All rights reserved. No part of this publication may be reproduced, stored in a retrieval system, or transmitted in any form or by any means, electronic, mechanical, photocopying, recording, or otherwise (except for brief passages for purposes of review) without the prior permission of Dundurn Press. Permission to photocopy should be requested from Access Copyright.

Editor: Shannon Whibbs
Design: Jesse Hooper
Printer: Webcom

Library and Archives Canada Cataloguing in Publication

Easton, Don
   Dead ends / Don Easton.

(A Jack Taggart mystery)
(A Castle Street mystery)
Issued also in an electronic format.
ISBN 978-1-55488-893-1

   I. Title. II. Series: Easton, Don. Jack Taggart mystery.
III. Series: Castle Street mystery

PS8609.A78D43 2011   C813'.6   C2010-907288-X

1   2   3   4   5   15   14   13   12   11

We acknowledge the support of the **Canada Council for the Arts** and the **Ontario Arts Council** for our publishing program. We also acknowledge the financial support of the **Government of Canada** through the **Canada Book Fund** and **Livres Canada Books**, and the **Government of Ontario** through the **Ontario Book Publishing Tax Credit** and the **Ontario Media Development Corporation**.

Care has been taken to trace the ownership of copyright material used in this book. The author and the publisher welcome any information enabling them to rectify any references or credits in subsequent editions.

J. Kirk Howard, President

Printed and bound in Canada.
www.dundurn.com

Dundurn	Gazelle Book Services Limited	Dundurn
3 Church Street, Suite 500	White Cross Mills	2250 Military Road
Toronto, Ontario, Canada	High Town, Lancaster, England	Tonawanda, NY
M5E 1M2	LA1 4XS	U.S.A. 14150

To those who suffer in silence ...

Chapter One

It was early afternoon when Gabriel Parsons glanced out the window of her front door. It was the last Thursday in January and although the snow that fell on Burnaby in December was gone, the weather was still cold and wet. She turned and smiled knowingly at her visitor who was putting on her shoes to leave.

Gabriel had been running a daycare out of her home for three years and she was familiar with the worried look of young mothers who were leaving their toddlers behind for the first time. Cecilia, like the others, procrastinated the closer she got to the front door. When Gabriel's husband died in a logging accident three years prior, leaving her with two children, she felt like God had forsaken her. Her son, Noah, was only ten years old at the time and Faith was one and a half.

Gabriel's frequent trips to church brought her comfort and eventually her prayers appeared to be answered, at least in a financial sense. Her two-storey house was forty years old, but relatively sound and had a full basement. At first she thought about selling, but Noah did not like the idea. Faith was too young to understand, but Noah was devastated over the loss of his dad. The home was something he still clung to, so Gabriel relented and decided to use the house to aid her financial situation.

She rented out the basement to two young men who ran a janitorial supply service. At first she was nervous about dealing with renters, but her fears were soon put to rest. They were polite, always paid the rent on time, and gave her free cleaning supplies.

Her church also brought unexpected support. Father Brown, who was retiring at the time, became a boarder and moved into a spare bedroom on the upper floor at the back of her home. He happily volunteered to babysit while Gabriel tried to find work.

Gabriel smiled as she paused to consider how the quality of her life was improving. Initially she found temporary shift-work as a short-order cook, but felt guilty using Father Brown to babysit when he refused to accept anything in return. Father Brown noted her love for children and came up with the idea of opening a daycare. It was the perfect solution.

Gabriel's thoughts returned to the present as Cecilia prepared to leave. Gabriel gestured to Cecilia's jacket and said, "It's raining. Zip up before you —" She caught herself and stopped. "I'm sorry," she added, feeling embarrassed. "I'm so used to looking after children I sometimes forget and try to mother their parents, too."

A pert grin flashed across Cecilia's mouth as she zipped up her jacket. "It's okay," she replied. "I knew as soon as I met you that you're the motherly type, which suits me fine."

Gabriel didn't reply, unsure of whether Cecilia was talking to her or simply uttering her thoughts out loud.

Cecilia took a deep breath as she looked around. The home was spotless. She gave Gabriel a warm smile and said, "When we first arrived, I commented to Emily about all the beautiful plants and bushes you have around your house. When you invited us in, I thought your home smelled cleaner than a hospital. Seeing how happy the children are ... well, I know I've found the perfect daycare."

Gabriel's home did look picturesque. Tomorrow would be different. Rolls of yellow crime-scene tape left by the police would surround the entire property.

Gabriel glanced at the crucifix hanging on the wall at the entrance to her home. For a few seconds she did not hear the rambunctious voices of the three pre-schoolers playing in the living room. Instead, she felt at peace. A friend once told her that she was kind to a fault. Gabriel didn't mind. She preferred to be that way. Her motto was: *Do good unto others and they* ... well, for Gabriel, her naïveté was about to change. Murder has a way of doing that.

"I meant to tell you," Cecilia continued, "that those pecan cookies you made were perfectly scrumptious!"

Gabriel gave a broad smile. She was forty-three years old, but had been cooking since she was a youngster. She also liked to eat what she cooked, as was evidenced by her wide girth and triple chins. "You can take some with you, if you like," she offered.

"No, thanks, I need to watch my … uh, sugar intake."

"Afraid you'll end up like me?" replied Gabriel, making a pretext of eyeing Cecilia suspiciously.

"No!" replied Cecilia abruptly. Too abruptly. "I … uh, you look good," she added, trying to sound sincere.

"Really?" replied Gabriel. Her voice was perpetually raspy, giving an impression of gruffness, but the merriment on her chubby, cherubic face said otherwise. "Its okay," she continued matter-of-factly as her smile revealed she had been teasing. "I know what I look like. I don't care. There are no men in my life now." She shrugged and glanced at the children and saying, "But there's lots of love, I can tell you that."

"I know," replied Cecilia warmly. "I could feel it as soon as we arrived."

The two women stared at each other briefly, both lost in their own thoughts.

Cecilia was the first to break the silence. "I'll be back at four-thirty to pick her up and see how she does. If everything goes okay, I'll drop her off Monday morning on my way to work."

"Everything will go okay," Gabriel assured her. "She looks darling … and is already playing with the other children. Father Brown and I will take good care of her."

A bemused smile played across Cecilia's lips as she watched Father Brown, who was sitting cross-legged on the floor amongst a pile of toys, nonchalantly allowing a four-year-old boy by the name of Jerry to use Father Brown's arm, neck, and head as a roadway for a toy car.

Cecilia's smile vanished and she appeared wistful as she turned her attention to Emily, who was playing on a plastic slide. The two boys had accepted their new playmate. There was a lot of noise as all three children enthusiastically tested the durability and limits of the plastic playhouse and toys in the room. It was a happy noise, she decided.

"You've already hugged her and said goodbye," said Gabriel softly. "Now might be a good time to slip away."

"Okay," replied Cecilia in a whisper. "You have my cellphone number ... if there is any problem ... if she doesn't behave, just —"

"Don't worry," said Gabriel, giving her a reassuring pat on her back. "Emily is in good hands."

Cecilia nodded and said, "Sorry, I know I'm worrying needlessly. It's just that she's — I've never left her alone before. She's only three."

"Worrying is what us moms do," replied Gabriel. "You never get over it, no matter how old they get."

Cecilia nodded and, after glancing at Emily one more time, she left.

Gabriel was pleased to be getting another child to babysit. Ostensibly she did it for the money, but even if she was rich, she would still want to do it. Before her husband died, they had talked about having at least six children. Now Noah was thirteen years old and occupied with school. Today, Faith remained in bed, complaining of a sore throat, but at four years of age, she would soon be in school as well.

Gabriel sighed as she thought about it. Some days she wished her children could have remained toddlers.

Her thoughts were interrupted when Jerry shrieked in protest as Father Brown picked up a toy tiger. The toy was for everyone, but Jerry was possessive. His shriek gave way to giggles as Father Brown pretended to attack him with the tiger.

Father Brown was a tall, thin man with a horse-shoe pattern of grey hair on his head. He never cared for bifocals and instead tended to wear reading glasses that sat low on the bridge of his nose while his eyes peered out from above. His eyes tended to be watery, but twinkled with delight at Jerry's giggles.

"Okay, Father Brown," said Gabriel, in mock admonishment, "remember to share the toys with the other children."

He raised his eyes in her direction and smiled, before relinquishing the toy to Jerry who retreated with it to a playhouse.

Emily, who had been watching Father Brown, approached him and with one finger, pointed at a grape-sized red birthmark on the center of Father Brown's forehead.

"Boo-boo," said Emily, softly.

"Not a boo-boo," replied Father Brown. "It's an angel's kiss," he said lightly.

Emily stared intently for a moment before leaning forward and kissing Father Brown on his forehead.

"Better now," she said matter-of-factly, before turning her attention back to the plastic slide.

Her unexpected kiss caused Father Brown to lean back abruptly. He looked up at Gabriel and said, "The new member of the flock isn't shy, is she?"

"You have a way with children," replied Gabriel.

"Apparently I do," he said. A smile flittered across his face, but he became sombre as he reflected on an incident from the previous night.

"Something wrong, Father?" asked Gabriel.

Father Brown frowned. "I have a way with children, but these children are not lost souls. If only I could find a way with the new arrivals God is sending our way. The ones who keep taking up residence in our back-yard," he lamented.

"Again?" asked Gabriel.

Two months ago a nearby liquor store opened for business at eight-thirty in the morning. Their clientele consisted of the down and out. People who had given up all hope and used the bottle to obliterate their thoughts. They tended to frequent an empty lot not far from Gabriel's house, but in the wet weather, some had taken to seeking refuge under a grove of large cedar trees in her back yard.

"You weren't woken last night?" asked Father Brown.

Gabriel shook her head and said, "I thought that yard light you put up would stop them."

Father Brown shrugged and said, "I think it is helping, but not everyone cares if the world sees them. An unfortunate soul stumbled into the garbage cans after you went to bed. I feared he would wake the whole neighbourhood up. I went out and asked him to leave. He did."

"I'm sorry," said Gabriel.

"You have nothing to apologize for."

"Maybe we should be calling the police."

"Incarceration isn't the answer. Give me time. I'm still working on the proposal to gather support for a new shelter. Besides, I was awake, reading the scripture." He paused for a moment, gave a small grin, and added, "However, it would not be good for business if a mom came by with her precious one and saw a man passed out in your yard."

Gabriel looked heavenward and replied, "I don't even want to imagine what that would do for business."

"Mommy," cried Faith from her room.

Gabriel glanced at Father Brown. "Go," he said, "I'll attend the flock."

Gabriel walked into Faith's room and saw her stumble while getting out of bed.

"You not awake yet, sweetie," said Gabriel.

"My neck hurts," whimpered Faith, rubbing her neck.

Gabriel sat on the bed and placed Faith on her lap. She felt her neck and detected a lump. "You had your mumps vaccination last week," said Gabriel. "Maybe you're having a small reaction. How about you come out and play with the others? There's a new little girl here to play with. Her name is Emily. I'll give you all some ice cream."

It was eleven o'clock at night and Father Brown reached to turn his bedroom light out when he heard the sound of breaking glass arise from the back of the house. He peered out the back window and saw an arc of light shine out from the basement door. The breaking glass had come from the renters in the basement. He was about to return to the comfort of his bed when he saw a man stagger out from under the cedar tree closest to the house. The man stood for a moment, looking about, before heading to a cedar tree that was farther away.

Father Brown muttered to himself as he put on his slippers and wrapped a bathrobe over his flannel pajamas before going outside. He passed by the cement steps leading down below ground level to the basement door. The door was wide open and Father Brown could hear the heated voice of one of the renters admonishing the other one for being clumsy. A portable fan was humming away at the door in an effort to clear a strong acidic odour.

Father Brown realized it was the fumes that had aroused the derelict and caused him to retreat to the tree farthest away. He was now sitting on the ground with his back against the trunk of the tree. He stared drunkenly up as Father Brown approached.

Father Brown took in a deep breath and slowly exhaled. He gave the derelict a friendly smile before crouching down to talk to him face to face. He wondered briefly if the acidic smell emitting from the basement could be any worse than the putrid smell of stale wine coming from the man's breath.

"Sir, we run a daycare here … young children. Your presence could frighten them. I'm afraid I have to ask you to leave."

The man stared silently for several seconds as his brain slowly processed the data. Eventually he mumbled something and stood, swaying on his feet. He stared at Father Brown for longer than was polite, as was the way of inebriated people.

Father Brown gently guided the man down the driveway to the back lane, but stopped as headlights appeared at one end of the alley.

"It's slowing down and parking," noted Father Brown. "It's safe for you to go. God be with you." He let go of the man's arm and watched as the man turned toward the lane.

As Father Brown walked back to the house, voices and shadows from the basement caught his attention. The voices were not loud, but someone was angry.

"You fuckin' idiot," seethed a voice. "We'll never get it done in time."

"It wasn't like I did it on purpose," replied the other renter. "Cocktail is supposed to drop by. Let's see what he says."

"Cocktail will be pissed at us for cooking outside the room. He won't help. More likely he will rat us out. What do you think the bikers will say when we only deliver half the meth? They'll kick our asses!"

Father Brown let out a small gasp. *Did he say meth? Lord no* — He stepped onto the lawn, knowing his footsteps would not be heard as he crept up to the basement stairwell. The yard light illuminated him from behind, so he crouched down to minimize his shadow on the house, while straining to listen over the noise of the fan. He knew he could scoot away unseen around the side of the house if either renter approached the basement door.

"Calm down. It was an accident," a voice from the basement pleaded.

"Calm down! Fuck you, calm down."

"It was me who dropped it."

"You think Satans Wrath will understand? They'll kick the shit out of us. We'll be lucky if we don't end up like Harvey."

Father Brown sadly realized his fears were true. *Gabriel will be upset, but the police will have to be —*

His thoughts were interrupted when he saw a shadow loom large on the back of the house in front of him. He spun on his heels and stared wide-eyed at the silhouette of a man who stood over him. The man was holding a cement construction brick high in the air with both hands.

Time slowed down for Father Brown. His jaw slackened and his mouth hung open in fear. He locked eyes with the man for what seemed like an eternity, but remained silently transfixed, as if resigned to his fate. He saw the first downward arc of the brick and his brain registered the sound of crunching bone.

Seconds later, Father Brown's body, now prone on the grass, received six more blows to the head. The brick dispensed a rivulet of blood up the perpetrator's chest and face with each upward motion. Other arcs of blood splashed high onto the back of the house. Upon impact the brick sprayed more blood in all directions.

The added blows were not necessary. Father Brown was dead from the first blow before his body even crumpled to the grass.

It was what happened to Father Brown's body next that revealed the real danger to Gabriel, Noah, and Faith as they slept upstairs in their beds.

Chapter Two

It was nine o'clock in the morning when Corporal Connie Crane, from the Integrated Homicide Investigation Team, arrived at Gabriel's home and parked. She was the first member of I-HIT to arrive, but six uniformed Royal Canadian Mounted Police officers were at the house.

As Connie stepped from her car, a young woman started her car and pulled out with tires screeching, causing Connie to step back.

"Hey!" yelled Connie. "Did you see that?" she asked, turning to a Mountie who was standing near the front gate.

"I saw," replied the Mountie, "but under the circumstances, I —"

"She even had a little kid in the car," interrupted Connie.

"Yeah, I know," he replied. "Her kid was one of the kids in the daycare here," he added, gesturing with his thumb toward the house. "You're Connie Crane from I-HIT, right?"

"We've met?" asked Connie. Her anger dissolved when she understood the young woman's instinct to protect her child and leave in haste.

"Didn't meet," continued the Mountie, "but I saw you at a murder of some guy in Coquitlam River Park last year. As I recall, you had a partner by the name of Dallas. A blood-splatter expert. You'll need him here."

"He's on his way. Sorry, I didn't recognize you."

"We all look alike in uniform," he smiled. "My boss is out back. He can fill you in."

Connie went to the back of the property and recognized a sergeant sitting in a patrol car in the rear alley. He motioned for her to join him.

"Hi, Bert. What have we got?" asked Connie, as her eyes scanned the lane. She was glad to see that yellow crime-scene tape had already cordoned off the alley.

"What do you mean … we?" smiled Bert. "This one is a homicide for you."

"You seem definite."

"You could try to write it off as suicide, but it won't be easy," said Bert, with a hint of sarcasm. "Bludgeon your brains out in the back yard with a concrete brick, after which you drag yourself down a set of stairs into a basement suite and lock the door behind you. Oh, yeah, the brick is also in the basement."

"Guess we — I can rule out suicide," replied Connie.

"Where are the rest of the troops?" asked Bert. "Thought they would be here by now."

"They'll be tied up for another couple of hours. There was another gang hit this morning."

"Another goddamned gang hit? I didn't even hear about it."

"Too many now to get much news coverage," replied Connie. "So in the mean time, what can you tell me about this vic?" asked, Connie, with a nod toward the house."

"No gang member, that's for sure. A retired priest. Living —"

"A retired priest?" reiterated Connie, unconsciously fondling the gold crucifix dangling from her neck inside her blouse.

"Yeah. He was rooming and boarding here. The owner, Gabriel Parsons, is a widow and lives here with her two children. She also runs a small daycare out of the house. Only three or four kids at a time. I talked to her briefly, but decided to leave the real interview to you."

"How did the call come in?"

"Gabriel said she was taking the garbage out at about seven-thirty and the first thing she noticed was a missing concrete brick out of the row of bricks lining her driveway. She turned and saw the sprays of blood up the back of her house. She dropped the garbage and headed back to her house. Along the way she saw the pool of blood and brain matter beside the base-ment stairwell. She ran back in the house and knocked on Father Brown's door to tell him. When he didn't answer she called 911. First member on the scene tried a key that Gabriel gave him for the basement door, but the lock had been changed. He kicked open the door and saw the body inside with a pulverized head. He didn't go in, so your crime scene is intact."

"Positive it's the priest?" asked Connie.

"Wearing pajamas and a blue silk bathrobe with a dragon. Gabriel said it was his."

"Did Gabriel look at the body? What was her response?"

"No. She waited at the top of the stairs. Started crying and broke into hysterics when she realized who the vic was. She's not crying now ... probably gone into shock."

"What prompted the priest to go outside dressed like that?" mused Connie.

"Gabriel said they've had a problem with winos sleeping under the cedars in her yard. Father Brown used to roust them on occasion."

"You thinking it was robbery? Doesn't make sense if he was wearing a bathrobe."

"I've got more. Gabriel rented the basement out about a year and a half ago to a guy who owns a janitorial company. She copied down his driver's license. The name given was a Bob Rimmer. I checked it out. The name, address, and driver's license number are all bogus."

"Son of a bitch."

"Gabriel says Rimmer ... or whoever he is, wasn't around much. He told her he owned the company, but two other guys by the names of Joe and John were the ones who were always coming and going. She never knew their last names, but thinks she could identify them. Joe is around thirty, slim, with short red hair. John is a little younger, muscular build, and a shaved head. She barely remembers Rimmer, but, as she recalls, he was around forty with collar-length dark hair. She says everyone tended to work nights and she seldom saw them."

"Joe and John gotta be bogus, as well. No matter, we should be able to get prints."

"That could be a problem. The place reeks of bleach. I think it's been wiped down. Whoever the renters were, they don't want to be found."

"Wonderful," muttered Connie.

"Maybe outstanding warrants on them," offered Bert.

"Could be. Maybe the priest found out and they whacked him."

"Possible," agreed Bert. "We didn't go in, but from what we did see, it looks like the basement suite has been cleaned out.

"Vehicles?"

"Joe and John drove a plain white van. No company logo. She can't remember what Rimmer drove. Guess he usually parked in the alley someplace."

"Figures," muttered Connie.

"There is one thing. They might be bikers, or maybe associated to bikers."

"They look like bikers?"

"No. She said the three of them looked real straight, but when they were first moving in, some biker-looking guy on a hog pulled into the yard. Gabriel said she heard Rimmer tell him in no uncertain terms to leave and never bring the bike around here again."

"Did she ask Rimmer why?"

"She presumed he knew the noise would bother the neighbours."

"Where's Gabriel?"

"Inside waiting for the last mom to arrive and take the remaining daycare kid away."

"I'll need a statement from her. You said she is in shock. Do you think she is up to —"

"I don't know. I guess she's holding it together. I think she has to for the moment. Besides still baby-sitting, she's got her own kids in the house. A four-year-old girl and a thirteen-year-old boy that she kept home from school."

"This has gotta be tough on her."

"At least she didn't see the body."

How about the pool of blood, bone, and brain matter on the lawn? She won't forget about that. Holding it together ... for how long? Still in shock — wait 'til it sinks in.

"You know any members that have a handle on the biker situation?" asked Bert.

Connie stared briefly at Bert as she collected her thoughts before lolling her head back and rolling her eyes. "Oh, crap," she whispered aloud. "That would be Jack."

Corporal Jack Taggart worked in and Intelligence Unit of the Royal Canadian Mounted Police in Vancouver. The unit specialized in organized crime. Jack knew a lot about bikers and in particular, Satans Wrath, who were world-renowned for having clawed their way to the upper echelon of organized crime families on the planet.

Connie Crane had past murder investigations where Jack, uninvited and against Connie's objections, had interfered. The problem, in Connie's opinion, was that Jack took certain investigations too personally. *Mind you, some were personal,* thought Connie, as she reflected back. *Bad guys with any smarts should have known better than to mess with a cop's family ... especially Jack's. Guess the ones who did were not smart. Not smart enough to know they would end up being corpses.*

Connie could understand bending the rules when bad guys crossed certain barriers, but with Jack, there was more to it. Both Jack and his partner, Constable Laura Secord, had received special training as undercover operatives. They were considered two of the best operatives in the RCMP. Connie had never worked undercover, but she had learned a little about Jack's personality from past investigations. She also knew Laura, and saw her personality change when she was assigned as Jack's partner.

What the brass did not seem to understand, Connie had decided, was that the real undercover training took place on the street. A place where survival becomes much more personal and where your methods of survival become more honed and deadly the longer you do the work. Jack had been surviving for a long, long time. The same couldn't be said for those he worked on. Many ended up in the morgue rather than court. Some said Jack's involvement was only coincidental to the growing body count. Connie knew better.

Connie thought about some of her past cases with Jack. *Some criminals became his informants ... or had they become his friends? Some good guys we thought were friends had become criminals. Through it all, Jack continues to weave and twist his way in pursuit of justice. His justice ... which has no resemblance to the law he was sworn to uphold.*

"You okay?" asked Bert. "Who's Jack?"

Connie slowly shook her head in response and sighed as she reached for her BlackBerry. *Past investigations with Jack saw me investigating more murders than I started with. God, I hope this time will be different ... I wonder if he is religious?*

Corporal Jack Taggart leaned back in his office chair as he talked on his BlackBerry to a friend. His desk and Constable Laura Secord's desk butted up to one other in an office designed for one desk and one filing cabinet. They had a dozen filing cabinets.

Jack's friend was a woman by the name of Ngọc Bích. She was brought to Canada by a smuggling ring on the pretext of working in the hotel industry. Upon arrival she was forced into prostitution. Jack had befriended her and convinced her to give evidence. Now Ngọc Bích was a nanny to another friend of Jack's. She was also taking music and learning to play the flute.

Many of the perpetrators associated to the smuggling ring had either been convicted or were dead.

Two Vietnamese brothers, both considered ringleaders, were still free, pending trial.

Ngọc Bích explained to Jack that she had shown up for court at ten o'clock, but the two accused didn't appear and the witnesses were excused. Warrants were issued, but Ngọc Bích later heard from the prosecutor who said that after the witnesses left, the defence lawyer appeared before the judge to say he had spoken with his clients and learned they had made a mistake and thought the court case was scheduled for the afternoon. The warrants were quashed and a new trial would be scheduled at a later date.

"I didn't sleep last night," lamented Ngọc Bích. "I really wanted this to be over. To see their faces when they are sent to jail for what they did to me and the others."

"I know. Me, too," said Jack. "I wish I could have been there with you, but I don't want the bad guys to see me and realize who I really am."

"I understand," said Ngọc Bích. "It's okay. I'm not alone. Another woman is testifying, too. She is also angry that the trial did not go ahead. I guess we'll have to wait a little while —"

"Hang on a second," said Jack as the phone on his desk rang. Laura took the call and as he wrapped up his conversation with Ngọc Bích, he could overhear Laura's cheery voice.

"No, I think Jack's an atheist," said Laura. "Me? I'm undecided. If I say I'm an atheist I'm afraid I'll never get any holidays ... hang on, Connie ... Jack, you still an atheist?" asked Laura as Jack put his BlackBerry away.

"Yes, God made me one," replied Jack.

"Yup, a heathen through and through," replied Laura into the phone. She paused and added, "Why is that a relief? ... Oh, you're kidding. Better speak to Jack. He knows more about them than I do."

Jack listened quietly as Connie quickly told him what she knew about the murder.

"Offhand," replied Jack. "I'm not aware of any full-patch members of Satans Wrath who operate a janitorial service, but I wouldn't be surprised. It would suit their MO to have such a company. They would use associates who don't have criminal records. Especially if they could get contracts in sensitive areas."

"Like police stations," suggested Connie.

"Or Motor Vehicle Branches, airports, Social Services ... any place to help them gather intelligence or gain entry to secure areas."

"You're thinking associates without records — so people you won't have photos of."

"I didn't say that," said Jack, chuckling. "I've got about a thousand pictures stored in a laptop. I've never been shy about keeping files on people who are even remotely connected."

"That would be you," said Connie. "Civil liberties be damned."

"You want photos but are accusing me of breaching civil liberties?" replied Jack, quietly.

Connie was silent for a moment, before saying, "Sorry. I didn't really mean that. It just came out. Guess I have a bit of an attitude with how you do things."

"With how I do things? What would ever prompt you to —"

"Yeah, yeah. Don't even start."

"Start what?"

"Well, I could go down a list, but I've seen and heard your act before."

"My act?"

"Yeah. The old show surprise, act concerned, deny, deny, deny routine."

Jack grinned to himself, but didn't respond.

"Don't know how some people can be so gullible around you. You better pray I never get transferred to Internal. I'd nail your ass in a minute."

"I don't pray. I'm an atheist, remember?"

"Good. Means you can be objective about this one."

"Can't say I'm partial to people who murder our senior citizens …"

"Jack —"

"I'm teasing. Do you want me to meet you at your office and show Gabriel the pictures?"

"She's running a daycare, plus she has her own two children. One of them is a little girl who is sick in bed. Could you could bring the pictures over here?"

"We'll be there in twenty minutes," replied Jack. "But to make it clear," he said, giving a wink to Laura, "it is you, the renowned Corporal Connie Crane who is asking Laura and I to assist. You are not going to accuse us of butting in? You're really asking … well, I'd say … begging for our help?"

"Just bring the goddamned pictures," replied Connie gruffly. Her brusque tone was not genuine and she smiled when she hung up. *At least this is one case that's not personal for him ...*

When Connie realized she had started to fondle the crucifix around her neck again, it gave her cause to remind herself to retain her own objectivity and professionalism. Her thoughts returned to the case. *What degenerate monster would murder a defenceless old man? A retired priest yet ... whoever you are, rest assured, I will track you down, you son of a bitch!*

"You okay?" asked Bert.

"Oh, yeah," replied Connie, with determination. "I'm on top of my game with this one," she added, while opening the car door.

"You going inside for a look?"

Connie paused to read an incoming text on her BlackBerry from the Forensic Identification Section. She looked at Bert and said, "That was FIS. They'll be here in thirty minutes. I'm going to take a look at what we've got. Send them my way when they arrive."

Connie stopped near the top of the stairs leading to the basement and stared at the dark stain in the lawn and the blood splatters on the back of the house. A large pinkish puddle had collected on the cement pad in front of the basement door. *Odd ... the murder took place outside ... should be a bloody trail leading down the steps to where the body was dragged to get it out of sight ...* The smell of bleach reached her nose to answer her question. *Bastards! They poured bleach on the steps on their way out to obliterate any footprints that would normally have been left in the blood. Whoever did this is calculating ... not the type to panic. Professional ...*

Connie's thoughts were about collecting physical evidence and figuring out what happened. She was wrong in her belief that the basement had been rented to a couple of men who were janitors. The idea of tripping a booby trap with a bomb never crossed her mind as she pushed open the basement door and stepped inside.

Chapter Three

Jack and Laura arrived at Gabriel's house as Gabriel stood on the sidewalk, apologizing to a mother who was strapping her child into a car seat.

Jack and Laura spoke to a uniformed Mountie who told them that Connie was around back and had gone into the basement suite. Jack watched Gabriel say goodbye and stood waiting to meet her. By the frightened look on the mother's face, Jack had little doubt that she would never bring her child back again.

Gabriel did not look frightened. Her eyes were puffy with streaks of mascara on her cheeks and blotchy red patches on her face and neck. She was too grief-stricken to be afraid. When she started to return to the house, Jack and Laura introduced themselves.

"We would like you to look at some pictures for us," said Laura, gesturing to the laptop she was holding.

"We are sorry to have to ask you to do this now, but time could be of the essence."

Gabriel turned as a young girl wearing pajamas came out the front door and stood at the top of the steps. "Faith! Go back in the house," yelled Gabriel.

"I want to see," wined Faith.

"No —" Gabriel stopped as Noah came out and put his arm around Faith's shoulders to guide her back into the house.

Faith protested, but gave in to her big brother and both children disappeared inside.

"I'm sorry," said Gabriel, turning back to Jack. "Could we do this at my kitchen table?"

"That would work better," said Jack. "Give us a couple of minutes to talk with one of the investigators and we'll be right in."

"I can't believe this happened," said Gabriel tearfully as they walked toward the house. "They seemed like such nice men."

"They told you they were janitors?" questioned Jack.

"Well, sort of," she replied, while heading up the steps. "They were more to do with supplying the right chemicals to other janitorial services who did the actual cleaning."

"I'll talk to you later. I need to talk to the lead investigator immediately," replied Jack abruptly as he turned and headed toward the rear of the house. Laura excused herself to Gabriel and hurried to keep up with him.

"Don't like the sound of that," muttered Jack.

"The chemical bit?" asked Laura. "You're thinking — not in a daycare! They wouldn't!"

Jack pointed to a row of rhododendron bushes planted alongside the house. They looked healthy, except for two plants in the center with leaves that were blackened and curled as if burned. "Look at that," said Jack. "They would and they did."

"I don't believe it," said Laura. "Maybe —"

"Connie!" screamed Jack, breaking into a run. "Anybody in the basement, don't move!" He rounded the corner to the backyard within seconds.

"Hi, Jack," said Connie, peering out from the basement door. "What the hell are you yelling about?"

"You don't smell anything in there?" asked Jack, looking down at her from the top of the basement stairs.

"Careful you don't step on anything," cautioned Connie. She looked puzzled and said, "Smell anything? Well, yeah. The whole place stinks of bleach or something. The assholes used it to obliterate their tracks. Noticed it when I first came in, but most of the smell is gone now."

"Like hell the smell is gone," replied Jack. "The fumes erase your sense of smell. Not to mention, killing plants."

"I don't understand. Why were you yelling at me not to move?"

"Connie, you're standing in a bloody meth lab," replied Jack. "I'm sure of it. If not meth, then something else as bad. A lot of these places are booby-trapped."

"Booby-traps? ... Christ, I don't think so. I've already been through it. The place has been cleaned out. But it is bloody, I'll say that much. You can come in and see ... but be careful."

"If *I'm* careful," replied Jack. He turned to Laura and said, "Wait out here."

"You don't have to convince me," she replied.

The smell of chemicals assaulted Jack's nostrils as soon as he entered. Within seconds he couldn't smell anything as his sensory organs became temporarily incapacitated. He looked at the diluted trail of blood leading to the prone figure on the floor. The victim's face had been literally pulverized. His silk bathrobe was halfway up his chest from being dragged inside by the ankles. A gold crucifix on a chain from his neck was resting on the floor above his head, with the chain held in place by his chin and ears.

"Wearing a bathrobe?" questioned Jack.

"They had trouble with winos sleeping under the trees in their backyard at night. Maybe he heard something and went out thinking he was rousting a wino and caught these guys instead."

"I'd say they caught him," replied Jack. "Nothing left of his face. Whoever did him must have a hell of a temper."

"The perp had to be doused in blood," commented Connie. "I'm not the blood-splatter expert, but if you noticed the splashes up the back of the house, I bet he was whacked at least half a dozen times." She gestured to a cement construction brick lying in a puddle of bleach nearby and added, "It was nice of them to leave the murder weapon behind."

"Wasn't so nice that they poured bleach over it afterward," noted Jack. "Anything in here to give us a clue who they were?"

"Not that I could see, but take a look and be my guest," replied Connie.

"A quick look," replied Jack. "We shouldn't be poking around in here without wearing hazmat suits. Let's make this quick and get out."

Jack saw a clean, square patch on the outside of a door leading to a separate room. Connie saw what he was looking at and said, "I told you they cleaned it out. Looks like they must have had a list or a picture or something on the door."

Inside the room were several wooden benches and shelves, all with chemical stains and circular burn marks where bottles had dripped. Jack saw where acidic fumes had blackened some of the walls and ceiling. High on one wall a small exhaust fan had been left with its frame screwed into the wall. The fan was blackened with a dark film of dirt and covered a fist-sized circular hole leading to the outside. Toxic fumes had burned the rhododendrons outside.

"I was right," said Jack. "This was their kitchen."

"Kitchen?" replied Connie.

"Not for making pasta," replied Jack, slowly gazing around the room. A small eyehole screw mounted in the corner of the room close to the ceiling caught his attention. His gaze followed the same height to a similar screw stuck in the wall above the door jamb. "You see that?" asked Jack.

"Couple of screws?" asked Connie.

Jack examined the top of the door and pointed to several small holes in the wood. "They had a switch mounted here," he said.

"What are you talking about?"

"Trip wire," replied Jack. This place was booby-trapped. Pretty common with labs. Nasty surprise for anyone wanting to rip the place off."

"What about cops?" replied Connie angrily. "I'd have walked right into it."

"Don't think they care about cops, either ... or nosy neighbours, for that matter. Some of these idiots don't realize they would get more time in jail for setting a booby trap than they do for the lab itself. Lucky for you they decided to take their stuff with them. Let's get out of here. The fumes are really carcinogenic."

"What's the proper procedure now?" asked Connie.

"Drug Section has specially trained members to dismantle clandestine labs under the direction of a chemist. This has already been dismantled so I would call in a Health Inspector who will cordon off the building. The place may only need a really good cleaning or it could require renovations. As far as Forensics go, see what the Health Inspector says, but you may need to tell them to wear hazmat suits, as well."

"What about the idiots making it? Don't the bad guys —"

"Some take precautions or wear masks, but that is a far cry from the proper protection of a hazmat suit. If

they stay at it, they end up with brains the size of wal-
nuts or blow themselves up before they die of cancer."

Connie nodded, but stopped to stare at Father
Brown's body. A ray of sunlight broke through the
clouds and glistened off the crucifix in sharp contrast
to the pool of blood.

"You Catholic?" asked Jack.

Connie nodded.

"Think maybe you should turn the investigation
over to someone who isn't?"

"Why?"

"If it goes to court the defence will say that because
of your belief you weren't objective in the investigation
and claim you framed whoever did this out of blind
rage."

"I may feel rage at what took place, but I'm not
blind. I'm seeing this through to the end."

Jack shrugged in response.

On their way up the outside steps, Connie gave
Jack a sideways glance and said, "I can't believe that
you, of all people, would be trying to slam me on
objectivity."

"I wasn't slamming you. Simply saying what the
defence will do."

"Well?" interrupted Laura, looking questioningly
at Jack as he and Connie stepped outside.

"Clandestine lab," said Jack.

Laura glanced at the upper portion of the house
before briefly closing her eyes and taking a deep breath.

Connie realized what Laura was thinking and she
turned to Jack to ask a question that she feared she

already knew the answer to. "You said carcinogenic ... what about the people who live upstairs?"

"Who knows," replied Jack. "For them it will be like living with a ticking time bomb. Never knowing if ... or when it will kill you. The bad guys used an exhaust fan ... maybe the people upstairs are okay ... maybe not. Everyone who has spent any amount of time in the place should get checked out."

"She was running a daycare," said Connie quietly.

"I know," replied Jack.

"Kids ... babies," said Laura, "everyone will have to keep checking to make sure they don't —" she stopped, choosing instead to bite her lip to maintain control of her emotions.

Unlike Laura, Connie's sorrow and fear was replaced with anger. "These sons of bitches killed a priest," she said vehemently. "They had the place booby trapped ... meth lab in a daycare ... they don't give a fuck about anything or anyone." She unconsciously clenched her fist as she stared at Jack. "I want these guys. I want them behind bars for the rest of their lives."

"You and me both," said Jack sombrely. "We'll meet with Gabriel and show her the pictures. Maybe we'll get lucky."

All three of them stared up at the house and took a moment to regain control of their emotions. Connie was the first to talk. "I'm told Gabriel is distraught and in shock," she cautioned. "Time is of the essence. I want her to be able to focus right now, so don't tell her about the cancer stuff. When you're done, I'll take a statement from her, after which I'll tell her to go to the doctor. The sooner we can find these guys the better."

Jack sighed and said, "Okay, the ugly part of introducing her to her future nightmares will be left to you."

"Along with contacting all the parents who brought their children here," added Laura.

Connie nodded in agreement and said, "The pictures might be our best bet. Got a feeling that Forensics will be a dead end. I'd like to get these assholes before they've destroyed any more evidence. With the amount of blood the actual killer would have on him, even if he showers, we might still find trace amounts under his nails or up his nose and in his ears ... providing we get him soon."

"We'll let you know in about an hour," replied Jack.

Jack and Laura spent the next forty-five minutes sitting with Gabriel at her kitchen table while Jack presented a slide show on his laptop of all the bikers he knew in British Columbia, along with their friends and associates.

During this time, Noah sat in the living room while Faith, not understanding what had happened, was content to lie under a blanket on the sofa and snooze.

"I'm sorry," said Gabriel, when the slide show ended. "I don't think any of these people are them." She wiped her eyes again, barely controlling her tears as she had during the entire process. Jack knew that her grief over Father Brown was genuine and her inability to help added to her grief.

"The men who were in my basement looked nice," sniffled Gabriel. "They didn't look dirty or have long hair and beards like most of the people in these pictures."

Jack nodded that he understood.

Gabriel leaned back in her chair, extending her arms by her side, and said, "I still don't understand. Father Brown was a beautiful person. He would read bedtime stories to Faith, help Noah with his homework. Babysit.... He went out of his way to help complete strangers. He didn't have money ... so why? Why would anyone commit such an ungodly act?"

"We'll do our best to find out who did it and why," replied Jack.

"Maybe it wasn't the people downstairs. Maybe it was one of those drunken men who keep coming to my yard. Some use very bad language and —"

"Everything has been cleaned out of the basement," said Jack. "Also the door was locked and Father Brown is inside."

Gabriel stared blankly at Jack. When her mind accepted his reasoning, she focused on another matter. "There's blood out on the lawn and the house. I'll need to clean it," she said, placing her elbows on the table and covering her face with her hands.

"Try not to think about that," said Jack, feeling lame. *How can she not think of it?* "You're going to need some emotional support. I'll put you in touch with Victim Services. They will help you. Is there a place ... relatives, somewhere you could stay for a few days?"

"I have a sister in North Van. She has a house ... but she's married ... children. I don't want to impose ..."

"Under the circumstances you should stay with her. You're still in shock. It's difficult to think clearly. You need to do what is best for you and your children."

Gabriel didn't respond. The silence was broken when Noah and Faith came in and Faith tugged on Gabriel's sleeve. "Mommy, my throat hurts," she whined, before coughing.

Gabriel lifted her onto her lap and looked at Jack and said, "She had the mumps vaccination last week and has a bit of a lump on her neck. Likely a small reaction."

Jack caught the look on Laura's face. He knew her concern was the same as his. She said, "Jack, why don't you call Natasha and ask her if that type of reaction is normal?"

"Natasha?" asked Gabriel.

"My wife is a doctor," explained Jack, getting up from his chair. He walked into the living room and called Natasha on his BlackBerry. He knew the reaction wasn't normal, but hoped he was wrong. Natasha confirmed that he wasn't.

"Can I look at the pictures?" asked Noah as soon as Jack returned to the kitchen.

"Sure," replied Jack. "Push this button each time you want to advance."

"I know how to use a computer," said Noah. "Are all these really bad guys?"

"Some are and some might be their friends," replied Jack.

"But if you're friends of a bad guy then aren't you a bad guy, too?" asked Noah.

"You don't always know who the bad guys are," replied Jack, glancing at Faith curled up on Gabriel's lap.

Gabriel stroked Faith's hair with her hand and asked, "Were you able to talk with your wife? What did she say?"

"Um ... she said that type of reaction is not normal and that you should have her checked out right away. It could be a lot of things."

"Like what?" asked Gabriel, her face revealing her worry.

"She, uh, didn't really elaborate. How long has she been sick?"

"Only a few days."

"Anybody else sick in the house?" asked Jack.

"No, thank the Lord," replied Gabriel.

"Jack," said Laura, "I don't think we should wait for Connie to take a statement if Natasha said —"

Jack put up his hand, signalling for Laura to stop and turned to Gabriel and said, "Does Faith have her own bedroom?"

"Yes," replied Gabriel, sounding puzzled.

"I would like to see it," replied Jack. "Would you mind?"

"I haven't cleaned it," replied Gabriel. "With her being sick ... the bed isn't made."

"That's okay," replied Jack. "We're not with *Good Housekeeping*."

"Okay ... I'll show you," replied Gabriel. She carried Faith down the hall as Jack and Laura followed. As they reached the bedroom door Gabriel asked, "What are you looking for?"

"Examining if Faith could be sick from an environmental cause," replied Jack.

"I told you I hadn't cleaned for a few days," responded Gabriel nervously, "but I am sure that my housekeeping is not such as to make anyone sick. If you are thinking ..."

"From what I can see, your home is impeccable," replied Jack, entering the bedroom. "I'm more concerned with fumes coming up from the basement."

"Oh, that," said Gabriel, sounding relieved. "I'm used to it and don't smell it anymore. What you're smelling is cleaning fluids that the men downstairs sometimes mix up for different cleaning solutions. They told me that different types of floors and rugs require different types of cleaning agents."

Jack spotted a discoloration on the wallpaper alongside Faith's bed. He got on his knees and looked under the bed. What he saw made him want to retch. It was a cold-air return vent coming up from the basement. He was conscious of Laura getting down on her knees and looking. Their eyes met and he saw her mouth drop open in shock as their eyes met.

"I found him!" yelled Noah, from the kitchen. "This is one of them!"

The excitement of Noah's discovery caused Jack and Laura to temporarily suspend their thoughts on the cold-air return. Seconds later, everyone huddled around Noah at the kitchen table as he proudly pointed to a picture.

"See?" said Noah, pointing at the picture with his finger. "That's Joe."

"Oh, no, honey," said Gabriel, while ruffling Noah's hair. "Joe doesn't have a beard. This man looks —"

"No, Mom," said Noah, sounding exasperated. "His hair is the same colour."

"Reddish-blond," said Gabriel. "Honey, lots of people have hair that colour."

"No," said Noah adamantly. "You never believe me. You're so dense sometimes," he muttered.

"Noah Parsons, you don't talk that way with me," replied Gabriel crossly.

"Mom, look closer at his eyes," pleaded Noah. "He even has the same freckles on his nose."

Gabriel looked again and after a few seconds she brought her face closer to the screen. "Good heavens, you're right," she said in amazement. "It is him!" She looked at Jack and added, "But his hair is short now and he is clean shaven."

"Told you so," said Noah, looking pleased with himself.

Jack knew the man in the photo. Herman Varrick. A year and a half ago Varrick ran one of seven labs on which Jack orchestrated raids after receiving information from an informant inside Satans Wrath. An informant he no longer had.

To make matters worse, Satans Wrath had an informant of their own. Someone working in Drug Section had tipped off some of the labs prior to the raid. Those who were arrested were released the following day. Some were still awaiting trial, including Varrick. So far, the dirty narc had never been identified.

Jack reflected upon the time of the raids and the time that Varrick moved into Gabriel's home. *Varrick relocated here as a result of what I did. I'm responsible for —*

Faith coughed and started to cry.

Jack stared at Faith. His brain tried to protect him from what his actions may have caused. *Maybe she has a cold. Could be nothing — the cold air return under her bed … still …*

He continued to stare as his thoughts gave in to the more likely reason for her illness. He clenched his jaw in an effort to control his own tears of frustration and sadness.

Chapter Four

Jack and Laura stood in the backyard and quickly told Connie what they knew.

"Herman Varrick," Connie said. "So he's a member of Satans Wrath?"

"Not a member," replied Jack. "They wouldn't risk having a club member take a chance like that. But Varrick was under their control before. I'm sure he and his fellow lab rats are still receiving their orders from Satans Wrath. Last time the bikers had a prospect handling the lab rats to act as a go-between with a member of the club. Things have changed since then, but Satans Wrath will still be in control … only more insulated."

Connie looked pensive so Laura said, "A prospect is like a probationary member of the club. Sometimes they call him a striker."

"Yeah, I know that," replied Connie dismissively. "I was deciding how to approach the situation. If

Satans Wrath are handling these guys, I know I won't
get any confessions, even if I do find traces of blood."

"You don't think traces of blood up some guy's
nose and in his ears would be enough to convict?"
asked Laura.

"I doubt it," replied Connie. "Defence would have
their client say they were there and tried to stop the
assault. Turn the murderer into a hero. I want more
than blood drops if we're dealing with Satans Wrath."
She turned to Jack and said, "What do you think?
You're the expert on these guys."

"You're right about not getting a confession from
them," said Jack. "Last time we caught them their
lawyer was waiting at the office before the narcs got
back with the prisoners."

"Wasn't that the same lawyer who later disappeared?" asked Connie, looking at Jack with suspicion.
"Rumoured to have been murdered by a Colombian
drug cartel?"

"That's the one," replied Jack. "Having to obtain
a new lawyer is a standard excuse the bad guys use
to drag out their court cases." He stared momentarily
at Connie and added, "And for your information, the
lawyer *was* murdered —"

Connie's eyebrows furrowed.

"— by bad guys," continued Jack. "At least,
according to a reliable informant we used to have."

Connie felt a little relieved. *Not that he wasn't
involved somehow …*

"Enough chit-chat," said Jack. "I'm taking Gabriel
and her kids to the Children's Hospital. She's in no

shape to drive. I've spoken with Natasha. Everyone who has spent time in the house needs to be checked, as well."

"We have priorities," said Connie. "We need to find these guys. I'll get uniform to take her. I want you to —"

"No, I'm taking her," replied Jack firmly. "For the next hour, Faith is my priority. I've got Natasha pulling some strings for us. It's better if I do it. In the meantime, Laura can go back to the office and start digging."

Giving in was not one of Connie's traits, but she had dealt with Jack before. Giving in was not one of his traits, either. She decided not to waste time arguing. *Besides, with Jack, I'll lose, anyway.* "Okay," she replied. "I'll save the statement taking for some other time."

Jack looked at Laura and added, "Grab a ride back to the office with uniform."

Laura nodded and said, "I'll talk to the narcs and see if we can come up with an address for Varrick. Also go through our intel and see who he was with when he was arrested last time."

"Careful about who you talk to in Drug Section," cautioned Jack.

"I know. I'll use Sammy's team and tell them to be discreet."

"You, uh, mind filling me in on that?" asked Connie.

"This stays between us," answered Jack. "A year and a half ago when we raided the labs, someone in Drug Section tipped off the bad guys and two of the labs had been cleaned out."

"Bastard," replied Connie. "Who did it?"

"Never identified as far as I know," replied Jack, looking at Laura for confirmation.

"That true, Laura?" asked Connie who knew that Laura's husband, Elvis, worked for the Anti-Corruption Unit, which handled the heavier cases coming out of Internal Affairs.

"Not yet," replied Laura. "I spoke to Elvis about it. He says they're narrowing it down. The office is broken into teams who work on different projects. By moving members around to different teams it basically becomes a process of elimination to figure out what is being leaked and who knew about it."

"The old shell game," commented Jack.

"So far they still don't know," added Laura. "Elvis does assure me that Sammy's team is clean. In fact, Sammy has been helping disseminate bogus info for Elvis on occasion."

"So we have a dirty narc to hinder us. Isn't that lovely," said Connie sarcastically.

"Do you want Varrick arrested if I locate him?" asked Laura.

"We need to identify his two playmates," replied Connie. "If you find him, do surveillance and see who he hangs with. I'd like to give Forensics a chance to see if they come up with something. The more nails we have to put in their coffins the better."

Jack sat with Gabriel at her kitchen table while Noah and Faith were in the living room. "The men in your basement were running a clandestine lab," said Jack.

"You found an illegal drug lab in my basement!" said Gabriel in astonishment.

"All their equipment and chemicals are gone, but they were definitely running a lab."

"No, you don't understand," said Gabriel. "I told you before. They were running a janitorial supply service. What you smell is —"

"No," replied Jack firmly. "I know the man that Noah identified. He is a criminal. I'm sorry, but I am positive they were not operating a janitorial service."

"Oh, dear," said Gabriel. She glanced toward the living room and said, "I really am dense."

"These guys are good at deceiving people," said Jack. "They easily manipulate judges and juries. It's their profession. We have found lots of labs operating right under people's noses."

Gabriel looked at Jack and muttered, "I really am stupid."

"No, you simply aren't familiar with how criminals operate. Hind sight is 20/20."

"They seemed so nice …" Gabriel sighed and added, "My sister often commented that I was a little too naive."

"Our concern is that these labs can be very carcinogenic," said Jack. "My wife feels it would be a good idea for everyone to be checked out as a precaution. I would like to drive you and your children to B.C. Children's Hospital."

"You want to drive us to the hospital now?" asked Gabriel, glancing nervously at Faith who was back lying on the sofa. She paused and stared at Jack briefly.

"What is it?" she demanded. "What haven't you told me? You looked in her room, under her bed ... what ... what is it? Tell me!"

Jack took a deep breath and said, "There is a cold air return under her bed that leads directly to a room in the basement that the men used for their lab."

"But you said everything has been cleaned out," replied Gabriel as her brain went into denial. "You can't be sure. You said the man used to be a criminal. It doesn't mean he still is."

Jack shook his head to show she was wrong.

"Father Brown said that there is not enough forgiveness in society," said Gabriel accusingly. "That we often expect the worst of people, making it difficult for those who have truly repented to be welcomed back into society."

"The person Noah identified is someone I arrested for running a meth lab a year and a half ago. It appears he moved to your house after he was arrested. I checked downstairs. There are still signs of what they were doing. I'm experienced in these matters. I have no doubt."

Gabriel looked at Jack as the realization sunk in. "You mean you knew about him a year and a half ago and let him go?" she said harshly. "Why didn't you keep him in jail? You're telling me that you allowed him to come here and murder Father Brown. Maybe hurt my family! How could you do that? What kind of person are you to —"

"Mom! What's wrong?" interjected Noah as he bounded into the kitchen at the sound of his mother's yelling. When he didn't get an answer, he stood between the two adults and looked defiantly at Jack.

Jack eyed him briefly. *You feel you had to become the man of the house when you dad died. Protective ...* "Son," said Jack quietly, "A terrible thing has happened. People, even adults, are upset. It will be okay."

"I'm not your son," said Noah defiantly. "Don't ever call me that."

"You're right," said Jack, "and I apologize. You're the one who found the bad guy for us. Pretty impressive that you could keep your cool after what has happened." Jack looked at Gabriel and said, "I bet you're awfully proud of him."

"I am," replied Gabriel. "I've always been proud of him."

Jack nodded. The break from the previous conversation served to calm Gabriel's voice.

"About the bad guy," said Jack, "the choice to keep him in jail was not mine to make."

"But if he didn't quit, why didn't you arrest him again? Why did you let him stay here?"

"I'm sorry," replied Jack sincerely. "About a year and a half ago, seven labs were raided by the police all in one day. Many people were arrested. They were all released shortly after appearing in court. I work for an intelligence unit dealing with organized crime. The majority of the people arrested that day were too low on the criminal ladder for me to keep track of. There are far more criminals than there are police officers. We simply don't have the manpower to keep following everyone we would like."

"These men commit murder and you're telling me they are too low on the ladder for you to work on?" she replied bitterly.

Jack sighed and said, "Maybe you have a right to condemn me, but I still need to drive you all to the hospital. My wife works in a medical clinic, but she has made arrangements to see that Faith receives priority."

Gabriel did not utter a word during the forty-five minute drive to the hospital. Noah was a little more inquisitive, but was content to hear that it was a matter of routine for everyone to be checked by a physician under such circumstances.

When Gabriel took her children to meet with a physician, Jack spoke to a grief counsellor at the hospital by the name of Phyllis. He gave her his business card and asked her to help Gabriel and let him know if there was anything he could do.

"I'll be glad to," replied Phyllis. "Gabriel is lucky to have you involved. So tell me, how are Holly and Charlie doing? Do you see them?"

Jack was taken back. He did not know Phyllis, but during a previous investigation he had dealt with Holly and her young son, Charlie, who had become paraplegic as a result of a bullet. A bullet meant for Jack.

"Holly opened up a small restaurant on the North Shore," said Jack. "I still see her on occasion. She and Charlie, and her daughter, Jenny, seem to be doing okay."

"Good to hear," Phyllis replied. "I saw her about a year ago when she brought Charlie in for a check-up."

"Have you and I met?" asked Jack.

"No, but I saw you coming to visit Charlie. Holly thinks the world of you, by the way."

"Thanks," said Jack. "Holly is a nice lady. So is Gabriel, so I would appreciate anything you can do for her. I would also like to be kept in the loop."

"I'll do what I can for her, but as far as keeping you apprised of anything medical ... well, I shouldn't really do that without Gabriel's permission."

"I'm not exactly in her good books. One of the men running a lab in her basement is someone I had arrested before. I never kept track of him after the arrest and he simply changed locations and set up a new lab in Gabriel's basement. He's still awaiting trial. Indirectly I am to blame for this."

"You're responsible? What about the man you arrested? Seems to me we should hold the criminals responsible for their actions."

Jack snorted and said, "Novel idea. You should suggest that to our judicial system."

"The point is, it wasn't you who would have released him." She pointed her finger at Jack's chest and said, "You're not responsible. Indirectly or otherwise."

Jack smiled politely. "Thanks, I guess you're right." *Except I know he was released to an unsuspecting public. Knowing all that and I still didn't do anything ...*

Phyllis agreed to keep in touch. Before Jack left the hospital, he once more met with Gabriel and handed her his business card.

She took it reluctantly and said, "I called my sister. We'll spend the weekend with her."

"My cell number is on the card," Jack said. "Call me when you need to go home."

"I don't need your help," she replied bitterly.

Jack stared at Gabriel momentarily and said, "I promise you that I will get who did this."

"That will not bring Father Brown back," replied Gabriel, "nor will it help my children. God will decide what mercy these men should receive."

Jack thought about Gabriel's comment on his way back to the parking lot. His self-incrimination became replaced by something else. Rage. Rage at a justice system he knew to be inept. By the time he arrived at his car, he lost his ability to hold his emotions in check. It resulted in a couple of bruised knuckles and a dent in his car door.

The trouble is, lady, your religious placebo might work for you ... but I don't believe in gods ... or showing mercy to people like Varrick.

Chapter Five

It was late afternoon when Jack returned to the office.

"How did it go?" asked Laura.

Jack shrugged and said, "Did what I could. Put Gabriel in touch with a grief counsellor. It'll be a few days before the doctors know anything. How did you make out?"

"The only address on Varrick is the one he gave when he was arrested last time. It's his parents' house in Port Coquitlam. He has the same address on his driver's licence, but doesn't have any vehicles registered to him. He was released without any reporting conditions. Connie has a team sitting on the parents' house, but it doesn't look good."

"I'm sure it's not. When's his next court appearance?"

"He's had his prelim and is scheduled for trial at the end of April."

"Three months away."

"Connie wasn't happy when she heard."

"We'll find him before then," replied Jack.

Laura gestured to a mound of reports on her desk and said, "I'm trying. I've collected every scrap of info I can on him and anyone he has been known to associate with."

"He could still be taking orders through some prospect with Satans Wrath."

"I know, but nothing is popping up to indicate who. I've been trying to triangulate any common denominators, phone numbers, anything I can find. Keeping track of Satans Wrath and their associates was bad enough before. Now that they are affiliating with all these street gangs it is worse. This is a mess," she said, gesturing at all the reports. "It didn't sound like he actually lived in Gabriel's basement, but where he is staying is anybody's guess."

"He probably didn't sleep at Gabriel's because of the danger to his health," said Jack. "Also it was booby-trapped, so that's another sign that they weren't there all the time."

"With what we've got it seems hopeless," lamented Laura.

Jack swept half the mound of paperwork onto his desk and looked at Laura. "We will find him," he said determinedly.

* * *

It was early evening when Connie stopped in.

"Anything on the surveillance?" asked Laura, glancing up from her desk.

Connie shook her head. "The parents are there, but no sign of Herman yet. He could be in the house, but the only car in the driveway is registered to his parents. I've got a feeling he isn't home. Let's hope he shows up later."

"I wouldn't count on it," said Jack. "How did Forensics make out?"

"No prints," replied Connie, while wheeling an office chair over and sitting down. "Not even a footprint or tire track." Her face brightened a little and she added, "Did find one black hair stuck to a piece of skull out on the lawn. Father Brown had grey hair, so it's not his."

"Varrick has red," said Jack.

"Yeah, I know," frowned Connie. "That's why I'm here. How are you making out? Did he have a buddy with him last time he was arrested? Someone he might be staying with?"

"He did," replied Laura. "I checked him first. Confirmed that he's been in jail for the last two months for assault."

"Another dead end," muttered Connie. "Tell me you've got something else. What about the prospect who was acting as a go-between last time?"

"Full-fledged member now," said Jack. "He wouldn't have any hands-on involvement. Times have changed. We have The Brotherhood to contend with, as do Satans Wrath."

"The Brotherhood? I've heard of that gang. What have they got to do with this?"

"Not *a* gang," replied Jack. "A conglomeration of gangs. Mostly gangs with mixed ethnic backgrounds. The Brotherhood started off as East Indian, but now encompass lots of other gangs, including Vietnamese, Chinese, Anglo-Saxon ... everyone. I've checked with the Gang Unit. Dozens of gangs have sprouted up in the lower mainland. About half a dozen gangs in particular are composed of hardcore seasoned criminals. Most of the gangs have an abundance of juveniles, as well, which means light or no jail sentences."

"And they call themselves The Brotherhood?" asked Connie.

Jack shook his head and said, "Several of the gangs don't have names. Just groups of criminals, both male and female. Many of the gangs once tried to unite under the banner of The Brotherhood, thinking it would cut down on the turf wars. As the gangs grew, it didn't work out. There's been a split within The Brotherhood. As you can tell by all the shootings, the turf wars are back on. The Gang Unit is overrun with work trying to keep a handle on all the hoods doing the drive-by shootings, let alone work on the bosses who are ordering the hits."

"Some are more than drive-bys," said Connie. "The body count is growing at an unbelievable rate. A lot of the cases have ended up in my office, but I wasn't assigned to them because I was busy at the pig farm." She paused and said, "But you didn't answer my question. Varrick was involved with Satans Wrath. What does The Brotherhood have to do with it?"

"The Brotherhood is dealing lots of dope, including meth. They're too much of a cash-cow for the bikers to ignore. Our latest intel indicates a common denominator between biker meth and the meth being sold by The Brotherhood. Our lab often identifies specific samples of meth as being made by the same chemist or at least the same ingredients and formula. The Brotherhood meth is matching the same meth coming from biker sources. There are also a lot more labs than there used to be. Seems like they're springing up all over the place."

"So Satans Wrath and The Brothrhood have formed a partnership?" asked Connie. "Maybe using the same chemists to make it?"

"Correct, except I don't know if partnership is quite the right word," said Jack. "Satans Wrath is one of the top organized crime families in the world. It is only a matter of time before they'll control The Brotherhood completely. The bikers had feelers out with at least the half-dozen or so bosses in The Brotherhood whom they consider worthy. With the dope starting to match up, it is obvious that it is more than feelers."

"Feelers?" asked Connie.

"Ambassadors, if you will," replied Jack.

"A bit like a corporate takeover," said Connie.

"Exactly," replied Jack. "The Brotherhood is penny ante in comparison to Satans Wrath. Extremely violent and stupid, but penny ante. Lots of young kids who lack conscience and think they're invincible. Also naive and stupid enough to think that using a gun will give them status as a real gangster. In reality, they're only cannon fodder for the real gangsters who are smart enough not to take stupid risks."

"In some aspects, that makes The Brotherhood more dangerous than Satans Wrath," added Laura. "Getting stoned and spraying bullets around isn't the bikers' style."

"If The Brotherhood is comprised of morons, how come Satans Wrath hasn't already taken over or kicked them out?" asked Connie.

"Satans Wrath aren't stupid. They've been learning the ropes for the last sixty years. They don't want to risk openly associating with The Brotherhood during all these shootings. Too much police attention combined with a lack of discipline on the part of The Brotherhood. The bikers will sit back and go with the winning side once the wars are settled."

"More like control the winning side," added Laura.

"Definitely," said Jack. "In the meantime, although the war is bad for business, it gives Satans Wrath a chance to appraise who they'll want working for them in the future. They could easily take out the bosses of The Brotherhood, but as I said, they're a cash cow. The Brotherhood has a lot of kids working for them. Kids dealing dope in schools, arcades, playgrounds, and everywhere else kids hang out. The Brotherhood is a good conduit for the bikers to control in order to make money. Let them take the risk while the bikers rake in the cash. Varrick was under the control of Satans Wrath and likely still is, but he could have been assigned to work with The Brotherhood. There has been a definite amalgamation with how they make meth. We have to presume that they are working together."

"Christ," said Connie. "Nothing is ever simple. Why couldn't I just once get a case where the wife comes home and shoots her husband for screwin' around on him ... then calls us to say she did it." She waved her arms in the air and added, "All this shit with gangs, juveniles, The Brotherhood, Satans Wrath —"

"Ah, come on, Connie," said Jack, with a grin. "Don't tell me you don't like a challenge. I know you better than that."

"I really want to solve this," replied Connie, sounding exasperated.

"Us, too," replied Jack, his voice becoming sombre. "If you saw the look on Gabriel's face after the doctors told her what they were testing for ... holding Faith in her lap ..." Jack concentrated on taking a deep breath and slowly exhaling in an unsuccessful attempt to block the memory before continuing. "Believe me," he said determinedly, "we will solve it."

"Well, you caught Varrick before," said Connie. "Let's catch him again. Any suggestions?"

"We need to find him and identify who was with him. With the evidence you have so far, you know there is no chance you could convict. If you haul him in for questioning he won't talk and all it would do is let him know we're on to him. Once we find him, maybe you could get a wiretap. We'll work together. Laura and I will liaison with Drug Section and the Biker Unit if the need arises. We still have some more reading to do. With The Brotherhood, it is going to take time to figure out who all the players are."

"I'll keep a surveillance team on the house," said Connie. "Maybe he'll show up. Let's see what another day brings."

It was ten o'clock at night when Jack arrived home and pulled into his parking space in the underground parking lot. He was glad to see that Natasha's parking spot was still empty, but knew she would be home from work soon.

Jack went to their apartment and returned a few minutes later with a toilet plunger. He was successful in that the plunger sucked the ding out of his car door, but as he walked back to the elevator, Natasha arrived.

She got out of the car and kissed him, before gesturing to the toilet plunger. "I always thought your expression of *you don't catch sewer rats with church mice* was what you said about your informants. I had no idea that you really were after sewer rats."

Jack sighed and said, "I used it take a dent out of the car door."

"Accident?" asked Natasha.

"I punched it," admitted Jack.

"Did it help?"

"No. Made me feel stupid."

"Bad day at the office, or did the door take a swing at you first?"

"Hasn't been a good day," replied Jack.

"Involving that family you brought to BCCH?"

"Yes."

"So you're after the sewer rats who lived in her basement."

Jack nodded.

"Sounds like tonight we should have a glass of wine and unwind a little."

"Make it a bottle."

Natasha eyed Jack's hand and said, "Break any bones?"

"No, I haven't caught them yet."

"I mean your hand, not —" She stopped when she saw Jack smile at her. "Do I need to worry?" she asked, convinced that Jack's smile was not genuine.

"I think I cracked a knuckle, but as far as the bad guys go, you don't need to worry."

Natasha stared at him silently.

"Hey, I'm smiling, aren't I?" added Jack.

"Yeah, and your upper lip looks a bit like a Frankfurter. It always does when you're trying to pull one over on me."

Jack's chuckle was genuine. "I love you, you know."

"I love you, too." She eyed Jack's hand again. Punching a car door was not his style. She gave him a quick kiss on his cheek and said, "Let's go find that corkscrew ... then we'll talk ... and don't try to bullshit me or I'll use that plunger on you."

"I could think of a nicer way to get a hickey," replied Jack.

"Hickey? Wasn't what I had in mind. You would need a proctologist when I was done."

It was seven o'clock Friday morning when Jack arrived back at Gabriel's house with cleaning supplies.

The blood was sprayed high enough up the back of the house that he needed to borrow a ladder from a neighbour. As he scrubbed the streams of dried blood off the aluminium siding he reflected on the violent, uncontrollable rage of the person who did the murder. *This is one animal I will find …*

Later that afternoon, Connie returned to Jack and Laura's office. Any optimism she had disappeared when they both gave her the thumbs-down signal.

"How about you?" asked Jack.

"Not a thing on the Varrick house. The parents went grocery shopping and to the liquor store and that was it."

"How about the crime scene?" asked Laura.

Connie shook her head and said, "We canvassed the neighbourhood and there was nothing of interest." She eyed Jack curiously and said, "I heard you were there this morning, making like a janitor."

Jack shrugged in response.

"You should have asked me," said Laura. "I would have helped."

"It was no big deal," replied Jack. "I was awake early." *More like I hardly slept from grinding my teeth all night …*

"It was good of you," said Connie. "Anyway, I've even taking to interviewing winos. I've talked to four of them so far. There's a liquor store about a block away from Gabriel's. I'm posting a member there every day for the next week. Also got Forensics collecting prints from empty wine bottles we've found in a vacant lot down the alley to identify others."

"Interviewing winos," mused Jack. "I heard recruitment for your section was down, but I hadn't realized how desperate you had become."

"Smartass," replied Connie. "No, from what we've been told, there were at least a dozen different winos who used Gabriel's yard to get out of the rain. I'm going on a possible theory, with the way Father Brown was dressed, that he might have gone outside to chase some winos away and saw something he shouldn't have. Then again, he might have seen one of the dopers doing something and went out to investigate."

"So you're hoping to come up with a drunk as a witness," said Jack. "Bet the courts will love that."

"Christ," replied Connie. "The reason I'm telling you is to show how desperate I am. We need to find Varrick!"

"If you're that desperate, want me to try a quick UC call to his parents?" asked Jack.

"If you could think of something that wouldn't heat him up, go for it," replied Connie.

"I'll think of something," replied Jack. "Wait in the hall and close the door and make sure nobody walks in during the call."

Jack waited until Connie left and closed the office door before glancing at Laura and saying, "I thought it better that Connie not hear. Don't want her to have to tell a judge and have the case thrown out by saying it put justice into disrepute."

"The lawyer act?" smiled Laura.

Jack nodded as he thumbed through a file. "I have Varrick's parents' number ... need to find out what lawyer is representing him on his drug charge."

"It's Basil Westmount from the law firm of Manhattan, Westmount, and Wilson," said Laura.

Seconds later, Jack punched in a phone number on his cellphone. "Good afternoon, may I speak to Mister Herman Varrick please ... oh, I see, you're his mother," he said. "Yes, I'm calling from Manhattan, Westmount, and Wilson.... Yes it is about his upcoming trial.... No, I'm sorry, his trial is still going ahead and it is imperative that we locate your son immediately.... I would call him, but the phone number we have is no longer in service.... Thank you, I would appreciate that ..." Jack quickly jotted down a number and asked, "That is a cell number, is it?... We don't need to talk to your son as much as we need to courier him some documentation. Could you confirm his current address?.... It's called *Headstones*? Yes, I've heard of the place. I believe we have the address on file from a previous client. Thank you very much.... It is a transcript from his preliminary hearing.... He already has that? Then I am extremely sorry for having bothered you. Our secretary should have made a notation on the file. We won't need to contact your son, then."

Jack hung up and winked at Laura before calling for Connie to come back in. When she did, he said, "It worked. I've got his cell number and address."

"Fantastic," said Connie. "How did you do it?"

"Pretended to be a friend looking for him," said Jack

"Man," said Connie. "I never thought these guys would fall for that old line. This is great, I'll find out who he's been talking with."

I didn't think they would fall for that either, thought Jack. He looked at Connie and said, "I wouldn't get your hopes up on getting much in the way of phone tolls. He gave this number to his mother, so it's his permanent number. He'll be using disposable phones for the stuff we're interested in. Cellphones that he'll toss out every week or so."

Connie frowned and said, "Hope you're wrong. What about his address?"

"Familiar with a place out in White Rock the bikers have nicknamed Headstones?"

"Nope," replied Connie. "Must not have had any murders there."

"None reported," replied Jack. "Headstones is a three-storey older house a couple of blocks back from the beach. It used to be a bed and breakfast place before it was bought by a close associate to Satans Wrath."

"More of a silent partnership," added Laura.

"It's a party place for people they don't necessarily trust enough to bring to their real clubhouse," continued Jack. "Also a crash pad for some. The bikers nicknamed it Headstones."

"Odd name," said Connie. "Sounds like a place where we should excavate the yard."

"You want another pig farm?" asked Jack.

"Hell, no," replied Connie, thinking of the killing ground of one of B.C.'s more notorious serial killers.

"Relax, I don't think the bikers are that stupid," continued Jack. "It got its name from a couple of large rocks on each side of the entrance to the driveway. A lot of prospective club members or associates live there and run the place. It has about eight bedrooms and Varrick is staying in one of them."

"The place isn't easy to watch," cautioned Laura. "They've got people coming and going all the time and some are the type who pay attention to anything that looks like it could be surveillance. On top of that, the prospects often do a walk-about checking for heat. There is a place Jack and I found where you can watch if you use binoculars, but if you get any closer you're liable to get burned."

"Suggestions?" asked Connie.

"How about you apply for a wiretap on Varrick while Laura and I try to identify what he's driving and who he is meeting," replied Jack. "If you get a wire, maybe we'll get lucky with a room or vehicle bug."

"He might be meeting his partners in Headstones," said Connie.

"Laura and I will photograph any new faces," replied Jack. "We'll pass the photos on to you and you can show Gabriel."

"And Noah," added Laura.

"Why don't you show her?" asked Connie. "You know them better than I do."

"I was the one who busted Varrick last time, which caused him to move into her place. I don't think she would appreciate me coming around."

"Don't tell her that."

"I already did."

Connie stared at Jack without speaking.

"It was the honest thing to do," he shrugged.

"You're a hard guy to figure out sometimes," muttered Connie. "But even if we get lucky and they pick out a photo, we'll still need to put a real name to the face or faces. I agree it is the way to go, but I still think we will have more luck with a wire."

"A wire might help," said Jack, "but we're in this for the long haul. The good news is that he will continue. Getting arrested didn't stop him last time."

"Last time he didn't take part in murdering a priest," said Connie. "It might cause him to change careers. If he goes straight, we may never figure out who his accomplices are."

"These guys don't give a damn about who they kill," replied Jack. "They may lay low for a few days to see if the heat is on, but as soon as the bikers think he's cool, he'll be put back to work. His expertise as a lab rat won't be wasted for long. Too much money involved. When he starts up again we'll find out who his running mates are."

"I've only got sixty days to run a wire," warned Connie. "If we don't get something substantial by then, I won't be able to get a renewal."

"I'm aware of that," replied Jack.

"I don't see any other options," added Laura.

Connie nodded in agreement.

Connie and Laura looked silently at Jack.

"Let's get to work," he said.

* * *

Jack and Laura found a place where they could park their car and use binoculars to watch the parking lot at Headstones. Several rooms on the second and third levels had lights going off and on during the evening. At three in the morning the last of the lights went out.

Jack waited another hour before driving through the parking lot as Laura used a tape recorder to obtain the license plates of half a dozen vehicles still left in the lot. Partway through the lot, Jack tossed an empty beer bottle out the car window. If anyone was watching, they would think they were partiers looking for action. As it turned out, none of the registrations gave any clue as to which one, if any, were being used by Varrick.

Surveillance over the weekend and the following few days did not yield any sign of Varrick. On Friday morning, Connie called Jack to tell him that she had a meeting with Public Prosecution Service of Canada and hoped to have a wiretap signed and running by the following day.

"What about phone tolls?" asked Jack. "Who has he been calling?"

"His parents and a few others that all look legit ... like fast food takeout places. The only ones who have a criminal record are his parents, and that was ten years ago for drug trafficking."

"I was afraid of that," sighed Jack.

"So I'm doing all this work to get a wire on the phone for nothing."

"The phone, yes, but if we can put him to a car we might be able to wire it or some other location where they might chat. Like I said, it is going to take time."

Early Friday afternoon Jack and Laura were slouched in their car watching Headstones and eating submarine sandwiches when Jack stopped chewing to answer his BlackBerry. It was the grief counsellor from the hospital calling to give him the news he dreaded to hear.

"Do you know anything about neuroblastoma?" asked Phyllis.

"No, but it doesn't sound good," replied Jack. He repeated the word in his mind. *Neuroblastoma* ... He felt like he had been whacked on the side of his head with a plank. He listened, guts churning, as Phyllis continued to talk. *Why didn't I keep track of the bastards? Faith has cancer. If only I* —

"You still there?" asked Phyllis.

"Yes. Sorry. What do you know about it?"

"It is a cancer of the nerve cells and can occur anywhere in the body. In Faith's case, it is in her nerve tissue alongside her spinal cord in her neck. There are no clear indications of what causes it."

"There are in this case," said Jack, harshly, then lowered his window for air. "What's her prognosis?"

"Don't know yet. A lot more tests will need to be done. Likely chemo."

"The rest ... what about Noah and Gabriel. The other kids ..."

"Things look good for them so far. They'll have to be retested every six months for the next few years. Jack, I'm sorry. Wish it was better news."

"I better go see Gabriel," said Jack.

"Uh, now is not the time."

Probably hates my guts ... and so she should ...

"She's still in denial ... doing a lot of praying. For you to see her ... well, from what you told me, it could evoke a lot of unwarranted anger. It wouldn't help either of you. Leave her to me. Don't worry, I'll be in touch."

"Jack!" interjected Laura. "It's Varrick. Heading to a black pickup truck," she said, without taking her eyes from the binoculars.

Chapter Six

Connie Crane skipped her lunch break to go to the Public Prosecution Service of Canada and meet with Bob, the prosecutor who had reviewed her application under Part VI of the Criminal Code for a wiretap intercept on Herman Varrick.

Connie made herself comfortable in a chair across from Bob's desk, and after the usual niceties were exchanged, Connie gestured to her application on Bob's desk and said, "Well?"

Bob grimanced and replied, "It's pretty weak, I—"

"Come on, Bob," interrupted Connie. "He was running a meth lab in the basement where the vic was found. Then he cleaned it out and took off."

"I know," replied Bob. "I did read it. Carefully, I might add."

"Sorry," sighed Connie. "I know it's not you. What are the issues you're worried about?"

"To start with, your affidavit says it wasn't Varrick who rented it. That it was someone else using a fake identity. You also say that Varrick was frequently in the company of yet a third unidentified person."

"These other two are who we want to identify," persisted Connie.

"And you say the only hair you found doesn't appear to match Varrick. There is nothing specific to indicate he had any involvement in the murder."

"He was running a meth lab for Pete's sake."

"Your Part VI is for a homicide, not drugs."

"You think I should rewrite it as a drug investigation?"

"No. There is no evidence to indicate he is still involved in the manufacture of drugs."

"So what are you saying? I don't have enough to get a wire?"

Bob paused for a moment and flipped through a couple of pages in the affidavit. He looked up and said, "Isn't there anything else you could give me?"

Connie shook her head and replied, "Nothing yet. We're doing surveillance, but so far it has been fruitless. We're hoping to get more evidence once we identify the other two guys. Which I am hoping a wire will do. There is also the other problem. Varrick is scheduled to appear in court for his meth lab trial in April. If he gets slam-dunked then, we'll really be left in the cold."

Bob slowly nodded and replied, "Well ... I said your affidavit was weak ... but maybe not impossible." He grinned and added, "Your victim was a priest. Maybe we'll get lucky and get a Catholic judge."

"I'd appreciate you trying. Otherwise we've got nothing."

"If we do get this signed, you better pray that you do get something within the next sixty days because I guarantee you won't get an extension otherwise." He looked sharply at Connie and said, "Are you sure you don't want to wait and see what else you might dig up?"

Connie glanced at her cellphone and saw an incoming call from Jack. "Give me a sec," she said apologetically to Bob.

"We're on him," said Jack. "Westbound on 99 in a black pickup."

Connie smiled and turned to Bob and said, "No, I don't want to wait. I want this son of a bitch!"

Connie got her wiretap order signed that afternoon. She immediately called Jack who told her that Varrick simply went to a bottle recycling depot and dropped off several dozen cases of empties, along with a few boxes of liquor bottles before going to a liquor store and restocking the booze supply at Headstones.

"If they've got him doing menial chores at Headstones when he is a cook for a meth lab, it is costing them money," noted Jack. "They're worried and are laying low."

"How long do you think they'll keep him on ice?"

"I'm surprised he isn't back to work already," replied Jack. "Although trained lab rats are valuable, they're not club members and are still expendable. My guess is they'll wait a week or two to make sure there is no heat before putting him back to work. Maybe they're looking to rent a new place for a lab."

"Hope so. The clock is running," added Connie ruefully.

"Did you hear the news on Faith?"

"Who?"

"Gabriel's kid … cancer."

Connie paused to let out a sigh before asking, "How bad?"

The pause gave Jack time to feel the rage simmer through his veins — his tendons and muscles going taut. For a brief second he allowed himself to fantasize that his hands were around Varrick's neck, choking the information out of him.

"Did you hear me?" asked Connie.

"I heard you," sighed Jack. "It's bad. Could be terminal but they don't know yet."

"I really, really want to nail these guys."

"Trust me, we will catch them. Justice will be served," he said coldly.

Connie's emotions were in turmoil when she hung up. She was saddened over the news about Faith, but at the same time, knowing Jack's reputation, she believed the culprits would somehow be identified. *Identified, perhaps. But with what evidence? And Jack's definition of justice … hope to God it is not Jack whom I have to testify against.*

* * *

The next month dragged by without any progress. Varrick continued to do menial chores around Headstones. Occasionally other men helped him and Jack and Laura photographed any of them who were new faces. Connie showed the photos to Gabriel and Noah, but none were recognized.

Sixteen days after Faith's cancer had been identified, she underwent surgery. Phyllis called Jack to let him know that the surgery was partially successful.

"Partially?" asked Jack.

"They got most of it, but some wrapped around her spinal cord had to be left. The doctors are optimistic that radiation will get what they missed."

"Think it would be okay if I paid Gabriel and her children a visit?" asked Jack.

"Give her a little more time," said Phyllis. "She put her house on the market last week and it has already been sold. There's a quick possession date. She has a lot on her plate right now. Don't worry, I think she is starting to accept and even forgive the men responsible."

"Forgive!" stammered Jack.

"It's her belief in the Bible. She's not as angry as she was. It's a good thing."

After Jack hung up, he thought about what Phyllis had said. *Forgive? I'll never forgive!* His knuckles, still sore, made him realize he had unconsciously clenched his fists at even the suggestion of forgiveness.

Chapter Seven

Another couple of weeks rolled by without identifying Varrick's accomplices. Connie called for a meeting with Jack and Laura at their office. She got right to the point as soon as she walked through the door.

"Okay, Jack. What's going on? The wire expires on April third! That's in two weeks! After that, Varrick goes to trial for the meth lab. You said the bikers would have him back in business soon. You call this soon?"

"Sorry, Connie. In the past they would have."

"Yeah? So what's changed?" asked Connie, violently shaking a chair to straighten the rollers before shoving it closer to Jack's desk and sitting down.

"I've been trying to figure that out, as well. To take this long ... the bikers are afraid of something. Maybe they're protecting someone. Someone a lot more valuable than Varrick."

"So what are you telling me?"

Jack shrugged and said, "I don't know what to tell you."

"Maybe the bikers are protecting that dirty narc you told me about," suggested Connie.

"Don't think so," replied Jack. "Two years ago we had a good informant in Satans Wrath who warned us we had the dirty narc. The bikers didn't slow down after the last arrests. I think they're protecting someone else."

"Your informant didn't know the narc's name?" asked Connie.

"No. The narc was recruited by a biker in the club who goes by the name of Pussy Paul. Runs lots of hookers and strip joints. We're looking for someone new. Someone who connected with Satans Wrath within the last two years."

"Speaking of the earlier labs," said Laura, "we tried to locate the lab rats from the other six labs that were busted. One is an unsolved homicide in Vancouver. He was found tortured and dropped in an alley."

"Who would do that to a guy connected with Satans Wrath?" asked Connie.

"Satans Wrath would," replied Jack. "Maybe they thought he was an informant, or perhaps got caught with his fingers in the till."

"What about the other lab rats?" asked Connie.

"They've disappeared, as well," replied Laura.

"Meaning?"

"Meaning they're likely running labs someplace else," said Jack. "Makes you wonder how many other innocent people are breathing in fumes from something they aren't even aware of."

"Then how can you be so damned calm?" asked Connie, as she glared at Jack. "Think about Gabriel's kid —"

"You don't have to remind me about Faith," said Jack, quietly. "I think about her every day. If I hadn't busted Varrick, she wouldn't be sitting in a hospital with her hair falling out."

Connie looked at Jack and caught the sombre reflection in his tone. *I was wrong to think he is calm — cold and calculating is more like it ...*

"Don't you have any other leads except Varrick?" interjected Laura. "Seems like we are putting all of our eggs in one basket."

Connie sighed as she picked up a pen and unconsciously started slapping the edge of the desk. Staring blankly down at the pen, she didn't look up to reply. "Nope. I've tried to get a description from anyone in the neighbourhood about what these other two look like. Nobody had anything of value. Talked to neighbours, delivery people ... nothing."

"What about the winos?" asked Laura. "If they were hanging around they might have seen people coming and going."

"Already tried," replied Connie. "I identified seventeen and we located all but three so far."

"Pretty good, considering most of them are homeless," noted Laura.

"Tell me about it," continued Connie. "I found one who was asked to leave by Father Brown. He said Father

Brown was a nice guy and wasn't mean about it. I think the wino, as much as his soggy, drunken brain would allow, did his best to help. Unfortunately, he couldn't even remember what day or even what week he had been there. He only knew it was Father Brown in the photo because of the small birthmark on his forehead. He never saw anyone else connected to the house except when a kid came out and threw some garbage in the can."

"Probably Noah," said Jack.

"You used to have an informant in the Satans Wrath," said Connie, as she looked up and tossed the pen down. "Can't you get another one? Or maybe talk to whoever used to help you?"

"That person repaid the debt owed to me. His loyalties are back with the club. All we would be doing is exposing our interest in Varrick. As far as getting an informant goes, it is rare to get one in the club. Our chances of getting one in The Brotherhood would be good, providing we can find someone connected with Varrick that could help us."

"So we keep doing what we're doing?" asked Connie. "I feel like we're spinning our wheels and going nowhere."

"If the bikers were going to cut Varrick loose, they would have already done so. They plan on using him, but are being unusually cautious."

"Hope you're right."

The morning of April 1 arrived and Jack and Laura were on surveillance at Headstones. When Varrick left in the usual black pickup, he started driving aimlessly around some of the side streets in White Rock.

"He's doing heat checks!" said Laura.

"Something's up," replied Jack. "See if anyone is around to help us. No use following him around in the residential area, we'll only get burned. If he doesn't come out, we can start a search later to see where he's parked. Let's set up on 152nd Street. That's the usual route for him to take if he's heading out. See if anyone is available to give us a hand. Get them to set up on 148th and 16th Avenue, as well."

Laura grabbed the police radio and a marked police unit pretended to work radar while watching for Varrick's truck.

Twenty minutes later, Jack and Laura saw Varrick driving northbound on 152nd Street and they followed. Minutes later, a couple more cars from Drug Section answered the call for assistance and joined in on the surveillance. They weren't needed. Varrick believed he had cleansed himself of any possible police surveillance and drove directly to a small strip mall in Port Coquitlam. He parked his truck and got in the passenger side of a white van. The surveillance team followed the van as it left the mall.

Jack radioed in the licence plate and the registered owner turned out to be a young woman who did not have a criminal record and lived in a house in Abbotsford.

"Anyone get a look at the driver?" asked Jack, as he drove several cars behind in traffic.

"Ten-four," replied a female voice. "Late twenties, bull-dog neck, bald, and wearing a gold fertility horn around his neck. Thought those things went out in the seventies," she muttered.

Jack smiled and said, "Is that you, Tina?"

"Ten-four."

"I owe you one. You just turned a cold investigation into a hot one."

"Hey, they don't call me the Asian Heat for nothing," replied Tina.

Jack chuckled. Tina was an undercover operative who was good at her job. She didn't look like a cop and was someone who could walk right past a target without them getting suspicious.

"He sounds like the one in Gabriel's basement who called himself John," said Laura.

Jack nodded and smiled with satisfaction. "Get the camera ready."

The van was followed to a small, older-style home and Jack got his first glimpse of the driver as both men walked up to the front door.

"Know him?" asked Laura.

Jack shook his head and said, "He looks vaguely familiar, but I can't place him yet."

An elderly woman answered the door and the van driver introduced her to Varrick. She handed a key to the driver and closed the door. Both men walked around to the rear of the house.

"Another basement suite," noted Laura.

"There's an alley in the back ... limited parking, want us to risk it?" radioed Tina.

"Negative," replied Jack. "Don't want to heat them up. Everyone keep their distance. There is a third guy that we still need to identify so keep your heads up."

Seconds later, both targets returned to the van while Laura discreetly stood between two houses across the street and snapped pictures. The van returned to the strip mall and Varrick went back to his truck.

The surveillance team followed the van to an apartment building where it pulled into a secure underground parking lot. It was not known which suite he went to and there were no names posted on the intercom system at the front door.

Later that afternoon, Jack called the surveillance off and returned to their office. Laura sent Connie the photos she had taken while Jack pulled out his laptop to study all the photos they had previously shown Gabriel and Noah.

Minutes later, Jack smiled and motioned for Laura to look at a particular picture. It was of a man with scraggly, long brown hair pulled back in a ponytail and sporting a bushy beard. Laura took several moments to look at the picture of the van driver and compare it to the photo on Jack's laptop.

"It is him," she breathed. "He's changed his appearance a lot. No wonder Gabriel and Noah couldn't recognize him. It's a definite match."

"David Zacharias," said Jack. "Goes by Zack. Long record for drugs and a close associate of Satans Wrath."

Within the hour, Jack received a call from Connie.

"The bald guy is him!" said Connie excitedly. I showed Gabriel the photos. She said there is no doubt he is the guy who said his name was John. Can we ID him?"

"Already done," said Jack. "Meet us at our office and we'll fill you in."

By the time Connie arrived, Jack had discovered that the young woman who owned the white van was actually Zack's sister and was married to a drug trafficker who had a record for dealing in methamphetamines.

"I don't want these guys for dope," growled Connie. "I want them for murder. Varrick is due to appear for his trial in two weeks and my wire runs out in two days. What can we do?"

"Put a bug in the place we found today," said Jack.

"The landlady handed them a key," said Connie. "Means they haven't even moved in yet."

"All the more reason to get the bug in quick before they do," said Jack. "I'm free to work tonight if you want teams to sit on Varrick and Zack to make sure you're not caught."

"You forgetting there's a person living upstairs?"

"She's old," replied Jack. "Probably doesn't hear well. Tell the team to go in with stocking feet."

"Yeah, well, even if we do get the bug in, what chance do you think there is that they'll actually talk about the murder? Especially in the limited time we have left."

"Maybe by then we can prove they're setting up a meth lab and can get a new wire for that," suggested Laura.

"Do you know the work involved to do that?" replied Connie. "Besides, proving it's a meth lab won't take long. If we keep a new wire running in the hope of getting evidence on a murder when the wire is for dope, then defence will claim we were on a fishing expedition and have it tossed out of court."

"Quit being so pessimistic," said Jack. "Get the bug in. I don't care if it is only for a couple of days. I think they will talk about the murder."

"What are you?" she snorted. "One of these guys who says the glass is half full?"

"Naw," replied Jack. "Who cares if it's half full or half empty. It's just beer. Slam it back."

Laura caught a glint in Jack's eye. She knew he had a plan.

The investigators were successful in placing listening devices in the basement suite late that night. Neither Varrick nor Zack returned or did anything of significance for another two days. It was nine o'clock at night before Varrick retraced his steps from Headstones and once more met with Zack at the strip mall before returning to the basement suite.

Connie stayed in the monitoring room to listen to the recorders. She had three hours before the wiretap would be disconnected. Jack and Laura were on surveillance and saw the men unloading boxes from the van. By the sound of glassware and a few comments she heard, Connie knew that they were setting up another meth lab.

"Jack," she radioed. "One of 'em said it was the last of the boxes. Also a comment about having a few days to set it up before they get the juice."

"Copy that," replied Laura in his place. "They're likely referring to the chemicals they need."

"They could be leaving soon," replied Connie. She waited a moment for a response, but there was nothing but silence. "This is it," she lamented over the radio. "Tonight is our last chance. At midnight we have to pull the plug." She waited for a reply, but didn't get one. "Jack? You there?" she asked.

Laura answered and said, "Jack left. You should hear his fist pound on their door any second."

As if on cue, Connie heard a loud thump over the recorder, followed by Zack's nervous whisper to Varrick, "Who the fuck is that?"

Connie let out an involuntary gasp as her stomach constricted. Her lungs froze and her mouth unconsciously dropped open as she strained to listen.

Chapter Eight

Several anxious seconds ticked past and Connie stared at the silent recorder. *Is it working?* Moments later, the sound of footsteps told her that it was.

"Who is it?" came Varrick's voice. "Who's there?"

Dead silence was followed by the sound of Varrick slowly opening the door.

"There's nobody here," he said. "What the fuck! Look what's hangin' on the knob!"

"A gold fuckin' cross?" responded Zack.

Connie heard the door knob rattle slightly before the door was closed again.

"There's a piece of paper tied to it," said Zack.

"A fuckin' gold cross," muttered Varrick, sounding bewildered.

"Someone's yankin' our chain over that dead priest!"

"His was real gold," replied Varrick. "This is painted wood."

"Who the fuck put it on the doorknob? Read the note."

Connie heard a rustle of paper and Varrick said, "*God knows what you did and is waiting ...*" Varrick started laughing.

"What's so funny?" demanded Zack.

"Cocktail is fuckin' with us."

"You see him out there?"

"No, but who else could it be?" answered Varrick.

"I thought he wasn't gonna show up until another couple of days," replied Zack.

"Come on," laughed Varrick. "There's nobody else it could be. It's him, fuckin' with us."

"Then why isn't he comin' in to laugh at us?"

"Probably will in a few minutes."

"Cocktail, you fuckin' bastard," grumbled Zack. "Man, what a fuckin' night that was," he added.

"Your fault for breakin' the glassware," said Varrick.

"It was you who cracked the door open for fresh air," replied Zack.

"I didn't know a fuckin' nosy priest would be outside listening," answered Varrick.

"He wasn't listening when we saw him. Too busy talking to God."

Varrick chuckled, but his voice became serious when he added, "Good thing Cocktail came along."

"I guess," replied Zack. "He wasn't laughin' then. Fuckin' near shit when we helped drag him in by the ankles."

"He's gotta be laughin' at us. Come on, let's go find

him. We're done here, anyway."

Connie closed her eyes for a moment. *Jack, you did it. Split this case wide open.*

Jack answered his BlackBerry and listened to Connie's excited and happy voice as she relayed what had transpired.

"Bad news," said Jack. "I don't know anyone with the nickname of Cocktail."

"You don't? Crap … well, I'm sure we will. Man … fantastic! Don't worry. With what we got tonight I won't have any problem getting the wire renewed. They said Cocktail is coming by in a couple of days. Jack, I'm so happy I could kiss your sweet little ass."

"I appreciate that, but I don't think Natasha would," said Jack, chuckling. "Also, it looks like we've got movement. Targets are leaving."

"Maybe they're going to meet with Cocktail," suggested Connie.

"Maybe. Or someone will. The problem is what will they do when they find out it wasn't Cocktail who hung the crucifix on their door?"

"Who cares?" replied Connie. "With what we've got on wire, this case is basically solved. Especially if we can lay a conspiracy charge. All we need is to identify Cocktail. Maybe tonight we'll do that, too."

Surveillance continued. Varrick retrieved his truck and went to Zack's apartment building where Zack parked and got in with Varrick before driving to Headstones.

"I don't like this," said Jack as he and Laura parked in their usual spot to watch.

"Maybe they're chatting with Cocktail," suggested Laura. "If we scoop the plates, we might identify him tonight. What's the worry?"

"The bikers kept these guys on ice a long time before deciding to set up another lab. I think they were protecting someone. Maybe Cocktail."

"So? Your point being?"

"If Cocktail is really valuable, they wouldn't risk having him go to Headstones. With what happened, Satans Wrath could be looking at Varrick and Zack as loose ends."

"Oh, man."

"Exactly."

Numerous vehicles came and went from Headstones. Jack and Laura snuck around on foot and identified several licence plates belonging to prospective members of Satans Wrath as well as numerous other criminals. None were associated with any name or occupation that would warrant the nickname of Cocktail.

It was four o'clock in the morning when the lights went out at Headstones. Varrick's truck remained parked.

"Maybe Zack decided to spend the night," said Laura hopefully.

"Above ground or below, is the question," replied Jack.

It was ten o'clock the next morning when Jack's question was answered. He arrived at work and saw a computer message saying that a Detective Wilson with the Vancouver Police Department had checked Varrick and Zack for criminal records earlier that morning.

Previously, Jack had entered Varrick and Zack on the Canadian Police Information Centre computer. The CPIC entry was done in a manner so that whoever checked the names would not know Jack was interested, but a message would be sent to Jack advising him of who checked the names. It would be up to Jack's discretion as to whether to inquire further. He decided to call.

"Homicide, Wilson," answered a gruff voice.

Jack identified himself, already knowing what he was about to hear. "I got a silent hit on CPIC," he said. "You ran two names this morning."

"Herman Varrick and David Zacharias," said Wilson. "Both murdered?"

"Yup, I think it was murder," replied Wilson. "Both found dead in an alley off of East Hastings about two hours ago. Time of death was about six hours earlier."

"Shot?"

"Nope. Looks like heroin overdoses. A needle was still in Varrick's hand. The thing is, neither had any tracks. Needles wasn't their thing. You got something that can help us, one way or the other?"

Jack sighed. *Do I tell them that it was me who got them killed?* "Um, in my opinion it was not accidental," replied Jack.

"Can you elaborate a little? Christ, if you're right, we're talking a double homicide here. Shit-rats or not, this landed on my desk. I want to solve it."

"They were associated with Satans Wrath —"

"Shit," said Wilson.

"And were in the process of setting up a meth lab," continued Jack. "I think the bikers may have clued in that we were on to them."

"So Satans Wrath severed the connection to protect themselves. Typical."

"You got it. Varrick and Zack are ... were of interest to I-HIT for another murder. I'll get Connie Crane to call you and fill you in. She's the lead investigator."

Jack barely hung up the phone when it rang. It was Connie.

"Hey, Jack. Good going last night. How late did you sit on them?"

"The lights went out at Headstones at four this morning."

"Zack stayed over too, did he?" noted Connie.

"His lights went out permanently around two. Same for Varrick."

"This is all great," said Connie, still filled with enthusiasm and not really listening. "I already spoke with PPSC. We'll get an extension on our wire."

"Connie, listen to me. I've got some bad news. Forget using Varrick and Zack to find Cocktail. We've hit a dead end as far as they're concerned."

"What are you talking about?"

"VPD found Varrick and Zack dead in an alley at eight o'clock this morning. Set up to look like heroin overdoses. They probably took them out of Headstones through the garage."

"Oh, God, no …" Connie felt the depression settle over her like a lead blanket. *My only leads to Cocktail are dead*. Her mind felt numb as Jack told her about his conversation with Wilson. She twiddled her crucifix around and around with her thumb and forefinger as Jack spoke. Eventually the chain tightened around her neck and cut into the skin before she stopped.

"Are you listening?" asked Jack, moments after he quit speaking.

"Yeah, I heard you," muttered Connie. "I was afraid this would happen."

"You guessed that the bikers would kill them?" asked Jack.

"No. I knew when I called you into this case that I would end up with more bodies than I started with."

"You haven't. Varrick and Zack are VPD's worry."

"You tryin' to be funny?"

"No, simply reminding you."

"Of what?"

"To stay focused. Our primary objective is to find and identify Cocktail. Forget about Varrick and Zack now."

"Yeah, but our evidence from last night's wire is useless. Where do we go from here? And who is Cocktail? One of Satans Wrath?"

"I've never heard of him. I ran his name through the system. Nothing matched."

"Varrick and Zack … you, uh, being straight with me on this?" asked Connie suspiciously.

"Hell, yes! I had no idea when I hung the crucifix on their door that it would get them killed. I figured the two of them were responsible for the murder. I was hoping to get them talking. I didn't know they'd go looking for Cocktail."

"Well obviously they did and he killed them, too."

"I doubt that Cocktail killed them. I think Satans Wrath did it to sever the connection and protect Cocktail. He has to be a major player to have the bikers jumping through hoops for him."

Connie's sigh was audible.

"Sorry, Connie," said Jack. "It was my fault. Last night I thought it was a good idea."

"Yeah, well ... shit happens. I'm not blaming you. If you hadn't done it, we would be nowhere. At least we know who we're after."

"We'll find out Cocktail's real name," said Jack, determinedly.

"That would be a start. Then we have to prove it. If he, or Satans Wrath, are jittery enough to whack Varrick and Zack, they're not about to be giving us any proof. I'll liaise with City and search their rooms where they were staying."

"You're dealing with Satans Wrath," said Jack. "The rooms will have been cleaned out."

"Yeah, I guess."

After a moment of silence, Jack said, "How about we set up a meeting with the Organized Crime Task Force and go over everything. Laura called them and they said they have a report that puts Zack at a house party a few months ago. Mostly kids, from what I gather. It doesn't seem significant, but let's see what else OCTF has and find out who else was at the party."

"Police work, all peaks and valleys," mumbled Connie. "Riding high one moment and crashing the next."

"We'll solve this. Don't worry, I'll think of something."

"Don't worry? You tell me you'll think of something and then say don't worry! Last night you thought of something and we ended up with two extra bodies."

"A consequence I didn't predict. Who would have guessed? You didn't."

"Yeah, well, maybe this time it was accidental," conceded Connie.

"What do you mean, *this time*?"

"You know exactly what I mean. Don't push me."

"Forget about Varrick and Zack. Stay focused on what to do next."

"A double homicide and you say forget about them!"

"There is another person who could die yet. Worry about that one."

"Another! Jack, what did I just say!"

"Faith."

"Faith? In you? Listen you —"

"No, Faith! Gabriel's four-year-old daughter. Will she die next?" Jack added harshly.

The mention of Faith shocked Connie and she was temporarily at a loss for words. After a moment, she heard Jack vow that they would identify Cocktail. She heard herself agree to attend the meeting with the OCTF and hung up.

Connie reflected on the cold tone of Jack's voice when he spoke of Faith. *If ... when we identify Cocktail ... then what? As of last night I thought I was working on three bad guys ... with Jack on the case, two are already dead ...*

Chapter Nine

On Friday morning a meeting was held with Jack, Laura, Connie, and Dan Mylo from OCTF, in Jack's office.

Dan outlined the gang wars in the lower mainland. "Province-wide," he said, "we've identified 118 gangs. The Brotherhood was an amalgamation of what used to be a dozen independent gangs. The gangs grew larger, some incorporated with each other, and the amalgamation split when turf issues developed. Basically, The Brotherhood is currently divided into two factions, with an estimated three or four bosses on each side controlling their gangs."

"No one guy has stepped up to take complete control, then?" asked Connie.

"Don't think it's that easy," replied Dan, glancing at Jack. "I think a certain degree of political backing is required."

Jack nodded in agreement and said, "The potential leaders are being watched and perhaps loosely guided by Satans Wrath. Although the leaders are adults in their twenties and thirties, the bulk of the membership are teenagers who were previously part of the independent youth gangs. They are violent, young, lack common sense, and have a total disregard for human life. They don't care who might get in the way as is evidenced by all the drive-by shootings."

"Which is our priority," said Dan. "We're spending all our time trying to take the guns off the street and work on the shooters."

"Where do the shooters rank in the organization?" asked Connie. "I would think they would be revered as top dogs."

Dan shook his head and said, "Not on the bottom, but not bright enough to ever be in charge. They're mid-level status. At the moment, we're too busy trying to keep a handle on them, let alone identify and work on the real leaders. Drug trafficking, prostitution, auto theft … all take a back seat to the indiscriminate shootings that are going on." He looked at Jack and said, "Out of curiosity, do you think Satans Wrath could be instigating some of these shootings?"

Jack shook his head and said, "Satans Wrath aren't impressed by indiscriminate shootings. It brings a lot of heat and is bad for business. At the same time, they appreciate the need to control and expand business. In some ways they're in a catch-22 situation. They know that police resources are limited and that all these shootings will take the heat off of them. At the same time, they are losing money because of the turf wars and its negative effect on business. Until the turf wars are settled, I don't think Satans Wrath will want to get too involved with who murders who. If history is any indicator, they will sit back and watch. Once the real victors are identified, they will step in and take over completely."

"Gives the bikers a chance to see who is worth their salt," concluded Dan.

"Exactly," replied Jack. "I presume you have most of The Brotherhood listed on CPIC as persons of interest?"

"We do," replied Dan.

"Could you include that I also be notified of any CPIC hits concerning them?"

"Consider it done," replied Dan. "Hope you like to read. With the amount of people connected to gangs and their ability to attract police attention, you'll be getting a lot of hits."

The meeting adjourned with everyone agreeing to keep each other informed of anything that might benefit one another. Dan Mylo had no idea who Cocktail was and said it wasn't a name that had come across any wiretaps or through any other sources. He provided a report from several months previous that showed Zack attending a noisy house party, but most of the people with him were teenagers who belonged to several different youth gangs.

After Dan left, Connie turned to Jack and said, "Any suggestions? It's obvious that OCTF have their hands full already. I think we're basically on our own."

"One of the lab rats busted a year and a half ago has his trial in three weeks," said Laura. "A fellow by the name of Kent Rodine. I talked to the narcs and they think the evidence is solid. Rodine was found inside the lab and his fingerprints are on the glassware. It's a jury trial so you never know. If he does go free we could follow him to find out where he hangs his hat. See if he meets with Cocktail. If he doesn't get off, maybe some of his friends will show up to see him off and we could follow them."

"Three weeks!" said Connie. "On a case where they expect a conviction? I don't want to rely on something that flimsy."

Jack looked at Laura and said, "Let's get more info on these gangs and watch how they deal. It might lead us to some of the labs."

"I investigate murders, not dope dealers," said Connie. "How do you go about it?"

"Through surveillance, arrests, informants —"

"I don't have the time or the manpower for all that," said Connie. "Even if I did, it would take a long time. Innocent people could be breathing in the fumes from these labs. There must be something we can do. Rodine and his buddies might not even be connected with Cocktail."

"I don't want to wait, either," said Jack. "We need an informant on the inside."

"Yeah, but how?" asked Connie. "You can't exactly run an ad in the *Vancouver Sun*."

"We need a clearer picture of what the meth situation is about," replied Jack. "Meth is a massive problem. Did you know that B.C. currently supplies the majority of our planet in meth? Australia, Asia … you name it."

"Heck of a thing for Canada to be known around the world for," muttered Connie.

"We can thank our provincial judiciary for their leniency and lack of foresight for that," replied Laura. "They aren't known for seeing the big picture, are they, Jack?" She gave a wry smile at employing a phrase often used by Jack.

Jack shook his head and said, "We're globally famous for both peacekeeping and supplying the world with methamphetamines. Hell of a combination. Men and women giving their lives for peace around the world while fellow Canadians destroy lives."

"I don't want to think about it," said Connie. "Too depressing."

"We do need to see the big picture," said Jack, glancing at Laura. "We have to find out everything we can. I'll check with Drug Section, VPD, and Toxicology to get info on anything to do with meth. This is the Easter long weekend. By Tuesday morning we should have enough reports to give us an idea of what is going on. Then we will target someone specifically. Maybe do a quick UC, buy some drugs and see if we can turn an informant. If we find one biker lab, surveillance may lead to more. Eventually we'll find Cocktail."

"Yeah … unless the bikers look at him as a loose end," said Connie.

"If they did, VPD would have found his body in the alley alongside Varrick and Zack."

"Too bad they didn't," replied Connie. "It would save us all a lot of time."

"Starting to think like me?" said Jack with a smile.

"I hope not," replied Connie, frowning.

"Even if he was dead, Satans Wrath would still have others running the labs," said Laura.

The dismal tone of her voice brought a moment of silence as the investigators thought about the situation. The meeting came to an end with Connie agreeing to see what they could learn over the next few days.

On Friday night Jack and Natasha sat on the balcony of their condo overlooking the city lights while sipping on a glass of Glayva. Jack snuggled closer to Natasha on the love seat while swilling a taste of the Scotch-based liqueur around in his mouth. *My life is great*, he thought.

He glanced at his watch. It was nine o'clock. It was a moment in time that he would remember.

Ai-li Cheung walked over to lock the front door of their corner grocery store. Her husband, Frank, had already plodded upstairs to the second storey that was their home for the last thirty-seven years. The sound of the toilet flushing announced where he was.

Ai-li, at sixty-four years of age, was two months younger than her husband. They both planned to retire next year. Up until a few months ago, they always kept the store open until midnight, but the neighbourhood was not what it once was.

Port Coquitlam, less than an hour drive from Vancouver, was no longer a quiet neighbourhood where people knew each other. Shoplifters had become bolder. Empty beer and liquor bottles were often smashed in their small parking lot. Frank often threatened to call the police, but in reality, he was afraid that if he did, the store windows would be smashed in retaliation.

Times had changed from when they used to give free candy to neighbourhood children or run small grocery orders to some of the elderly who lived nearby. The elderly had moved on. Ai-li understood. She did not mind that they closed three hours earlier now. She was looking forward to the day they would close for the last time.

Ai-li was reaching for the door when it was yanked open in front of her. A tall, skinny man with droopy eyes stepped in, waving a syringe containing a bloodly liquid in her face.

"The money," the addict said. He did not yell, but there was the sound of determination in his voice. "Or I'll stick ya with this ... and believe me, AIDS ain't somethin' ya want to have."

Ai-li nodded her willingness to comply. She was too afraid to talk as she hurried to open the till. The addict followed, but remained on the opposite side of the counter.

"The money," he repeated. "Hurry up." He stared intently at Ai-li's face as his body rocked back and forth.

Ai-li quickly took the money from the till and put it in a bag and pushed it toward him.

He remained rocking back and forth, staring at her.

"That's all of it," she whimpered.

He stared back at her in a stupor before his face contorted in rage. Without warning, he grabbed her wrist and plunged the needle into her arm, injecting the bloody liquid. "I told you to hurry!" he yelled, before letting go and stepping back, still holding the syringe.

Ai-li stood paralyzed in shock as the addict stepped back and waved the empty syringe in the air. The rage left his face and he said, "The money ... or I'll stick ya with this. AIDS ain't somethin' ya want ..." He stared at the empty syringe and blinked his eyes in confusion.

Ai-li's mouth hung open as she looked at her arm. "I did!" she cried, gesturing to the plastic bag.

Chapter Ten

On Tuesday morning, Jack listened to the details over the phone as the uniformed Mountie from Port Coquitlam told him about the robbery. As he listened, Jack thought about his own life and his time with Natasha on Friday night. *Life can change in a heartbeat … value every second.*

"Canine Unit tracked him down," the Mountie said. "The guy does have AIDS, so I guess it's a good thing the dog didn't bite him."

"AIDS cannot be transferred from an infected person to an animal," replied Jack.

"Yeah? Good to know. Too bad it isn't that way with people. Personally I cringe every time I have to arrest someone who is combative."

"Don't you pack a Taser?"

"Are you kidding? With the crap we get for using Tasers these days I'd be better off shooting them.

Anyway, the guy wasn't a problem. The asshole was so stoned he was lying in some bushes. Said he couldn't remember if he dreamed he did it, or actually did. He had a small amount of meth in his pocket. CPIC says you are interested in him so —"

"Anyone talk to him to see where he got the meth?" asked Jack. "I'm trying to track down any labs or even rumours of labs at this point."

"I don't have any info on any labs," replied the Mountie. "As far as where he got it from, you have to be kidding. Around here kids can buy that shit easier than they can cigarettes. If you want to know who the dealers are, go down to the schools and see who are driving the muscle cars. Sure as hell isn't the teachers."

"That's a sad state of affairs."

"Tell me about it. I've got kids of my own. As far as this guy goes, CPIC says he is gang-connected."

"Bottom end," replied Jack.

"You have time to work on the bottom end?" said the Mountie. "Must be nice, we don't have the time or manpower to go after the bigger fish, let alone the small fry."

"I understand," replied Jack. He briefly thought about Varrick and his previous opinion that he was too small to work on. *A four-year-old girl may die because I didn't make the time.*

When Jack hung up, he sighed as he thought about Ai-li. *Bet she doesn't think the guy who injected her was too small to work on ...*

Jack picked up the next report from a pile on his desk. It was about some youths were joyriding in a stolen car. They lost control and drove onto a sidewalk where a man was walking with his wife. He pushed his wife out of the way in time, but the car mutilated his legs against the side of a building. He would never walk again. The youths escaped, but a small quantity of meth was found in the car. The investigation was still continuing.

As Jack picked up the next report he glanced at Laura and their eyes met. "I don't know how much more of this I can stand," she said, gesturing to the reports. "Feel like a coffee?"

"You go ahead," replied Jack. "To me, it's like taking off a Band-Aid. Do you do it slowly or rip it off all at once? I prefer to get it over with."

"Hadn't thought of it that way," replied Laura. She grimaced and continued reading.

Jack's next report was about an incident in the early hours of Sunday morning. The police in Richmond were called by a husband to a domestic dispute. Their sixteen-year-old daughter, due home at midnight, arrived forty minutes late. His wife and daughter argued and the mother punched the girl in the mouth, breaking her tooth. The husband attempted to intervene, but his wife, who had prior convictions for prostitution and was addicted to meth, threatened him with a butcher knife. The man locked himself in the bathroom and used his cellphone to call the police. The mother was arrested and a small quantity of meth was found in her purse, along with a phone number for a known Brotherhood dealer.

Jack threw the report down in disgust and said, "A few years ago there were only a few labs. Today it's everywhere. The Ministry of Health should list meth as an epidemic," said Jack, facetiously.

"More like the World Health Organization should declare it a pandemic," replied Laura. "You coming up with anything?"

"Nothing except a sour stomach. Doesn't anybody care about what is going on?" he lamented.

"Someone does," mused Laura. "I've got a Crime Stoppers report that indicates someone with a reliable history has been giving tips about drugs and dealers at Queen Elizabeth Secondary School in Surrey. Uniform has made several small-time busts."

"Glad someone is doing their bit," replied Jack, dismissing the information as his thoughts focused on the next report. A Dave Valentine of the Victoria Police Department had responded to the CPIC entry concerning one of the lab rats that Jack had arrested a year and a half ago. This particular lab rat was in jail, but Jack had listed him as a person of interest in the event he was granted day parole. Victoria PD reported they had heard he was receiving drugs while in jail through a Victoria dealer by the name of Cory McCall.

Jack called Valentine and learned that Cory McCall had a lengthy record, including seven previous drug convictions, three of which were for trafficking. He was currently on probation in Victoria and had only been released from jail the previous week. He was known to be a close friend of the lab rat and they had been in the same jail together.

"Cory isn't a huge dealer," said Valentine, "but he is a thorn in our side. Out only a week and we're told he's got dealers putting out for him all over town."

"Meth?" asked Jack.

"No. Coke. Small amounts up to the pound level."

"His friend in jail used to run a speed lab," explained Jack. "Labs are what I am after. I'm trying to identify a person by the nickname of Cocktail who is connected with the labs and is likely working for Satans Wrath. Cocktail was involved in a murder of an innocent citizen who happened to be in the wrong place at the wrong time."

"Sorry, I don't know of any labs and have never heard of Cocktail."

"Any objection if I do a UC on McCall and try to turn him?" asked Jack. "If they were in jail together and are friends, McCall might know who Cocktail is."

"I'd rather see the asshole busted and put back in jail. He has a dangerous reputation ... but seeing as you're talking about a murder, I don't have any objections."

"Good. Do you know where he hangs out at?"

"His dealers float around town, but usually on weekends McCall goes to a club in the basement of the Strathcona Hotel."

"My partner and I will be over this weekend."

"Like I said, he is dangerous. I think he has a screw loose. You'll need a good cover team. We can help you with that."

"Great. Really appreciate it."

Jack's next call was to Connie. She was in full agreement with the idea and reiterated that she was anxious to get something going rather than wait and take their chances when Kent Rodine went to court.

"This could be the one time the judge puts Rodine in jail," said Connie. "Rolling McCall could be our best and maybe only option."

At eleven o'clock on Friday night, Jack and Laura descended the steps below street level into the club beneath the Strathcona Hotel. They had seen a photograph of McCall and knew that he was tall, tattooed, and had used his time in jail to lift weights. He was someone who would easily stand out in a crowd.

Once Jack's eyes adjusted to the dimness of the lights, he saw that the majority of the crowd were young people who appeared friendly and were there simply to have a good time. Many were university students while a few were tourists who were checking out the nightlife that Victoria had to offer. There was no sign of McCall.

"Music is a little loud," commented Laura as they took a seat.

"I agree," replied Jack. "Some say if the music is too loud it means you're too old."

"Don't even go there," replied Laura. "No sign of our friend."

"It's early yet."

Over the next hour the crowd continued to swell. Jack and Laura discreetly watched and eventually identified two or three drug dealers who were making frequent trips to the washroom with some customers or simply doing exchanges under the tables with others.

It was one-thirty when they spotted McCall saunter in and sit with two of the dealers. Jack saw them whisper and both dealers handed money to McCall.

"Bingo," said Jack. "Time to score."

Jack waited and approached one of the dealers after he left McCall.

"Hey, I moved from Edmonton," said Jack. "Don't know anyone yet." Jack touched his nostril and said, "Do you know where a guy could get something a little stronger than booze?"

The dealer stared at him briefly, sizing him up, and asked, "How much ya lookin' for?"

"An eight-ball," replied Jack.

"Meet me in the can in three minutes," said the dealer.

The transaction went smoothly and the dealer sold Jack one-eighth of an ounce of cocaine. Five minutes later, Jack returned and sat with Laura.

They watched as the dealer returned and spoke with McCall. Over the next hour, three dealers periodically met with McCall.

Jack waited until he saw McCall walking back from the bathroom before approaching him and blocking his path. "I got something to say to you," said Jack.

"Yeah?" replied McCall, staring down at Jack.

"The coke your guy sold me better be good or you'll be losing a lot of business."

McCall's face showed instant rage and he said, "I don't know what the fuck you're talking about!"

"Oh, don't give me that," replied Jack. "I'm in the business, too. I can see what is going on with the guys you got working for you."

McCall stepped closer to Jack and cocked his fist. The violent response caught Jack slightly off guard and he could feel the spittle spray on his face as McCall spoke. "You shouldn't be fuckin' talkin' to me! I just got out of jail two weeks ago! I don't know you!"

"Yeah?" replied Jack calmly. "Well I don't know you, either. But I want you to know that I'm looking for a steady connection so I can send good quantity back to Alberta. Right now I'm scoring small samples to see who has the best stuff. If your stuff is shit, then you'll be losing a chance to be making big bucks down the road."

McCall stepped back, panting heavily as he tried to decide whether Jack was a provocation or a business opportunity. Jack recalled the warning he had received earlier about McCall. *He is dangerous ... and unpredictable ...*

"What weight ya talkin' about?" asked McCall.

Jack shrugged and said, "Well, as you said, I don't know you, either. I'd prefer to start off small. Maybe a pound to begin with. If it is good and everything goes well, then I'd have no trouble handling a few keys every month."

McCall said, "Well the stuff you got tonight has been stepped on, I'll tell you that now. But if you're buying quantity I won't dilute it. How about we meet tomorrow around noon and I'll sell you an ounce as a sample?"

Jack agreed and the following day he waited in an alley behind a Victoria restaurant. Eventually McCall arrived and motioned for Jack to get in his car. Jack complied and was not too concerned as Dave Valentine, along with several other members of the Victoria PD, were hiding in close proximity.

"You got it!" yelled McCall looking wild-eyed as Jack sat in the car and closed the door.

Jack wondered if McCall was planning on robbing him so he nodded toward his own car in the alley and said, "I've got my end together, how about you?"

McCall's demeanour changed abruptly. "Yeah, right here," he replied softly while reaching in his pants pocket to retrieve a small plastic bag of cocaine.

"A beautiful day," said Jack, eyeing McCall curiously.

"Yeah, it's nice here," replied McCall. "You'll like Victoria."

Jack nodded and said, "Actually I've got the money with me." He passed McCall a wad of cash and in return received the cocaine.

As McCall was counting the money a seagull flew low over the car and landed on the ground. "What the fuck?" screamed McCall. The muscles in his face twitched and he bounced around on the seat looking out all the car windows.

"Just a bird," said Jack.

"Oh," replied McCall as he started counting the money over again.

"So this stuff is good?" said Jack. "Better than what you sold me last night?"

"Oh, yeah. I didn't step on it at all."

"You do some yourself?" asked Jack, wondering if cocaine was responsible for McCall's mood swings.

"Fuck, no. Don't do dope."

You act this way without being on drugs? You are nuts ...

"You do dope?" asked McCall.

"Nope. That's for chumps. I'd rather make money."

"That's how I look at it, too."

Jack returned to his own car and watched as McCall drove slowly down the alley, but before reaching the end he abruptly stepped on the gas. His tires squealed as the car burst wildly out of the alley and onto the street before disappearing amongst a honking of horns.

Moments later Jack met with Laura and members of the Victoria PD.

Jack turned over the plastic baggie of cocaine to Valentine and said, "This guy is dangerous."

"I know. I warned you."

Jack looked at Laura and sighed.

"What is it?" she asked.

"In all good conscience I don't think we should give McCall the opportunity to stay out of jail."

Laura stared briefly at Jack and said, "It's your call. I respect your opinion on that. Connie won't be happy."

"Neither will some citizen when they cross paths with McCall. He's a ticking time bomb waiting to go off." Jack looked at Valentine and said, "Bust him. I'll testify when the time comes."

Later, Jack called Connie.

"How did it go?" she asked. "Did he roll? Does he know who Cocktail is?"

Jack sighed and said, "Sorry, Connie. For your investigation, consider McCall a dead end. He's too dangerous. I'm not giving him the opportunity to talk. We'll need to find some other way to pursue this."

"What are you talking about? We need to identify Cocktail!"

"I know that," replied Jack as he hung up.

Chapter Eleven

On Monday morning Jack received an unexpected call from Gabriel Parsons, inviting him over for tea.

"I don't know if you know," said Gabriel, "but we've moved to a new home in Richmond. Well ... not exactly new. About the same as our other place, but new to us. A new start, I pray."

That was fast, thought Jack, before realizing three months had passed since Father Brown was murdered. *Three months and we're no further ahead ...*

Jack arrived at the new address and Gabriel invited him inside for tea and freshly baked chocolate-chip cookies.

"I wanted to apologize," said Gabriel. "I believe I was rude to you when ... well, when we first met. I was blaming you for allowing these men to make drugs in my basement."

"I'm the policeman, not the judge who let them out," said Jack.

"I realize that. I also spoke with my neighbour before I moved. Was it you who came and cleaned the back of my house?"

Jack nodded and recalled the numerous sprays of blood that he had scrubbed off. It made him conscious of how much time had passed while a monster remained on the loose.

"That was a very Christian thing to do. Out of curiosity, what church do you belong to?"

"I'm an atheist."

"Oh … I see," replied Gabriel, with a frown.

"How is Faith?" asked Jack, intentionally changing the subject.

"She's still in hospital. She has one more round of radiation to go. The doctor seems optimistic. I have been praying that God does not take her from me this soon."

"And your son? How is he doing?"

"Noah is … well, he's had to adjust to a new school. He's been fighting. I think he is angry at the world. He and Father Brown were close. It was like he lost his father all over again. At least the doctors say he is healthy."

"Would you like me to talk to him?"

"Thank you, but no. Together, our faith in God will see us through these troubled times. The school counsellor is also involved."

"I see. And your daycare? Have you started up again?"

"I have one dear little toddler for three days a week when her mother works. Hopefully more will come later. All of my previous clients have taken their children elsewhere. I can't blame them, I suppose."

"It wasn't your fault."

Gabriel shrugged off his comment and said, "I also have a basement suite, but have been afraid to … well, after last time … would you happen to know anyone? Perhaps a young police officer or someone who would be interested?"

"Not offhand, but I will ask around," replied Jack.

The rest of the visit went well, but Jack felt mixed emotions when he left. He was relieved that Gabriel was not blaming him, but at the same time he spotted a photograph of Faith and felt frustrated that he was no closer to identifying Cocktail than he was months earlier.

Two more weeks passed with little activity until the day that Kent Rodine appeared for his trial over his charges stemming from when seven labs were raided. Jack and Laura, both parked outside the courthouse, waited for a call from one of the Drug Section investigators. The call came early in the afternoon.

"Jack. Sammy here. You wouldn't believe the performance. Rodine's girlfriend looks like she's going to give birth any moment. They were being all kissy-face and he was patting her stomach. Once, when Rodine was being cross-examined I think she had a contraction. The jury couldn't take their eyes off of her."

"Do you know her name?"

"I heard the lawyer refer to her as Miss Venice when he asked if she was okay."

"Is the jury still out?"

"No, they're back already. It's the fastest I've seen a jury reach a decision. Guess they didn't want to watch a baby being born in front of them. No big surprise, they found Rodine not guilty. Didn't matter that his fingerprints were on the glassware. Good news for you, but to me the whole thing sucks."

"You got an eye on them?"

"Yeah, they should be coming out soon. He groomed for court and is clean shaven with short hair and wearing a blue, pin-striped suit. She is as big as a house. You can't miss them. Hang on ... the lawyer is walking with them. You should see all of them in about half a minute."

"Who is the lawyer?" asked Jack.

"A biker lawyer. Basil Westmount."

"Same one that Varrick had," replied Jack. "That's a good sign. Could mean that Rodine is close to Satans Wrath."

"Good luck."

Rodine, Venice, and Westmount left the courthouse together and walked to a nearby lounge. Jack and Laura walked in as their targets sat down in a booth. Connie, along with several other I-HIT members, remained outside to continue the surveillance when they left.

Although the lighting was dim, there were no other customers and Jack knew that they could not sit beside them in the next booth and listen without attracting attention.

"What do you figure?" whispered Laura. "Maybe we should wait outside."

"I'd like to know if Cocktail's name comes up," replied Jack.

"They'll burn us if we try to listen in on —"

"Come on," said Jack, taking Laura by the hand and walking over and sitting at the booth adjoining Westmount, Rodine, and Venice. Westmount, who had been talking, became quiet as soon as Jack and Laura sat down. Laura looked at Jack and grimaced.

"Let's sit farther back where it's darker," said Jack, standing up. "Your hubby works around here. If he walks in, it's better if we see him first."

Westmount watched quietly as Jack and Laura moved to a table farther away before resuming their conversation. Rodine and Venice did not seem to notice and were still excited from their victory in court.

"Told you sitting next to them wasn't a good idea," said Laura.

"Guess you were right," replied Jack.

"Oh, man," muttered Laura. "Venice ordered a beer. I want to go over there and tell her off."

"And you thought sitting next to them would heat us up," replied Jack. "Forget that idea."

After three drinks each and an hour later, Rodine, Venice, and Westmount left the lounge. Jack was glad that neither man gave them a second look. His actions earlier hadn't caused them concern.

Laura used her BlackBerry to call Connie. "Got 'em?" Laura asked.

"Ten-four," replied Connie. "They meet anyone?"

"No. Jack and I will have to play catch-up." As she spoke, Laura saw Jack go over to the bench that

Westmount had been sitting on. Laura continued to talk to Connie and said, "We'll call you when — oh, man!"

"What is it?" asked Connie.

Laura watched as Jack bent over and retrieved an object from under the bench.

"Laura? What's wrong?" asked Connie.

"Uh ... nothing. Almost broke a nail."

By the time Jack and Laura returned to their car, Connie called to say that Rodine and Venice had said goodbye to Westmount and were getting in a car. The car was registered to a low-level drug trafficker in Richmond. Jack wondered if the car was "loaned" because the owner was behind on a drug payment. Not an uncommon practice in the drug business.

As Laura wheeled through traffic to catch up to the surveillance team, she said, "Okay. Let's hear it."

"Hear it?"

"Your voice-activated recorder. Smooth, I didn't see you do it."

"Taping Rodine without a judge's order ... Laura, I'm aghast. That would be illegal."

"It would be illegal, anyway. Conversation with his lawyer is privileged." She snapped, "Quit pretending! I saw you go back to where Westmount was sitting."

"This is strictly between the two of us," said Jack, as he took the recorder out of his jacket.

"It had better be," said Laura seriously.

"We listen once and I erase it."

"Erasing a problem is easier than burying it in a cemetery," replied Laura.

Jack put his finger to his lips, gesturing to Laura to be quiet as he played back the recorder.

The first conversation they heard was Venice laughing as she said, "Well, do you think it's time for me to give birth to an eight-pound pillow?"

"I would prefer if you waited until you were back in the car," said Westmount. "I wouldn't like to take a chance that we run into the judge or juror members when we leave."

"If you insist," giggled Venice. "How was my performance?"

"Outstanding," said Westmount. "I'm tempted to hire you for other cases. Next time maybe you could babysit someone's infant and bring it to court."

"You think I'm that good?"

"You were really good, honey," said Rodine.

"Cute touch on your part, too," said Westmount, "by patting her stomach."

Jack paused the recorder and said, "And you thought she was going to be a bad mother. Jumping to conclusions like that. Shame on you," he said, with mock admonishment.

"I don't know whether to be happy that she isn't pregnant or angry at her deceit."

Jack clicked the recorder back on. The rest of the conversation was uneventful up until Westmount ordered the bill from the waiter.

"Speaking of bills," said Westmount, "do you want to pay me now? I never know where to send your invoice."

"Tomorrow is Friday, which is delivery day for me," replied Rodine. "I've got the ol' cookie sheets full. Tomorrow morning I'll bag and deliver. I can bring you the cash then."

"I've got a trial scheduled for ten tomorrow morning," replied Westmount.

"Not a problem. I'll be on the road by six. Gotta have it delivered by eight. I could still make it to your office by nine."

"Perfect," replied Westmount. "I'll give you the invoice then."

"Wish the invoice really matched what I have been paying you," grumbled Rodine.

"Hey, we talked about that. I've warned you that leaving a paper trail could put you in jeopardy if they ever go after you with a proceeds of crime investigation."

"Don't give me that bullshit," chuckled Rodine. "You're saving yourself from paying taxes."

"Okay, so our partnership is of a mutual benefit. Besides, you're a fine one to talk about paying taxes. At least I pay some."

"I would pay taxes, but I'm still waiting for my T-4s to arrive."

The conversation ended in laughter. Jack looked at Laura to see what she was thinking. Her smile said it all.

"We better not lose them," said Jack.

"With the army that Connie has out?" replied Laura. "They better not. Too bad we can't tell her what we heard."

"Let her worry. I told her this case would take time."

"As long as it's not us doing time," shot back Laura, with a nod toward the recorder in Jack's hand.

The surveillance team followed Rodine and Venice to an older home in Burnaby. As the surveillance team waited, Connie got in the back seat of Jack and Laura's car.

"Figure he might have a lab in there?" asked Connie.

"Time will tell," replied Jack.

Over the next couple of hours, numerous people showed up and most were carrying in cases of beer and liquor.

"Celebrating his court case," said Jack. "He won't have a lab in there."

"Christ, we need something," said Connie. "You think we'd make a green light sooner or later. I'm getting sick of all these dead ends. What if he's not even in the meth business anymore? Then what the hell —"

"Trust me," said Jack. "He's still in business."

"You sound very confident," said Connie, leaning forward in an attempt to see Jack's face.

"Guys like this don't quit," he replied.

"Oh," she said and sat back in the seat.

Over the next couple of hours a few more people arrived, but from the licence plates gathered, most appeared to be petty criminals or small-time drug traffickers.

At midnight Connie looked at her watch and said, "Guess there is no sense wasting manpower. I think I should call it off. With all the booze going in there, I bet he sleeps the day away tomorrow. I've still got a court brief I have to study tonight for a trial tomorrow morning. Maybe we can sit on Rodine again tomorrow night or the next day."

"Uh … I've known some of these guys to be early risers," said Jack.

"Really?" replied Connie. "Most of the criminals I know sleep until at least noon. What are you trying to pull?" she asked suspiciously. "Hoping to gaff a bunch of overtime?"

"No, I'm serious," replied Jack. "With labs, sometimes certain chemicals have to be added at specific times. I think we should stay on him for at least forty-eight hours straight."

"You shitting me?"

"Jack is right," said Laura. Considering the time he spent in court, if he has a lab … and I'm sure he does, he'll have to check it soon."

"Put it this way," said Jack. "Laura and I are going to sit on him all night, but it is your case. If he goes mobile and we lose him, it will be your fault."

"Don't you two ever sleep?" Connie asked.

"We take turns sleeping in the car," replied Laura.

"Okay," sighed Connie. "I'll tell you what. I'll leave two guys behind tonight and will put a full team back on at eight tomorrow morning. That good enough for you?"

"Guess it will have to be," replied Jack reluctantly.

Connie got out of the car and closed the door, but paused before turning and knocking on Jack's window. When he opened the window she leaned in to look at their faces. "Anything you're not telling me?" she asked.

"Nope," they both replied in unison.

"Yeah ... that's what I thought," she said. "I'll leave you four people instead of two."

"Hope she never switches over to Internal," said Jack, as they watched Connie walk away.

At six o'clock in the morning Jack reached into the back seat and shook Laura awake and said, "He's out to the car. We're about to be mobile," he added, while reaching for the police radio to alert the others.

For the next half-hour, Rodine drove in and out of parking lots while constantly monitoring his rear-view mirror. Eventually he headed off and at seven o'clock he drove down an alley behind an older house in Burnaby and pulled up to an attached garage.

"Has to be the lab," said Laura.

"Can't see him driving in circles for any other reason," replied Jack, while wiping the sleep from his eyes.

The police radio squawked again to announce that Connie had arrived at work. "I hear you guys are mobile. What's going on?"

"He did a bunch of heat checks and we followed him to a dumpy old house in Burnaby. Close to the PW Brewery."

"Think it's a lab?"

"Good chance."

"Did he switch vehicles like Varrick did?"

"No, but the car he's driving isn't registered to him."

"I need grounds for a warrant. Can you smell anything indicating chemicals?"

"All I smell is the brewery."

"My court case isn't until ten. I'm on my way."

Rodine was in the house half an hour before driving away. The surveillance team followed him to a six-level apartment building in White Rock and watched him park out front.

"Anybody able to go on foot and walk in with him?" radioed Connie.

Jack and Laura drove past the front of the building and Jack quickly grabbed the radio. "Cancel that," he ordered. "There's someone standing six in the lobby. Two more punks are walking out front. Everyone stay back."

"What is this place?" asked Laura. "The Canadian Mint doesn't have this much security."

Jack didn't respond as he was busy copying licence plates into his recorder as they drove down the block.

Seconds later, Rodine returned to his car, only to drive into the apartment's underground parking garage. Five minutes later he drove back out onto the street and was followed to downtown Vancouver. After stopping at Basil Westmount's office, he returned home.

Connie remained in Vancouver for her court case. It was later adjourned so she returned to where the surveillance team was parked at Rodine's house. Connie got in the back seat of Jack and Laura's car as Jack was calling in the licence plates he'd recorded from the apartment building.

Many of the plates were associated to gang members in The Brotherhood. Jack's next call was to Dan Mylo in the Organized Crime Task Force who said that the apartment building was of particular interest. The apartment manager was a man by the name of Sy Sloan, who was the leader of one of the gangs.

"We think Sy controls the whole building as far as who is allowed to live there," said Dan. "Sy is out of shape, but he is monstrous in size and looks intimidating. The apartment building is like a fort. He picks and chooses who lives there. You won't get inside without them knowing. All the straight citizens have been driven out."

"You have any wire on the occupants?" asked Jack.

"Not at the moment," replied Dan. "Not enough grounds. If you can help us in that regard it would be much appreciated."

"I think Rodine is delivering meth to someone in the apartment, but I don't know who."

"That's the problem we've been having. We've had targets come and go, but once they're inside that place, who knows what is going on or who they're meeting," said Dan.

"We need an informant," said Jack.

"That we do, my friend, that we do."

Jack hung up and told Laura and Connie what he had learned.

"Figure Rodine is delivering meth to The Brotherhood?" asked Connie.

"Positive," replied Jack. "My guess is he got paid for it and then went and paid his lawyer."

"Think maybe we should bust him next time and see if he'll talk?" suggested Connie.

"He won't talk," replied Jack. "There is no incentive. Not with what he would get in court, Satans Wrath would deal out a far worse punishment. Plus we don't have grounds to stop and search him. His first call would be to Basil Westmount."

"Maybe you could make a UC buy from him?"

"This guy is a cook, not the dealer. Besides, even if I did, there is no incentive strong enough for him to talk."

"Isn't there something we can do?"

"We should do surveillance on the apartment building," said Jack. "Figure out who more of the players are. We could get lucky. Maybe Cocktail lives in the building or visits here."

"If we get lucky … but then what? I need evidence. Bullshit gossip doesn't stand up. Hang on, I'm calling PPSC to see what my chances are of getting a wire on Rodine."

Connie spoke for several minutes with a Crown Prosecutor before hanging up. She was quick to the point. "Goddamn it! Goddamn it! God-damn it! He says I don't have grounds for either a search warrant or a wire …" She drove her fist into the back of the seat and said, "Christ this is bullshit. We don't even know if his place near the brewery is a lab."

Jack made eye contact with Laura and stared silently at her as Connie complained. Laura paused for a moment before giving a subtle nod.

"We're all tired," said Jack. "Let's go home early and reintroduce ourselves to our spouses."

"The day has turned out pretty good," said Laura. "We've discovered his lab and know what apartment building he is delivering it to."

"We only think we've discovered his lab," replied Connie. "And what good is that if Rodine won't talk? We don't even know if he knows Cocktail."

"As I said," repeated Jack, "we're all tired. A few days of surveillance on Sy and his people could turn up something." He turned and stared at Connie and said, "Trust me, we will come up with something. I'm nauseated from the reports rolling in every day on what meth is doing to people. A lot of innocents are getting hurt."

"Hope you don't think I'm blaming you," said Connie. "I feel so frustrated. Maybe a good night's sleep would help."

It was two o'clock in the morning when Jack took the small leather case out of his jacket pocket. Laura, holding a flashlight, stood quietly as Jack picked the lock. When the door opened, they caught the strong smell of an odour that they knew did not come from the brewery. Seconds later, their sense of smell had been annihilated. It would be several hours before they would be able to smell again.

"Not healthy in here," whispered Laura.

"I know. A quick peek and we're gone."

The first room was a kitchen with an old table and chrome chairs with ripped plastic seat cushions. Down the hall was a bedroom. The door was open and Jack could see a grubby mattress lying on the floor. Opposite the bedroom was another door that was closed. Laura shone her flashlight on the door and Jack saw a picture of a small animal.

"What's that?" he said.

"It's a picture of a hamster," replied Laura. "Gee, it's really cute." Her mind came back to the reason they were there and she gestured to the door. "What do you think?"

"The lab room in Gabriel's basement had something taped to the outside of the door," said Jack. "About the same size. The room was also booby trapped."

"You think the hamster is a terrorist?"

"I don't know what the picture has to do with it. He does have beady eyes."

"How do you know it's a he?"

"He has whiskers."

Laura snickered and said, "Well, one thing is for certain. You've convinced me not to open this door. From what we smelled when we first came in, we know the lab is here."

"I'd feel better if I could see it," replied Jack. "Go back and wait. I'll be done in a second."

"No! You come, too. I'm not bringing you home to Natasha in a garbage bag."

Jack chuckled and said, "The booby trap was dismantled at Gabriel's, but they left behind some eyehole screws above the door. I'm sure you can open the door a little to turn it off, but I want you to go."

"I'll stay and hold the light," she replied.

"I'll hold it in my mouth. Get out of here."

"If you think it is safe enough for you, then it is safe enough for me."

"You're really stubborn, do you know that?" said Jack in exasperation.

"Must be contagious. Hurry and get it over with."

"Okay, but at least stand to one side … and there won't be any hurrying," replied Jack, as he slowly turned the door knob. They both winced as the door clicked open a crack.

"I'm going to hold the door steady," said Jack. "Shine the light at the top of the jamb."

Laura did as instructed and Jack saw a slim metal lever extending up from the far side of the top of the door. He ran his fingers up the piece of metal and detected a strand of wire passing along the far side. He gently pushed on the side of the metal lever until it moved below the height of the wire. After exhaling audibly, he slowly pushed the door open.

The room contained the lab. The wire wound its way through a couple of eyehole screws to a large glass carboy filled with liquid. There were several benches containing glassware and numerous bottles of chemicals. A wooden rack contained numerous cookie sheets with traces of white powder. "Don't think that was cookies he was making," commented Laura.

"We've seen enough," said Jack. "Too bad we have to keep this to ourselves."

* * *

Over the next few days, the surveillance team discovered that Rodine would go to the meth lab during the day, only to return home at night where he and Venice would spend their time watching videos.

It was Thursday afternoon and a week had passed since Rodine had won his court case. As usual, Connie sat slumped in the back seat of Jack and Laura's car where they were parked down the street from Rodine's house. Her disposition had become grumpier as the days passed.

Occasional surveillance of The Brotherhood apartment building identified numerous criminals coming and going, including three prospects for Satans Wrath. Nobody had any name or occupation that would warrant the nickname of Cocktail. Jack believed that Rodine was the key and surveillance concentrated on him.

"He's not meeting anyone," said Connie. "At least no asshole by the name of Cocktail that we know of. Maybe we should follow the prospects from Satans Wrath."

"Those guys are too well trained to lead us to Cocktail," replied Jack. "Relax, I've got a plan to get an informant. Hopefully soon."

"What? This is the first I've heard of it," said Connie. "Who? How —"

"*Who* is on a need to know basis. Sorry, at the moment you don't need to know. It would be better in court if you never knew."

"I suspect there are a lot things where it would be better if I didn't know about you two," said Connie. "Dare I ask how you're going to do it?"

Jack remained silent.

"Okay," said Connie. "Never mind ... just do it."

After Connie left, Jack looked at Laura and said, "You free for a date with me tonight?"

"Sure. You buying dinner?"

"Only if you like baking soda."

"You've piqued my curiosity. Who is this new informant?"

"Rodine ... if he lives."

Chapter Twelve

On Friday morning, the surveillance team watched Rodine make another trip to The Brotherhood apartment. Minutes later, he returned home.

"Nothing changes," said Connie.

"Nice to confirm he has a schedule," noted Jack. "You're right, though. No use wasting manpower. Last Friday and Saturday he spent all day at home. Let's break off the surveillance. I'm sure you have things to do and Laura and I need to do some things."

"Things like working on getting an informant?" asked Connie, hopefully.

"Exactly."

"Sounds good to me. I've got a ton of paperwork and an upcoming trial to prepare for. Call me if you need a hand."

Jack and Laura drove away as Connie broke off her surveillance team.

"Thought you would want to stay around for the action," said Laura.

"I want Connie to think we left. She's too ethical. If the bikers realize they bought baking soda and show up and decide to torture and possibly kill him, I don't want to take a chance on Connie putting a stop to it."

"Good chance they might kill him."

"I hope they don't because we would need to find another informant, but if they do, it seems like a fair punishment for running a meth lab."

"I agree, so don't be hauling out any pictures of Faith in the hospital or something. I couldn't stand it."

"I don't have any."

"Only because you knew I would be on board with this. Rodine's girlfriend is in there. It could be a double murder. Did you think of that?"

"She put herself into this. If you fly with the crows —"

"If they're both killed, Connie will blame us."

"Act surprised … show concern … deny, deny, deny. It was an unfortunate coincidence that we broke off surveillance."

"She won't believe that for a second."

"I know, but she won't be able to prove anything."

Minutes later, Jack and Laura returned and parked where they could watch the front of Rodine's house with binoculars.

The hours slowly ticked by. Once, Venice, wearing a pink tank top and skin-tight blue jeans over her thin figure, strolled outside and picked some flowers growing near the house and went back inside.

Late in the afternoon a black SUV arrived and three prospects from Satans Wrath got out and approached the house.

"Showtime," said Jack. He was unable to see who answered the door, but he did see one of the bikers deliver a fist to the person's face before all three disappeared inside.

"Ouch," said Laura, watching through her own set of binoculars. "No hello, how are you, nothing …"

Twenty-five minutes passed before the three bikers left the house and drove away.

"They left Rodine and Venice in the house," noted Laura. "Maybe a good sign."

"That and they didn't light the house on fire. I'm betting things went according to plan."

Minutes later, the front door opened and Rodine limped out onto the porch landing.

"Broken nose," commented Jack, looking at the blood streaming down the front of Rodine's shirt. "Holding his side … maybe broken or cracked ribs."

"Heading for his car," said Laura.

"Oh, crap," interjected Jack sadly, more to himself than Laura.

"What?"

"Check the porch … Venice came out … she wants him to stay."

Laura focused back on the porch. She saw why Jack was distressed. Venice clutched a bathrobe to her naked body. She had received more than a beating.

Jack and Laura followed Rodine as he drove back to his lab.

"Rush order, I bet," said Laura.

"Will take a couple of days," replied Jack. "Starting Sunday we'll check every night."

"We're taking tomorrow off? I won't know what to do," teased Laura.

"Do you remember Ngọc Bích?"

"Of course. Your Vietnamese friend. Isn't the trial coming up soon on the two brothers who owned the brothels?"

"It got moved to June 15. The same day I'm scheduled to testify in Victoria against Cory McCall."

"It will be good to put McCall away. Sounds like you and Ngọc Bích will have something to celebrate that day, as well."

"Hope there are no more adjournments with Ngọc Bích."

"How has she been doing?"

"She's a bit like a wounded bird, but is slowly getting it together. Good days and bad. She's been enrolled in music lessons since we rescued her. She plays a flute."

"Probably therapeutic," said Laura.

"Tomorrow she is giving a free performance in Stanley Park at noon."

"Elvis and I will be there," said Laura.

"Natasha and I were going to bring a picnic lunch."

"Sounds good. I'll give Natasha a call after and we can figure out what to bring."

* * *

The following morning, Jack walked out of the shower and saw Natasha lying naked in bed with a sheet pulled up to the bottom of her navel. She was performing her monthly ritual of doing a self-examination of her breasts as she carefully checked for any lumps.

"Wish you would teach me how to help you with that," said Jack, marvelling at how beautiful she looked.

Natasha looked up at him and said, "I did try to teach you once. As I recall, you became sidetracked."

"Sometimes I have a hard time with concentration."

Natasha continued her exam, but quit a moment later and said, "Quit staring at me! I can't concentrate."

"I bet you're remembering the last time I tried to help you," said Jack, teasingly.

Natasha paused, furrowing her forehead as if trying to remember, before saying, "That was a long time ago." She smiled and said seductively, "My memory could use refreshing."

Jack felt the blood pulse to his groin. No further invitation was needed.

Later that afternoon, Jack and Natasha and Laura and Elvis sat on a blanket in Stanley Park and listened to Ngọc Bích play her flute.

"She plays beautifully," commented Natasha, sitting with her back pressed up against Jack's chest.

Jack wrapped his arms around her and kissed her on the back of her neck. The day was captured in his memory as one of the most beautiful he'd ever had.

When Ngọc Bích was finished, she joined them for the picnic and received a bouquet of red roses as a gift from Jack and Natasha. The afternoon was warm, sunny, and peaceful. Jack was glad that Ngọc Bích did not discuss the upcoming trial scheduled for the following month. Everyone needed the break.

Sunday morning came and Jack read the newspaper. He wished he hadn't. An article reported a young man being randomly attacked outside a grocery store by four guys who slashed his face with a knife. The attackers were alleged to be high on meth.

"Something wrong?" asked Natasha. "You're frowning."

Jack sighed and said, "Laura and I hope to turn an informant this week. The guy runs a meth lab. If he cooperates, I'm going to have to allow him to continue running his lab. At least for a while."

"For the greater good, I presume. The big picture."

Jack smiled, despite how he felt. "You sound like Laura."

"Maybe we sound like you."

"Maybe," said Jack, tossing the paper aside.

"Yesterday was really a perfect day," said Natasha. "Romantic."

Jack smiled. It had been good to see how far Ngọc Bích had recovered from her months of torture. The delay in the trial only gave her time to get stronger. He knew she was looking forward to her day in court and confronting the monsters responsible.

His thoughts turned to Faith and he knew there was another monster to catch.

Chapter Thirteen

Kent Rodine's next batch of methamphetamine was on the drying racks Tuesday night. At seven o'clock Wednesday morning he returned to his lab and used the privacy of the garage to load the kilos of meth into the trunk of his car. As he raised the garage door to leave, a man with a gun shoved him violently against his chest, knocking him back onto the trunk of the car. At the same time, another car pulled in and parked in the driveway.

Seconds later, Rodine was handcuffed and sprawled over the hood of his car. He watched sullenly as Jack opened the trunk and retrieved one of the kilos. Laura, standing with her pistol pointed at the base of Rodine's neck, quietly stepped back as Jack approached.

"Got some good news and some bad news for you, Kent," said Jack. "Bad news is we're seizing all the dope from your car. Good news is we're not going to arrest you. You might want to start thinking of an excuse to your friends to explain how you lost the dope."

"What? You can't do that! You have to arrest me!"

"Why? It isn't like you would get any real time and it means a bunch of paperwork for us. Kind of a nuisance, really."

"No, you don't understand," said Rodine. "These people ... they're not my ... they wouldn't understand or believe ... they ... last week ... Christ, man, you gotta bust me."

"We are not going to arrest you, that I can promise," said Jack.

"They'll kill me," he pleaded.

"I know. I simply don't care."

"Why? Why me? This ain't right!" he cried.

"Jack, it really isn't right that we don't give him a chance first," said Laura. "He doesn't seem like that bad or stupid of a person. Maybe he would want to co-operate with us. Tell us stuff so we could catch enough people to make it worthwhile."

"I, I can't do that either," whined Rodine. "Without the dope they would kill me, anyway. You don't understand. Last week something went wrong. Someone must've cut the shit after I delivered it. The bi— ... these guys I work for, they think I tried to rip them off. They came over and kicked the shit out of me. Then tied me to a chair and made me watch as they took turns fuckin' my girlfriend every which way —"

"I don't care and I don't feel like listening to all this bullshit," said Jack.

"It's not bullshit!" Rodine stopped talking and his mouth hung open for a moment as he looked back and forth at Jack and Laura. His eyes settled on Jack and his voice turned pleading. "I'd help ya. Believe me, I'd help ya ... but I can't. You gotta bust me. Please."

"Maybe he would be a suitable candidate for Witness Protection," suggested Laura.

"No," cried Rodine. "If you put me in Witness Protection, they know where my folks live and my brother's and sister's families. They'd whack them if they couldn't find me. And if they did find me, last week would be a picnic compared to what they would do next time. No, you gotta bust me. It's the only way I'll stay alive. I've been working my ass off these last few days. Started the second batch going before this one was done. It was dangerous as shit in there."

"What if you help us and we let you keep the dope and keep making it?" said Jack.

"You would do that?" replied Rodine with a glimmer of hope.

"Only if you're absolutely honest with us about everything ... do exactly what we tell you and keep us in the loop. When I figure you've paid your debt, you'll be cut loose."

"But if you bust these guys they'll know it was me. I can't take a chance that —"

"I will make you a promise that we will never do anything to burn you," replied Jack.

Rodine paused and said, "It ain't exactly like I got a choice, is it?"

"You could be a hero and kill yourself," said Jack, indifferently. "It might spare your girlfriend."

"I ain't no hero. What do you want to know?"

"Everything. Start from the beginning since your last bust. Who do you sell to and who do you get your chemicals and glassware from?"

"Will you take the cuffs off me?"

Seconds later, Rodine sat on the hood of the car with one hand holding his rib cage.

"Did these guys break your ribs?" asked Jack.

Rodine nodded and said, "Broken or cracked. Either way they hurt like hell every time I take a breath."

"Tell us who attacked you last week."

Rodine paused, grimaced and looked at Jack and said, "There were three of 'em. Bikers with Satans Wrath. Well, either with them or workin' for them. I only know them as Croaker, Hamburger, and Chugger."

"How long have you been hanging out with Satans Wrath?"

"I don't really hang out with them. I just work for them. I got connected with them about three years ago. Then two years ago I got busted in a lab ... but I beat the case." Rodine looked at Jack and said, "Guess you already know that?"

Jack nodded.

"Yeah, well shortly after that bust, I was approached by a guy by the name of Herm. He's in tight with Satans Wrath. Has been for years. He got busted on the same day in a different lab."

"What's Herm's last name?" asked Jack.

"I'm not sure. Something like Warwick."

"How about Varrick?"

"Varrick?... Yeah, that's it. He taught me how to set up a proper lab. It was like taking a course. Meth 101. Varrick followed written instructions. A step-by-step document."

"So Varrick is the brains behind everything?" asked Laura.

"Naw. He isn't that smart," replied Rodine. "He was trained by someone he calls the Grandmaster Cocktail."

"The Grandmaster Cocktail?" asked Jack, trying to sound only slightly interested. He also realized Rodine was still taking about Varrick in the present tense and did not know he was dead.

"Yeah, or just Cocktail, as he usually refers to him. Cocktail knows how to make the purest form of meth going and do it real professional-like."

"Interesting," said Jack, trying not to let his excitement show. "Tell us everything you know about Cocktail and then work down from there."

"I'm told Cocktail is an expert at making other stuff, too, like ecstasy and GHB, but I only make meth. Other labs make the other stuff."

"GHB," said Jack in disgust. "Gamma-hydroxybutyrate. Better known as the date rape drug. So who is this guy?"

"I've never met him. Varrick said Cocktail originally approached him after the last bust because he read his name in the paper and happened to know where he lived. Cocktail had some smart ideas and a business plan. He knew all about how to make dope and also had access to all the right chemicals. He wanted Varrick to introduce him to someone from Satans Wrath."

"So Varrick did that?" asked Jack.

"Yeah, but there's more. Cocktail also knew names of guys connected with The Brotherhood. His idea was to get the bikers and The Brotherhood to work together and expand sales. Cocktail didn't want to deal with The Brotherhood directly."

"How come?" asked Jack.

"From what Varrick told me, Cocktail knew who a lot of 'em were, but didn't want 'em to know he was involved. A lot of The Brotherhood members are kids … teenagers. He was afraid they would blab. He knew the bikers wouldn't."

"Sounds like Cocktail isn't stupid," said Jack.

"Not according to Varrick. He says the guy is a real brain. Like a scientist. At first Varrick was skeptical of the idea that the bikers would get involved with a bunch of kids or guys who were still in their twenties. Cocktail said they weren't all that young and gave him Sy's name."

"Sy?" repeated Laura.

"Yeah. Sy is the guy I deliver to. He's boss of one of the gangs in The Brotherhood. Anyway, to get the ball rollin', Cocktail agreed to go with Varrick and run the idea past Sy, who jumped at the chance. Then Varrick took Cocktail to meet with the bikers who also liked the idea. The bikers brought Cocktail in under their wing and made inroads into The Brotherhood through Sy. After that, Cocktail developed a training course. Varrick said Cocktail taught him and the rest is history."

"Where is Varrick's lab?" asked Jack.

"I dunno. Never been there. Lab locations are kept real secret. Varrick did mention it's in the basement of some woman's daycare, though."

"Cocktail knew it was a daycare?" asked Jack.

"Oh, yeah. That was like Step One in Meth 101. Location. The first time, Cocktail rented a place with a fake driver's licence he got from the bikers and used a cover story of a Janitorial Supply Company. Guess he proved himself because the bikers were impressed. After that, the bikers used other guys to rent places."

"Cocktail didn't care that it was a daycare?" asked Laura.

"Naw. The thing is, it's close to an industrial area. Cocktail told Varrick to try and put a lab in an area that would help hide the smell." Rodine gestured with his hand and said, "It's no accident that this place is close to the brewery. Varrick said Cocktail laughed about the daycare and joked that a bunch of tots crappin' their pants would also help hide the smell."

"I take it, Cocktail doesn't care about kids getting cancer," said Jack coldly.

"I hadn't really thought about it. I think most of the labs are in rented spots. Nobody wants to use their own place. When I work in the lab I usually wear a mask."

"Aren't you the smart one," said Jack, knowing the cheap paper masks he previously saw inside would do little to stop the carcinogenic fumes from entering his lungs.

"Yeah, thanks," replied Rodine, not realizing Jack was being sarcastic. "Anyway, Step Two is setting the lab up the proper way and learning how to make the shit. Cocktail taught that to Varrick who then taught others, including me."

Rodine paused as Jack jotted down some notes, before continuing, "Oh, yeah, all the labs are booby trapped as per Cocktail's instructions. Wrong person enters and the whole place goes up in a big fireball. It will destroy all evidence and whoever enters, as well."

"Like a cop," said Laura.

"Yeah, or someone trying to rip us off. I can take ya inside and show ya, if you like?"

"Later. Is there a Step Three?" asked Jack.

"Yeah, the most important step. Marketing. We hand a percentage off to Satans Wrath, but also flood the high schools, universities, and colleges with the shit at bargain-basement prices. That's why it's nice to have an in with The Brotherhood. Most are the right age and in school."

"Why sell so low?" asked Laura.

"So they get hooked. When they graduate and get good jobs the price will go up."

"That's if the dope doesn't cause them to flunk out," said Jack.

"Yeah, there's always that possibility," agreed Rodine.

"Any other steps?" asked Jack.

"That's about it. At least how Varrick laid it out to me. Satans Wrath liked the marketing idea, as well.

They distribute the chemicals they get from Cocktail and get a cut of all the action, plus a percentage of all the dope. I don't know how big of a percentage. Sy looks after that."

"Do you deal with any of the bikers direct?" asked Jack.

"Not normally. Things have changed since the last time we were busted. Different bikers for contact with different labs. Even then, the bikers usually use a go-between and rarely have anything to do with the cooks … unless they want to beat the shit out of someone," he added ruefully. "Sy manages an apartment complex. All of the tenants in there work for him in one way or another. That's who I deliver to."

"But Cocktail and Sy know each other," said Jack.

"Only sort of."

"Sort of?" questioned Jack.

"Cocktail knew who Sy was, but, according to Sy, hadn't met the guy before then. Still doesn't know his real name. It was Varrick who first started calling him Cocktail. Sy likes to brag a lot about who he knows and his connections with Satans Wrath, but he is tight-lipped about Cocktail. He knows what the bikers will do to him if he ever spilled the beans."

"Does Sy still meet with Cocktail?" asked Jack.

"I don't think so. The bikers act as the go-between. They taught Sy how to be really careful, like using lap-tops and other people's wireless signals to communicate through chat rooms. On rare occasions, he'll text a coded message on his BlackBerry, but you'll never get him talking about anything on the phone. Doesn't even talk in his apartment. If something needs saying, he takes you for a walk down the hall. Sy has lots of people he deals to. Even his half-brother, Tommy, is the main supplier for his school."

"School!" noted Jack. "How old is Sy?"

"I think thirty-two. Tommy is seventeen."

"What school does Tommy go to?" asked Jack.

"Queen Elizabeth Secondary in Surrey. He still lives at home with his mom and Sy's dad."

Jack and Laura glanced at each other. Crime Stoppers had received several tips about dealers in that school.

Jack looked at Rodine and continued. "How many labs are Satans Wrath getting a percentage from?"

"I don't know. Lots. I do know it ain't wise to try and rip them. Not even a little bit, 'cause either the solutions wouldn't add up or it would have to be diluted. When they were beating on me they said I diluted it with baking soda. I told them I wasn't stupid enough to try and rip them. The fuckin' bastards. I trust Sy, so it had to be one of the bikers who ripped me."

"You said the solutions wouldn't add up if someone was ripping them off?" asked Jack.

"Do you know the main cook we had when we got busted with all those labs last time?"

"Yes."

"Cocktail examined the records that the police turned over to his defence lawyer. From all the empty chemical containers the cops seized, Cocktail calculated that more dope was being made than the bikers knew about."

"So Satans Wrath were being short-changed on their percentage," said Jack.

"Exactly. Varrick told me the cook took a long time to die."

"His body was found in an alley," said Jack. Seeing the nervous look on Rodine's face, he quickly changed the subject and said, "So basically, a network of labs has been set up, with the original training, expertise, and chemicals coming from some guy by the name of Cocktail."

Rodine paused for a moment, reflecting upon the situation he found himself in, and what the future would hold if the bikers found out.

"Trust us," said Jack. "We will never do anything to divulge who you are. Never. So answer our questions."

Rodine swallowed, took a deep breath and slowly exhaled. "Yeah, we follow Cocktail's instructions like he's the great guru. Varrick and Zack run their own lab. Me, I gotta do it myself. Varrick gets the chemicals from Cocktail and passes them on to the bikers for delivery. Find Varrick and Zack and you'll find Cocktail."

"Is there anybody else you know who deals with Cocktail?" asked Jack.

"No, except for the bikers, I think Varrick is the only one who knows who Cocktail really is and the only guy who acts as a go-between for Cocktail and the bikers. Satans Wrath don't want anyone to know that Cocktail is associated with them. The odd time, like maybe once or twice a year if Cocktail can't get all the right chemicals, we sometimes have to change the formula. When that happens, Varrick gets his instructions from Cocktail. Sometimes the new stuff is checked out on a couple of kids to see if they croak or anything. If everything is okay, then Varrick passes on the new recipe to the rest of us."

"Cocktail is the head chef and the rest of you are like the sous chefs," said Laura.

"What's a sous chef?"

"Never mind," replied Jack. "Do you know if any kids have died from the experiments?"

"Varrick once told me that a couple have. I don't know who. Varrick is who you guys should be watchin' if you want to get a handle on everything."

"Varrick and Zack are dead," said Jack. "Both died of a drug overdose two months ago."

"Yeah? Those dumb shits. I wonder what they cranked up?"

"Heroin," replied Jack.

"Stupid bastards. I thought they were smarter than that. Sell dope, don't use it."

"We don't believe it was an accident," said Jack. "Varrick and Zack may have been getting careless. Perhaps drawing police attention," he added.

"Shit ... and here I am talking to you."

"Don't worry. It won't happen to you as long as you stay on our good side. Screw with us, hold anything back ... well, I think you know what will happen."

Rodine nodded silently.

"We would really like to find Cocktail," said Jack. "Do that for us and we're square."

"That may not be easy," replied Rodine. "It ain't healthy for me to be asking questions about him. As I said, Sy is a very cautious dude."

"Don't do anything to get yourself killed," said Jack. "We'll work through this together. What bikers do you get your chemicals from?"

"I place the order through Sy and usually it's different bikers who deliver. Not full-fledged dudes. I forget what they call them."

"Prospects or strikers," said Jack.

"Yeah, that's it. As far as I knew, the bikers got the stuff from Varrick, but if he's dead, then I don't know who the go-between would be."

"Where, when, and how do you get your chemicals?" asked Jack.

"Fuck, the pickups are at weird hours and in different remote areas. That way everyone can check and make sure nobody is being followed."

"Is Sy expecting this delivery right away?" asked Laura, gesturing to the trunk of the car.

"Yeah, I should have it to him around eight. Not much time. Next one is due Saturday morning."

"Okay, I want you to give us a two-minute tour inside the house and then make your delivery," said Jack. "Keep on running the lab like always."

"For how long do I run the lab?"

"Not long. I hate what it is doing to people," said Jack, making no attempt to hide his anger.

"But then what happens?"

"We'll bust your lab when you're not there. You could even say you spotted police surveillance. If you keep your prints and stuff off the glassware, you'll win another court case."

"I don't think I want to chance winning another court case if you plan on busting Sy or any of the bikers. It would be better if I go to jail, too. That way nobody will suspect I ratted out."

"Not a problem," replied Jack. "We'll figure something out when the time comes. I'll give you my cell number. Memorize it. Anything I should know, day or night, call me."

After a quick tour of the lab, Jack and Laura returned to their car.

"Looks like we have someone on the inside," said Laura. "Connie should be happy with what we know."

"Except he's not really on the inside or he would know who Cocktail really is," said Jack. "We're going to have to get to Sy somehow. Doesn't sound like wiretap or surveillance will work."

"Thinking of doing a UC on Sy?" asked Laura.

"It may be our only option. Get our new friend to introduce us. I'd also like to see where and how far spread this dope is going. Maybe Toxicology could help," said Jack, picking up his cellphone and calling the RCMP Crime Lab.

"Toxicology … Lucy, it's Jack Taggart. Sorry, I don't have much time. Is there something we could use to spike a shipment of crystal meth? Something that wouldn't be noticed or hurt people, but at the same time show up like a beacon to you if any of it came back for analysis? It would help us figure out where it is being distributed."

Jack talked for a moment more before smiling and hanging up. He did not realize his decision to chemically tag the drug was about to have a devastating affect on his moral decision to allow the lab to continue operating.

Chapter Fourteen

Connie was mildly pleased when she met with Jack and Laura at their office and learned what their *new friend* had told them.

"Puts us one step closer," she said.

"Sy Sloan has a record three pages long," said Laura, as she slid the criminal record across the desk to Connie. "Includes a dozen drug convictions, several assaults, and possession of restricted weapons."

"But no charges in the last three years," noted Connie as she scanned the documents.

"According to OCTF he is one of the more prominent leaders in The Brotherhood," said Jack. "He's reached the point where others take the risk for him."

"That includes his seventeen-year-old half-brother, Tommy," said Laura. "According to our friend, Tommy is the main meth dealer at Queen Elizabeth Secondary."

"There has been a steady flow of Crime Stoppers tips coming in regarding teenage dealers at QE," said Jack. "Uniform have made several arrests, but Tommy has not been caught yet."

"From what your source says, I'm not optimistic about Sy being caught through surveillance or on a wiretap," said Connie. "And if Sy isn't in contact with Cocktail anymore, then what —"

"Sy is still the stepping stone we need to focus on," interjected Jack. "Looking at his record, he's not overly intelligent. The reason he is a leader is because he is twice the age of most of the punks."

"Also twice the size," said Laura. "OCTF says he's monstrously huge. He rules by intimidation, not brains."

"So what do we do?" asked Connie.

"I think Laura and I could get close to him through a UC," replied Jack. "We could get our new friend to introduce us."

"He would do that?" asked Connie.

"We wouldn't exactly give him a choice," replied Jack.

"Some of the bikers know you," said Connie. "What if you're recognized?"

"It is only the prospective bikers who deal face to face with The Brotherhood. The current prospects don't know us. We'll change our appearance and names. I'll introduce myself as 'Jay.' If I bump into someone from my past who still doesn't know my real occupation and calls me Jack, I can say that Jay is short for that." Jack turned to Laura and said, "How about you? Want me to call you 'Princess' or something?"

"Princess!" Laura gave a pretend giggle before her voice became serious and she said, "Knowing the mentality of those in The Brotherhood, I guess Princess would be appropriate."

"I'll also contact Drug Section and see if Sammy's team can help us out on occasion," said Jack.

"Are you planning on doing a UC right away?" asked Connie.

"Actually, after what happened," cautioned Laura, while looking at Jack, "they might be a little paranoid that our friend is not on the straight and narrow with them. Introducing new faces right away could raise the alarm."

"What happened?" asked Connie.

"Apparently someone ripped off some drugs and our friend took some heat over it," said Jack, noting that Laura gave a slight grimace of self-retribution for making the comment in front of Connie.

"Apparently," repeated Connie, nodding as if she understood something.

"Let's give it a week or two and dig up all the background info we can on Sy," said Jack, then talk to our friend and work out an idea for an introduction."

"Well, apparently, I guess that is all we can do," replied Connie.

Saturday morning came and Rodine made his next delivery to Sy. This time the shipment had been chemically tagged to make it identifiable in any future police seizures.

Jack and Laura each made it home for dinner Saturday night and decided to take Sunday and Monday off. Jack felt optimistic that things were coming together and bought a bottle of wine to enjoy with dinner.

It was nine o'clock Sunday morning and sixteen-year-old Julie Goodwin's cereal had gone soggy as she stared down at the bowl. Her mom and dad and twelve-year-old brother, George, had finished their breakfast, but were still at the table making small talk.

Julie knew that in a few minutes they would go off to church and leave her alone. She was too sick to go anywhere. She felt like she was still in a trance. Dark, puffy folds of skin beneath her eyes stood in sharp contrast with the paleness of the rest of her face.

"Are you sure you are going to be okay, dear?" asked her mom.

Julie nodded.

"Yesterday, when you went to ... your new friend ... Lorraine's house for dinner, what did you eat?" asked her dad.

"Pizza."

"Bet it was off," he commented as he stood up from the table.

"We'll check on you when we get home," said her mom, reassuringly.

"I think she's faking it to get out of going to church," said George as he walked past and cuffed her lightly on the back of her head.

Normally his action would have provoked an angry retort in their traditional brother-sister feud ... but this morning was different. Julie reached out unexpectedly and hugged George and kissed him on the cheek.

"I love you, Georgie," she whispered, before quickly letting go.

"Don't you ever do that again!" he protested.

Both parents looked at each other and smiled. Julie was growing up.

Julie waited until they left before getting a notepad and pen. She stared down at the blank pad and thought about the day before. Her new friend, Lorraine, did not turn out to be a friend. She had gone with Lorraine to the house of someone she did not know, although several students she recognized from school were there.

She had one drink. Lorraine said it was a *virgin* Caesar. She felt embarrassed at Lorraine's comment and wished she had never confided in her. She could not remember if she drank it all.

The next thing she remembered was staring up at a bedroom ceiling. She could not move or speak. It was as if she was having an out-of-body experience. Several young guys were having sex with her. They were laughing. One said he had to go last because he had a STD.

Lorraine walked her home later. She told her not to do anything stupid and to consider it a rite of passage.

Lorraine also handed Julie a small baggie of crystal meth and told her to take some, that it would make her feel better. Julie refused and flung it back at her.

Julie squeezed her eyes shut to block out the memory. It didn't work and she stared at the blank piece of paper in front of her. Eventually she picked up the pen and began to write. Her tears smeared some of the ink, but it was still legible.

Dear Mom and Dad,

I am really sorry. Please don't hate me. You two have been the best parents anyone could have. I did something really stupid. The whole school will know. I could never face going back. I am really sorry. Please forgive me. I love you all.

Chapter Fifteen

On Tuesday afternoon, Jack sat at his desk reading reports about minor meth seizures from across the lower mainland.

Laura glanced up and asked, "Any of the seizures from our friend's lab?"

Jack shook his head and said, "Personally, I don't know if that makes me feel good or not."

"I feel the same way. A relief to know that the stuff we're allowing isn't showing up, yet at the same time it makes it difficult to track."

"Obviously there are a lot of other labs running besides ours," replied Jack.

"Ours? Oh, man … I guess you're right," said Laura. "It's awful to think of it in that context."

"If we shut our friend down it won't make any difference," said Jack. "If we don't catch Cocktail they'll start another lab somewhere else."

"I know. At least *our* lab isn't in the basement of a daycare."

"I think we better quit referring to it as ours," said Jack. "Somebody hears that and Internal will be all over us."

"Again."

Jack smiled and said, "Yes, ag—"

His telephone interrupted his conversation and he answered. Laura listened closely when she heard Jack talking to Lucy from Toxicology.

"Our first hit," repeated Jack while looking at Laura and giving her the thumbs-up sign.

"Sixteen-year-old girl by the name of Lorraine Calder," said Jack, while writing down what he was being told. "The police went to interview her as she was arriving home … she tried to chuck a small baggie from her purse … did it match the stuff we tagged? Who was the arresting officer? Gotcha. Thanks a bunch."

Jack hung up and called a constable in Surrey. Laura knew by the look on Jack's face that what he discovered did not make him happy. When he hung up he stared silently at Laura for a moment to collect his thoughts.

"Let me have it," said Laura solemnly.

"They were investigating the suicide of a sixteen-year-old kid who attended QE by the name of Julie Goodwin," said Jack. "An honour student whose brains likely made her a bit of an outcast. She became friends with the girl, Lorraine Calder, and spent last Saturday with her. On Sunday, while her parents were at church, she got the key to her father's gun locker and shot herself. Her parents came home and were reading the suicide note when her younger brother found her body."

"And it was our dope that Lorraine had in her purse," Laura reiterated.

Jack nodded. "Lorraine said that Julie Goodwin gave it to her. Lucy talked to the pathologist and said there was an indication Julie may have been sexually assaulted. Also traces of GHB in her body."

"Date rape," whispered Laura to herself.

"No sign of meth in Julie's body. I think Lorraine is a liar."

"Our friend mentioned that some of the other labs made ecstasy and GHB," said Laura.

Jack was already dialling his cellphone.

Rodine walked the three blocks to a small neighbour-hood playground. He saw Jack and Laura parked nearby and got in the back seat of their car.

"You guys knew I was over drinkin' with Sy last night?" asked Rodine. "That's why you called?"

"Tell us what you found out," replied Jack, wanting to keep Rodine on edge as to how much they did know of his activities.

"Didn't find out much," replied Rodine. "Tommy showed up and was really pissed off. Two of his deal-ers got busted in the parking lot at school yesterday. Tommy thinks a teacher is ratting them out. Says he has it narrowed down to one of three. They might kill the teacher if they find out."

"You serious?" asked Laura.

"Damn rights. They'll kill me, too, if they find out I'm rattin'."

"Previously you mentioned other labs were making ecstasy and GHB," said Jack. "Any idea at all where the labs could be or who the cooks are?"

"No, but Cocktail would be the one who arranged their training on how to make it."

"We want you to introduce us to Sy," said Jack.

"I can't! He'd kill me!"

"Laura and I work on an Intelligence Unit and rarely go to court. We would never do anything to bring heat down on you. If arrests were ever made over anything you were involved in, we would not do it without your permission."

"Really?"

"Really. I want you to tell Sy that you've met someone who you think is connected to the Irish mafia. Tell him we moved here from back east."

"Irish mafia ... fuck, that would impress him. Sy is always watching those old *Godfather* movies. He even talks like Marlon Brando half the time."

"Tell him we move stolen property in a big way and say you think we have connections in the trucking and shipping industries."

"Why not say you're into dope instead?" asked Rodine curiously.

"To protect you. With the bikers hanging a beating on you, they may be a little paranoid if all of a sudden you have new friends wanting to buy dope. We also don't want to come across as competition. I'm five years older than Sy. I want him to to look up to us and not be treating us like a couple of underlings. I want him impressed enough to start confiding or bragging to us."

"How do I say I know you?"

"Tell him you met us a year ago at a really nice restaurant. Say you think we are silent partners in the place and like to party hearty and have lots of cash to throw around."

"What restaurant?"

"Have you been to any classy ones?"

"Yeah ... maybe ... a year ago for my girlfriend's birthday ... let me think."

"Tell Sy you've partied with us often," said Laura. "Introduce Jack as Jay and me as Princess."

"You know," said Rodine, starting to warm up to the idea, "there is an empty apartment in Sy's building that he is looking to fill. Maybe I could tell him that you are interested as a scam to meet him. You wouldn't really have to rent it, but it might be a way for you to invite him to party with you. He likes his booze."

"Perfect," said Jack. "Is the apartment on Sy's floor?"

"Like next door?" asked Laura hopefully.

"No, it's directly above him. The problem is the building isn't very soundproof. Sy gets really pissed off if someone disturbs his sleep. He would prefer to rent it to an old person, like a grandparent of one of his guys. He was doing that, but the old fart croaked last week."

"Tell him you think we are planning on using it to store stuff and won't really be living in it all that much."

"That might work. When should I do it?"

"Immediately, before he rents it to someone else," replied Jack. "Talk to him and give us a call. I'd like to meet him tonight."

After Rodine left the car, Laura said, "Tonight is really pushing it. Not much time to get the UC plan approved."

"Let Connie do the paperwork on that. We don't have time if we want to save a teacher from being murdered."

Chapter Sixteen

Morris Bloomquist had arrived at his apartment and was opening a Chinese food takeout container when the intercom buzzer sounded. He was tired and glared at the intercom speaker on the wall in a subconscious desire for his look to silence it. However, his glare did not have the same success as it did on his staff at Queen Elizabeth, where he was the principal.

Jack identified himself and the buzzer beeped to let him and Laura inside.

"Morris Bloomquist?" asked Jack, while he and Laura showed their badges at the apartment door.

"Mister Bloomquist," he replied. "Did you come to tell me my ex is dead?"

"No," replied Jack, puzzled. More so, when he saw a flash of disappointment cross Bloomquist's face.

"Our apologies," replied Jack. "It can't wait."

"You've interrupted my dinner. I trust you don't mind if I eat it while it is still warm. You may sit if you like."

Jack and Laura sat down and Jack said, "There are two reasons we did not come to the school. First, we both work undercover and would prefer to keep our identities secret."

"Good God!" said Bloomquist while manoeuvering a fork full of noodles into his mouth. "You both appear to be in your mid-thirties and you're telling me you are working undercover on children?"

"Our targets could be the parents of some of these children," replied Jack. "The other reason we are here is out of concern for a teacher. There may be a degree of urgency to this."

"What teacher? Why?"

"We don't know which teacher. That is why we came to you. Crime Stoppers has received several tips over the last year concerning students at your school who have been trafficking in drugs. Several arrests have been made."

"And you are going to accuse me of not maintaining control over the students," said Bloomquist harshly, while plucking a wayward noodle from his lips and sucking it back inside his mouth.

"Not at all," said Laura quickly.

"We are concerned that some of the people involved in drug distribution at your school are beginning to figure out who is talking and are planning to respond with extreme violence," said Jack.

"The person phoning Crime Stoppers ... male or female?" asked Bloomquist.

"Crime Stoppers didn't say," replied Jack. "They are very protective about maintaining the confidentiality of the system. It has to be someone the students trust enough to confide in. Could you give us the names of teachers who are popular with the students?"

"Lyle Ryker comes to mind," said Bloomquist. "He was very active with the students over the tsunami in Thailand a couple of years ago. They raised a considerable amount of food, clothing, and money."

Bloomquist paused to slurp another mouthful of noodles. Jack didn't mind. It gave him time to write in his notebook.

"The second name is Marie Sainsbury," continued Bloomquist. "She gets along well with most of the more troubled students. The third is Bob Dunn. He teaches math but is also a phys. ed instructor. He coaches sports and sees the students after hours. Sometimes they go on road trips together."

"Anyone else?" asked Jack.

"Possibly Amanda Flowers. She is new to teaching. She did her practicum with us last year and came on full-time in September. She's young, single, and pretty. A lot of the male students probably have a crush on her."

"You said that Bob Dunn teaches math and phys. ed. What do the other three teach?" asked Jack.

"Bob replaced Lyle as a math teacher when Lyle ended his term with us last June."

"The information the police are receiving is current," said Jack. "I believe we are looking for a teacher who was here last year and this year. What about Marie and Amanda?"

"Marie teaches English, but is also a guidance counsellor. She talks to a lot of the students. Amanda teaches history and art."

"I see," replied Jack, while jotting down the information in his notebook."

"If you plan to interview my staff, I would like to be present," said Bloomquist. "It is most upsetting that someone would deal with the problem in such a devious manner and without consulting me. I'm sure the whole issue could have been dealt with a lot more effectively. Explains this nonsense of why police officers keep storming into my school."

"Oh?" replied Jack. "I wasn't aware that police officers had been storming into the school?"

"So far they've only made arrests in the parking lot and on the street out front," replied Bloomquist. "It is only a matter of time. I know how these things work. After all, my second wife was a cop."

"And how do these things work?" asked Laura, sounding innocent.

"There is no need to be facetious," replied Bloomquist. "What's your next step? Busting into student lockers?"

"Were there certain lockers that you think we should —" Laura stopped when she felt Jack's knee nudge her leg.

"I forgot to mention something," said Jack. "I was provided the times of when the tips were called in. Most were received between two and two-thirty in the afternoon. Would that narrow it down?"

Bloomquist looked smugly at Jack and said, "Had you bothered to tell me that to start with, we would not have needed to waste everyone's time. All our teachers are busy teaching during that time. They wouldn't be making calls of that nature. The person who is 'reporting' is no doubt a student. Perhaps skipping class."

"I'm sorry," muttered Jack. "I should have thought of that. I feel like an idiot for wasting everyone's time."

"I married an idiot. Lived with her two years before we divorced. Perhaps you should get together with her," smiled Bloomquist.

Jack locked eyes with Bloomquist and within seconds Bloomquist looked down and said, "Obviously I am only joking."

"Well, Morris, I'm sure I will be seeing you again," said Jack coldly. As he slowly arose he placed his hands on the table and leaned closer to Bloomquist and stared into his eyes. Bloomquist instinctively cowered back in his chair and looked down.

"What a jerk!" said Laura, as soon as they returned to their car.

"He's a bully," said Jack. "I hate bullies. I understand why the teacher didn't go through the normal channels. That's why I made up the story about the calls coming in during class hours."

"That's what I figured."

"We need to protect her."

"Her?"

"Amanda Flowers. Let's find out where she lives and talk to her right away."

"Why her?"

"The tips are recent enough that we know it's not Lyle Ryker. Bob Dunn is a coach and I don't see jocks and kids in sports as being the type to know the details provided to Crime Stoppers. That leaves Marie Sainsbury and Amanda Flowers. Sainsbury is a guidance counsellor. She wouldn't want to risk her credibility with the students by taking a chance on saying anything. That leaves Amanda. Young, idealistic, and trying to make a difference. Not burned out yet. My money is on her."

Jack checked the Motor Vehicle Branch and came up with Amanda's address. Her driver's license said she was twenty-five years old, but upon meeting her, Jack saw that she looked younger. He could see why many of the students would have a crush on her. She had flowing, shoulder-length blond hair, a cute figure, and a pretty face accented by large blue eyes.

After initial introductions, Jack said that they would like to speak to her concerning some of the students. Amanda invited them inside to the living room.

"Nice home," commented Jack as they were led inside. "Do you live here alone?"

"I live alone, but unfortunately the house isn't mine. The owners are a retired couple who are travelling around the world for a year. I'm house-sitting. Doesn't cost me a dime as long as I look after the place."

From the tidy yard and clean interior, Jack knew that Amanda was fulfilling her end of the bargain.

Once they were comfortably seated, Amanda offered tea or coffee. Jack and Laura politely declined and Jack said, "We are here to talk to you about your Crime Stoppers tips."

A look of irritation crossed Amanda's face. "I thought that was supposed to be confidential!" she said.

"It is," said Jack. "We didn't find out from Crime Stoppers. We received a tip that the bad guys have narrowed it down to three teachers. We met with Morris Bloomquist and he —"

"Mr. Bloomquist knows that it's me?" said Amanda fearfully.

"No, not at all," hastened Jack. "We asked him for a list of teachers who are popular with the students. Your name was one of them."

"How did you know it was me?"

"Logical deduction. We left your principal thinking it was a student, but if we figured it out, so might the bad guys."

Amanda gave a large sigh of relief. "I think Mister Bloomquist would fire me if he knew. He is against having students arrested. He believes it gives the school a bad name."

"I'm not impressed with the man," said Jack.

"He's not really a bad person … it's … well, his ex-wife was a police officer. A messy divorce may have clouded his judgment."

"Our concern is that the bad guys are narrowing down their list of suspects," said Jack. "We have received information that they are willing to murder whoever is tipping off the police."

"That doesn't surprise me," said Amanda bitterly. "But something has to be done. QE has turned into a zoo. Kids stoned out of their minds ... violence, gangs. Last weekend we had a top student commit suicide. If we had made QE a safer place where kids would open up ... I don't know ... none of us saw it coming. I —" Amanda stopped to wipe a tear from her face.

"We know about Julie Goodwin," said Jack, sadly. "I applaud you for your efforts to clean things up, but you need to back off. We have reason to be genuinely concerned for your safety."

"Lots of students confide in me," said Amanda. "I'm pretty careful because I don't want a student to get into trouble. I know what these gangsters are about. When I've called Crime Stoppers with information, I have been really careful to ensure that there is nothing passed on that would endanger any individual student. The information I have provided has been common knowledge to lots of students."

"If we figured it out, so might the bad guys," repeated Jack. "In the future, I would appreciate you calling us and not Crime Stoppers.

"And you will do something about it?"

"That's a promise," replied Jack.

* * *

Jack and Laura were leaving Amanda's home when Jack received a call on his cellphone.

"Hey, Jay! How ya doin'?" said Rodine. "Is Princess with you?"

"I'm doing great," replied Jack. "Any luck with that apartment?"

"Ya, I'm with Sy now. Told him about ya. If you want, you can come over and check it out right away."

An hour later, Rodine introduced Jack and Laura to Sy as they entered the apartment lobby. Sy stood with his arms folded over his chest and gave Jack a hard look.

"They're okay," whispered Rodine nervously to Sy. "I told ya, Jay is my cousin for fuck sakes. I've known him all my life."

Inwardly, Jack cringed. Rodine had made a serious error by saying they were related. Later, if he and Laura were identified, there would be no way for Rodine to say that he had been duped.

Sy nodded, but his attitude was one of suspicion. They took the elevator to the fourth floor and Sy used a key to let them inside the apartment.

"There's still someone's stuff in here," noted Jack.

"The owner's dead," said Sy. "His relatives have until the end of the month … two weeks from now … to get the shit out of here. I'm still not sure if I'll be renting it to you. A friend of mine has expressed an interest."

"Suit yourself," said Jack. "I've been looking for a place with underground parking and Rodent says you're a good guy, but if you have someone else that —"

"Rodent?" answered Sy.

"Yeah," smiled Jack as he looked at Rodine. "That's what I've always called him."

"Yeah," chuckled Sy. "His little face does look a bit like a rat's."

"Fuck you," replied Rodine, while glaring at Jack.

"Anyway," continued Jack. "I prefer to pay cash. No receipts and no name on the intercom. If your friend isn't interested, I'm willing to pay you two Gs a month."

Sy sucked in a little wind. Two thousand dollars a month was double what the apartment was worth. He rubbed his chin with his hand as if in deep thought and said, "Cash, eh? You know, I've always been a believer of first come, first serve. If you got a thousand-dollar damage deposit to put down, it's yours to move into at the end of the month."

It was nine-thirty the following morning and Tommy Sloan was late for school when he gunned the engine of his purple Trans Am and drove through a stop sign. His action did not cause an accident, but it did come to the attention of Constable Dale and Constable Button who were in a nearby patrol car.

"See that?" said Button. "I stopped that kid once before. The little asshole has a real foul mouth. Hit the lights, I'm going to write him up."

Seconds later Tommy turned on his signal and pulled over to the curb.

"Yes, Officer, I know I didn't stop," he said. "I'm late for school," he said, as an explanation.

"Too bad, but you're getting a ticket," said Button.

"Yes, sir. I guess I deserve it," replied Tommy.

"Another thing," said Button. "Shut the car off and hand me the keys."

"I'm not going to try and outrun you," smiled Tommy, as he did as instructed.

"Good. One more thing. Step out of the car and place your hands on the roof."

"You fuckin' pigs got no right to search me!" yelled Tommy.

Twenty minutes later, Constable Button placed Tommy into an interview room where he was allowed to call a lawyer.

"Tell your lawyer that the quarter-pound of meth we seized out of your shorts was individually grammed up," said Button as he closed the door.

Twelve hours later, Chugger, a prospect from Satans Wrath, picked up Sy at his apartment. After an hour of counter-surveillance tactics, including switching cars, Chugger parked behind a car wash called Wet Willy's. It was closed for the night.

"The rear door is unlocked," said Chugger. "Go on inside. I'm supposed to wait here."

Sy did as instructed. He recognized Cocktail who was seated in the customer waiting area with another man. He did not know who the man was, but the gold insignia ring on his hand said he was a full-fledged member of Satans Wrath.

"You think it is a teacher from QE who is talking to the police?" asked Cocktail, dismissing any small talk.

"According to my brother it is. He said the cops tried to make it look like nobody tipped them, but too many guys have been busted lately. Three or four teachers are the only common denominator."

"Which ones?" asked Cocktail.

Sy gave Cocktail all the surnames.

The biker looked at Sy and said, "Sit here, while we make a call from the office."

Sy waited as the biker and Cocktail entered an office and closed the door behind them.

Once inside the office the biker looked at Cocktail and asked, "Any ideas?"

"It's Amanda Flowers. She could pass for Playboy material and struts around with a real attitude. She isn't much older than the students. There isn't a straight boy in that school who wouldn't want to fuck her. They talk to her like she's their friend and not a teacher. She needs to be taught a lesson."

"Not a fatal lesson," said the biker. "We don't need the heat."

"Not kill her," said Cocktail. "She lives alone, house-sitting and looking after someone's cat. The owners are away. I have an idea that will leave a lasting impression upon her. Something to make a lasting impression on any others who decide to stick their noses where they don't belong."

The biker listened to Cocktail's plan and said, "Sounds good. Tell Sy to carry it out."

Sy stood up when Cocktail and the biker returned.

"We know who it is," said the biker. "It's the bitch by the name of Flowers."

"How do you know?" asked Sy.

"How we know is none of your business."

"Should we do something?" asked Sy.

"Yes," replied Cocktail. "Miss Flowers needs to be taught a lesson."

Sy listened carefully to Cocktail's plan and saw the biker give his nod of approval.

"I'll arrange it for tomorrow night," said Sy, getting up to leave. He glanced at Cocktail before heading toward the door as Cocktail's plan rolled around in his brain.

Sy was no stranger to violence, nor did he shun it, but the evil grin on Cocktail's face convinced him that this was one person he would never cross.

His plan, it's gonna be bloody ... bloody and fuckin' cruel. Every time she looks in a mirror ...

Chapter Seventeen

It was ten o'clock the following night when three youths crept across the lawn behind Amanda Flowers's home. Being the third week of May, the sun had set an hour earlier and the yard was mostly in darkness. A few lights were on in the house. The back porch light was also on, but a large shrub blocked most of the light to the yard.

Two of the youths were fifteen years old and the third was sixteen. All of the boys had lengthy juvenile records for assault, drug trafficking, and auto theft.

The youths were both giddy and nervous about the instructions they had received from Sy. A brutal and multiple rape was to be followed by carving the word RAT on her forehead.

The youths ducked low in the yard when they heard the back door open. It was followed by a soft feminine voice that yelled, "Kitty, kitty, kitty! Come on, Whiskers!

I'm leaving the door open. If you're not in by the time I scrub my teeth, you can spend the night outside!"

The youths heard the footsteps fade back into the house and a moment later, an upstairs bathroom light came on.

"This is gonna be fuckin' easy," said the oldest, pulling a pistol from his belt. The pistol was only a pellet gun, but it looked real and he knew Flowers would be too scared to tell the difference.

He glanced at his two friends who nodded and smiled back as they each pulled out hunting knives.

The one youth brandished his knife in the air, simulating carving the letters *R-A-T*. "Easy and fun," he said.

"Too bad Tommy couldn't be here," said the other.

"Sy is smart," whispered the oldest. "He'll make sure Tommy has a good alibi for tonight. Come on ... time to put on our masks."

The youths placed their weapons on the lawn in front of them, dug in their pockets, and each pulled out a ski mask.

Instantly, three powerful beams of blinding light illuminated the backyard. The mouths of all three boys simultaneously hung open.

"Police! Don't move!" screamed a command as black-clad men appeared out of the darkness pointing Heckler & Koch MP5 submachine guns at them. The favoured automatic weapon of the Emergency Response Team.

The youths gasped simultaneously, their eyes wide with fright as the members of the ERT circled them. Seconds later, the boys were all handcuffed and laying face-down on the grass.

Jack and Laura heard the scenario play out from where they sat with an ERT commander in the back of an ERT van parked a block away.

At noon the day before, Amanda had called Jack to thank him for having Tommy arrested. Jack said that he knew nothing about it. After hanging up, he called Rodine and told him to have a beer with Sy and find out what he was thinking.

Later, Rodine had called Jack back and said, "Sy met with Cocktail and some biker. They figure a teacher by the name of Flowers has been ratting and got Tommy busted. I'm surprised Sy told me, but I think he was so freaked out by Cocktail's plan that he had to tell someone."

Jack winced when he heard the news, but wasn't surprised. He found out so they could also figure it out. He asked Rodine what Cocktail's plan was and listened as Rodine told him about the intended rape and mutilation with a knife.

At first Jack had felt nauseated because he knew that to identify Flowers as the intended victim would compromise Rodine. Then he came up with a plan to protect Flowers and Rodine.

Jack told his bosses that Tommy was an important figure in The Brotherhood because his brother was a leader. He said it was rumoured that The Brotherhood blamed a teacher for Tommy's arrest, but that he did not know which teacher.

Jack suggested the possibility that a drive-by shooting of a teacher's house could occur, or perhaps The Brotherhood would break into a teacher's home and commit a violent assault. Jack added further fuel to the fire by telling Morris Bloomquist, who panicked and demanded protection for himself. He also provided a list of several other teachers' names, including Amanda Flowers.

ERT was assigned to protect the teachers and Jack assured everyone that it would only be for a couple of days because if The Brotherhood did retaliate, they would do it when the anger was still high.

"These guys aren't smart enough to wait and plan things out over time," said Jack. "They're comprised of impulsive hotheads. If the rumour is right, they won't wait."

Jack knew that the information he provided would be immediately given to defence lawyers upon arrests. The police, who were providing protection to several teachers and without having any knowledge of the intended rape and assault with the knife, would make the arrests appear innocuous enough to protect Rodine from discovery.

Now, Jack sat in the back of the van and closed his eyes while massaging his temples with his hand as he thought about the arrest.

"What is it?" asked Laura, sounding concerned.

"They screwed up," replied Jack.

"You got that right," replied Laura. "All of them busted."

"Not the punks," said Jack, looking up. "The arrest was screwed up."

"What do you mean, we screwed up?" said the ERT commander.

"Damn it," replied Jack. "The bust was premature. Defence will say the kids were there to slash her tires or something. I told you to wait until they were inside. You had what, one policewoman pretending to be Amanda and three other officers in there? You could easily have handled three punks."

"That was before one of them pulled a gun out of his pants," replied the commander. "I'm not going to risk the lives of my people over some assholes who, even if they had gone inside, would likely end up with, at best, a few months in Juvenile Detention."

Jack reflected on the information he had received from Rodine. He knew the gun was only a pellet pistol, but it was a detail he could not share in advance with the other officers. He sighed and looked at the commander and said, "You're right. I'm sorry. You made the right call."

"Damn right I did." The commander was silent for a moment before adding, "Guess you did, too. Your rumour was right."

Forty-five minutes later, Jack received a call from Connie asking where he was.

"In Amanda Flowers's house," he replied. "Where are you?"

"I'm at the Surrey office. The three punks have already lawyered up. Basil Westmount is defending one and other lawyers from his firm are representing the other two. None of the little assholes said a word. Turns out the pistol was only a pellet gun."

"Too bad," replied Jack. "It is going to be tough for some prosecutor to try and prove they intended to harm her. They were busted in her backyard, not in her house."

"Yeah, but they were in a teacher's yard at night with weapons and ski masks," said Connie. "That ought to count for something."

"Yeah ... a reasonable person would think that," said Jack, sarcastically. "I have to go. Laura's upstairs helping Amanda pack. I've convinced her to move to a new place."

"Relatives?" asked Connie.

"No, her parents live in Victoria. I want her to quit and move away, but she is being stubborn."

"Hope she finds a safe place. The Brotherhood may try again."

"I know. I told her that these guys might not give up. It would make them look bad, like they were incapable of handling business."

"I hope she isn't planning on continuing teaching! Doesn't she realize how dangerous these guys are?"

"I told her. I said with the items they were caught with ... masks and knives ... that in my opinion they were going to sexually assault her and cut her up."

"Do you really think that or were you trying to scare her?"

"I really think that ... and it did scare her. She agreed to take some time off. I'm hoping she will at least take the rest of the semester off and start next year in a different school."

"Will she?"

"She's too stressed at the moment to decide. She's already worrying about how long court will take. She wants the whole matter over with so she can get back to teaching."

"I'll talk to the prosecutor. Maybe see if we can expedite matters."

It was midnight when Jack and Laura arrived with Amanda and introduced her to Gabriel Parsons, who took them around to the back of the house and into the basement suite. The bed had already been made up for her and there were towels and linens available.

"You've got your own kitchen," said Gabriel, "but I know you haven't had time to shop. In the morning come and knock on my door. I'll make you breakfast."

"That's not necessary, but thank you," replied Amanda.

"I don't mind. You would be doing me a favour. I could use the company. I also put a quart of milk and some almond-chocolate-chip cookies in the fridge for you. I baked them this afternoon so they're fresh."

Amanda smiled in spite of how she felt.

When Gabriel left, Amanda turned and said, "What a sweet lady. Thank you so much for helping me."

"Gabriel has been through a lot," said Jack.

"So you told me on the way over."

"I appreciate that it hasn't been easy for you, either. I'm hoping you will be good for each other."

"I hope her daughter is going to be okay," said Amanda. "The stress must be terrible."

"Maybe you could help out by tutoring Noah. Gabriel said he was still suffering the loss of his father when Father Brown was murdered. He was a father figure to Noah. Gabriel said Noah has been fighting at school and that his grades have dropped."

"I'd be glad to help tutor him. What grade is he in?"

"Grade eight. He attends Cedar Woods Secondary. He's never been to QE, but to be on the safe side, I want you to use your mother's maiden name while you are here."

"If you think it's necessary."

"I do," replied Jack. "I can't reiterate strongly enough. Don't tell anyone where you are staying. Give us a month or so to see what is happening. The punks who planned to attack you tonight are with The Brotherhood.

"I know about The Brotherhood," replied Amanda. "I've had to deal with their BS on a daily basis."

"Then you know they are dangerous."

"Anyone listening to the news about all the shootings knows that."

"They're not all kids. Adults are in charge. Dangerous adults. I really wish you would move farther away."

"Your parents live in Victoria," added Laura. "That's a beautiful city."

"At twenty-five I don't want to be moving back in with my parents," replied Amanda. "Let's see what happens in court."

Chapter Eighteen

Over the next couple of days, Jack and Laura spent their time in the back of a surveillance van identifying people coming and going from Sy's apartment building. Most were teenagers and most had criminal records. Of interest, one of the teenagers was identified as Lorraine Calder, the same person who had been with Julie Goodwin the day before the girl committed suicide.

Rodine told Jack that Lorraine was a girlfriend of one of Sy's top lieutenants. A man who went by "Brewski" and who lived in the apartment next to Sy. Jack was able to identify Brewski's real name as David Brewster. A twenty-nine year-old man who had a long criminal record for violent assaults and drug trafficking.

Three days before Jack and Laura were to move into Sy's apartment building, Jack received a phone call from

Connie. He spoke quietly on the phone in case someone should happen to walk past the van and hear his voice.

"You like your bad news straight up?" asked Connie glumly.

"What have you got?" whispered Jack.

"Crown and defence made a deal for the three punks we caught going after Amanda Flowers. Half an hour ago they all pled guilty to criminal harassment by engaging in threatening conduct."

"That's better than I thought," replied Jack. "I figured it would be along the line of vandalism."

"That might have been better. At least there would have been an admission that they intended to damage something."

"Maybe defence thought the masks and weapons wouldn't make the pretext of vandalism quite as plausible. I hope those details were mentioned."

"They were. The prosecutor told the judge how they crept into her yard with masks, knives, and a pellet pistol. Westmount spoke for the defence. He told the judge that the young boys had an ill-conceived idea to put the masks on and yell at the teacher from the backyard. Their plan was that when the teacher looked out her window, the boys would hold the knives and pellet pistol up in the air to scare her and then run away. He said it was a schoolboy prank which was obviously wrong. He said all three young boys feel very foolish, ashamed, and extremely sorry for what they have done. He said letters of apology have been written to the teacher, but the police have stopped them from giving her the letters."

"What did these *young boys* get?" asked Jack.

"All three received two years' probation. They were already on probation for other crimes and this probation is to be served concurrently with the other."

"So they received nothing?"

"You got it."

"Is the Crown going to appeal the sentence?"

"No," replied Connie. "With the evidence at hand the prosecutor says we're lucky as it is. Who knows, maybe that was all the punks really intended to do."

"Oh, Connie," said Jack, sadly, "you're sounding naive enough to be a judge. That is not what they intended to do."

"What makes you so sure?"

"Seeing as you're not going to court, I'll fill you in."

"Fill me in on what?" asked Connie suspiciously.

"I am trusting you to keep this to yourself. Someone's life depends upon it."

"I understand."

Jack told her about Sy meeting with Cocktail and the real plan which had been foiled.

"That evil prick! We gotta get this guy!"

"Trust me, we will."

"Wait a minute. Did you bullshit us when we had ERT sitting on all —"

"Just found out from our friend a few minutes ago," lied Jack.

"Yeah, I bet."

"Does Amanda know what happened in court?" he asked, changing the subject.

"Not yet. I can tell her if you like, but I thought you and Laura had a better rapport with her, so –"

"We'll tell her," sighed Jack.

Jack and Laura met with Amanda. She invited them in for tea, but Jack did not want to wait to tell her the news. He watched as her face went blank, repeating his words over again as she tried to make sense of what happened.

"They're still out there," cautioned Jack. "You should move out of the lower mainland."

"Why?" yelled Amanda. "It's not like they should be angry!"

"Several of them have been arrested over the last year," said Jack. "They might try again to send a message."

"What message?" she demanded.

"Intimidation," said Laura. "To scare anyone else from talking to the police."

"This is bullshit!" Amanda looked at Jack and said, "Even with masks, they would never have gotten away with it. I know their voices. Two of them are not even in any of my classes, but I know them to hear them." She looked intently at Jack and said, "Tell me, their apology letters … do you think they were genuine?"

"No. It is a common ploy by defence to impress the judge. Believe me, these guys are not repentant, which is why I would like to see you move somewhere else."

"This really sucks." Amanda brooded for a moment and said, "I want to be alone. Goodbye."

"Amanda, I know you're angry," said Jack. "So am I, but —"

"Don't worry. I'll take the rest of the year off and try to find a different school to work at next year. Please, just go."

As Jack and Natasha were making dinner, Natasha asked, "Bad day?"

"Why do you say that?"

"You're slamming the cupboard doors. You always do when you're subconsciously trying to take control of a situation."

Jack smiled to himself, once again realizing how easily Natasha could read him. "It wasn't that bad of a day," he replied. "Things turned out as I expected, just not as I would have liked."

Over dinner, Jack told Natasha about the three punks receiving probation and how much it had affected Amanda's life. He realized that Natasha was unusually silent over dinner and when they finished eating he asked, "Something on your mind?"

Natasha sighed and said, "You've had a bad day …"

"Doesn't matter. What is it?"

"There is something I want to tell you. Let's go sit on the sofa."

Jack nodded and Natasha held his hand and led him to the living room. As they sat down, Jack's BlackBerry vibrated. He glanced at the call display. It was Gabriel Parson.

"I better answer," he said.

Natasha forced a small smile and nodded.

Gabriel was in hysterics. It took Jack several seconds to calm her down before she spoke coherently.

"Noah and I were at BCCH visiting Faith," she sobbed. "When we returned home ... Noah saw a bloody footprint on our sidewalk coming from Amanda's."

"Did you go in?"

"No! Not after —"

"Did you call 911?"

"Yes. The ambulance is taking her away. That's their siren in the background ... or maybe the police. I heard the paramedics talking. She was gagged and tied to her bed. Naked ... her face ... blood everywhere."

"Is she alive?"

"Yes, yes, she's alive. I heard her voice."

Jack heard Gabriel's voice turn from the phone and she said, "Yes, Noah," before speaking to Jack again and saying, "The police are here. I need to go."

Jack called the Major Crimes Unit, while quickly explaining to Natasha what had taken place. MCU had already been called and Connie Crane who was on her way to the hospital.

Jack didn't know if he wanted to cry or to vomit as he placed his next call to Laura.

"Laura, something —"

"Jack, it's Friday night and Elvis and I are out having a romantic dinner. The waiter is setting our meal down right now. Can whatever —"

"No it can't wait!" Jack yelled harshly, before pausing to apologize and blurting out the details.

"We'll head home immediately," said Laura. She was still in shock over the news. Her mind was still reeling, trying to grasp the reality of it all. She felt like she was listening to someone else's voice telling Jack where she was, robotically repeating some of the details, hoping somehow that she was still sounding professional.

"Wait at the restaurant," she heard Jack say. "It's closer for me to pick you up there than go to your house. I'll be there in twenty minutes. I'll also call our friend and tell him to get over to Sy's and see what he can find out."

Jack's call to Rodine went unanswered and he cursed out loud. He was heading out the door when he glanced at Natasha and said, "What was it that you were going to tell me?"

"With what you've got going on ... be careful. I want you to stay focused."

"I always am. What was it you were going to tell me?"

Natasha briefly reflected on her thoughts and said, "About how much I love you."

"I love you, too." Jack quickly kissed Natasha and hurried to his car. He tried to call Rodine several more times as he drove to the restaurant.

Laura was with Elvis in the restaurant foyer when they heard the squeal of tires approaching. Laura stuck the tissue back in her purse that she had been using to dab the smeared mascara off her face. Without thinking, she automatically used her hands to brush a wrinkle out of the front of her skirt before giving Elvis a quick kiss on the cheek. He watched as she ran in her high heels out to the car to join Jack, leaving Elvis thinking that under any other circumstances, it might have appeared funny.

"Where we going?" Laura asked, as soon as she closed the door.

"Over to Sy's and see who he's with. Tell him we want to see him about the apartment or something. Our friend isn't answering. I left him a message to —" Jack stopped to answer his BlackBerry.

"Sorry, I couldn't pick up," said Rodine. "I was with Sy. You gotta get over to that teacher's place. She's been attacked and is tied to her bed. Probably less than an hour ago. I just found out."

"We know. She's at the hospital. Who did it and where are they?"

"Three kids. Juvies. I'll be burned if you bust them."

"I won't burn you. Are they the same three as were in court today?"

"No, those guys are apparently at some Pizza Hut so they have an alibi. The three that did it just left here."

"They were already there! Who are they?"

"I don't know who two of them are, but the oldest one, Ray, lives in the apartment on the floor below Sy. He's only seventeen, but looks older than the other two."

"I've seen Ray coming and going from the apartment building," said Jack. "What about the other two. Did you see them?"

"Yeah, I saw them, but they're not from around here. They look to be about fifteen or sixteen years old.

One has a purple Mohawk hairdo and the other has long black hair parted in the middle. Ray called Sy to meet him out front of the apartment. That's when Sy told me what they did, so I walked out with him. Ray and the two others were waiting in Ray's red Camaro. Sy gave them a case of beer and they drove off."

"Son of a bitch," muttered Jack through his rage. "Any idea where they might have gone?"

"Not really. Sy asked Ray what they did with the masks and knife. Ray said they put it all in a plastic bag and tossed it into the bushes when they drove past some park. Sy was pissed. He told them to go back and bury it so it would never be found."

"What park? Do you know the name of it?" asked Jack, his mind pleading for the right answer."

"I don't know. They didn't say. They left a couple of minutes ago."

"Jesus fucking Christ!" yelled Jack.

"They did say it was about a ten-minute drive from the teacher's house, if that helps."

Jack felt relief. "That helps a lot. Coming from Sy's they'll be using Highway 99, which means they're coming in our direction. We'll be waiting when they get to Richmond."

"Man! You do that and I'm dead! You promised —"

"I know what I promised. Don't worry, I keep my promises."

Chapter Nineteen

Jack told Laura what he had been told while driving to intercept Ray.

"We can't let them get away with this," cried Laura. "Informant or no informant. We can't sit by."

"Do you really think I will sit by?" answered Jack tersely. "You know me better than that. We will protect our friend though. We gave him our word."

"Then what can we do? Any arrest and they'll know who told. Especially if we wait until they pick up the bag of evidence."

"I've got an idea," said Jack, coldly, "and it doesn't involve arresting them."

"Jack ... no, we can't. I know how you feel. I'd like to kill them, too. But we can't. They're still just kids."

"Kids committing adult crimes," replied Jack. "You know how things went in court today ... and that was with the masks and a pellet pistol. What do you think will happen in court if they're arrested without the hard evidence of the masks and knife?" Jack paused and when Laura didn't respond, he said, "I can hear it now. If we get DNA to prove they were there, lawyers will get the kids to say they were enticed to Miss Flowers's home on the pretext of tutoring them. She used her position to seduce and introduce them to the world of bondage. The kids went along with her, but one kid threatened to tell his buddies about it. They'll say Miss Flowers threatened to charge them all with rape if that happened. The kid panicked and things got out of hand. They'll cap it off by saying the kids were actually the victims of an adult. A teacher yet ... a person in authority who used her power over them."

"That's far-fetched. A jury might not believe that."

"Yeah, *might* being the key word. Especially without the masks and the weapons."

Laura sighed and said, "Okay, okay. Even if you're right ... I don't even want to think about it. But what do we do? Killing them isn't an option. Anything else I would go along with."

The rage Jack felt caused the tendons to go taut in his neck and his eyebrows furrowed, darkening his face. "I'll tell you what the option is —" He stopped talking and Laura wondered if he was too angry to speak. "Hang on, incoming call," he snapped, answering his cellphone.

"Jack, it's Connie. The office said you called. You know what happened?"

"I know," replied Jack tersely.

"You told me you were moving her to a safe place. How did you let this happen?"

"I don't know," replied Jack. His mind continued to cycle every detail in a futile attempt to figure out how he screwed up.

"You better find out, because so far, we got nothing."

Jack realized he was clenching his jaw and that his fist was gripping his phone like a vice. He relaxed his muscles, but the vengeance he felt was as powerful as ever. "Believe me, we'll find out," he replied. "I've picked up Laura. How's Amanda?"

"Her injuries aren't life-threatening, thank Christ. I only spoke to her briefly. She said she was tied to her bed, repeatedly raped by three guys, and then they slashed her forehead multiple times with a knife. She'll be badly scarred."

"Where is she now?"

"She's laying on a gurney in the holding area. A doctor is working on her face. After that, they'll get her a private room where, hopefully, if she's not too sedated, I'll be able to talk to her in detail."

"Not life-threatening if the nightmares don't drive her to suicide," said Jack, bitterly. "Do you really think she will be up to talking to you?"

"She's traumatized, but not hysterical. She did say she is good with voices and is positive none of the three were the same guys as before."

"Good with voices, is she?"

"Yeah, but she didn't recognize any of them. Maybe they were adults or kids from some other school."

"Cocktail used juveniles last time to alleviate any jail time if they were caught."

"Do you have any leads for us?"

"No, we don't have any leads at all."

"Oh, man ..." murmured Laura in the background.

"Then what are you doing?" asked Connie

"Talking it over with Laura. Trying to figure out who is responsible."

"Responsible! You know it's Cocktail! Probably went through Sy again. What's wrong with you? Have you called your informant?"

"It's kind of touchy talking to the informant right now," replied Jack.

"Kind of touchy? I can't believe this! Don't you realize what happened?"

"I'm fully aware of what happened," replied Jack. "We'll do some digging and get back to you."

"Yeah, well —"

Jack hung up his phone mid-sentence.

"Do some digging?" asked Laura. "Oh, man," she muttered again.

"Not the type of digging you're thinking of," replied Jack, "but a skirt and high heels isn't exactly the right thing to be wearing for what I have in mind. You wearing nylons?"

"Yeah, why?"

"Hang on, I'm going to phone Natasha."

Jack rapidly punched the buttons on his BlackBerry. Laura listened as he asked Natasha if she could convince the hospital to delay moving Amanda to a private room.

"There's no time to explain," he said. After a pause, added, "Convince someone that you're a doctor from another hospital. Say there's been a multi-vehicle accident and it may be necessary to transfer some patients. Ask them to hold any rooms they can for an hour to give you time to assess the new arrivals."

Laura saw Ray drive past in his red Camaro, as did Jack.

"Gotta go," said Jack. "Use a payphone. Hopefully in an hour I'll get you to call again and say the transfer isn't necessary."

"Take 'em off!" he yelled to Laura as he sped through traffic to catch up to the Camaro.

"Take what off?" asked Laura.

"Your nylons. Now!"

Chapter Twenty

Connie Crane looked down at Amanda Flowers as she lay on the gurney and tried to console her. Amanda's forehead was swathed in bandages to stop the bleeding while they waited for a plastic surgeon to examine her.

"They're supposed to move you to a private room," fumed Connie, once more sliding open the white drape and peering out. "They don't seem that busy." She caught sight of the doctor who first examined Amanda and said, "Hey! You forget about us? You said we would be moved to a private room in a couple of minutes. That was forty-five minutes ago."

"Sorry, something came up. A multi-vehicle pileup. Rooms are on hold for the moment until the situation can be assessed. We're working as fast as we can."

Connie walked over to the doctor and said, "Sorry, but it's critical that I get a formal statement from the victim as soon as possible. Under the circumstances, I need to talk to her in private."

"I'm sorry," replied the doctor. "I appreciate your situation and have kept the spots on either side of you empty. That's the most privacy I can offer at the moment and even that could change soon. I'm told we have three more patients being brought in with multiple injuries, so it is about to get busy. You may want to use what time you have now to talk to her."

Connie grimaced, but nodded in agreement and returned to Amanda and pulled the curtain shut before taking out her notebook.

"Okay, Amanda, you've told me some of the details, but I need a full statement. You said you were in your kitchen near the back door when three guys in ski masks kicked the door open. They were brandishing knives and said they would kill you if you screamed. Is that right? So —"

Connie shook her head at the sound of running feet and loud voices as gurneys were slid in on both sides of the curtained enclosure. "This isn't going to work," she muttered, sticking her head out once more. She saw two uniformed RCMP officers, with notebooks in hand, about to enter the enclosures beside her. A young man was laying on a gurney out in the open and it was apparent that all of the private enclosures were occupied.

She recognized one of the officers. "What's going on? An MVA?"

"No, this was no car accident. Some lunatic attacked three kids in a park with either a tire iron or a pipe. They said he was wearing pantyhose over his head."

"Must've looked like a deranged rabbit."

"He accused them of getting his daughter hooked on dope and started wailing on them. We have two victims with broken legs above their ankles, the other with a broken arm, and all three with broken collarbones. Actually, the oldest kid had both his collarbones broken. At least, that's what the paramedics say."

"Broken collarbones," mused Connie. "Easy to do and it would disable a person's ability to use their arms and hence their hands. Sounds like your perp has been trained in hand-to-hand combat. Could be a soldier. Did you catch him?"

"Not yet. We've got the dog handler out looking."

"Sounds like they sold dope to the wrong person."

"It could be mistaken identity. These kids claim it was their first time to the park. They'd gotten their hands on a case of beer and were drinking it and minding their own business when the attacker appeared out of the dark and started beating them. Must have been crazy … although he did have some conscience."

"Why do you say that?"

"When he was finished, he used one of their cellphones and jabbed in 911 and put the phone in the kid's hand so he could scream for help."

Connie shook her head. *What the hell is the world coming to?* She looked at her colleague and said, "Well, good luck. Hope you catch him."

Moments later, Connie saw the startled reaction on Amanda's face when the voices of the new patients could be heard.

"It's them," she gasped, sitting up and grabbing Connie by the sleeve.

"Who?" asked Connie.

"The guys who attacked me," she whispered. "I recognize their voices. Out there." She pointed. "I'm positive."

Connie looked at Amanda and whispered, "Lay quietly. I'll check it out."

Connie slipped out from behind the curtain to have a closer look at the three teenagers. She fought the urge to believe they could be that lucky. *Amanda is in shock ... could be a false reading to any young men's voices she hears ...*

Connie looked at the youth who was laying on the gurney out in the open. Her pulse quickened when she spotted blood on the bottom of his running shoe. *More on his shirt ... but they were attacked ...could be his own.* She bent to examine the blood on his shirt sleeve.

"You a cop, too?" asked the youth, who had seen Connie talking with the uniformed officer.

"Yup."

"You better catch the guy. Look what he did to me! I'm really hurtin'."

"The uniformed officers are investigating what happened to you. I'm not here for that." Connie made direct eye contact with the youth and added, "I'm investigating a woman who was attacked in her home tonight." She saw his response. *A flicker of fear ... or could it be a reaction to a jolt of pain?*

"I had a nosebleed earlier," the youth said, instinctively trying to pull his arm away. He yelped in pain as the effort to move his arm was stopped by a broken collarbone.

Connie heard the crackle of the portable radio as the uniformed officer spoke. *Could it really be them? To get a lucky break like this* ... She was only partially aware of a conversation droning over the police radio in the background. *Nosebleed, my ass. Doesn't explain how the blood got under his bicep and he's acting nervous* ... She momentarily forgot the blood on the sleeve as her brain triggered a response to the radio conversation. *Something about a bloody plastic bag with ski masks found buried in the park?*

"Yeah," crackled a voice over the radio. "The police dog found it buried in the park close to where the youths were attacked. Contains ski masks ... latex gloves ... a bloody knife ... the blood is fresh."

Connie stared at the young man in front of her who glanced at the officer with the portable radio before looking sullenly back at her.

"That fuckin' sucks!" he said, defiantly staring back. "Figures, the only way you pigs could catch anybody is by a fuckin' fluke! Get me my lawyer!"

Chapter Twenty-One

It was midnight when Jack dropped Laura off at the office so she could retrieve a surveillance van. She was going to watch Sy's apartment in the hope that the arrests might spark some activity. In the meantime, Jack was going to pay Gabriel a visit. He knew she would still be up.

"I'll join you as soon as I'm finished," said Jack.

"That might be soon if Gabriel slams the door in your face," replied Laura.

Gabriel's home was still a buzz of activity with the Forensic Identification Unit still hard at work in the basement. Any fear that Jack had about not being welcome was quickly overcome. Gabriel peered through a window after he knocked and flung open the door and hugged him.

"How is Amanda?" she asked.

"Her wounds are not life-threatening. She will, however, be scarred for life … emotionally and physically."

"I hope she finds comfort in the Lord," said Gabriel while using her fingers to wipe tears from her eyes. "Thank you for coming back tonight."

"Thank me for coming? Gabriel, it was me who introduced you to Amanda. This wouldn't have happened here if I hadn't brought her over."

"I guess not," replied Gabriel. "Where do you suppose it would have happened, then?"

Jack found himself at a loss for words.

"Please. I'm glad you're here. Come in and I'll make you some tea. I … I need to know if we're in danger."

"No, you're not in danger," replied Jack. "Amanda was their target."

"Because she was helping catch bad men who were selling drugs to the kids in her school?"

"Yes … something like that."

"Are the same people who attacked her the ones who murdered Father Brown?"

"The youths who attacked Amanda tonight are not the same people, but belong to the same group … or groups of people that we suspect are behind Father Brown's murder."

"I don't understand how someone could do that to another human being. Amanda was so nice. Still a child, really. If whoever did it doesn't seek forgiveness, they could go to Hell."

"Tonight, if I had my way," replied Jack.

Gabriel looked at him sharply and said, "Vengeance is not ours. It's God's."

"So I've been told," replied Jack.

"Good. Come in. I'll pour some tea."

The next morning a meeting was held with Jack, Laura, Connie, and Sammy from Drug Section. Neither Jack nor Laura had been to bed yet, having spent the night watching Sy's apartment building in a futile attempt to learn more.

Connie was late so Jack used the time to update Sammy on the investigation.

"You're moving into Sy's apartment this coming Friday?" asked Sammy.

"Yes. That's when Laura and I become known as Jay and Princess. Will you still be able to help us out with surveillance or maybe a quick UC if the need arises?" asked Jack.

"Not a problem."

"I still feel sick about last night," said Jack. "Only Laura and I knew where Amanda was staying."

"What about the landlady?" suggested Sammy. "Maybe she blabbed."

"Gabriel?" replied Jack. "Not a chance. I went to her house and spoke with her last night. She's too upset over what happened to Faith. There is no way she would say anything."

"What about her other kid? The boy?"

"All Noah knew was that they had a new border. He didn't even know her last name, let alone the circumstances of why she moved to —"

"Sorry I'm late," announced Connie, striding into the room.

"Hey, Connie," said Jack. "Where you been?"

"Doing police work," she replied, pulling out a chair. "And speaking of police work," she said, looking at Laura, "aren't you a little overdressed?"

"Last night interrupted a date with Elvis," replied Laura.

"You come up with anything?" asked Jack.

"As a matter of fact, I think I did," Connie replied as she sat down. "I may have figured out how they found Amanda."

"How?" said Jack, feeling the guilt contract his stomach and paralyze his lungs.

"I interviewed her this morning. She said she told the secretary at Queen Elizabeth her new address so some mail could be sent to her."

"I told her not to tell anyone," lamented Jack.

"I know. She told me, but said the secretary is an older lady, really nice, and would never tell anyone. I met with the secretary at her house. She is a nice lady. Unfortunately, too nice to think like a criminal."

"Meaning?" asked Jack.

"Her office is open to everyone passing by. She stores the files in a cabinet that she locks at the end of the day. She doesn't lock her office at lunchtime and can't even remember if she put Amanda's address away promptly or left it on her desk until later."

Jack put his elbow on the table and covered his eyes with his hand. He wished he were alone right now. *I should have told her that someone else would get her mail...*

"It's a big school," continued Connie. Lots of students and lots of teachers coming and going. Everybody busy and nobody paying attention. You know how it is."

"Yeah, I know how it is," replied Jack, looking up. "How is Amanda doing?"

"Okay, all things considered. They are releasing her this morning. Her parents showed up and are taking her back with them to Victoria."

"Seems soon," commented Laura.

"I thought so, too, but I guess the hospitals are busy and her injuries are not serious. She will need to make a lot of visits to a plastic surgeon."

"I suggested she go live with her parents before, but she refused," said Jack.

"She's not now. She doesn't even want to go back to Gabriel's to pick up her stuff."

"I don't blame her," said Laura.

"When we're done here, I'll call the hospital and see if Laura and I can pick up some of it for her," said Jack. "At least her purse and some clothes."

"No need," replied Connie. "I got uniform to do it." She glanced at her watch and added, "Actually I imagine she's on her way to the ferry as we speak."

"What about her car?" asked Jack.

"Uniform delivered that to the hospital for her, as well. Her mother is driving it back so everything is looked after for the moment."

"Anything from the punks who were arrested last night?" asked Sammy.

"No," replied Connie. "They were demanding lawyers before I could finish reading them their rights."

"Any evidence to link them to Sy?" asked Jack.

"Nothing," replied Connie, tapping her pen on the edge of the desk while she pondered what could be done next.

"At least you guys got lucky last night," said Sammy. "Hell of a good coincidence that the slimeballs ended up in the hospital next to their victim."

"Yeah, sometimes we get lucky," responded Connie. Her mind toyed over the word *coincidence*. She looked across the table at Jack. Coincidence was a word she knew all too well from past investigations. There were always coincidences when Jack was involved.

"So what's next?" asked Sammy.

"We're no further ahead on identifying Cocktail than we were months ago," replied Connie. "I hate to think that your UC is our only option. It might be easier for your informant to wangle a meeting with Cocktail than either of you. Maybe your informant could wear a wire."

"Out of the question," replied Jack. "We promised our friend that we would never divulge his or her identity."

"Witness protection?" suggested Connie.

Jack shook his head and said, "Our informant has lots of family members in the lower mainland. The Brotherhood knows a lot of them. If our source is burned, they'll kill someone else if they can't get their hands on the source. You saw what they did to Amanda. Imagine what they would do to one of their own who turned. Laura and I should be able to gain Sy's trust. We've worked on smarter people than him."

"Don't forget," said Sammy. "We've still got a dirty narc someplace."

"I always presume there are dirty cops someplace," replied Jack. "It pays to be careful all the time."

"Even if you gain Sy's trust," said Connie, while glancing at Laura's bare legs, "how do you plan on getting him to introduce you to Cocktail?"

"We'll cross that bridge when we come to it. Sy met him before. With Varrick out of the way, maybe Sy will be meeting him again."

"So what will you do?" asked Connie, while watching Jack closely. "Follow Sy and hope he meets Cocktail someplace like a *park* where you could bump into them or something?"

Jack's face remained unchanged and she wondered if her suspicions were unfounded.

"We need Sy's trust first," said Jack. "Then I'll say we have a buddy, maybe Sammy, who is interested in setting up a lab. Do something to see if we can draw Cocktail out."

"I could handle that roll," replied Sammy. "How big is your buget?"

"Connie says we're only authorized for twenty grand."

"That's not much," commented Sammy.

"They're not buying dope," said Connie. "It should be lots to rent an apartment for a couple of months." She looked at Jack and said, "Isn't it? Things are tight. I had to beg to get that much."

"We'll see," replied Jack. "I've already spent half of it."

"What the hell you talking about? You haven't even moved in yet!"

"Damage deposit, months rent in advance, furniture rental, renting a moving truck, dishes ... other stuff," replied Jack.

"That shouldn't be much more than five grand," said Connie. She looked at Jack and said, "What's the other stuff?"

"Two new plasma televisions and two cases of Russian vodka," replied Jack with a grin aimed at Sammy.

"What? You're not serious?"

"Laura and I can never agree on which channel to watch, so we decided we would each get our own set." Jack cast another smile at Sammy and added, "Also thought we should have some booze around in case we throw a party."

"Yeah, right," replied Connie. "You had me going there. I thought you were serious."

Sammy grinned also. He was a trained undercover operator. He knew that Jack was serious ... at least for what was purchased.

"Anyway," continued Jack, "as long as we remain in the background and make sure we stay out of court, it could work. Speaking of court, I have a trial coming up in Victoria in a couple of weeks. The nutcase I bought coke from. It won't interfere with doing the UC here."

"One of the punks arrested last night lived in Sy's apartment building," said Connie. "I expect the three of them will be released soon to await trial."

"So what," replied Jack. "He's never seen my face."

Connie looked at Jack. *I wonder if he's ever heard you ...*

"What are you thinking?" asked Jack.

"Doesn't matter, I guess," replied Connie. "The guy has two broken collarbones. He can't even wipe his own ass. I heard the nurses say he was moving back home with his parents so they could look after him."

"Certainly a couple of lucky breaks last night," said Jack.

Connie ignored the pun and said, "Getting Sy to introduce you to Cocktail won't be easy."

"We'll figure out a way," said Jack. "We're operators. It's what we do. Sy isn't all that bright. He uses the kids, but in reality, Cocktail and the bikers use him. Getting him to trust us will be ... like a walk in the park," he added, giving Connie a shallow smile.

His remark caused her to drop her pen. She stared back at Jack, not bothering to pick it up. His face was without expression but she thought she saw a slight nod.

Coincidence, my ass!

Chapter Twenty-Two

At nine o'clock Friday morning, Jack and Laura, driving an SUV, arrived at Sy's apartment complex followed by a local moving truck. Sy gave them the keys to their apartment and the underground parking garage. By three o'clock that afternoon they were completely moved in and unpacked. Their furniture was rented and their dishes and cutlery had been purchased from Walmart.

The two men who drove and unloaded the moving truck had another purpose. They were with a specialized unit of the RCMP. All rooms in the apartment would be bugged for safety.

At midnight Jack and Laura left the apartment and returned an hour later. They used a two-wheeled moving dolly to haul two new television sets up to their apartment. Jack left one television on the dolly outside in the hall and the other one on the floor inside the front entrance.

"Good as time as any," said Jack, walking in to the bedroom which he knew was above Sy's apartment.

Jack checked his watch and then jumped high in the air and landed with a loud thud. Fifteen minutes later he jumped again. A repetition of four more followed before they heard Sy bang on the ceiling with a broom handle.

"He's really getting mad now," commented Laura.

Two jumps later, an enraged Sy appeared in the hallway outside their apartment. Jack pretended not to see him as he struggled with the dolly and said, "This is the last one, Princess."

Sy appeared behind his shoulder and saw Laura dragging a large cardboard box that she had lifted by one end. She spotted Sy and let the box drop, making a loud thud.

"What the hell are you two doing?" seethed Sy. "It's after two o'clock in the fucking morning!"

"Damn it, Princess!" said Jack. "Were you dropping them all like that? This is an apartment. You have to remember to keep the noise down."

"They're heavy," she said. "I'm not a weightlifter."

Jack turned to Sy and said, "I'm really sorry. A friend of mine was supposed to move this stuff tonight and his truck broke down. He called me at midnight in a big panic to help take a few sets off his hands."

"Consider this your first and last warning," replied Sy. "I live right below ya. No more fuckin' noise or you're out!"

"I understand completely," replied Jack. "As an apology, I'll give you this last set."

Sy looked at the box and said, "It's a fifty-inch plasma television set ... the box hasn't even been opened. You're giving it to me?"

"Yes, I think it should be a good set," replied Jack. "My friend is ... uh, in the electronic business. These are ... uh, extra sets that nobody wants. Out of date or something. Give me a hand and we'll haul it down to your place. The only thing is there is no warranty. If something ever goes wrong with it, don't try to get it fixed on warranty."

Sy smiled. Rodine had told him that Jack was connected to the Irish mafia and into moving stolen property. He had a feeling that he and his new tenants would become good friends. At least, he hoped they would.

The following Monday night, Sy awoke to one loud thud coming from above. After that, everything was quiet. At noon the next day he answered a knock on his door.

Jack stood there with a sealed case of Russian vodka.

"Hi, Jay. What's this?" asked Sy.

"I dropped one of these last night," said Jack. "Sorry about that. I bet it woke you." He handed the case to Sy and said, "A gift for you."

"You're giving me a dozen bottles of vodka?"

"Yeah. I ... uh, have a friend in the liquor business. It didn't cost me anything."

"No warranty?" said Sy with a smile.

Jack chuckled and said, "Yeah. No warranty against headaches."

"If you're not up to anything, how about having a drink with me?" suggested Sy. "We could watch a movie on my new television. It works great, by the way."

"That's good. A drink sounds good, too. Mind if I go get Princess?"

"Not at all. I think we have enough," replied Sy, hoisting the case of vodka for emphasis.

"Well, if we run out, I've got more," said Jack.

By mid-afternoon, Sy had guzzled enough vodka mixed with Red Bull that he had loosened up a little. He looked down at his dirty jeans and rumpled shirt and cast a glance at Jack and Laura, who were dressed in trendy clothes.

"You guys do alright, doncha?" Sy said.

"We do all right," admitted Jack.

"Yeah, I can tell. Come with me a sec, will ya? Want to take a little walk. You don't mind, do ya, Princess? I'll bring your man right back."

"I don't mind," replied Laura. "It will give me time to pour another drink." *One without vodka.*

Outside in the hallway, Sy said, "I make a rule of never talkin' business inside my place. You never know who is listenin'."

"Good rule," said Jack. "Back east I used to have my places swept once a month. Then I figured it was smarter not to say anything inside."

"You had your places swept ... man ... your cousin told me that ... you know, you were connected. I didn't realize how big. Plus I thought that was back east."

"The world is getting smaller," replied Jack. "We have a lot of friends. Some are out west."

"Shit, I can see why ya got friends. You are one generous guy."

"Ah, hell," said Jack, brushing off his comment. "That's nothing. Chump change. My friend did get his truck fixed, so most times we'll use a proper storage place. The other night with the truck breaking down and the storage locker closing, we were in a bind."

"Chump change? That television ain't no chicken feed to me." Sy looked at Jack suspiciously and said, "The way you're dressed and everything ... your watch ... necklace ... you got money."

"I get by."

"So why move into a dump like this?"

"This isn't our only place," replied Jack. "I don't believe in putting all my eggs in one basket. Along with my friends, I've also made a few enemies along the way. I like having more than one place to hang my hat. Rodent said you were a solid guy. Someone who could keep his mouth shut. Figured it would be a safe place if we needed one."

"Your, uh, other place is a little nicer, I bet," said Sy.

"One is. I'm not exactly the trusting sort. Only Princess knows the location of my other places."

"One is?" repeated Sy. "Man, that's smart. Maybe somethin' I should think of."

"You have enemies?" asked Jack.

"Did your cousin tell ya much about me?" countered Sy.

Jack shrugged and said, "I know my cousin is a chef."

"A chef? Oh, yeah," chuckled Sy.

"I presumed you were in business with him."

"We do some stuff together," admitted Sy. "But do I have enemies? Fuckin' right. Things are gettin' hot. A guy has to be careful."

"Hot! If you have heat then I'm not staying here," said Jack, sounding angry. "Rodent didn't say anything about the police sniffing around."

"No, no. Not that kind of heat," Sy assured him. "It's the competition. People encroachin' into places they shouldn't."

"Ah, I see," replied Jack.

"We've been tradin' messages back and forth."

"Good to communicate," said Jack.

Sy smiled and said, "Not the type you're thinkin' of. The kind where you drive fast …" As he spoke, Sy used his hand to simulate firing a gun. "You ever do that?"

Jack shook his head and said, "Nope. That attracts the police and usually doesn't accomplish anything. I prefer the magician's act."

"The magician's act?"

"Make the bunny disappear."

Sy smirked and said, "You are one cool dude. You into the powder?"

"I don't use. I like to keep my brain intact."

"No, I don't mean usin'. I mean making money off it."

"Dope is something I've kept away from. Too risky for me. I have an aversion to going to jail."

"Fuck, man. You're not back east now. We're in B.C. Things are different out here."

"So I heard."

"Besides, if a guy is smart, he don't take risks himself. You get the YDUs to do that."

"YDUs?" asked Jack.

"The young, dumb, and uglies," laughed Sy. "Come on, let's go back inside. Maybe I'll invite a couple people I know."

The drinking in Sy's apartment lasted several hours. During that time, a few young people came and went. They were of mixed ethnic background, including Asian and East Indian. Jack doubted that few of them were older than their early twenties.

One exception was Brewski, who lived next door to Sy. He showed up with a teenaged girl hugging him around his waist. The girl had a good figure and wore a low-cut sweater to show off her ample breasts. Her light brown hair was curly and cropped short. *She could be attractive*, thought Jack, *if she didn't look like a hardened slut*.

"Brewski is my right-hand man," slurred Sy in a drunken whisper to Jack. "Not like all these other fuckin' YDUs."

Brewski heard the comment and stood a little straighter. He was proud to be identified as being important to Sy. Jack smiled to himself. *Sy isn't overly bright, but Brewski is even slower.*

"Meet my girl," said Brewski. "Lorraine, say hi to Sy's new buddy."

"Well helloooo," Lorraine crooned, unwrapping herself from Brewski and running her hand down Jack's chest.

Jack remembered Lorraine Calder from the investigation into Julie Goodwin's suicide. It was difficult to feign friendship. "Time for me to check with my own girl," he said, and walked over to join Laura.

"Time to slip away?" Laura asked. She had witnessed Lorraine's arrival and knew that it would not be good to make an enemy out of Brewski.

"Yes, I've had about all I can stand."

"You're telling me," whispered Laura. "I'm old enough to be most of these kids' mother. If I hear one more sentence start with, *so like, this is cool dude* or *so like, this is rockin'*, I think I'm, *so like*, going to slap someone."

Over the next week, Jack and Laura became better acquainted with Sy, who was beginning to open up more and more. One afternoon, Jack walked down the one flight to visit with Sy and saw him talking to a man in the hallway. The man, in his early thirties, was obese with a shaved head that showed the rolls of fat on the back of his neck. He quit talking and nudged Sy as Jack approached.

"Hey, Sy," said Jack. "Princess is out shopping. I hate sitting alone, so wondered if you were up to having a beer?"

"Hell of a good idea," smiled Sy. "We're done business here, anyway." Sy introduced his acquaintance as "Munch."

"You want to join us?" Sy asked Munch.

Munch shook his head and said, "Gotta take care of business."

"What, you headin' to a buffet someplace?" asked Sy with a smile.

"Fuck you," said Munch, chuckling. "I did that at noon."

As Munch walked away, Sy looked at Jack and said, "He's a good guy. Someone solid who is on my side of The Brotherhood."

"The Brotherhood?"

"We used to be independent gangs, but there were problems. We thought if we met and talked, maybe we could resolve our problems. Like in the movies with those New York families."

"Sounds professional."

"Yeah, that's what I thought. It was my idea. So the seven biggest gangs formed a coalition and we called ourselves The Brotherhood. For a little while, things were great. We even did business with each other."

"What happened?"

"Ah, next thing ya know, squabbles started breaking out over new territory. Then we started fighting over what had long been our own turf. It's gotten that you never know when some fucker will drive by and take a shot at ya. Two of the other gangs are on my side. Munch is the boss of one of 'em. The boss of the other gang is a guy called Mongo."

"You mentioned last week that you were involved with drive-bys," said Jack. "It's good that you have some allies. Are you at war with all of the other gangs?"

"Three for sure. The fourth one is riding the fence."

"Sounds like you should convince the fence-rider to go your way. Make it four against three."

"I've tried."

"Maybe he's trying to play you against each other and is hoping to come out on top when the smoke clears," suggested Jack.

Sy's face darkened and he said, "The fuckin' dirty Indo'! You think so? That would be Rashard's style."

"I don't know the guy, but I've encountered similar problems back east."

"What did you do about it?"

"Start making friends. People you can trust. The more the merrier. The bigger your group, the less chance someone will want to mess with you. It isn't any fun if you're worrying about dodging bullets all the time. The idea is to make money and enjoy life. If you have to share a little of the profits ... well who really cares as long as you're still making lots."

Sy stared at Jack momentarily and said, "I like how you think. Some day I'd like to be top boss of all these fuckers. The thing is, I know of six other guys who want the same thing."

"Mongo, Munch, Rashard, and three others?"

"Yeah, three others," replied Sy, looking irked that Jack had paid such close attention.

"Well, glad I'm not involved," said Jack. "I'd never want to be the boss. Too much pressure. It was one of the reasons I moved out west. People wanted me to step up and be boss. For a while I made all the right moves, but after meeting Princess, I decided I didn't want it. I like feeling safe and comfortable. Speaking of which, it makes me nervous hearing about stuff that's none of my business. How about a beer and watch a movie or something?"

Sy studied Jack briefly. *Good, he doesn't really want to talk about it. Can't be all that interested.... Maybe I didn't fuck up by sayin' too much*. "Yeah, sounds like a perfect plan," replied Sy. "Come in to my place. I got a two-four of Lucky."

Over the next three cans of Lucky beer, Sy brooded more and more about what Jack had told him. *Curious background*, he thought, glancing at Jack. *He is one smart fucker. If I can get him to trust me more, I bet he could help me with some of the right moves. Like in* The Godfather *movie ... I'd be the top boss and maybe Jay could be my fuckin' consigliere or whatever the fuck it is called.*

Sy looked at Jack and said, "You up to anything Saturday night?"

"That's two days from now. I don't think I am, but I'm not sure, I'd have to check with Princess. Why?"

"My YDUs are havin' a party at a house that a couple of my guys are rentin'. I gotta make an appearance. I tell ya, it would really be doing me a favour."

"I'm not much for hanging out with kids," replied Jack.

"Me, either. That's the point. I feel like a loser at my age showing up alone at a party with a bunch of bubble-gummers. With you there, I can make an excuse. Say we're goin' someplace else after."

"Why not go with Brewski?"

"He's got some business to take care of."

Jack nodded and said, "Okay, as long as I drive. If you decide to stay, then Princess and I can leave."

"Thanks, man. I appreciate that. I don't want to stay long, either. Drop by and throw a few goodies around, have a couple of beer, give a few dumb fucks a pat on the back and then split."

Later that night, Jack and Laura had a meeting with Connie, Sammy, and Dan Mylo from the Integrated Task Force. Everyone was pleased with how much progress had been made. With the information Jack provided, Dan and Sammy agreed to apply for wiretap authorizations on all the main people.

"The bug monitors are going to be swamped," said Sammy.

"At least now we know who some of the guys are who are calling the shots," said Dan. But you're right, they are going to be busy."

"Make sure you keep Laura and me out of court," said Jack.

"I'll check with the prosecution," said Sammy. "If it goes to court we will try to keep it on a case-by-case basis. Worse comes to worse, we withdraw a charge."

"Speaking of which," said Connie, "Don't you have a court case tomorrow?"

"In Victoria," replied Jack. "Not to worry, I'll be on the seven o'clock ferry in the morning and should catch an afternoon ferry back. I checked with Victoria. None of McCall's current associates know me, so even if they do show up, I should be okay."

"Good," replied Connie.

"It's going to be good when they slam the door on McCall," said Jack. "Victoria PD is concerned. They want me to wear Kevlar and are assigning a four-man bodyguard team to accompany me to court."

"What do you figure he will get?" asked Connie.

"His record includes three convictions for dealing cocaine and he was only out of jail two weeks when he sold to me. In any other province I would expect him to be sent away for six or seven years, but knowing our justice system here, I'm guessing more like three or four years."

"Good luck," said Sammy.

"I've also called Amanda," said Jack. "I'm going to meet her for a coffee after court. I've got a bunch of her effects that I gathered up from Gabriel's."

"I've been wondering how she is doing," said Connie. "Hope she is well enough to give a strong testimony when the time comes."

"I hope so, too. I'll let you know. Tomorrow is also when Ngọc Bích testifies against the two Vietnamese brothers for the rape, beatings, and imprisonment in one of their brothels. I'd appreciate it if you stayed close to her tomorrow."

"I know about her trial," said Connie. "I've been assured that there is extra security already."

Jack stared at Connie without speaking.

"Okay, I'll be there, too," said Connie.

Jack breathed a sigh of relief and smile. *The system is working as it should ...*

Tomorrow would drastically change Jack's opinion regarding that.

Chapter Twenty-Three

Jack walked into the Victoria courtroom and immediately saw a look of disappointment cross McCall's face, followed by anger as he whispered to his lawyer, who glanced at Jack, before turning back to McCall.

Jack quickly surveyed the courtroom. His four bodyguards moved past him and took up strategic positions. Jack smiled to himself. He was pleased for two reasons. The first was that McCall actually showed up. The second was the sight of the young lawyer with McCall.

Jack guessed it was the lawyer's first year of practice. Jack was a seasoned veteran in the courtroom and knew he would come out on top with any comments the young lawyer would throw at him while testifying. *The truth will prevail!*

Perhaps the lawyer sensed so, as well. He changed the plea to guilty. Jack listened as the prosecutor read in the circumstances of the drug sale, McCall's lengthy record, his only being out of jail two weeks before the crime and — what Jack thought was a nice touch — the fact that McCall had remained legally unemployed ever since his arrest. *Someone did their homework ...* Jack glanced at Dave Valentine who grinned and gave him the thumbs-up.

Jack listened as the fresh-faced lawyer stood to address the judge. He explained that the reason his client had not been able to obtain employment was because of the severe psychological stress that his client had been subjected to by the RCMP.

Jack glanced at the members of the Victoria PD who were in the courtroom. He could tell by the puzzled look on their faces that they were also confused.

"You see, your Honour," said the lawyer, "Corporal Taggart, the RCMP officer who purchased the drug from my client —" The lawyer paused to point at Jack who returned the judge's gaze. The lawyer continued, "— did not tell my client that he was an undercover operative prior to the sale. As a result, my client has been left emotionally scarred and has a strong distrust for people, leaving him unable to obtain employment."

Jack did his best to suppress a chuckle. *Being a new lawyer is one thing, but to say something as ridiculous as this ... the judge is going to eat him alive.*

The judge reflected on what he had been told. His brow furrowed and he glowered at Jack.

Jack's mouth dropped open in shock. *Something is terribly wrong! The judge is looking at me with utter disdain; like I'm a piece of dog shit stuck to his shoe ... he can't be going along with this!*

Jack stood in a trance as the judge handed down his sentence. McCall was given four months of house arrest.*

"What does this mean?" a bewildered Jack asked the prosecutor.

"It means McCall will have to be home by nine o'clock at night if he isn't out working or seeking employment."

"You'll appeal?"

The prosecutor shook his head and said, "It wouldn't do any good."

Jack stumbled out of the courtroom like a blind man with a lobotomy. He felt like he was in another world. A place without any logic or common sense.

Amanda answered the door at her parents' place and gratefully accepted several boxes of her personal effects that Jack had brought with him. Her parents were out shopping and after Jack had unloaded the car, she invited him inside for a coffee.

Amanda was wearing bangs down to her eyebrows. She was much thinner than before and her face was pale. It was obvious she wasn't going outside much.

"How did your court case go today?" she asked.

---

* As outrageous as it would appear, the circumstances concerning this court case are factual and were personally experienced by the author. Only the names have been changed. Circumstances of a court case involving "Ngọc Bích," which follow later in the chapter are also based on fact.

"He plead guilty," replied Jack, hoping she would drop the subject. "How are you really doing?"

"Not well. Guess it takes time." She looked inquisitively at Jack and said, "You once told me that you were in an Intelligence Unit and didn't go to court."

"This was an exception. I had originally hoped to gain some information to help solve Father Brown's murder. My target had connections to The Brotherhood. I'd hoped to turn him into an informant, but after meeting him, decided he was too dangerous to let off. Anyway, I'm sorry that you're not doing well. Do you want to talk about it?"

"What did he get?"

"Who?"

"The cocaine dealer you were in court for."

"Nothing, really," said Jack, trying to keep his emotions in check.

"Nothing?"

"Four months' house arrest. If he's not seeking employment he is suppose to be home by nine o'clock at night."

Amanda stared hard at Jack for a moment and asked, "Why do you bother?"

"I don't know," replied Jack, hearing his voice crack. "I feel ridiculous. Risked my life for nothing."

"The Brotherhood were also responsible for having me attacked," said Amanda. "So you were here working undercover on something that might have helped me."

"Guess you could put it that way, but at the time, it was to help Homicide find someone they are looking for."

"You shouldn't say you risked your life for nothing," said Amanda. "You risked it for me and people like me."

"Still doesn't change the result," said Jack.

"You said Homicide *are* looking for someone. Can you tell me anything about it? It sounds like you know who you are looking for?"

"How are you at keeping secrets?"

"You have to ask?" replied Amanda, as small grin flashed across her face. "I'm the one who went behind Mister Bloomquist's back to try and see justice served."

"Have you ever heard the nickname 'Cocktail'?"

"No."

"We're trying to identify him. We've heard a rumour that he has control over some of The Brotherhood. He is the same person who ordered your assault. If anyone finds out that we are looking for him, he may disappear forever. It is also imperative that my real identity be kept secret from The Brotherhood."

"I won't tell a soul." She stopped talking and stared off into space as her body started rocking back and forth in her chair.

"Tell me about your therapist," said Jack, gently. "Do you get along well? Sometimes you need to meet a couple of therapists before you find someone you click with."

"Maybe. She seems nice, but it's not really helping yet."

"It's going to take time."

"I know. My therapist told me. Years. She warned that going to trial could upset things further. Reliving the memories could cause any progress to backslide completely."

"Sometimes you have to take one day at a time. If you need someone to talk to, I'm only a phone call away. The trial could be a long way off. Time will make you stronger. Another friend of mine was beaten and sexually assaulted. She is testifying today. A couple of years ago she felt like you, but today is looking forward to seeing her attackers held accountable."

Tears came to Amanda's eyes and she blurted out, "I'm not that strong." She paused to take a couple of breaths and to regain her composure before continuing. "Even if Cocktail is identified, I've decided I'm not going to testify. Against him, or the three who did this to me," she added, brushing her bangs to one side to reveal the ugly red scars across her forehead.

"Are you afraid they'll come after you again?" asked Jack.

"No. I'm too angry and depressed to worry about that. I just don't see testifying as doing any good. It would just depress me further. I know you think I'm a terrible person. I should worry about who they'll attack next ... but I'm not up to it."

"I don't think you're a bad person," replied Jack, "but knowing the judges, if you refuse to testify, there is a good chance they would put you in jail for contempt of court."

"They would put *me* in jail?" Amanda gave a shrill-sounding laugh.

"They take it as a personal affront if you disobey a subpoena."

"A personal affront?" Amanda started crying and Jack sat beside her and put his arm around her shoulder.

"Then I don't want you to find him," sobbed Amanda. "Same for the three who attacked me ... promise you'll find some way to drop their charges if they don't plead guilty."

Jack briefly closed his own eyes to block the tears. "Charges have already been laid against the three," he said. "I'm sorry, it is out of my hands, but under the circumstances, I doubt that any defence lawyer would want to chance you taking the stand. They will likely plead guilty on the pretext of feeling bad for what they have done. I imagine that they will be sentenced to a couple of years in juvenile detention."

"And Cocktail? He won't plead guilty. No way. He may have ordered it, but you know damn well he'll never admit it."

Jack didn't respond. He didn't know what to say.

"I bet you wouldn't convict him regardless," added Amanda. "Or if you did, maybe he would end up with four months' house arrest like your cocaine dealer."

Briefly, Jack wondered about telling Amanda that if Cocktail was convicted of bludgeoning a retired priest to death with a rock, he would likely plead guilty to Amanda's case and serve a concurrent sentence. *What am I thinking? We don't have any evidence that he committed the murder, either. He'll likely walk on both charges.*

Jack glanced at Amanda's face. He felt sickened and angry. *How can I go on, pretending to represent justice? I really should quit. Why waste the taxpayers' dollars with this charade?*

"You never answered," noted Amanda. "I'm right, aren't I? Cocktail will never face justice for what he did to me."

Jack remained silent for a moment, before gripping Amanda by both shoulders and staring intently into her face.

"What is it?" she asked.

"I don't make promises I can't keep ... so believe me when I say I will find Cocktail and that ... justice will be served."

Jack caught the three o'clock ferry home. It was cold and windy, but he didn't notice as he stood outside on the upper deck and stared into the waves. His BlackBerry rang and the call display told him that it was Ngọc Bích. He quickly answered and stepped inside where it was quieter.

Ngọc Bích was crying, but managed to blubber out that the court case had gone ahead. The judge, in his summation, said that he could not accept the credibility of Ngọc Bích and the other witness over two respected businessmen. After all, said the judge, both witnesses had been prostitutes. The case was dismissed.

Jack tried unsuccessfully to console her. When he eventually hung up, he went down to his car and wept.

Chapter Twenty-Four

Jack told Natasha over dinner about the two court cases and Amanda's desire not to go to court. She sat quietly, slowly chewing her food.

"Nothing to say?" asked Jack.

"What can I say? It's horrible," she replied.

Jack watched her eat and said, "It's not like you to be so quiet. You have been a lot lately. Is there something bothering you?"

"I'm bothered that you are so unhappy and stressed about your work."

"I'll get over it."

Natasha shook her head and put her fork down. "I doubt you ever will, but you better find a way to deal with it emotionally. The stress will affect your health. Eventually cause you to make decisions you regret."

"Decisions such as …?"

Natasha chose to ignore the question. She picked up her knife and fork to attack a piece of steak and said, "I love you. I always want you to come home alive."

Jack saw her eyes water. He felt guilty that his work was affecting her.

"I want you to be the happy," she continued. "I want to spend more time with the loving and caring guy I know. Is that too much to ask?"

"No, it's not too much to ask. I'm sorry. Maybe I shouldn't have unloaded on you."

"Of course you should unload on me. I'm your wife, but even if I wasn't, as a doctor, I know enough about stress and what it can do to the human body."

"I'll take it easy."

"Don't give me that bullshit," she said crossly. "I know you better than that. But you do need to learn to accept the things you can't change. You did your job. Don't blame yourself for what some judge decides."

"Yeah, I know. Life isn't fair."

"It certainly isn't," replied Natasha.

Jack spent the rest of the evening staring at the television. He didn't really watch any programs. It was a way to try and blank out his brain and give it a rest. Natasha understood the ritual, but wasn't pleased when Jack told her that he would be working Saturday night. She had that night off and valued what precious time they had together.

It was a long night for Jack. It took several hours to fall asleep. When he did, he found himself on a ladder washing Father Brown's blood off the back of the house. It became more smeared and spread farther as he scrubbed. It was hard to reach because the ladder kept sinking into the ground. Eventually his cleaning worked and the blood disappeared. No, it hadn't. Like magic, as only a nightmare could be, the blood kept reappearing. More streaks and splashes than before. He climbed the ladder again ... it kept sinking.

It was nine o'clock Saturday night when Jack and Laura drove Sy to the party. The house turned out to be a ramshackle rental with an overgrown yard and a single-car garage. The house had been painted yellow, but huge chunks of paint had peeled away. Street lights illuminated a couple dozen other cars parked nearby. Several young people milled around outside on the front porch.

"Guess we're not the first," commented Jack. He glanced in the rearview mirror as he parked on the street and made eye contact with Laura in the back seat. She smiled at the sound of the heavy metal music vibrating the gutters on the house.

As they entered the house, Sy introduced Jack and Laura to two men in their early twenties who went by the nicknames of "Roach" and "Bagger."

"These are the guys who rent the joint," said Sy, while handing Bagger a flat of canned beer.

Jack nodded and glanced back at the street before stepping inside. He saw a brown van arrive with dark tinted windows on the side and rear. He knew that

Connie and Sammy were inside to watch and scoop licence plates. Hopefully many of Sy's gang would be identified. Unfortunately, they knew that the people above Sy would not be attending.

Sammy immediately left the van and pretended to walk away. Later he would return to slip unnoticed through a side door on the van. On his way back to the van, Sammy took the opportunity to jot down a licence plate of another carload of young people who had parked near Jack's SUV and gone into the party.

Movement caught his eye and he saw that a teen-aged boy with a ponytail had stepped out from behind a nearby pickup truck and was staring at him.

"You kids cause any vandalism tonight and I'm gonna call the cops," said Sammy, before walking away.

"Fuck you," replied the boy, taking a long drag on a joint before walking back to the house.

Sammy later snuck back to the van and lightly tapped on the side door. Connie unlocked it and let him inside.

"Might have been spotted writing down a plate," he said. "Any action in the last couple of minutes? Anyone come out to look around?"

"Nothing out of the ordinary," replied Connie.

"Good. Maybe the little asshole was too stoned to see straight."

A moment later the van rocked as it was nudged by a car parking behind it. The car was full of young people who were laughing as they got out and headed for the party.

Sammy saw that the car had blocked them in. He chuckled and said, "It looks like we may be here until the party is over. When does our overtime kick in?"

Roach and Bagger's house was filled with young people. Jack and Laura split up, with Laura mixing with the young women while Jack tried to socialize with the males.

Sy enjoyed the attention he received and Jack knew it gave him a sense of power. Jack also had the feeling that Sy was trying to impress him. *A good sign. The more he tries to impress me, the more he will open up.*

"Hey, Bagger!" yelled a female voice from the front door. "Where are ya?"

Jack turned and recognized Lorraine as she arrived with a younger girl.

"Hey, Bagger!" yelled Lorraine again. "Come and meet Cassandra. She's the one I was telling you about."

Bagger appeared through the crowd and made a show of ogling Cassandra, who blushed. Bagger smiled at Lorraine and asked, "Where's Brewski?"

"He might come later."

Bagger nodded and looked at Cassandra and said, "Get ya a drink? I make a good margarita."

"No," replied Cassandra. "My parents would smell it. I'm not allowed."

"Vodka won't smell. One won't hurt," said Bagger.

"Yeah, come on, Cassie," said Lorraine. "Don't embarrass me by acting like a geek."

"Okay, I guess one won't hurt."

Jack moved through the crowd for another hour before returning to the living room to sit on the sofa. He was quickly joined by Lorraine.

"So, like, you are Sy's new buddy?" she asked.

"We're getting to know each other," replied Jack.

Lorraine stared at him as if trying to make her mind up about something, before saying, "You know, I like older guys. You got more money and know how to please a woman."

Before Jack could reply she ran her hand up the inside of Jack's thigh and said, "Come with me out to my car. I think I lost my contact lens in the back seat. You could help me look."

"Not interested," replied Jack.

"Why?" replied Lorraine in surprise. "You gay? Nobody has ever turned me down before. I can't believe this."

"I'm not gay, but I've got a girlfriend. She's around here someplace. You've met her before."

"So who gives a shit? I've got a boyfriend, too. We won't be missed. Come on," she said, reaching over to caress his groin.

Jack slapped her hand away.

Anger flashed across Lorraines face and she said, "I know your problem, you're too old. Need me to lip-start it for ya?"

Before Jack could reply, Lorraine muttered, "Fuck you," and stood up abruptly and walked away.

* * *

Outside, Connie and Sammy saw a four-door green sedan parked nearby, with two young men in the front seat and a third in the rear.

"What are they up to?" asked Sammy. "It's cold tonight. I don't see any exhaust. They've shut the car off."

Connie adjusted her binoculars and saw a telltale red glow. "Smokin' a joint," she replied. "Wonder why they don't go inside?"

"Maybe they have a better appreciation of music," replied Sammy, "and are too stoned to know how cold it is."

Jack tried to pretend that he was enjoying himself and mingled as best he could in the crowded room. Later, he overheard Bagger talking to Lorraine.

"Where is she?" asked Bagger, looking around.

"Went upstairs to use the bathroom. What do ya think?"

"She's fuckin' beautiful. Roach thinks so, too."

"Told ya so. Hope you have fun."

"That's guaranteed."

"Good. So, you got a present for me?"

"Of course," replied Bagger, digging into the pocket of his cargo pants. "A deal's a deal. The blow is on me," he said, passing her a small paper flap. "Got a new rig for ya, too."

Jack saw Lorraine put the cocaine and needle in her purse as he departed for the kitchen to find Sy.

Sy was in the kitchen playing a drinking game with several young men. Jack saw Laura standing behind them. She rolled her eyes at him as she gestured to Sy. The men were sitting on the floor in a circle, each with a bottle of beer in front of them. On top of each bottle was an upside down bottle cap. They took turns, flicking other bottle caps with their fingers to try and knock off the cap on their opponent's bottle. If successful, the loser had to gulp down the beer and start with a fresh bottle. Judging by the empties beside Sy, he had been losing a lot.

Jack bent over and patted Sy on the shoulder. "What time were you thinking of leaving?"

"I don't know. How about after one more beer," replied Sy, before falling over on his side. Everyone laughed and Jack pretended to be amused as he helped Sy back into a sitting position.

"We should go," suggested Jack.

"Yeah, I do feel polluted," replied Sy, "Give me ten more minutes to finish this last drink, will ya?"

"Ten minutes and Princess and I are gone," replied Jack, looking at his watch. "I'll use the washroom and be right back."

Jack went to use the washroom on the main level, but someone had vomited on the floor.

"There's another one upstairs," said a young man with a ponytail.

Jack went upstairs and came upon a group of guys standing in the hall outside a bedroom door. He made his way past and into the washroom. Moments later, he heard the bedroom door open and Bagger say,

"Hey, she was a virgin. Can you believe it! Another one."

"Bullshit," said another voice.

"Ain't bullshittin' yeah, man. Go take a look."

"Fuckin' A. Wished she had popped her cherry with me instead of you."

"What the fuck, you're next, anyway."

"Still not the same. Ain't never had a virgin."

When Jack left the washroom he happened to follow Bagger down the stairs and into the kitchen. Upon arriving in the kitchen Bagger raised his fists above his head and danced a little jig.

"Bagger! Ya bagged another one," laughed one of the youths who was sitting on the floor. Before Bagger could reply, the youth flicked a beer cap between his fingers, striking Bagger in the face.

"Hey, Fucker!" yelled Bagger, tackling the youth and rolling around on the floor, knocking over drinks as the two combatants laughed at each other.

"Time to go," said Jack, grabbing Sy by the arm to help him stagger to his feet.

Sy agreed and they made their way out to Jack's SUV. Laura got in the back seat, while Sy climbed into the passenger side as Jack started the engine.

"So," said Jack, while pulling out of the parking space, "I was wondering how Bagger got his nickname. I thought it was from selling baggies of weed."

"Oh, fuck no," replied Sy. "He got it for all the chicks he bags. He's always getting laid."

"A real smooth talker with the ladies, is he?" asked Laura.

"Not much talkin' involved," mumbled Sy. "I know a guy, Cocktail, who keeps us connected with GHB. Ya know what that is?"

Jack nodded.

"There's a reason they call it the date-rape drug," slurred Sy. "Bagger's too fuckin' ugly to get laid without it."

The conversation between Lorraine and Bagger and the introduction of Cassandra flashed into Jack's brain. The realization and the rage he felt instinctively caused him to slam on the brakes. He briefly wondered who he wanted to kill first. Bagger and the other young men standing in line waiting to take their turn with Cassandra, or the slobbering drunk sitting beside him.

"Jay," said Laura quietly from the back seat, "didn't you say you had a friend who was in the market for GHB?" She sensed his anger and her question was meant to both caution and remind him that their real objective was to identify Cocktail.

"Why ya stopping?" asked Sy, looking around, completely clueless as to the rage Jack felt.

Jack took a deep breath and slowly exhaled.

"Why we stoppin'?" Sy asked again.

"A cat ran out in front of us," replied Jack, as he commenced driving again. "You mentioned a guy by the name of Cocktail. With a name like that, what is he, a bartender?" asked Jack, feigning a chuckle.

"No. Forget about him."

* * *

Connie and Sammy had watched as Jack, Laura, and Sy came out of the house and got into their SUV to drive away. As soon as Jack pulled away, the green sedan also drove off in a hurry.

"Coincidence?" suggested Connie. "They did start their car a couple of minutes before Jack and Laura came out."

"Shit!" yelled Sammy. "They're unrolling the rear windows! Hang on," he added, throwing the gear in reverse and ramming the car behind them.

"What the hell you doing?" yelled Connie.

"They're smokin' a joint. Not likely they're going to let the smoke out of the car without reason. Besides, it's cold out." He rammed the car behind them a second time and said, "Damn it, we'll never catch up in time. Why are you sitting there? Call Jack!"

"Tell him they're being followed?"

"Being followed? Jesus, Connie!" yelled Sammy.

"I don't work drugs. What the —"

"It's a hit!" screamed Sammy. "They're going to shoot them!"

Chapter Twenty-Five

Jack stopped behind a car parked in the centre lane at a red light when his BlackBerry rang.

Laura caught the eye contact Jack made with her in the rear view mirror. *Something's up …*

"Hi, Aunt Connie," she heard Jack say. "Calm down. Take a breath and talk quietly," he added, pressing the receiver tight to his ear so Sy wouldn't hear.

"You're being tailed," said Connie excitedly. "Three assholes in a four-door green sedan. They were sitting in the car watching the house and smoking a joint. They left as soon as you did and rolled the rear windows down. Sammy thinks they might be getting ready to shoot you."

Laura saw Jack check the side mirrors before riveting his attention back to the rearview mirror. This time he wasn't looking at her.

"Your pit bull is missing again?" replied Jack. "You can't find it? That's a dangerous animal to have on the loose." He saw Laura's head swivel as she looked out the windows.

"What are you talking about? Did you hear me?" asked Connie.

Jack saw the green sedan slowly pulling up alongside the passenger side of his SUV.

Sy drunkenly looked at Jack and said, "Your aunt has a pit bull? Good breed to have, man. She got a grow-op or somethin'?"

"Everyone down!" screamed Jack, ducking down. Through his peripheral vision he saw Laura scrambling to the floor.

"What the fuck ya doin?" roared Sy, when Jack clenched his collar with his fist and jerked him below the dash.

Jack's verbal response was not necessary as a barrage of bullets sent a shower of broken glass on everyone inside.

Jack cranked the steering wheel hard to the right and stepped on the gas. His car rammed the sedan, temporarily knocking the shooter off balance as the SUV sped forward. The sedan's squealing tires announced it was in hot pursuit as both vehicles raced down the street and turned a corner.

"Princess," yelled Jack, tossing his BlackBerry into the back seat. "Talk to Aunt Connie. I'm kind of busy."

"Busy! You fuckin' nuts?" screamed Sy.

"Hi, Aunt Connie," said Laura. "Sorry to hear Fang took off on you again. Where are you looking for him? … Oh, yeah. Remember last time he was about two blocks west of there. You'll probably hear him bark if you call and listen."

As Jack wheeled through the traffic, he glanced over to see Sy with a pistol in his hand while winding down what was left of the passenger window.

"Hey, fuckers!" Sy screamed, while drunkenly leaning out the passenger window and trying to aim.

"Don't!" yelled Jack, grabbing Sy by the belt on the back of his pants and yanking him back inside while swerving into the right lane to block Sy's target from view.

"What the fuck? Who's side ya on!" yelled Sy angrily. "Stay on the left side so I can shoot these fuckers!

"I've got a better idea," yelled Jack, not wanting a drunken Sy to let loose with a handgun and endanger the wrong people. "I'm going to brake and ram. If you're hanging out the window they're liable to shoot you. Either that or you'll fall out when I brake hard."

"Brake and run? What are ya talkin' about?" screamed Sy, his words barely intelligible from a combination of alcohol and fear.

"Not *run*. Ram! Keep your head down and trust me. You'll see shortly."

Jack veered back to the left lane and drove as if he were intent on racing away. The sedan was more powerful and soon started to edge up along the passenger side once more. Jack slammed on the brakes and the sedan surged past before the driver had time to brake.

It was what Jack was waiting for. He stepped on the gas and rammed the left rear corner of the sedan, sending it spinning clockwise out of control before smashing sideways into a power pole. Steam billowed out from the crumpled hood of the sedan and one wheel was bent over from a broken axel. Seconds later, the occupants were climbing out and running in different directions.

"That's Weasel!" yelled Sy, pointing to the shooter who had bailed out of the back seat. "I recognize that fucker! Back up so I can finish him!" he said, once more hanging out the window with his pistol.

Jack grabbed him by the belt and hauled him back inside. "Some other time!" Jack yelled. "The cops are here. I see a red light on the dash of some van comin' up fast behind us. Time to split."

Moments later, when they were safely away from the scene, Sy looked at Jack and Laura and said, "You two gotta be the coolest two people I've ever met."

"That shit was nothing," replied Jack, as casually as he could.

"What do you mean, nothing! Fuck man, you saved my life."

Don't remind me, thought Jack. He glanced at Sy and said, "You ever hear about the west-end gangs out of Montreal?"

"Oh, yeah. Old time gangs ... Irish ... heard they used to cut off body parts."

"My old man was a member all his life," said Jack. "I was raised in that shit. This is nothing. More annoying than anything. One of the reasons Princess and I moved out here was to get away from it."

"Man ... how you both handled that back there."
He looked back at Laura and said, "You too, talking
to your aunt like we were out for a Sunday drive."

Laura shrugged, pretending it was nothing. *Hope
I didn't pee myself ...*

"Who does Weasel work for?" asked Jack.

"He's part of Balvinder's gang," replied Sy.

"You once told me that there were three gangs you
were at odds with. Who are they?"

"Besides Balvinder, there's Fateh and Quang's
gangs, but I know Weasel is with Balvinder," said Sy.

Jack nodded as he wheeled through traffic. His
adrenaline was still high and he kept one eye in the
rearview mirror.

"Where did you learn to drive like this?" asked Sy,
with a tinge of suspicion. "You handled yourself back
there like you drove NASCAR."

"Used to drive a cab once," replied Jack.

"That figures."

"Know anyone in the auto body business?" asked
Jack.

"Damn right. Don't worry about the bullet holes.
I'll have it fixed for you first thing Monday. No charge.
I owe ya, man."

Jack parked the SUV in the underground parking lot at
the apartment complex and they went to Sy's apartment.

Brewski, armed with a pistol and a sawed-off shotgun, said he would spend the night with Sy. Jack told

Sy that he and Princess were going to return to their other apartment until they knew things were safe. Sy understood their concern. He said he would be calling a meeting with some people tomorrow and asked Jack if he would come. Jack said he would think about it.

Jack called a taxi and he and Laura were driven to an expensive apartment complex near Stanley Park. After a brief walk to ensure it was safe, they called Connie who gave them a ride back to their office.

Jack and Laura then spent the next two hours typing reports. Jack also called his boss, Staff-Sergeant Rosemary Wood, who demanded a meeting with him at eight in the morning.

It was two-thirty in the morning when he arrived home. He was surprised to see Natasha awake and reading in bed. She quickly put her book away and gave him a warm smile as he entered the bedroom.

"How are you doing? she asked.

"I'm great," he replied, still feeling euphoric that he was alive.

"You sound happy. Have you gotten over yesterday's court cases?"

"I don't think I will ever get over it," said Jack reflectively, "but I do appreciate that some things in my life are more important."

"Oh? Such as?"

Jack paused and said, "Coming home to you."

Natasha stared intently at Jack for a moment before smiling and saying, "Glad you finally have your priorities straight. How soon will it be before you're finished this assignment? A week? A month? Longer?"

"The bad guy I was with tonight mentioned the nickname of the man I'm trying to identify. It shouldn't take long. Some stuff is happening. I have to work tomorrow ... early. It could wrap up within the week. Why?"

"Selfish reasons. I want you to myself. Sounds like I won't have you tomorrow, either."

"I'm here now," Jack replied, reflecting on how close he had come to catching a bullet or two.

"Physically, yes, but I can see your thoughts are elsewhere. They have been a lot lately."

"Sorry. It's hard to concentrate sometimes. I really want to catch this guy."

"I understand that part. There is always someone you really want to catch. I accept that and I want you to be able to concentrate on your work and come home safe. I don't see you a lot, so when I do, it would be nice if you thought of me and not some criminal."

"I'm sorry." Jack stared briefly at Natasha and said, "Are you okay? You've seemed really tired lately ... kind of run down."

"It's late. Damn right I'm tired."

"You shouldn't have waited up. I could have slept at the UC apartment."

"No, when you called at midnight, I said I wanted you to come home. It's Saturday night ... I want my guy to sleep with."

"To sleep?" said Jack, suggestively, as he bent over and kissed her on the nape of her neck.

Natasha smiled and said, "That, too. So hurry and come to — hey, you've got broken glass stuck in your sweater. Looks like windshield glass."

"Oh ... that," replied Jack, as he stood up and saw where Natasha was pointing. "I was in a fender bender tonight and rear-ended somebody. Nobody was hurt."

"I thought you sounded strange when you called. Sounding all lovey-dovey."

Jack shrugged and smiled in response.

"A rear-ender ... sounds like your fault. See? You do need to concentrate on what you do."

"I'd like to concentrate on your body."

Half an hour later, Natasha's breathing told Jack that she was asleep. He felt too anxious to sleep and wondered what tomorrow would bring.

Car chase and shoot-out on the streets.... The brass will go nuts. Sy was going beserk when I left him.... Somebody is going to die ...

Chapter Twenty-Six

Whiskey Jake was the president of the east-side chapter of Satans Wrath. It was not yet eight o'clock on a Sunday morning when he arrived at the mansion belonging to Damien, the national president of the club. He didn't question the order to attend.

He stopped at the electronic gate outside of Damien's estate and looked into the closed-circuit television camera. Seconds later, the gate swung open and he drove inside. He parked his Mercedes beside a green Jaguar that belonged to Lance Morgan, who was the president of the west-side chapter. He then walked over and pressed the intercom button beside the main entrance and stared into another camera.

"Hi, Whiskey Jake," responded a woman's voice. "They're out back. Go around the side. I'll bring you a coffee."

Vicki was Damien's wife. At thirty-seven, she was

eighteen years younger than Damien. Whiskey Jake thought she was sexy and attractive, but even though he was a giant of a man who towered over Damien, he knew better than to even fantasize when it came to Vicki. His loyalty to the club was above all else.

Whiskey Jake lumbered around to the back of the house and met up with Damien and Lance who were sitting in a gazebo near Damien's swimming pool. Whiskey Jake hadn't sat down yet when Vicki brought him a coffee.

"Black," she said matter-of-factly, "two sugars," before returning to the house.

Without comment, Damien and Lance stood up and the three men went for a walk. Damien had his house swept for bugs on a regular basis, but even in his gazebo he would not take a chance.

"Okay," said Damien. "Sounds like The Brotherhood are at it again. First thing I hear on the news when I wake up is about a car chase and shoot-out on the streets last night. The police haven't made any arrests, but are speculating that gangs involved in a turf war are responsible."

"Yeah, I heard it on the way over," said Whiskey Jake.

"First, what is the plus side?" asked Damien.

Whiskey Jake said, "The drive-by shootings have taken the heat off of us. Last night will help some more. The cop's Organized Crime Task Force will focus on the shooters in The Brotherhood. Strictly bottom-end people. Maybe they'll make a few arrests, seize some guns, get some publicity, and try to make themselves look good. Nothing to affect our club."

"And the negative side?" asks Damien.

"Might affect our business to a small degree," responded Whiskey Jake.

"Could do more than that," said Lance. "Politicians could use public fear to posture for votes, maybe strengthen gang laws under the Criminal Code and give the OCTF more funding and manpower as a result of the shootings."

"And?" prompted Damien.

"The OCTF might find out that we are supplying The Brotherhood with meth and GHB," continued Lance. "Once the OCTF knock off the dumb shits in The Brotherhood, they're not going to want to disband and lose their power. They're bound to come after us next."

"Exactly," said Damien. "We need to educate The Brotherhood. The harder it is for the police to nail them, the more insulation we have, and the more police resources will be spent on The Brotherhood."

"They're a bunch of punk kids," said Whiskey Jake. "Hard to organize and they won't like it if they realize we're taking over. We know the leaders, but we don't know who all they control or how many they got."

"Exactly why we should make a move. Discreetly start grooming a leader to take over The Brotherhood. Someone to gain power over them and make it easier for us to control."

"Like a mole," said Lance.

"Exactly," replied Damien. "Pick someone we already control. End their war before the police use it as an excuse to ask for more money and resources.

Allow The Brotherhood to set up a couple of dummy bosses underneath whoever we pick as a protective layer for us."

"Like the canary in the coal mine," said Lance.

"Precisely. At the moment, they have too many bosses, which is another reason there is so much conflict."

"Right now they have seven bosses," said Whiskey Jake.

"Which are too many idiots if we are to control them properly."

"Maybe we should cut their number down?" suggested Whiskey Jake.

"Exactly what I have in mind, but with all the heat over these shootings, the timing isn't good for us to openly do it ourselves. It could also have the potential of backfiring on us. The Brotherhood might realize we are the bigger threat and unite against us."

"So how do we do it?" asked Whiskey Jake.

"We need to figure out which side is winning and go with them," replied Damien. "We need someone with more brainpower than the current bosses to move things along. How about Cocktail?"

"He's got the smarts," said Lance. "Both sides of The Brotherhood deal with him and know we back him. They trust him and know he would never expose himself by being a boss. Makes them trust him more. He's also smart enough not to double-cross us."

"Good," replied Damien. "Tell him to pick who he thinks is going to be the winning side, then offer to help them out. Set the losers up to be taken out all at once. Professionally. No more idiotic drive-by-shooting shit."

"You got it," said Whiskey Jake.

"In the meantime, except for Cocktail and his action, tell all our guys to stay clear of The Brotherhood."

"After last night, the heat will be all over them," agreed Lance.

"Plus, the dumb shits will probably retaliate immediately instead of waiting," said Damien. "Give everything a few days. Once the air clears a little, tell Cocktail to meet the bosses and provide us with an assessment. Make sure our prospects are around to ensure secrecy and security with Cocktail. If there is any doubt, abort. I don't want the police to ever connect him with us or The Brotherhood."

"So once a stronger side emerges, we'll eliminate the weaker side," said Whiskey Jake.

"Yes, but not us personally," replied Damien. "Get them to do it. We'll give Cocktail some ... professional advice that he can pass along. Get the losers in one spot. Take care of them all at once and make sure their bodies never surface."

"He could use a pretext that we have ordered a truce meeting for them to straighten things out," suggested Lance.

"That would work," replied Damien. "Anything to get them all together in a place without witnesses. Won't be as much heat if they disappear. Especially if their money disappears at the same time."

"I think they're smart enough not to use banks," said Lance.

Damien nodded and said, "But I doubt they are sophisticated enough to launder or use offshore accounts. Tell Cocktail to get the losers to give up their cash before they dispose of them."

"Torture the fuckers first," said Whiskey Jake, as if he was going over his own mental checklist.

"Cocktail can split it amongst himself and the winning side," continued Damien.

"If we take out three or four of their bosses," said Lance, "with the number of punks out there and a lack of leadership, there could be a lot of retaliation on an undisciplined level."

"If shit really goes wrong, we'll claim Cocktail was acting on his own," said Damien. "If it goes well, the winning side should feel indebted. As far as retaliation goes, without their leaders the kids will fold pretty fast. For a brief time it might draw a lot of police scrutiny, but all we have to do is wait it out and make sure we don't get caught in the middle."

Satans Wrath would not have to wait long to see who the weaker side was. Jack would be placed firmly on that weaker side … and targeted for assassination.

Chapter Twenty-Seven

Jack and Laura arrived at the office at quarter to eight on Sunday morning and saw that their boss was already there.

"Come in, have a seat," said Staff-Sergeant Rosemary Wood, gesturing to the two chairs in front of her desk. She waited until they were seated and said, "Well?"

"You read our reports?" asked Jack, pointing to the papers on her desk.

"I read them," she said, matter-of-factly. "Driving like a couple of lunatics while shooting and smashing up cars on our public streets. It must have been quite a night."

"It was," admitted Jack.

"Both of you feel you are okay to work?"

"We're fine," both Jack and Laura said in unison.

"You'll need to see the Force psychologist."

"We know."

"I'm sure you do. Be nice to the man, he is only trying to help."

"Don't worry, Rose. We'll be nice and say the right things," said Laura.

"For sure," agreed Jack. "I don't want him recommeding stress leave."

"I know you will say the right things," replied Rose, shaking her head. *These two make a living out of fooling some of the toughest people on the planet. Our poor shrink won't stand a chance.* She looked at them and said, "About last night, it was a miracle nobody got hurt."

"The incident was over within thirty seconds," said Jack.

"A lot of people can get hurt in thirty seconds," replied Rose.

"I know, but under the circumstances I did what I thought was best."

"You never shot back ... I take it you weren't armed?"

"No. Seldom are when we're undercover."

Rose nodded and said, "After you called me last night, I called Isaac."

Jack sucked in a deep breath and slowly exhaled. Assistant Commissioner Isaac was the criminal operations officer who oversaw all the operational investigations in the Pacific region. He wasn't someone you would bother at home without serious consideration. More so, when the call was made after midnight.

"How did he take it?" asked Jack.

"Well, he wasn't exactly happy," replied Rose, "but you won't be kicking your Stetson up the highway to Nunavut Dog Sled Patrol, if that's what you're thinking."

"Good. What did he say?"

"When I woke him up to say that you had been involved in a … situation, he groaned and muttered, "not again" and asked who was dead. When I said that the situation did not result in anyone's death … that is correct, isn't it?" asked Rose, while scrutinizing Jack's face.

"So far," replied Jack.

"So far?"

"Sy is planning retribution. He asked me to attend a meeting with him today."

"You mentioned that last night and Isaac is in agreement that you do attend to find out what you can and to defuse the situation if possible."

"If possible," replied Jack.

"Naturally, you won't take part in any retribution yourself."

"Naturally," replied Jack.

"Good. Isaac wanted that made clear. Also, he was relieved that nobody was hurt, but was irate that none of the perpetrators would be charged. I explained that you two couldn't go to court because it would burn your informant. He didn't like it, but agreed. Maybe later other evidence will surface where charges could be laid without you having to appear in court."

"Sy would never co-operate," said Jack. "Even if he did, with his record of violence, a jury wouldn't exactly feel sorry for him."

"Well, in the end, Isaac said perhaps it was a blessing you two weren't going to court because he knew how it would play out with the media if they ever found out."

"So everything is okay, then?" asked Laura.

"In my view, Isaac's response was pragmatic. He said that under the circumstances, it would appear that what you did was reasonable given the situation."

Both Jack and Laura exhaled loudly and smiled at each other.

"He told me to tell you, Jack, that his response may have been different if someone had been killed." Rose looked sharply at Jack and said, "I am to tell you specifically that he means citizens, good guys ... and bad guys."

"That goes without saying," replied Jack, furrowing his eyebrows slightly as if indignant.

"I'm not the Force shrink," said Rose. "I know you better, so don't try to con me."

"Sorry," replied Jack. "Force of habit."

"Are you going over to see Sy when we're done here?" Rose asked, changing the subject.

"I'd like to hold off until later in the day. The Organized Crime Task Force has some wire up and running. It would be nice to know if anything comes across the phones that might help us figure out if more attacks are planned. I'm also concerned that Connie and Sammy saw Weasel and his cohorts start their car before we left the party. I don't believe in coincidences."

Rose snickered in spite of the seriousness and said, "You of all people say you don't believe in coincidences?

Hell, that's been your middle name ever since I arrived in this office."

"You know what I mean," said Jack. "There's a good chance Sy has someone in his gang who is working for the other side."

"And we don't mean our side," said Laura.

Rose nodded, sighed, and said, "Be safe, the both of you."

"Yes, Mom. Both hands on the wheel," replied Jack.

Rose furrowed her eyebrows to feign anger at the remark.

Jack looked at her and said, "Deception doesn't suit you. Maybe that's a good thing."

Rose pursed her lips before saying, "Go. You've got work to do." She waited until they left the office before smiling at how easily Jack had seen through her.

It was suppertime when Jack and Laura arrived at Sy's apartment. In the previous hour Sy had called Jack a couple of times, but his calls were ignored. It was a control issue and Jack wanted to be in control.

"Where the fuck you been all day?" asked Sy, as they entered his crowded apartment. There were only males in the apartment and the atmosphere was a combination of excitement and tension.

"Princess and I had to go rent a car and then we went to help my aunt find her dog," replied Jack. "Why?"

"Why? This is fuckin' why!" said Sy, picking up a sawed-off shotgun and waving it in Jack's face, before nodding toward the door and saying, "Come on, let's you and I take a walk."

Laura kissed Jack on the cheek and said, "Don't be long. Princess might get bored."

As soon as Jack and Sy were alone in the hallway, Sy said, "We found out where Weasel is stayin'. We're gettin' him tonight."

"Tonight!" replied Jack.

"Yeah. He's staying with his girlfriend."

"Have you ever heard the expression, 'revenge is a dish best served cold'?" said Jack. "There'll be lots of heat. If you wait, they'll relax their guard."

"We're gonna do it. If you don't want to come, then don't." Sy looked suspiciously at Jack and said, "Fuck, man, they shot at you and Princess, too. I thought you would want in."

"I do, but something stinks," replied Jack.

"What are you talkin' about? The only thing that is gonna stink is Weasel's corpse!"

"Who told Weasel and his buddies about the party?"

Sy shrugged and said, "I dunno."

"How did they know it was you last night when it wasn't your car?"

"Probably watchin' the place. Saw us leave."

"It was dark when we left. People coming and going. Easy to see silhouettes, not so easy to see faces."

"What the fuck are you tryin' to say?"

"That you have a leak. Someone tipped them off last night. This could be a trap."

"Naw, ain't no trap," replied Sy. "Roach and Bagger got lucky. Rounded up a guy by the name of Raven who knows Weasel's girlfriend. Raven talked as soon as they rammed a gun in his face. He told us Weasel is staying with his girlfriend in the basement of her parents' house."

"Roach and Bagger kill Raven?" asked Jack, non-chalantly.

"Naw, not necessary. Roach and Bagger are holding him at their house so Weasel can't be warned. What Raven told us checked out. I had one of my guys drive past the house half an hour ago. Weasel's car was parked in the alley behind the house."

"Same car as last night?" asked Jack.

"Naw, didn't you hear the news? They used a stolen car last night. His is a blue Honda. If it's there, we'll sneak up, kick in the door, and blast the shit out of him and his bitch."

Jack took a deep breath and slowly exhaled before saying, "I'm telling you, after last night … you heard the news. The cops could be watching everyone. If they know it was Weasel, they'll be expecting someone to take revenge. You should wait until things cool."

"Fuck that." Sy cast a sideways glance at Jack and said, "You saved my life last night, but now you're actin' weird. If you're worried about us gettin' hurt, don't. I got a team of seven guys, not countin' you an' me. We got enough firepower to blow the whole house to smithereens. So … you comin' or not?"

Jack sighed and said, "Yeah, I'll come. Give me a minute to tell Princess I'm steppin' out. How long will we be?"

"The place is out in Maple Ridge. Better count on being gone a couple of hours."

"What you got for wheels?"

"Brewski will drive a van with cool plates. Me, I got a little five-litre Mustang that the guys boosted. Goes like a bullet. The owner is on holidays, so it won't be reported."

"Hope it's not white?"

"It's black. Why?"

"Good. Harder to spot at night. If we're going to do it, let's do it right. Start with letting me drive and have the van follow."

"Why?"

"Because when we leave, I'm going to drive in circles for awhile. Make damn sure nobody is following us. Tell Brewski to do the same."

"Okay, you proved your driving ability last night," replied Sy. "You can be the wheel man, but when we get there, I'm first through the door."

"Wouldn't want it any other way," replied Jack.

Jack quickly updated Laura as they walked back to their rented apartment above Sy's.

"Oh, man," said Laura. "Bust them and we're burned. Don't and we're party to murder. Any ideas?"

"OCTF should be able to come up with an address on Weasel's girlfriend. Tell the narcs to drive over there and empty the garbage off their floor mats out front and in the alley behind. When we arrive, have the

Emergency Response Team do a takedown. I'll stall as long as I can to give everyone time to set up."

"You're going to have them arrested? We'll be burned. They'll figure it out."

"Maybe … maybe not. I have an idea."

Minutes later, Sy opened the trunk of the Mustang parked in the underground parking lot. "Take a look," said Sy, as he smiled and pointed to a duffle bag.

Jack opened the bag and saw four handguns, four sawed-off shotguns, and an AK47 automatic machine gun. "Hell of an arsenal."

Sy nodded and kept the AK47 for himself, along with one of the shotguns for Jack, before passing the duffle bag over to his gang members, who were parked beside the Mustang in a van. Seconds later, Sy ordered two of his people to ride in the back seat of the stolen Mustang while the others went in the van with Brewski.

"Let's roll!" ordered Sy.

Jack spent an hour driving around in circles before an exasperated Sy told him enough was enough. Jack drove as directed to a residential area in Maple Ridge. When they arrived, Sy indicated a house halfway down the block. "Pull over," said Sy. "I see his blue Honda parked out front now."

Jack pulled over to the curb and Brewski pulled in behind him. At the opposite end of the block a set of car headlights came on and the driver sped away. "One of your guys?" Jack asked.

"No," replied Sy. "I didn't want Neighbourhood Watch or someone reporting anything suspicious. That's probably a neighbour. Don't worry about it."

"It pays to worry sometimes. Tell the guys in the van to drive around the area and check things out. It's not good for both of us to be parked together. While Brewski is doing that, I'm going to park on the next block and you and I will walk back. Let's see if anyone is sitting in parked cars."

"Fuck, man, you're paranoid."

"You stay alive that way … and out of jail."

"Yeah, okay," muttered Sy, before giving the order for Brewski to circle the area.

Jack parked the car in the next block and said, "Let's leave our artillery in the car. I don't want to be seen walking down the street carrying these cannons. If it is the cops they're liable to see it and grab us."

Sy agreed and left the AK47 in the car and told his two associates to wait while he and Jack checked things out.

As Jack and Sy arrived at the end of the block from Weasel's house, Jack pointed to the ground and said, "Damn it, I knew it." He pointed to the empty parking space at the end of the block where the car had driven away when they first arrived.

"What?" replied Sy. "I don't see nothin'."

"Cop droppings," said Jack, pointing to the sidewalk and road.

"Cop droppings?" replied Sy with a snicker. "What the fuck are you talking about? Looks like sunflower seeds."

"A buddy of mine got busted once," replied Jack. "They had his house under surveillance first. He told me later he knew where they had been parked by all the sunflower seeds they ate and the husks they spit out while watching his place."

"You shittin' me?"

"No. We should get the hell out of here. Tell the boys in the van to scram."

"Over some seeds? You gotta be kiddin'. Hang on."

Jack listened as Sy ordered the van to cruise through the area and check.

"That could draw heat," cautioned Jack.

"You're fuckin' paranoid," replied Sy with a chuckle. "Come on, we'll head back to the car. If the boys haven't spotted anything suspicious by then, we're goin' in."

"Let's walk down the back alley first and check it out," suggested Jack.

"Yeah, okay, but if the alley is clear, we're gonna do this fucker."

"Sounds good," replied Jack.

They had barely made it into the alley when Sy received a call.

"The cops got us pinned!" screamed Brewski. His warning wasn't necessary as the sharp, piercing sound of sirens cut the night air from several different locations.

Two police cars with lights flashing entered each end of the alley simultaneously and zoomed toward Jack and Sy.

"Come on," yelled Jack. "Over the fence!"

Jack and Sy both clamoured over a wooden fence and raced through someone's backyard, out through the front and crossed the street to another yard and kept going. Three blocks away they were in another yard and about to run out a gate into a rear alley, but the sound of another car speeding up the alley caused them to crouch down behind some bushes while peering through the back fence.

Jack glanced at Sy and saw he was holding a pistol at the ready.

"Jesus, Sy," whispered Jack. "I thought we left the artillery in the car in case the cops searched us."

"After last night I started carrying an ankle holster," Sy whispered.

Both men froze as a flashlight beam cut through the darkness behind them. Jack looked over his shoulder and saw the distinct yellow stripe on the uniform trousers of a policeman who walked toward them. His beam was still probing the bushes when Jack saw Sy raise his pistol and take aim.

Chapter Twenty-Eight

Laura sat in the back of a surveillance van with Connie and the commander of the Emergency Response Team. The Organized Crime Task Force gave them an address in Maple Ridge for who they thought were the parents of Weasel's girlfriend, but had added a disclaimer that their information was a month old. *Did Weasel still have the same girlfriend?*

With the address being in Maple Ridge, Laura felt relatively confident that it was the same, but when she saw Jack arrive in the Mustang, followed by Brewski in the van, she breathed a sigh of relief.

The surveillance van was parked across the street one block down from where Weasel was living and offered a relatively good view of the front street and one entrance to the alley.

The ERT commander groaned when Jack parked the Mustang and the van started to circle the neighbourhood. "Wished we had more time to set up and organize," he said.

"What do you mean?" asked Laura. "Jack made them drive around for an hour before they even left the city. I thought you guys were good? How much more time did you need?"

The commander ignored her comment as their earplugs crackled a message from another member of the ERT.

"T-1 and T-2 out of the car and walking back toward the house."

Laura used binoculars to watch through the one-way glass in the surveillance van and soon saw Jack and Sy come into view as they walked along the sidewalk. She smiled when Jack stopped and pointed at the sunflower husks while talking to Sy.

"These two are the guys we let escape, right?" crackled their earphones.

"Affirmative," replied the commander.

Laura continued to watch as she relayed what was happening to Connie and the commander. "They're heading back down the street," she whispered. "If they follow the plan they should be going down the alley." Seconds later, Laura confirmed that Jack and Sy were entering the alley.

"Teams one and two, are you in a position to take out the vehicles?" radioed the commander.

"Team one, ten-four."

"Team two, ten-four."

"Team three, ready for the alley?" asked the commander.

"Team three is ready."

"All teams go!" radioed the commander. "Team three, make it look good but let them run."

"Copy that," replied several voices barely heard over the eruption of sirens.

Seconds later, Laura smiled when they received the first report.

"This is team one. We have five targets secured and kissing asphalt."

Moments later, the second team also reported that the arrests of two more targets had gone without incident.

The radio crackled again and Laura heard, amongst laughter, a voice say, "Team three here. We got two rabbits leaping fences and backyarding it northbound from the alley."

"Copy that," replied the commander. "Stay in the alley and make some noise."

Laura heard the sound of a garbage can being kicked over and saw lights come on in several houses as people awoke to the sound of the clamour taking place.

"This is team one," the radio announced, "we've recovered enough weapons to start a small war."

"Likewise for team two."

Laura smiled at Connie and said, "Perfect. I love it when a plan comes together."

"Yeah, and the law didn't come into it," said the commander

"The law?" asked Laura.

"Murphy's law."

"Guess all your worrying was for nothing. Mind dropping me off at my car? I should be getting a call soon."

"Not a problem," replied the commander, gesturing for Laura to hold on for a moment as he received a radio call from the telecommunications centre.

"Are you still at the same location?" asked a feminine voice.

"Ten-four," replied the commander. "Just mopping up."

"Uniform spotted two men running through someone's backyard three blocks north of your location. We have one member in pursuit on foot and the other circling the block in the car."

Laura's eyes flashed her concern as she looked at the commander.

"They were told to stay clear!" replied the commander into his transmitter.

"I advised them that," replied the woman, "but they said they heard sirens and believed your takedown was finished. They said two were escaping, so they decided to help."

"What channel are they operating on?" asked the commander.

Laura felt her stomach knot as the commander contacted the patrol car and said, "Who am I talking to?"

"Constable Gibson," came the reply.

"Clear the area at once! Leave the pursuit to us!"

"Uh … I can't get hold of Constable Farthington," replied Gibson. "He turned his portable radio off to sneak up on someone."

Laura grabbed the radio and said, "Gibson, this is Constable Secord. I don't have time to explain. You need to get Farthington back to the car immediately. Get out and fire three shots into someone's lawn. Do it now!"

Chapter Twenty-Nine

As the flashlight beam came closer, Jack stood up and walked between Sy and the officer.

"Hi, officer," said Jack. "I'm glad you're here so fast!"

Jack blinked as the flashlight beam found his face. "Who are you?" demanded the voice behind the flashlight. "Keep your hands where I can see them!"

"It's not me," said Jack indignantly. "I'm the one who called 911. There were two of them," he said. "They ran through my yard a moment ago. They went that way," he added, pointing back between two houses.

"Oh … uh, I see," replied the officer. "Okay, uh …" he didn't finish as he took a step in the direction Jack pointed, before turning around.

Come on! Go! Jack thought, while smiling and giving a slight nod of encouragement for the officer to continue his search elsewhere.

"First, I'd like to see some identification."

"It's inside my house," replied Jack. "They're getting away for Christ's sake! Why aren't you chasing them?"

The officer's reply was interrupted by the sound of gunfire. By the third shot, the officer vanished from view in the direction the shots came from.

"Fuckin' bloody hell," said Sy, standing up from where he had been crouched behind a bush. "Hope those shots were some cop being plugged and not one of my guys!"

"Come on, we better keep moving," said Jack. "I'll call Princess and have her pick us up."

"Fuck, I know I've said this before, but you gotta be one of the coolest dudes I've ever met. That fuckin' cop don't know how close he came. You shouldn't have done that, though. Fuck of a chance being in the middle if the shootin' started."

"I probably saved your life ... again," replied Jack.

"Bullshit! I had the drop on him. He didn't even know I was there."

"Don't be stupid," replied Jack. "Think about it. He's trained and wearing body armour. He'd see your muzzle flash ... you're crouched and would probably fall back on your ass with his first shot. His second shot would take out your nuts and intestines." Jack paused to let the image sink in and said, "And for what? If you gave yourself up, what would you get? Probation? Hardly worth killing anyone over. Especially a cop."

Sy eyed Jack carefully and said, "What you did was stupid, too. Putting yourself in the middle like that.

You could have been shot. Makes me wonder who you were trying to save? Him or me?"

"I wanted to save all of us," replied Jack. "Those punk kids you've got working for you wouldn't stand up to the heat if a cop got killed. They'd rat us out in a jiffy. We'd both spend the rest of our lives in jail."

"Their lawyers would protect them. They wouldn't need to rat."

They eventually made their way far enough out of the area and Jack called Laura to come and pick them up. Jack and Sy spoke little as they waited. It was clear that Sy was going over everything in his head. On occasion, he cast a suspicious glance in Jack's direction.

Forty minutes later, Laura drove up and Sy quickly climbed into the back seat while Jack sat in the front with Laura.

"What happened?" asked Laura, as she started driving.

"I think we were set up," said Sy. "The cops were waiting." His voice was grave and Jack turned in his seat and saw Sy's blank face staring at him, pondering over what had happened.

"They had to know that Weasel was one of the shooters last night," said Jack. He spoke as if talking to Laura, but studied Sy's face for a response. "They were obviously waiting to see if someone would retaliate," he added.

Sy scowled and looked at Laura and snapped, "Find me a payphone! I don't trust ..." He paused to look at Jack before continuing, "this BlackBerry."

* * *

Minutes later, they found a payphone and Sy ran over to it while Jack and Laura waited in the car. He glanced back at them as he dialed a number.

Sy's first call was to Mongo, one of the other two bosses who was still on his side. Mongo owned a pizza outlet, but Sy placed the call to a cellphone number that Mongo had given him earlier that day. Soon Mongo's gruff voice answered.

"This is Sy. This number still cool?"

"Yeah, one of my guys got it yesterday. What's up? How did it go tonight?"

"My guys got busted outside Weasel's house. I was lucky to escape. Cops got most of my good artillery. I heard shots, too. Don't know what the fuck happened. Hope none of my guys got wasted."

"Fuck, no. Tell me you're joking."

"Do I sound like I'm jokin'?"

"Fuck," muttered Mongo. "How did it happen?"

"I made the mistake of trusting two people who moved into the apartment above mine. Jay and his bitch he calls Princess. They're sitting in a car waiting for me to finish talking with you."

"What do you want to do?"

"Take 'em both out tonight. One of them has to be a rat. Maybe both, who knows."

"How ya want to do it?"

"They don't realize I figured out it's them. I'll bring 'em over to your pizza joint. Meet us in the alley and we'll go in your back office. Call Munch, too. The three of us gotta unite if we're gonna win this war. May as well have Munch join us and get started."

Laura sat in the car with Jack and watched as Sy jabbed the numbers into the phone. She glanced at Jack and said, "Connie will be expecting us to call soon. She'll be wondering what Sy has to say and be worried."

"She'll have to wait. I'd like to know what Sy is thinking myself."

"Something is going on," she said, looking back at Sy. "He looks upset."

"After what happened, I expected he would be upset," replied Jack. "But is he on to us?"

"That's the big question," replied Laura.

"We'll play it by ear, but keep your head up. He's packing a pistol in an ankle holster. Once he's back in the car, if it looks like he's going for it, I'll grab him, beat the hell out of him and toss him out. As long as he's not arrested, our informant should be safe."

"And if he pulls the gun out before he gets in?" asked Laura.

"Drive like hell. Here he comes."

Sy got in the back seat again and Jack turned to face him, acting nonchalant as he draped one arm over the back of the seat. "So, what do you figure?" asked Jack. "Maybe come back to our place and we can figure out what happened."

"Maybe after," replied Sy. "There's someone I want you to meet, first. He's waiting."

"Who?" asked Jack, hoping to hear the name Cocktail.

"A guy you've never met. I told him about you two. He has a plan of what to do next."

Sy's evasive manner set off a warning bell in Jack's brain. *Is he introducing us to Cocktail ... or the Grim Reaper? If I say no, and he's suspicious, it will make things worse. If I'm innocent, I need to act that way and should go along.*

Jack glanced at Laura for her reaction. She stared straight back at him, without expression. Jack sighed. She was leaving the decision up to him. Jack turned to Sy and asked, "Where is this place?"

"A restaurant called Pizza 24-7, near the Guildford shopping centre in Surrey." Sy looked at Laura and said, "Take the 152nd Street exit and cut across on 96th."

Jack smiled to himself. *Good, a restaurant. Public location should be safe.* "Sounds good," said Jack. "I could use a bite. How about you, Princess?"

She felt numb. *Something isn't right ... but I trust Jack ...* She looked at Jack and nodded. *Oh, man ...*

Chapter Thirty

Half an hour later, Laura parked in a back alley behind a steel door with a sign saying PIZZA 24-7. She tapped on the horn as directed and the steel door opened as the three of them got out.

Jack followed Laura toward the steel door and looked at the two men who were waiting for them at the door. He recognized Munch's fat face from having seen him with Sy previously. The other man was large and muscular with short black hair and a goatee. There were some Asian features to his face and Jack recognized him from a previous mug shot as the one they called Mongo. *So much for meeting Cocktail ...*

Jack glanced back at the vehicle. He knew things were looking bleak when he got out of the car and saw Sy hesitate and bend over in the car before climbing out. Sy maintained a safe distance as he followed Jack and Laura, while keeping one hand behind his back. Jack had little doubt about what Sy was holding.

Mongo sneered at Jack and Laura and said, "Follow me into my back office."

Inside a short hallway, Jack tried to sound naive and spoke to Sy without looking back. "Who are these guys," he asked. "Are they cool to talk in front of?"

"Oh, yeah," chuckled Sy. "They're cool. Cool enough to kill for me."

They entered a small office containing a wooden desk marred by numerous cigarette burns. Behind the desk was a green plastic patio chair. Two more plastic chairs were in front.

"Jay and Princess, sit down," said Sy, standing behind them after he closed the door.

"Thanks," replied Jack, taking a seat beside Laura before he looked back at Sy and said, "So, the cops obviously knew Weasel was the shooter from last night and were set up on his place to see if someone would retaliate."

Sy smiled and said, "That would make sense except I forgot to mention to you that Weasel only moved in with his girlfriend this afternoon. The cops wouldn't have known that."

"Oh, I see," replied Jack. "Makes it obvious who the rats are."

"Sure as fuck does!" snarled Sy.

"Good," replied Jack. "After the shit you got me into tonight, I expect two things."

"Really?" replied Sy looking puzzled. "And what is that?"

"First, you buy the pizza and second, you take care of those two rats!"

"What the fuck, Sy?" said Mongo. "I don't understand. I thought you said —"

Sy put his hand up, gesturing for Mongo to be quiet, before looking inquisitively at Jack and saying, "Do you want to run that one past me again?"

"Sure. Pepperoni, mushrooms, black olives, and green pepper."

"Not the fucking pizza. The part about taking care of two rats."

"That's why we're here, isn't it?" asked Jack. "To decide how to take out Roach and Bagger?"

"Roach and Bagger!" replied Sy, looking incredulous.

"Yeah," replied Jack, before gesturing with his hands and saying, "Duh ... as if you didn't figure it out. Well, I'm not stupid, either." He turned to Mongo and Munch and said, "Last night we *just happened* to leave Roach and Bagger's when we fuckin' near get killed."

Mongo looked at Sy and said, "Didn't you tell me earlier that the cops were there, too? That someone saw some guy and later realized he might have been writing down licence plates?"

"What?" said Jack loudly, looking at Sy. "You didn't tell me that!"

"Wasn't sure if it was cops or a neighbour," replied Sy, defensively.

"Figures," said Jack. "Fuckin' cops were probably laughing when we were getting our asses shot off."

"I said it might not have been cops," said Sy.

"Either way," Jack said, continuing his conversation with Mongo and Munch, "Then it *just happens* that Roach and Bagger find the place for us to whack Weasel tonight and the cops *just happen* to be waiting for us. Guess I don't need to tell you that it *just happened* that Roach and Bagger weren't there with us!"

Munch looked at Sy and said, "Is that true? They weren't with ya?"

"They're sittin' on a hostage," said Sy. "Couldn't let him go until we took out Weasel."

Jack looked at Sy and said, "Guess I'm the dumbass for agreeing to go with you tonight. I tried to talk you out of it. I could have *just happened* to stay behind, too … you gave me that option, but I went with you."

"Sy? What the fuck?" asked Mongo.

Before Sy could respond, Jack pointed a finger at him and said, "First I damn near die saving your ass last night and then I have to save it again tonight. You're lucky we're not the rats or you would be dead. Either that, or in jail. I think Roach and Bagger are tied in with your enemies and the cops. Being the leader, I'm sure you were the grand prize of who the cops wanted to catch. Lucky for you I talked you into checking things out first."

Sy stared back. His face was blank as his mind grappled with what happened.

Jack shook his head in admonishment and said, "Yeah, I would say you owe me. As I said, two things, first you buy us some pizza, and then go take care of Roach and Bagger. I'm hungry and tired. Let's eat."

Sy hesitated before sticking the pistol in the back of his waistband. Jack knew that he and Laura were safe for the moment.

"You think they're both rats?" asked Sy. "Roach and Bagger both?"

"Definitely," replied Jack. "One couldn't pull it off without the other guy knowing. I bet they're talking to both the cops and at least one of the other gangs who are trying to take you out. Either that Balvinder guy you mentioned, or one of the other two, Fateh or Quang."

"Or maybe Roach and Bagger are talkin' to all three and the cops," said Mongo.

"I'm gonna call those two fuckers and get them over here," said Sy.

"Forget that," said Jack. "There's already too much heat. How do you know they won't bring the cops trailing along with them? I'd do it another way."

"How?" asked Sy.

Jack eyed Mongo and Munch suspiciously before standing up and looking at Sy. "Come on, let's you and I talk in the hall. You know these guys, but I don't."

Laura forced a smile at Mongo and Munch as Jack and Sy stepped out into the hallway. Moments later they returned and Sy stood in one corner of the room and whispered to Mongo and Munch while Jack sat down beside Laura.

When Sy was finished, Mongo looked at Jack and asked, "What the fuck is in it for you? Why have you been hanging out with Sy all of a sudden?"

"I'm not interested in belonging to any gangs," replied Jack. "I try to be independent. I do, however, have a lot of connections. I'm an entrepreneur. Sometimes there are things people want. Some times I can get them for them ... cheap."

"I can vouch for that," said Sy, with a smile. "Anything from televisions to Russian vodka. I'll tell you, Jay, after tonight, if there is anything you need ... and I mean *anything*, you just ask."

"You know," said Jack, "there might be something you could help me with. Maybe in the next few days if —"

"Fuck the small talk," said Mongo, looking at his watch. "Fuck the pizza, too. We got some loose ends to take care of before the sun comes up."

Sy looked apologetically at Jack and said, "He's right. Let's talk tomorrow."

Laura waited until she was alone in the car with Jack before saying, "They were going to do us."

"I know, but with Sy behind us holding a gun in his hand, I figured it was better to play dumb. Speaking of which, I should call Connie. She'll be freaking out."

Connie answered her BlackBerry on the first ring. "Where are you?" she asked anxiously.

"We're okay."

"You get any heat? Scared the shit out of me when I heard uniform were after you."

"Everything is fine," replied Jack. "Sy doesn't suspect us."

"Good. Did Laura tell you we seized a lot of weapons tonight?"

"I saw them earlier when Sy handed them out. Tonight's arrests were most of his top people. Seizing their guns is like taking the teeth out of one faction of The Brotherhood. At least for the moment."

"Don't know how long we can keep them in."

"At least they're identified. They might be hesitant to try it again."

"Hope so."

"Sy introduced us to Mongo and Munch."

"Mongo and Munch? They're bosses of two other factions in the group. What's going on? Why would Sy meet them tonight after what happened?"

"I think they're trying to figure out what went wrong. I passed it off as the police already knew Weasel was the shooter from last night and were waiting to see if anyone would retaliate."

"Good thinking. They buy it?"

"Looks like it. They still think Laura and I are cool. Sy said if there was anything I need, I simply had to ask. I'll meet with him tomorrow. I have an idea to draw Cocktail out."

"How?"

"It's time to tell him I've got a friend who wants to set up a meth lab. We'll use Sammy."

"Fantastic. These other guys are pissing me off, but it's Cocktail I want to hang for murder."

"And running meth and GHB labs. I'm certain there was another date rape last night at the party."

"Makes me sick."

"Believe me, Cocktail is going down."

"Think your idea will work?"

"Hope so. After what we've been through with Sy in the last two days, I shouldn't have any problem convincing him to help us with a lab. Cocktail might show up."

"Maybe the narcs can concentrate on Roach and Bagger, too. They both sound like they are in the thick of things. It might give us another avenue to pursue if your lab idea doesn't work."

"Roach and Bagger are low-level punks," replied Jack. "Watching them would be a waste of time. Let's talk about it later. I'm going home."

"Which one?"

"To Natasha. See you in about six hours."

After Jack hung up, Laura looked at him and asked, "What was your other way?"

"Other way?" replied Jack. He was exhausted and knew he wasn't thinking clearly.

"In regard to Roach and Bagger. When Sy was going to call them over and murder them, you said you would do it another way. Then you went in the hall. What did you tell him?"

Jack paused, wondering how best to articulate the matter.

"I have a feeling," said Laura, "that Roach's and Bagger's futures hold more than, say, four months' house arrest."

Jack nodded and said, "As far as Roach and Bagger go, they don't have a future. Not after their performance in the bedroom last night."

"You don't need to convince me. I saw Cassandra. She didn't belong with that bunch. So what did you say to Sy?"

"I told him, hypothetically speaking, of course, if I were him I'd make it look accidental. Call Roach and Bagger and tell them to set Raven free and that you're all going over to their place to have a drink and try to figure out what went wrong. At that time give Roach and Bagger a taste of their own medicine."

"GHB?"

"Exactly."

"So they'll end up … dead drunk … but how?"

"After they're unconscious, order a pizza for pickup and leave." Jack paused, looking at Laura's reaction. Her expression gave the impression of mild interest, as if she were studying a dinner menu. *Only she is putting her trust in having me place the order.*

Laura paused and thought about what Jack said. "Sounds like a gas," she replied.

"It will appear they started the car in their garage, but passed out before opening the door. Accidental carbon monoxide poisioning." Jack gave a grim smile and added, "You figured it out. Means you're starting to think like I do. Doesn't it scare you?"

"A little," she admitted.

"What I suggested … no, not suggested, what I *said* to Sy was all hypothetical, of course. Simply musing about different ways to dispose of people. I don't believe for a minute that he would actually do it."

"Of course not ... for the record. Act surprised, show concern —"

"Deny, deny, deny," said Jack, finishing her sentence.

Chapter Thirty-One

It was five o'clock in the morning before Jack and Laura finished their paperwork at the office and an hour later before they each made it home to their own beds. About the time Jack was climbing into bed, Cocktail was slurping coffee out of a Styrofoam cup as he sat in a car in Kitsilano Beach Park overlooking English Bay in the heart of Vancouver.

Cocktail was waiting to meet Balvinder, one of the prominent leaders in The Brotherhood. He was told to gain Balvinder's trust and bait the trap. He knew his orders came from the upper echelon of Satans Wrath. *Appraise who is stronger and set up the losers to die.*

Prospective members of Satans Wrath had arranged the meeting to ensure security from both the police and the warring factions of The Brotherhood. One prospect sat nearby on a park bench. He was a giant of a man with a short, cropped beard that did little to hide the multiple scars on his face. Cocktail knew he went by the nickname of "Hamburger" and it wasn't because of his ugly face. Hamburger liked to fight. His nickname came from what other people's faces looked like when he was done with them. Other prospects also roamed the area on foot and in vehicles.

Cocktail didn't have to wait long. One of the prospects pulled up and dropped off Balvinder, who ambled over and got in beside Cocktail.

"Well, Balv, how's it going?" asked Cocktail. "I understand some of your boys tried to take out Sy a couple of nights ago?"

"Yeah, they should have got him. Sy was so drunk he fell over in the house before he left the party. Came with some guy by the name of Jay and a broad. Jay was driving and was obviously sober. My guys said that when the shooting started he drove like a professional demolition derby driver. Sy was lucky. His time will come."

"I need to be kept informed."

"Why?"

"Think of who brought you to meet me. It's them who asked."

Balvinder glanced over at the biker who had brought him and saw Hamburger scowling at him from the park bench. "Mother of god," breathed Balvinder under his breath.

"It's not a good idea to make these guys angry," continued Cocktail. "You know we do business with Sy's, Mongo's, and Munch's guys too. What you're doing is attracting police attention. If it keeps up,

Satans Wrath will cut business with you guys because it could reflect police attention on them."

"What are you saying? Quit the war? Ain't gonna happen. It's already started and there are too many of Sy's people who keep moving into areas they don't belong. That's why we picked him first."

"Conflicts happen. That's life and the bikers know that, but don't expect much business from my end if you guys keep dragging this out."

"So what are you saying?" asked Balvinder.

"I work for them," said Cocktail, while giving a sweep of his hand in Hamburger's direction. "What I'm saying is if we want the money to keep rolling in, you better end it pretty quick, one way or the other. I'm going to be telling Sy the same thing. He'll pass on what I tell him to Munch and Mongo. I want you to pass this on to Fateh, Quang, and Rashard."

"So which is it? Does Satans Wrath want us to make peace or have an all-out war and get it over with?"

"Let's say they won't be doing business with people they don't respect. If they think you are weak, you will soon be cut out of the action."

"My gang is not fucking weak."

"I know. Yours isn't. That is why I'm talking to you. Trust me, my friend. I shouldn't say this, because Satans Wrath want me to treat everyone equal, but out of all the others, you're the one I respect the most."

"Glad to hear that."

"But I need to know what is going on. If you're doing something to help bring things to an end, then it would help if I could explain that to the bikers.

Even with Fateh and Quang who are your allies today, things change in time."

"Tell me about it. We formed The Brotherhood in the first place so we could get along. That didn't last long."

"If there is an all-out war, there will still be survivors. Satans Wrath will want the survivors to sit down and split up what turf belongs to whom. After that, if someone starts raising shit and brings police attention on everyone, they will have more than the police to deal with." Cocktail, paused, pointing a finger at Hamburger and adding, "You want to take guys like him on?"

"No … and what you're saying makes sense. But how do you decide who gets what turf?"

"Eventually there will be a meeting and I'll be the referee. Besides, what is the worst that could happen? If you all disagree, you end up no different. But it could work. In the meantime, if you have something happening that we need to talk about, go through the regular channels and the bikers will arrange for us to meet. Everything is to come my way. Satans Wrath is looking to do business with someone who is solid and strong. Let's make sure that person is you and the people who are on your side."

"I'm all for that."

"The sooner it is over with, the sooner we can all get back to making money. Real money. Especially if some of the … uh, less respected gangs, are not around to demand pieces of the pie."

"I understand," said Balvinder. His white teeth flashed a smile against his dark skin and he said, "I'll tell Fateh and Quang. They might listen to me. As far as Rashard goes, maybe you should talk to him."

"I thought you were winning Rashard over to your side?"

"Not yet. That fuckin' Jamaican is still not claimin' allegiance with anyone. He's gonna have to decide pretty quick, but right now, I don't trust him."

"I'll talk with him. As far as what happened two nights ago, you know there will be retaliation. Things could get hot."

Balvinder's teeth flashed again as he gave a short burst of laughter.

"What's so funny?"

"They already tried," replied Balvinder. "It's not on the news yet. Weasel was one of my guys who tried to take Sy out two nights ago. Sy recognized him and somehow found out where he was staying. A couple of hours ago Sy and a bunch of his guys snuck over to try and shoot him. Well guess what?"

"What?" asked Cocktail.

Balvinder laughed again and said, "The fuckin' pigs were on to them. Busted their asses! From what I hear, they damn near got Sy, too. He barely escaped and lost most of his heavy-duty guns and a lot of his top guys."

"How do you know if it's not on the news? Did Weasel see it happen?"

"Weasel never even got out of bed. We got someone on the inside. Sy's not even home yet, but he called what guys he has left and is whimpering like a fuckin' baby. The pigs did a real number on his outfit.

I should send them a thank-you card. Now it's just Mongo and Munch we gotta take care of. In fact, with what happened, I bet the fuckin' Jamaican will join up with us."

"Interesting," mused Cocktail.

Sy was on his way home after leaving Roach and Bagger's house when he got a message on his BlackBerry. He recognized the coded message and sighed as he changed direction and drove off to meet his contact from Satans Wrath.

An hour later, Sy entered an office at Wet Willy's Car Wash while his car was slowly dragged through the wash cycle inside the building. Cocktail was the only other person in the office and sat behind a desk as Sy took a seat in front of him.

"How's it going?" asked Cocktail. "Heard someone took a shot at you a couple nights ago?"

"Yeah, I figured you would have heard," mumbled Sy. "Fuckin' lucky I happened to have a friend with me who knows how to drive."

"Oh? Who is that?"

"A guy by the name of Jay. He lives in the apartment above mine."

"You never mentioned him before."

"He's Rodine's cousin and moved here recently from back east. He's a smart fucker and knows the game real well."

"Our game?"

"Naw, he's not interested in dope. Hot property is his thing."

"What? Boosting items from stores?"

"No, not what you're thinking. Jay is rich, has class, and is well-connected. Docks … railway … trucking lines. This guy ain't small-time. Has got a real looker for a lady. Calls her Princess. Jay is rich. I'm thinking of asking him to partner up with me, but I don't know if he will. He likes to be independent."

"I have to tell you, Satans Wrath are really getting pissed off with all this chickenshit drive-by shooting crap."

"It doesn't seem chickenshit when you're the one being shot at."

Cocktail chuckled and said, "No, I guess not. The point is, it is attracting police attention and affecting the profit margin. Satans Wrath want to do business with someone they respect. Someone who knows how to make money. I've been hinting that you're the guy. With all our action, your mattress must be stuffed."

"I'm doin' all right."

"All right?"

Sy couldn't resist the urge to brag. "Close to a million hidden away." Sy saw that Cocktail was impressed. *So I lied a little. What the fuck, I'm halfway there.*

"Got it in a safe spot I trust," said Cocktail.

"For sure. Some place where the cops won't find it."

"Good. Your new friend sounds interesting. Are you serious about asking him to partner up with you?"

"Things haven't been going well, especially after tonight."

"So I heard."

Sy's face darkened as he glanced out the office door at Hamburger standing in the hallway. "Yeah, I figured you had. Bad news travels fast."

"That it does. Sorry for how it turned out tonight. I'm also really glad they missed you the other night."

"Yeah?"

"Keep that to yourself. I'm supposed to be impartial. Satans Wrath want the war to end. In the next couple of days they're planning to orchestrate a truce. It will be decided then who gets what territory."

"So I'll get to sit down with the honchos from Satans Wrath?" asked Sy.

"Not directly," replied Cocktail. "They still look at you guys as amateurs. Hopefully if things go as planned, that will soon change. They're looking to see who the smart leaders are and who is best suited to be making money. Certain guys might get selected to run additional enterprises and make more money. For now, I'm to treat everyone equal because they want me to referee the meeting."

"What about security?"

"The bikers will look after it. I might be the referee, but everyone knows who I'll be representing. If anyone does something stupid, they're dead."

"Gotcha."

"I really shouldn't say this, so keep it to yourself. Out of all the others, you're the one I respect the most. I want you to do well at the meeting."

Sy's face brightened. "Thanks. I really appreciate that."

"It would be a good idea if you kept me informed of what you're up to. Go through the bikers to arrange a meet, if need be, but I'm the point man. If you're making any moves it will help if I know so I can convince the bikers that you're not some dunderhead flailing around."

Sy nodded and said, "Thanks, Cocktail. I could use all the friends I could get. A good reason I should take on someone smart like Jay. He is one cool dude. Knows how to get rid of people to make it look like an accident. It would be good if he joined up with me."

"Bet your guys who got busted last night won't be in jail long."

"I talked with Basil Westmount. He expects he'll get them out this afternoon. Problem is, they'll be heat bags with the cops at a time when I need 'em most. That's if none of them squealed."

"Think any of them would?"

"Fuckin' Roach and Bagger did. Don't know what the cops had on them. As far as last night goes, well, I know Brewski would never turn."

"What? Roach and —"

"Yeah, those two. Don't worry about it. They've already been taken care of."

Cocktail waited until Sy left before speaking to Hamburger.

"Pass it on to your boss that I know who the losing side is going to be. The police arrested a bunch of Sy's guys last night and wiped out his top people. The ones who are left are pointing fingers at each other. They took out two of their own a couple of hours ago."

"I'll pass it on," replied Hamburger.

"I realize that the, uh, selected individuals for the final ... shall we say, *execution* of this plan is up to you guys, but I think the choice is obvious. With that in mind, I gave Sy the bullshit line about getting everyone together for a truce talk."

"Think he went for it?"

"Like a hungry gull after a school bag-lunch."

"I'm sure we'll be in touch soon, but in the mean time, carry on business as usual."

"One other thing. Sy has a new friend he is thinking of partnering up with. Don't know anything about the guy or who might be backing him. He lives in the apartment above Sy with his girlfriend. They go by the names of Jay and Princess. Might be a good idea for you guys to check them out."

Chapter Thirty-Two

Balvinder's meeting with Fateh that afternoon did not go as smoothly as he had hoped.

"Fuck runnin' stuff past Cocktail," said Fateh vehemently. "How the fuck do you know he won't pass it on to the other side?"

"He won't," replied Balvinder. "If he was doin' that, he could have had me killed this morning. Satans Wrath don't give a shit about which side wins as long as they're not caught in the middle. I spoke with Quang about an hour ago. He thinks the three of us should come up with a game plan."

"I don't need fuckin' Quang's help to kill anyone."

"It is better if we coordinate things under a united front. If we don't resolve it quick, Cocktail says the fuckin' gravy train we've all been riding is going to come to a halt."

"Satans Wrath would cut off the chemicals?" asked Fateh.

Balvinder nodded.

"That would cost them money, too."

Balvinder shook his head and said, "Man, the bikers got lots of other action. They deal coke by the ton and got labs right across the country. They can afford to put our labs on hold, but we can't. Besides, where else could we get chemicals that cheap? Even if they didn't kill us, their prices would put us out of business. If our people quit making money ... pretty soon they won't be our people."

Fateh thought about it for a moment and replied, "Okay, when it comes to keepin' our pipeline for chemicals coming, I agree. But I'll be damned if I'm going to be running to them if I decide to pop somebody. When there is opportunity, you grab it. If you had told me where Sy was partying the other night, he would already be dead."

"My guys tried."

Fateh smiled and said, "Yeah, I heard. With little girlie guns. Like I said, you should have called me. I'd have introduced Sy to Big Bertha."

Balvinder was surprised. "It came through? You got it?"

"Yup. Had it smuggled across the border last week. Fifty-calibre. Fuckin' bullets bigger than your thumb. Capable of bringing down an airplane. Got it mounted in the back of a van. All we gotta do is pull up alongside, slide open the side door and blow anything we want into fuckin' smithereens. There wouldn't be enough scrap metal left of a vehicle to make a paperweight."

"Un-fuckin' believeable! Why didn't you tell me?"

"Just did. You still got someone close to Sy?"

"Yeah."

"I don't want to risk Big Bertha hanging around Sy's apartment. The heat is obviously on him and I'm not taking a chance of the cops grabbing it. Next time you pinpoint when he'll be someplace else, give me a call."

"There's Mongo and Munch to consider, as well."

"We can deal with them after ... that's if there is any fight left in them. It was Sy's people who invaded our turf. That is who should get the message first on not to fuck with us. The bikers want this war over? Fine! Consider it fuckin' over when Big Bertha opens up."

Late that afternoon, Jack returned to Sy's apartment and the two men did their usual walk down the hall.

Sy looked at Jack and said, "Roach and Bagger ... done."

Jack ignored the comment and said, "That was a hell of a night last night. We were lucky to escape. Sorry you lost so many of your guys."

"You tried to warn me. I should have listened. Everyone from the van, including Brewski, got let out a few minutes ago. The guns were stashed in a duffle bag. Our lawyer says it will be hard for the cops to prove who they belong to. The two YDUs in the Mustang are still being held."

Jack didn't respond until they had walked farther. "Something else on your mind?" he asked.

Sy coughed and said, "I know things don't exactly look like they're going well for me, but I think it is going to pick up."

"That's good."

"Remember I once told you I knew a guy by the name of Cocktail?"

"Yes," said Jack. He felt his chest tighten and realized he was holding his breath.

"I met with him this morning."

"You're a busy guy. Thought you'd be a little tired after last night."

"Sometimes I don't get a choice. Certain people call and ya gotta go."

"Certain people like Cocktail?"

"Certain people like Satans Wrath. They acted as my chauffeurs. You know about them, eh?"

"Who doesn't?" replied Jack. "Is Cocktail one of them?"

"No, but he works for them. Cocktail helps me. He supplies the chemicals and the training for the labs we run. I've been making a lot of money. Still am."

"You shouldn't be telling me this. If Cocktail gets popped, you'll be giving me the hairy eyeball."

"Hear me out. I'm not blabbin' without reason. It's like you said before, I need to gather as many allies as I can. Cocktail says the bikers are going to force us to accept a truce and decide what turf belongs to who."

"Sounds smart. What's that got to do with Cocktail?"

"He is going to represent the bikers at the meeting. Act as a referee. Guess the bikers don't respect us enough yet for a face to face."

No shit ... "When is this meeting?"

"In the next couple of days. It will be better for me if I have as many people on my side of the bargaining table as possible. With your connections and everything ... I would be willing to cut you in on the action. I know dope isn't your thing, but we could still work something out. Even if you were to act as a silent partner or something, with your connections maybe I could expand. Claim more territory to make me look good at the meeting. We could make a shitload of money."

"I should meet Cocktail."

"He's more into the lab side of things. Not your bag."

"Remember earlier when I said there was something you could help me with? When we were at Pizza 24-7?"

"Yeah, but I was busy going out to take care of Roach and Bagger. What do ya need?"

"I've got a friend who also moved here from back east. He's into the dope scene. The guy is meticulous and good at calculation. With a little training, he would be ideal to run a lab."

"Fuck, that fits right in with what I am asking you. Like I said, you obviously know people."

"My friend's name is Sammy. I spoke to him about it and he was thinking we could pipe the product back east. That way it wouldn't step on any toes out here."

"That's even better yet." Sy paused as he thought about it, smiled and said, "Hell, yeah, I'll be glad to help. Provide the chemicals, training … how to set the lab up proper. Even find him a place to do it."

"Sounds great. I'll tell Sammy. How much money will he need to get started?"

"Fuck, don't worry about that. We'll front him what he needs to get started. Once he's cooking he'll be workin' on commission. As long as he maintains his deadlines and makes it how he is supposed to, everything will be fine."

"Sounds perfect. I'm sure he'll be pleased. When could he get started?"

"Give me a day or two to arrange things. Too bad you hadn't said something earlier. I could have mentioned it to Cocktail this morning."

That evening, Jack and Laura met with Connie and Sammy and debriefed them on Jack's conversation with Sy.

"God, we are going to get this guy," said Connie, once more fondling the crucifix on her neck.

"You talking to us, or Him?" said Jack with a grin.

"You and Him," replied Connie.

"I've hedged our bet," said Jack, becoming serious again. "We have at least two chances. If he doesn't show up to teach Sammy how to run the lab, then I will try to wangle a meeting with him through Sy at the truce conference."

"So all these drive-by shootings should come to a halt," said Connie.

"The truce is supposed to take place within a few days," said Jack. "When it does, we can all breathe easier."

"Maybe I'll get a weekend off some day," said Connie, happily. Her gaze drifted back to Jack and she said, "How the heck do you pretend to run a lab?"

"I know a guy who owns an old farmhouse on an acreage in Langley," offered Sammy. "He used to raise chickens, but is retired now and travelling. The chicken coops are gone, but the house is usable. Months ago he rented it to some guys who started a grow-op. He clued in as to what they were doing and reported it. I'm sure I could convince him to let us use it."

"Perfect," replied Jack. "We can't do any arrests involving the lab because it would lead back to our informant. Once we identify Cocktail, Laura and I will find an excuse to disappear."

"We can't be trafficking in meth!" said Connie.

Jack laughed and said, "Don't worry, we won't. In theory, it should take Sammy a week to get up and running before they expect product. By then, the truce meeting should have taken place."

"And if it doesn't or we still need more time to ID Cocktail, what then?" asked Connie.

"It will be easy to stall," replied Jack. "Sammy could say he has to get out because the owner is on a round-the-world trip, but is coming back unexpectedly. Or we could arrange a fake bust on the lab. Have it done when Sammy isn't there. It would be an excuse for him to flee."

"This could work," said Connie. "It might draw Cocktail out so we can identify him. Even if he doesn't appear, if we follow Sy, he might lead us to him."

"I don't recommend you do that," said Jack. "Cocktail is tied in with Satans Wrath. They are too adept at switching vehicles and spotting surveillance. If they spot a tail, we may never get another chance."

"Plus," said Laura, "Sy will be extremely kinky after being shot at the other night, not to mention his own guys being busted. They are all going to be looking over their shoulders. At least until a truce is finalized and who knows how long that will take."

"Speaking of that, what about the risk that you might get caught in a crossfire again?" asked Connie.

"We'll be careful," said Jack. "When Sy says it is time to get the chemicals, I'll rent a van that nobody will have seen before. When we leave the apartment, I'll have Sy duck down so he won't be seen by any of the opposition if they are watching."

"Between the bikers, Cocktail, and the turf war, everyone is going to be paranoid as hell," noted Sammy. "First time dealing with them, they're going to be worrying about you doing a rip-off, as well."

"For sure," replied Jack. He looked at Laura and said, "Wear something tight and skimpy so they know you're not packing a gun. The bikers will likely ensure we're not being followed. You guys sit back and wait until we call you. I'm confident Sy trusts us, but I won't be armed, either, in case we're searched."

"Sounds bloody dangerous," said Connie. "I don't like the idea of you not having backup. You know what policy says in that regard."

"We'll have you for backup," said Jack. "Way back ... waiting in Langley close to Sammy."

"A lot of good that will do," grumbled Connie.

"I don't want anything to happen that could scare Cocktail away. Even if he doesn't show up at the lab, there is still the backup plan over the truce meeting. I'm sure I can convince Sy to let me tag along for that."

"Which is even more dangerous," said Connie. "Going to a meeting with a bunch of guys who are at war with each other."

"They may be at war with each other, but I think they will all respect the wishes of Satans Wrath," said Jack. "Besides, they say there will be security to make sure nobody is armed."

"If Cocktail shows up at Sammy's lab, the meeting may not matter," said Laura.

"One day at a time," replied Jack.

"Maybe we should put a bug in the van you rent," suggested Connie.

"Not a chance," replied Jack. "Satans Wrath is liable to do a sweep. If they find a bug, we're all dead. It's bad enough having our apartment bugged, I'm not going to risk the van."

"Speaking of bugs," said Laura, "how is it going with the wiretaps?"

"Good," replied Sammy. "I spoke with OCTF. All new names have been added to their Part VI. The judge signed it this morning so if anyone is dumb enough to use their phones, we should hear."

"Tell them to keep their ears open," said Jack. "If they hear of anyone that might be moving chemicals, I'd like to know about it."

"I spoke to them," replied Sammy. "I also didn't want them busting us by mistake."

"The two of you will be entirely on your own," said Connie, looking back and forth at Jack and Laura.

"We know."

Everyone sat for a moment in an uncomfortable silence. Eventually they all silently nodded in agreement.

Sammy placed a call and discovered that he could use the farm house in Langley any time he wanted.

"We're set," said Sammy. He looked at Connie's worried face and lightheartedly said, "Hey, cheer up kid! What could possibly go wrong?"

Jack was driving to Sy's apartment when his BlackBerry rang again. It was Gabriel Parsons.

"Hope I didn't catch you in the middle of anything?" asked Gabriel.

"I'm not busy," replied Jack. "What can I help you with? Is it Faith?"

"Faith is doing okay. Too sick to do much, but at least she's home now. No, the reason I called is because of Noah. I would like your opinion on something."

"My opinions are free. What is it?"

"Lately he's been wanting to dress all in black like he is a vampire or something pagan. I simply won't allow it. Now he's bugging me to allow him to get a ring put through his eyebrow. It's like he's trying to make himself ugly. I know some of the kids at his school pierce their faces with jewellery, but Noah is only thirteen. What do you think?"

"He's been through a lot for such a young guy. I realize he is still a child, but he is also reaching the age where he wants to show his independence. You need to talk to him. Maybe you could compromise a little. Perhaps allow him to wear certain clothing, but hold off on the face jewellery."

"I try to be a good mother," replied Gabriel, as her voice cracked.

"You're a great mom. I admire you. Considering what has happened in your life ... the stress you must be under ... I've seen people fold under a lot less."

"Well ... thank you. I do find comfort in God. I pray that the man who killed Father Brown will turn to God and beg forgiveness."

Jack thought about her comment after he hung up. *Glad she didn't ask for my opinion on that ...*

Jack met with Sy and told him that Sammy had a good spot already rented for a lab.

"Where at?" asked Sy.

"Somewhere out in Langley. An old house. It used to be a chicken farm. The owner is retired and is travelling around the world. Sammy is anxious to get started."

"That's great. Finding the right place is the hardest part. Chicken farm, eh? Cocktail will like that."

Oh, I thought he would have preferred a daycare ... "How soon before we can get started?" asked Jack.

"I gotta clear it with the bikers first. You staying upstairs tonight?"

"I'm not sure. Princess is afraid someone will come looking for you and start shooting up the place."

"They didn't get all my guys. I've got people guarding the place twenty-four-seven. I hate using phones. Why don't you at least stay and I'll come up and see you in a couple of hours. I might know somethin' by then."

An hour after Sy met with Jack, he took another stroll down the apartment hallway with two prospects from Satans Wrath, Chugger and Hamburger. Sy quickly told them about his new friends, Jay and Princess.

Hamburger did not tell Sy that Cocktail had given him the names earlier that morning.

"Jay is really connected," said Sy. "He could make us a lot of money if I can convince him to partner up with me. He wants to set up a lab for a buddy of his. Good chance to impress him."

"Yeah?" replied Hamburger. "You trust them both?"

"Fuckin' A. They're rock solid. Stake my life on it."

"You will be," said Chugger.

"Not a problem," replied Sy. "They're ready to go. Got an old farmhouse already."

"We'll front you what you need to get started," said Hamburger. "First payment is seven days after delivery. If anything goes wrong …"

"I know."

"How long have you known them?"

"Not long, but we've already done a lot of shit together. They came recommended to me by Rodine. They're cousins. He's known them all his life."

"Tell 'em we'll do it tomorrow. Take them both on a little trip while we check them out. If they're not okay, you won't be bringing them back."

Chapter Thirty-Three

Later that night, Sy met with Jack and told him that things were set for the following morning. Jack left the apartment complex immediately and he and Laura had another brief meeting with Connie and Sammy.

"Sounds like everything is a go," said Connie.

"My team will supply some of the cover out at the farm," said Sammy.

"Make sure it is only your team that does," said Jack.

"Still no word on the dirty narc?" asked Connie.

Sammy shook his head.

"Nothing unusual has come over the monitors from our UC apartment," said Laura.

"Not yet," said Jack. "It would really surprise me if Satans Wrath doesn't check us out before tomorrow. Maybe tonight we will get lucky. I mentioned to Sy that I would be staying in our other apartment tonight. I know he has a pass key."

* * *

The following morning, Jack and Laura rented a van and drove to Sy's apartment complex and parked in the underground lot. They went to Sy's apartment and saw a note on the door telling them he was next door at Brewski's. Moments later they were let inside by Lorraine and saw Sy and Brewski slurping coffee at the kitchen table. The apartment was covered with empty beer and liquor bottles.

"Good to see that you got out," said Jack, giving Brewski a friendly pat on his back. "Looks like we missed a good party."

"You did," said Sy. "I went back to get you last night, but you were already gone."

"I got sprung yesterday afternoon," said Brewski. "Gotta appear in court next week to enter a plea. Should be able to drag it out for a couple of years. My lawyer says the cops aren't saying why they searched us. Could be because of a wiretap or somethin'. He thinks we have a good chance of getting it tossed under a charter argument."

"That's great," replied Jack.

"Same goes for the two in the Mustang," said Sy. "It hadn't been reported stolen yet so the cops had no legal reason to search it."

"Excellent," replied Jack.

"So, I hear you're introducing Sy to someone to go into business with us," said Brewski.

Jack nodded and said, "A buddy of mine by the name of Sammy."

"And what business would Sammy be in?" smirked Lorraine.

"It's called none of your business," replied Jack.

Lorraine mouthed the words "fuck you" and smirked again.

"Speaking of which," said Sy, "You both ready to go?"

"Both of us?" replied Jack. "I was thinking we didn't need Princess."

"Hey, I don't want to be stuck sitting in the apartment by myself," protested Laura.

"Not really any choice," said Sy. "You have to come. My friends said they wanted to meet the both of you. You get a van to use?"

"Got one from Budget. It's in the underground lot. You better duck down when we leave."

"You don't have to tell me. I'm doing a lot of ducking these days. Give me a minute to go back to my place and use the can. I'll meet you both downstairs."

When Jack and Laura left Brewski's to go to the van, Laura grabbed Jack by the sleeve and said, "You try to cut me out of the action again and I'll kick you in the nuts."

"It just occurred to me, why should we risk the both of us if there's no need?"

"That's bull. You thought of it before and waited until we were in front of Sy, hoping he would agree with you."

Jack frowned and said, "Okay, you're right, but think about it. Why risk your life if we don't need to?"

"Because I'm your partner. That's why."

* * *

Balvinder received his second call that morning and passed it on to Fateh. After that he sent the second text that morning to his contact with Satans Wrath, asking to meet. He received a text message back saying: "Like before. I'm busy. Meet this afternoon."

Balvinder shrugged. He had done what was asked. *Besides, by this afternoon the war might be over …*

There was a reason why the prospects couldn't meet Balvinder right away. They were waiting in Sy's apartment to confirm that Jack and Laura had left with Sy, before using the pass key they had been given.

The prospects weren't the only ones waiting. In a wooded area close to the United States border, Fateh bounced along in the back of a van with one arm draped over Big Bertha. A gang member by the name of Hadad drove, while three other gang members sat with him in the back of the van.

Fateh looked out the window as the van approached an uprooted tree beside the road. Rutted wheel tracks led past the fallen tree into the woods. "This is it," he said. "Hadad and I checked it out early this morning. There is only one way in and out." He looked at Hadad and said, "Drive past the entrance and find a place where we can watch. They're in a Budget van. Once they arrive, give 'em a minute to get in there and park. Then we introduce them to Big Bertha."

* * *

Jack and Laura gave Sy a curious look when he arrived and climbed in the rented van. He was carrying a box made of thin plywood that he set in the back of the van.

"What's that?" asked Jack, hearing a scratching noise come from the box.

"That my friend, is Harry the Hamster."

"You've got a hamster in there? What on earth for?" asked Laura.

"It's a safety thing," replied Sy. "Something my friend Cocktail came up with for the lab."

"The old canary in the coal mine?" asked Jack.

"Yeah, something like that," replied Sy, laying down on the seat behind Jack and Laura as Jack drove toward the exit.

Shortly after Jack pulled out from the underground parking lot, Sy sat up and directed Jack to drive to a rural area near the United States border, which was about a thirty-minute drive from their apartment.

"Why down there?" asked Jack.

"They didn't want to do the deal around my apartment. There's a place in the bush we are to go to. I've never been there, but I drew a map," said Sy, taking a piece of paper out of his coat pocket. "They always pick different places," he continued. "They know what they're doing. Don't worry, there won't be anyone around to bother us."

Part way to the destination, Jack realized that a car was following them and told Sy.

Sy glanced back and said, "Yeah, I recognize Croaker, the guy driving. The bikers are pretty cautious. They do that sometimes. I told them what you were driving. Last night they gave me the route we're taking. They put guys out along the way to make sure we're not being followed."

Minutes later, Croaker passed them, slowed in front and turned off.

"Just got the okay," said Sy. "If he had turned on his four-ways, it would have meant we were being followed and to abort."

"Good," said Laura. She swallowed and added, "I feel safer already knowing how careful these guys are."

"Is your friend Cocktail going to be there?" asked Jack, glancing in the rearview mirror at Sy's face.

"Naw, Cocktail turned the chemicals over to them. He won't be coming."

Jack glanced at Laura who also tried to hide her disappointment by turning to look out the passenger window.

"I thought Cocktail was going to help train Sammy," said Jack. "We were supposed to meet him."

Sy shrugged and said, "He's trained me. Don't worry, I can set it up. Also got the recipes with me," he added, gesturing to his BlackBerry.

Back in the RCMP Headquarters building in Vancouver, a monitor saw an indicator light go on in Jack and Laura's undercover apartment and turned up the volume.

"Hey, we've got some action," she said to her colleague. "Sounds like several men are searching the place." A man's voice over the recorder soon announced who they were.

"Hey Taco! Look what I found," yelled the voice. "Got a broad's driver's licence."

The monitor checked her list of names. Taco was the nickname of a Satans Wrath prospect.

"What ya doin'?" asked Taco.

"I almost missed it," said the voice. "It was taped to the bottom of the desk drawer and fell off when I opened it. Look, there's more. We got some of the guy's ID too."

"Fuckin' A," replied Taco's voice. "Take a look and see who Jay and Princess really are. Get on your BlackBerry to Pussy Paul right fuckin' now."

Both monitors in the RCMP building smiled.

"Snoopy bunch, these bikers," said one.

"Yeah, we should talk."

Jack drove as instructed and turned down a rutted lane past a fallen tree leading into a wooded area. Moments later they reached a small clearing where a scattering of empty beer bottles and the blackened remains of a fire pit told him the location was no doubt a favourite hangout for young people looking to party. He parked the van and shut off the engine.

Another van immediately appeared from behind them and Jack realized it had been parked in a location hidden from view on the far side of the clearing.

"That was quick," said Jack."

Sy peered out the window and said, "Yeah, that's Hamburger who is driving. He's big enough to lift a full barrel by himself. That's Chugger beside him. He's no wuss, either."

Hamburger backed his van up and parked so the rear doors of both vans were facing each other.

"You two wait while I go chat with them first," said Sy.

Jack and Laura watched as Sy stepped out of the van and met with Hamburger and two other bikers who got out to meet him. Jack opened the door and looked at the group and Sy motioned for him to step out of the van.

Before Jack could move, the roar of an engine caught everyone's attention as a third van bounced into the clearing and came to a broadside stop.

"What's going on?" asked Laura nervously.

"Don't know," replied Jack. "Maybe more bikers for security."

"Hope so, or — oh, man!"

Jack looked in disbelief as the side door of the newcomer's van slid open. Inside they saw a 50-calibre machine gun mounted on a tripod. Fateh looked like a raging fanatic as he swung the muzzle around in their direction.

Chapter Thirty-Four

One of the monitors in the RCMP building started to panic. She had replayed two calls that had come in earlier that morning. The calls were related to the investigation by the Organized Crime Task Force on gangs, but were low priority because the intercept was on the cellphone of a low-level gang member who worked for Balvinder.

The first call was from a young woman who said, "Your phone cool?"

"Yeah, it's in my mother's name. What's up?"

"Sy will be leaving his apartment tomorrow morning with a guy named Jay and his fuckin' bitch. They're supposed to go meet some friend of Jay's to do something. Probably sell him dope. If you meet me, I copied a rough fuckin' map of where they're going."

"Who is this fuckin' Jay?" asked the man.

"The same guy who drove that night when I called you from the party. I don't like his attitude. He wanted to fuck me, but I told him he was so old I'd have to lip-start him. Freaked him right out," she laughed. "I was hoping you would get him that night, too. Today is your chance. Put one right up his ass for me and do his bitch, too."

The second call was between the same people and the young woman said, "They're heading out in a couple of minutes. Jay's got a Budget van. Him, his bitch, and Sy will be inside. Don't fuck up this time."

"Don't worry, with Big Bertha on the scene, a fuckin' cockroach wouldn't survive."

"Who's Big Bertha?"

"A big fuckin' boy's toy. These guys will be maggot food by lunchtime."

The monitor fought back the tears as she reached for the phone. Investigators from OCTF had cautioned her to listen carefully for any mention of Big Bertha. Intelligence reports indicated it was the nickname of a 50-calibre machine gun that the gang was attempting to get. She also knew Jay's real identity.

Connie was sitting with Sammy in a pickup truck parked down the road from the rented farm house going over last-minute details when she received a call from the monitor, telling her about Big Bertha and the plan to murder Jack, Laura, and Sy.

"That fucking whore! Who is she?" demanded Connie.

"We don't know," replied the monitor. "It was an incoming call from a cellphone."

"Damn it, find out! If Jack and Laura get killed, she is going down for conspiracy. I'll call Jack. Better hope we're not too late!"

"Let me call him," said Sammy, who had his ear pressed close to Connie's phone. "If Sy hears it's me he won't be so suspicious."

"That's if anyone is left alive to hear," said Connie, winding down the window for a sudden need of fresh air while Sammy dialled.

Back at the clearing, Fateh hesitated when he recognized Hamburger. Jack looked at Laura and said, "Stay cool. See what happens, but on the first shot, bail out the door, stay low, and head for the bushes. Try to keep the engine block of our van between us and that gun."

"It's too far. We'll never make it," said Laura.

"I know."

"You know? Then don't you have a better idea?"

Fateh spoke to the other men in the van with him and gestured toward the bikers. It was obvious he hadn't expected Satans Wrath to be present.

As if reading his mind, Hamburger barked out an order. Both the other prospects took their windbreakers off to reveal they were wearing club colours. They only had the bottom rocker, but it was enough to show they were prospects for Satans Wrath.

Fateh waved his arm at Hamburger and shouted, "You three better take off. I got business with these others!"

Jack saw Hamburger nod.

"Jack, the bikers are going to leave," said Laura. "We'll be massacred!"

Jack jumped from the van and approached Hamburger and took him aside, under the watchful aim of Fateh.

Hope you're good at making friends fast, thought Laura.

After a terse and whispered conversation, she saw Jack hand his BlackBerry to Hamburger who threw it to the far side of the clearing, before shoving Jack back toward the van.

Oh, man ...

Hamburger shouted, "Hey! You! The broad in the van! Get the fuck out here!"

Laura quickly got out and stood with her back to the side of the van next to Jack and Sy. She watched as Hamburger sent a text message on his BlackBerry.

Laura felt her BlackBerry vibrate and quickly shut it off. She expected it would also be thrown, but Hamburger simply glanced at her and said, "Smart move."

A full two minutes ticked past before Hamburger received a reply, during which time Fateh manned the gun with both hands, staring at Jack and Sy with murderous intent.

Hamburger looked at the text message, subconsciously nodding his head as he did so. When he finished, he told Jack and Sy to remain where they were while he and his two associates stepped back to talk in private.

"What's going on?" shouted Fateh from the van.

"Shut the fuck up and watch," replied Hamburger, while walking back and standing in front of Sy.

"You are a stupid fuck, do you know that?" roared Hamburger as he punched Sy in the gut. Sy slumped and two more punches saw him fall to the ground where Hamburger started kicking him. Sy curled into a fetal postion and cried out in pain while loud cheers emitted from Fateh's van.

After delivering a stomp to Sy's kidneys, Hamburger spun around and punched Jack in the mouth. Jack fell back against the van, stumbling to the ground on one knee before slowly getting up. He knew better than to fight back and was relieved when Hamburger stepped away.

The other two prospects, with pistols drawn, searched Jack, Sy, and Laura. Jack's rented van was searched next. The only weapon they found and took was a pistol they removed from Sy's ankle holster.

Fateh smiled as he took one hand off the machine gun and gave the bikers the thumbs-up sign.

Hamburger smiled back as he and his two associates walked over to talk with Fateh.

"Think we should try to run for it?" cried Sy. "Fateh is looking at Hamburger ... the bikers are between us. Maybe —"

"Wait," mumbled Jack, with one hand checking his bloody teeth.

Seconds later, Fateh's smile was replaced with a look of panic as Hamburger reached in with one meaty hand and grabbed him by the shirt and hurled him out onto the ground.

Hamburger then beat and kicked Fateh while the other two prospects held Fateh's other four gang members at gunpoint. Moments later, they were searched and the bikers found five more handguns. After this, Fateh and his gang members were beaten and pistol-whipped with their own weapons.

After the beating, Hamburger ordered Fateh and his crew to get to their feet. Fateh stood, looking dumbstruck as one of the prospects drove away with Big Bertha.

"You really think you can get away with driving in here and pointing that fuckin' cannon at us?" snarled Hamburger.

"We didn't know you guys were here," pleaded Fateh.

"Shut the fuck up! The cannon is ours. Consider it payment for fucking with us like that. Now fuck off! All of you!"

Fateh didn't have to be told twice.

Hamburger and the remaining prospects returned to where Jack, Laura, and Sy were standing. Hamburger gestured to Jack's bloody mouth and said, "That was to let you know we don't like being used ... although, under the circumstances, you made a pretty cool move."

Jack held his jaw with his hand. Four of his teeth were loose, but he was glad they were still in place. He had seen the punch coming and jerked his head back to minimize the impact. He smiled wryly as he saw Fateh and his followers looking back over their shoulders while limping off down the lane.

"And you!" Hamburger yelled at Sy. "How the fuck did they know about this place? Who the fuck did you tell?"

"I ... I ... I —" Sy repeated and stopped. He was too afraid to think clearly.

"We'll talk about it some other time," said Hamburger. He gestured with his thumb to the van and said, "We got shit to unload, but I tell ya, any more fuck-ups like this and I'll personally cut your head off and kick it up your ass."

As soon as the chemicals and numerous boxes of glassware were loaded, Jack, Laura, and Sy stood at the back of their van and watched the bikers drive away.

Jack looked at Laura in silence.

"I'm okay," she said. "How's your mouth?"

"Bleeding a bit. I'm sure it looks worse than it is. I didn't swallow any teeth."

"So what the fuck did you whisper to Hamburger?" asked Sy. His voice had reached a higher pitch and he was trembling.

"I told him that I had already called my people and said it looked like Satans Wrath had declared war on us and had lured us into a trap. He denied it and said they would never put themselves in the middle like that. I told him it wouldn't look that way and he should talk it over with his boss. Guess the boss agreed with me."

"Fuck! How did you know the biker boss would think that?"

"I didn't."

"Man, we're lucky. You saved my life again."

"Ditto for me," said Laura.

"Saved mine, too," replied Jack. "But the question remains. How did Fateh know we were here? Who did you tell?"

"I never said much to anyone," said Sy.

"Someone knew. You even needed a map to get here."

"Last night we were partying at Brewski's with the guys who got released from jail. I may have said I was doing a deal with you, but that was all. I also took the map out to look at it because I wanted to make sure we didn't get lost."

"You put it back in your pocket after?" asked Jack.

"Well, I was interrupted, what with the partying an' all. It was on the kitchen counter for a while." He looked intently at Jack and said, "You think Brewski is playin' me for the other side?"

"We were set up when we left the party at Roach and Bagger's. Brewski wasn't there then."

"You figured Roach and Bagger set us up that night? That's what you said!"

"I'm sure Roach and Bagger set us up to the cops the night we went to Weasel's. Looks like someone else is trying to feed us to the other side. You know the guys better than I do. Out of the other four guys who were at Brewski's last night, how many were partying at Roach and Baggers that night?"

"All of 'em were there."

"You've got a mole. You better find out who, or you're dead."

"More like all of us are dead," added Laura.

"Come on," said Sy. "I gotta take a quick piss, but then we better hurry before Fateh and his crew decide to return. They might still have their phones."

Sy's mention of phones reminded Jack that he still didn't have his. He walked across the clearing to get it and saw a folded piece of paper on the ground where Fateh had been beaten. It was a roughly drawn map of their location. Directions were also written on it … in female handwriting. On the other side of the paper were the partial notes of a school assignment.

"Hey, Princess," yelled Jack. "Help me find my phone, will you?"

As soon as Laura joined him, he turned his back to where Sy was urinating in the bushes and said, "Take a look."

Laura glanced at the paper and said, "Lorraine. She's the mole. What do we do? Sy will kill her. She's only sixteen."

"I know and if Connie finds out, she will demand that she be protected. It will blow everything."

"It will for sure. Maybe burn our friend as well … but if we don't do something, she may get us killed."

"We've only got a couple of seconds to decide," said Jack, glancing back over his shoulder at Sy who was zipping up. "I know she's young … so were Cassandra and Julie Goodwin."

"Oh, man."

"Well?"

Laura tilted her head back, briefly closing her eyes. *A sixteen-year-old girl ... am I ready to go that far? What is the right thing to do?*

"We don't have time," said Jack. "We need to decide. You know what I would do, but not if you don't agree."

Laura looked at Jack and said, "I guess if she's old enough to play with the big boys, she's old enough to face the consequences."

Jack nodded, scooped his BlackBerry off the ground, and they returned to the van as Sy climbed into the back seat behind them.

"Take a look at what fell out of Fateh's pocket," said Jack, handing Sy the piece of paper.

Sy's mouth dropped open. "A copy of my map!" He studied the paper, flipping it over and added, "It's a girl's handwriting. That fuckin' Lorraine! She was the only girl there last night! That devil bitch! She's dead!"

"We've got business that needs taking care of first," said Jack, with a jerk of his thumb toward the chemicals.

"I can't believe it," seethed Sy. He punched his hand with his fist and said, "Yeah, okay. Let's drop this off with your buddy. Make sure you drive slow. Between the chemicals and the bomb stuff, we don't want to take any chances."

"Did you say *bomb*?" asked Jack and Laura simultaneously.

Chapter Thirty-Five

Jack was driving out of the lane when he remembered to turn his BlackBerry back on. It rang immediately.

"Hey, Sammy. How ya doin'?" asked Jack.

"Okay to talk?" whispered Sammy, as Connie listened in.

"For you, sure."

"You have no idea how relieved I am to hear your voice. Something came over the lines. A young woman tipped off Balvinder's people that you, Laura, and Sy were leaving to do a dope deal this morning. She even gave them a map of where you were going. They're going to try and take you all out with a 50 calibre."

"We don't have to worry about *that*," said Jack. "*That* is already taken care of."

"*That?*" said Sammy. "Don't tell me you've got another problem."

"We certainly do," replied Jack.

"What else is going on? Can you give me a hint?" asked Sammy.

"Canada Day?" said Jack. "Not much. You planning a party?"

"Canada Day?" replied Sammy. "I don't get it."

"Sure, a party will be fun ... You got what ... fireworks ... those really big ones? Sounds like a blast. Be careful nobody is drunk or stoned. Make sure someone is around who knows how to handle the stuff."

"Are you serious?"

"Yup. See you in about an hour."

"What the hell was that all about?" asked Connie as soon as Sammy hung up.

"Don't know what happened with Big Bertha, but somehow it has been taken care of."

"Oh, great," muttered Connie. "That will probably mean there are more bodies someplace. What is all this about Canada Day?"

"Call bomb disposal and have them standing by."

"Bomb disposal! Oh, mother of Jesus!"

When Jack hung up, Sy looked at him and said, "This is embarrassing. I'm shakin' like a leaf. You two ... even you, Princess ... no offence, but you act like it was no big deal."

"I did find it disconcerting," said Laura.

"Disconcerting! I was scared shitless! Did you see the size of that bazooka? One bullet would take your whole head off!"

"Doesn't help to dwell on it," said Jack. "Learn from the past, but think about the future."

"I am thinking about the future," said Sy. "I gotta tell ya, I don't know how much longer I can handle this shit. I've never been shot at or threatened like this before in my life until I met you."

He's got a point there, thought Laura.

"My nerves are shot," continued Sy. "I've been thinking of moving back to Ontario. Maybe get back in with my ex and our little girl."

"You're a dad?" asked Jack.

"Yeah. Got a six-year-old. Haven't seen her in four years." Sy strained to looked back and forth in the side mirrors and said, "You making sure we're not being tailed? They never took Fateh's phones."

"I'm making sure," replied Jack. "But speaking of that, what do you intend to do about Lorraine?"

"Stop at the first pay phone we come to. I'm gonna call Brewski. It's his slut. He can take responsibility."

"You can't talk over a phone," warned Jack.

"No worries. We have a system. I text him on my BlackBerry and tell him to pick me up a coffee and a doughnut. I give him ten minutes to go down the block to a coffee shop and I call him there."

Minutes later, Sy spotted a pay phone and Jack pulled over and parked. As soon as Sy left to use the phone, Jack turned to Laura and said, "Sammy and Connie already know about the ambush."

"How?"

"It came over the lines. Lorraine called someone to

pass on the info. Connie and Sammy haven't identified her yet, but Sammy called to warn us."

"They'll want us to hear the voice. What do we do?"

"We can't tell Connie about what we did …" Jack glanced out the window at Sy and added, "Or what we are doing."

"She'd have us up on conspiracy to murder," replied Laura.

"It will also be hard to say that we don't know her voice."

"So what do we do?"

"Hope Sy works fast," said Jack. "Wait while I go check with him."

Sy called the coffee shop and was telling Brewski what happened when Jack walked up to him.

"When and how do you plan on doing it?" asked Jack, interrupting Sy's conversation.

"The fuckin' devil bitch is at Brewski's place," said Sy. "He wants to take her out to where we were. Says he'll slash her up about a thousand times, then gut her with a knife and let her crawl around in the dirt until she dies."

"Bad idea," whispered Jack. "That will bring the cops down on everyone. They know she is Brewski's girlfriend. If they end up getting him on the murder beef, he's liable to turn on you to try and get a reduced sentence."

"She's gotta die! She's gonna pay for what she tried to do to us!"

"To start with, I bet it was Brewski who got her hooked and mainlining coke," said Jack.

"So what? Who cares about that?"

"You and he both should. You can't trust an addict. For a free fix, they would turn in their own mother, which is likely how Fateh got to her."

"You think we should wait?"

"Waiting is too dangerous. Lorraine might try it again. You need to act immediately."

"So what the fuck are you saying we should do?"

"No torture. Nothing to draw heat. Let her kill herself."

"How?"

"Give her something she will take and overdose and drop her somewhere. Make sure none of your guys are even around when she does it."

Sy thought for a moment and nodded in agreement.

"Princess and I won't be coming around until we know it's done and things are safe."

"I'll tell Brewski to do it right away."

"Send me a text message on my BlackBerry. Punch in the numbers 6660 and I'll know the job is done."

"Six, six, six ... sign of the devil," said Sy. "What's the zero for?"

"The devil is in the hole."

"Cool."

"This whole situation isn't at all cool," replied Jack.

"Yeah, I know. I fucked up."

"One more thing ..." said Jack, pausing to lock eyes, "don't you or Brewski tell a soul about Lorraine, got it?" he said, while jabbing his finger into Sy's chest.

Sy nodded sombrely.

* * *

Forty minutes later, Jack introduced Sy to Sammy.

"You took longer than you figured," said Sammy. "Any problems?"

"Some of the competition were around," replied Jack, "but they chatted with the bikers and left. No big deal."

Sammy saw Sy's mouth gape open at Jack's comment, followed by a look of awe as Sy stared at Jack. Sammy smiled to himself. *Well, you've got his respect, Jack. Reeled him in, hook, line, and sinker.*

Sammy gave everyone a quick tour of the farmhouse and Sy appeared satisfied with an inner room where Sammy had installed shelving units and table.

"Got a good lock on the door, too," said Sammy, "in case someone comes by."

"We get a percentage of everything you make," said Sy. "Jay said you are planning on shipping it back east. What doesn't go back east goes to us. Understood? No side deals with anyone around here."

"I understand," replied Sammy. "Who do I contact for dropping off the product and ordering more chemicals?"

"Me. That's what the bikers want." Sy smiled and gave Sammy a slap on the back. "Really glad to meet you. Any friend of Jay is a friend of mine. Now, let me show you how to set a lab up like a professional. Even comes with a booby trap."

"Wonderful," said Sammy lamely.

Over the next several hours, Jack and Laura watched as Sy gave Sammy an in-depth course, complete with instructions on how to run a meth lab. He also screwed a small metal lever inside the door at the top. A wire ran past the lever through small eyehole screws over to a large glass carboy set on a shelf on the opposite side of the room. A rubber bung plugged the hole at the top of the carboy. The bung had been punctured with a grouping of small nails so that the spikes from the nails hung down inside the carboy. Sy threaded the wire through the small hole in the bung and let it dangle inside the carboy.

"We tie a small glass vial to the end of the wire in the carboy," said Sy. "If someone comes in and doesn't lower the lever above the door, it will yank the glass vial up where it will shatter against the nails. The stuff in the vial falls in the carboy and … ka-boom!" he yelled.

"Is this really necessary?" asked Jack.

Sy shrugged and said, "The fuckin' fireball will wipe out everything. No DNA, no fingerprints … not nothin'. This is how Cocktail said to do things and the bikers say so, too. Anybody comes in that ain't supposed to … well, there won't be anything left of 'em but ashes."

"Sounds like Cocktail and the bikers are protecting themselves more than the one doing the cooking."

"Gotta play by their rules," said Sy. "Sometimes the bikers are waiting when you arrive. If it ain't hooked up right, you're in for a hell of a beating. Besides, it's easy to do. There is enough give in the line to open the door a little. If the lever is up, then the top of the lever is behind the line and the bomb is activated. All you gotta do is flick the lever down when you enter and back up when you leave."

"Hope I don't forget," noted Sammy.

Sy chuckled and said, "Everybody says that. If I thought you would forget, I'd have asked you to pay the money up front."

Sammy's face paled as he studied the apparatus.

"Don't worry," said Sy. "You won't forget after what I show you next. Let's go outside around back." He glanced at Laura and said, "This is guy stuff. Might be better if you wait in the van."

Laura did as suggested while Sy retrieved the plywood box containing Harry the Hamster, before going behind the house with Jack and Sammy.

Sammy set the box on the ground and took the lid off.

Jack saw the hamster sit back on its hind legs as it peered up at them. The box had a small glass bottle containing a liquid in one corner of the box. Sy took the lid off the bottle and picked up a plastic straw and an eyedropper.

"Watch this," said Sy. He took a pill bottle containing a clear liquid from his pocket and removed a couple of drops with the eyedropper. "Don't bend over too close," he cautioned, before using the eyedropper to place a few drops in the end of the straw and tip it so the drops ran down the straw and into the bottle inside the box.

Immediately a small explosion ignited an inferno inside the box. Harry the Hamster instantly became a squealing ball of flame and bashed and clawed against the side of the box for a moment before succumbing.

"They always panic and keep running into the wall," said Sy. "Haven't had one jump out of the box yet."

Jack and Sammy traded grim glances over the odour of burned hair and charred flesh.

"Awful, ain't it?" said Sy. "I almost puked the first time Cocktail showed me, but as he says, you won't forget to disarm the door. He also said to put a picture of a hamster on the door to remind you each time you enter."

Jack and Sammy knew a picture would not be necessary. Neither man would ever forget.

Chapter Thirty-Six

Jack and Laura drove Sy back to his apartment and waited in the underground parking lot while Sy went up to speak with Brewski. When Sy returned, he said, "Brewski gave her some stuff and dropped her off at her parents' place about two hours ago."

Jack nodded silently.

"He said she had asked where we were. He said he didn't know and was worried because we should have been back. The little bitch pretended to worry, but it was all an act. Her mom and dad get home from work in another hour. I'm guessing she took it right away so they won't see that she's stoned. I'm sure she's a goner."

"I want it confirmed."

"Will do. What are you up to?"

"Got some more business to take care of. Merchandise that needs moving. Call me when you know."

"Six, six, six, the devil's in the hole."

As soon as Jack and Laura were alone, Jack called Connie and told her what had happened, except for anything to do with Lorraine or that they knew it was her who told.

"Get back here, pronto," said Connie. "We need to find out who tried to set you up. I'm sure you'll recognize her voice. She's someone who knows you both. Sounds young."

"What do we say to Connie?" asked Laura, while returning to the office.

"Stall until we know Lorraine has been taken care of."

"What if she doesn't OD? Maybe someone finds her in time?"

"Then we have to stall. Try and talk Connie out of doing anything that would heat us up until we know she's dead."

Laura nodded and was quiet. As Jack was driving, he saw that she was trembling and there were tears in her eyes.

"Want to talk about it?" he asked.

"I wouldn't know where to start," she replied. "Everything that happened today. Even the thing with the hamster. How can someone be so cruel? Why do people act the way they do?"

"Abusing pets ... lighting fires ... violence ... classic symptoms of sexual abuse. Maybe Cocktail has some real demons lurking inside," suggested Jack.

"And what about all the other stuff he's responsible for? Gabriel's little girl with cancer. Setting up labs everywhere and putting bozos in charge of them. Sending kids to rape and mutilate Amanda Flowers." She looked at Jack for a response, but he remained quiet so she added, "I don't know who to hate more, Cocktail or Sy."

"Sy is a moron," replied Jack. "He does whatever Cocktail says. Regardless, you have to face the facts. Even if we could prove Cocktail is behind all the labs, he wouldn't get as much time as he would for murdering a priest. That has to be where our priority lies."

"Yeah, and how much time will that be? It wasn't premeditated, so what? Fifteen years max with parole in ten? You think that is enough? Will Gabriel's kid even be alive in ten years? Think Amanda will ever forget?"

They stopped talking as Jack sat waiting for a traffic light. Jack stared at Laura for a moment before responding. "Sounds like you're trying to convince yourself of something. Why don't you talk about what is really bothering you?"

Laura looked at Jack, took a couple of halting, deep breaths and said, "She's only sixteen. I know she tried to kill us, but … but I'm not sure what we're doing is right."

"I don't think there is a right thing. I try to look at it like destroying a rabid dog."

"She's not a dog. She's a human. Someone's sixteen-year-old daughter."

"Imagine a sixteen-year-old in a clock tower with a rifle killing people. Imagine you're a police sniper. Do you wait and hope the kid runs out of ammo?

Somewhere along the way something went terribly wrong with this kid. Maybe she was born a psychopath ... who knows. She may not have a rifle, but she's just as deadly."

"It would be easier if she were older," replied Laura quietly.

"Compared to most other sixteen-year-olds, I would say she is a hell of a lot older."

"I know, but where does it end? Where do we draw the line?"

"I don't know. We have to decide in each given situation. You and I see and know things the rest of the world doesn't. We need to survive and protect the people who work for us. To me, morality is a big issue and the more I do this job, the more I think morality and the law are polarized opposites."

"We were sworn to uphold the law."

"What about justice? I try to balance all three. Morality, the law, and justice. Sometimes it doesn't work, but I try to do what I think is right."

"It scares me."

"It scares me, too. It would be easier if twelve informed people could think about it for as long as was needed. That is what the law intended. We don't have that luxury. What we are doing now seems wrong. If she were to live and kill someone else, that would be wrong, too. Somehow we have to live with what we decide."

* * *

Jack buzzed the security button to allow them access to the monitor's main office and hallway leading to the monitoring rooms.

The door opened and Connie said, "There you two are. We were about to send out a search party. You both know Dallas, don't you?"

Jack and Laura nodded. They knew Dallas was one of Connie's partners and a blood-splatter expert.

"Hi, Jack," said Dallas. "It's been a while. Last time I saw you was behind that woman's house where the priest got slaughtered. Remember?"

"Remember? I wish I could forget. I still dream about the blood. Doesn't it bother you?"

"Not really," replied Dallas, "but I don't deal with the people end of things. I do my analysis and split."

"And your analysis of this perp?" asked Laura.

"Prone to violent rage. Probably had a pretty bad childhood." He looked at Jack, chuckled and added, "He's not afraid of blood, that's for sure. Not to mention what he did after —"

"Can it, Dallas!" said Connie sharply. She turned to Jack and Laura and in an apologetic voice said, "Sorry, there's hold-back information I don't want out. All you need to know is that 'prone to violence' is an understatement."

"Not a problem," said Jack. He knew that most homicide investigators kept information back. It made damning evidence in court if the accused admitted to something that only the killer knew about.

"Enough chit-chat," said Connie. "I want you to listen to this girl's voice and — Christ, you stink, Jack.

Smell like burned hair. Anyway, come in and join the party. Third room down the hall. You said on the phone that all went well with Sammy and Sy?"

"Sammy is a good operator," replied Jack. "Sy trusts him."

"Good. Bomb disposal called a few minutes ago. They've neutralized the bomb. I don't know what it was made of."

"Some of it was ether," replied Jack. "Highly flammable. I don't know what the other ingredients were."

"The lab will tell us," replied Connie. "In the meantime they've put something else in the carboy to smell and look real."

"Good," replied Jack. "I think Sy will be dropping by in a few days with a prospect to see how Sammy is progressing."

"How long before they expect their first shipment?" asked Connie.

"One week," replied Jack. "I'm hoping to meet Cocktail long before then."

"He didn't show his face today," noted Connie.

"With Sammy running a lab, Sy is even more comfortable with us. He already indicated that he would like me to be a silent partner. I'll push that angle and demand to meet Cocktail. It only makes sense that I should meet him if I'm going to be Sy's partner."

"Providing this girl on the phone doesn't kill you first," said Connie, as she opened up the door to the monitor room.

As soon as Jack and Laura entered the room a young woman with teary eyes took off her headphones and said, "I'm really sorry. I should have been more on top of things over someone trying to set you up. I was backlogged and didn't get around —"

"It's okay," replied Jack. "Not your fault. Everyone is short of manpower these days. Let me listen to who tried to set us up."

"Got some other news for you, too," said Connie, while waiting for the monitor to find and replay the conversations. "Satans Wrath searched your apartment this morning. They found the identification."

"Perfect," said Jack. "Love it when a plan comes together. Did you notify Anti-Corruption?"

"Already done. Someone checked your aliases on CPIC and saw the fake criminal record."

"Someone?" asked Laura. "You mean we still don't know who the dirty narc is?"

Connie smiled and said, "I talked with your husband. He said it gave them the lead they needed. They had six possibilities. Today, your aliases were checked using an access code belonging to the secretary in Drug Section."

"The secretary?" asked Jack.

"Wasn't her. She was gone on her lunch break when it happened. Elvis said only two of their suspects were working day shift and one was in court. They've finally figured it out."

"Who?" asked Laura. "I used to work in that section."

"Me, too," echoed Jack.

"Constable Mark Cabot," replied Connie.

"I know him," replied Laura. "Very annoying type. Would start to drool any time a woman came close to him."

"His dad is a Member of Parliament," said Jack.

"I know, Elvis told me," said Connie. "His application to join had been rejected, but someone pulled some strings."

"Typical," replied Jack. "I'd better give Elvis a call. Make sure he knows they still can't bust him because it would identify our informant."

"Elvis is on top of the situation. Their plan is to have him transferred to a small detachment up north where he can't do as much harm."

"Too bad our pretend war on drugs didn't allow us to execute spies," replied Jack.

"I agree with you there," replied Connie.

"Speaking of spies," said the monitor, "Listen to this."

After the two conversations were played, Connie looked at Jack and asked, "Who is she?"

Jack furrowed his eyebrows and shook his head.

"She said you came on to her?" noted Connie. "At the party at Roach and Bagger's house. You've got to know who she is."

"Her name is on the tip of my tongue," said Jack. "After what happened this morning, I'm too rattled to remember. The house was packed with people that night. I do remember some kid of about sixteen making a pass at me."

"How about you, Laura?" asked Connie.

Laura shrugged and gestured with her hands to indicate she was at a loss.

"Sweet sixteen sure doesn't apply to this little darling," said Connie. "I thought this would be a piece of cake for you. How many people could have known about this morning?"

"We asked Sy the same question. Turns out he was at a party last night with a bunch of his people. Celebrating their short stay in jail over the incident at Weasel's house. These guys aren't the brightest. They talk a lot."

"You can tell by her voice that she's young," said Connie. "Sy is bound to figure out who it is."

"Possible," admitted Jack.

"Which means we've got a girl out there that we need to identify and protect," replied Connie.

"This isn't the type of girl who will listen to you," said Jack. "She will tell you to fuck off and all you will have accomplished is to heat everyone up."

"I'm sure you're right, but we still have to follow policy. It would look bad if we knew and didn't at least try to help her."

"We are so close," said Jack. "A couple of days is all we need and we'll find out who Cocktail is. Once that happens, Laura and I will fade away and you can warn the girl."

"Fade away! If this kid stays on the scene you could both disappear for good." Connie paused as she thought about the situation further and said, "Matter of fact, it's too dangerous. I'm going to talk to my boss. I think we should pull the plug. If we keep tabs on Sy, sooner or later he'll take us to Cocktail. I don't want to risk your lives any further."

"I appreciate your concern," replied Jack, "but you can't count on Sy leading you to Cocktail."

"Why? He could have today."

"Could have ... but didn't. Something stinks. Maybe the war is causing Satans Wrath to pull back a bit. Cocktail is a valuable commodity. They may decide to keep him back for protection."

"It's you, Laura, and Sammy who need protection."

"We're too close to back off."

"We are close and I owe that to you two, but after this morning — things have gotten way out of hand. I'm sure if we put round-the-clock surveillance on Sy he'll lead us to him."

"Unless your surveillance is burned and they kill Sy to sever the connection. They did it last time. Not to mention the fact that I've bailed Sy out a couple of times. He may not survive. If he ends up dead, where do you go from there?"

"That's just it. You talk like you're only worried about Sy getting whacked. With someone in Sy's gang feeding information to his enemies, other gangs shooting each other ... things are too dangerous. A dead priest is one thing. Don't put me in the spot of having to investigate the murder of you and Laura, too."

"So how would you try and find her?" asked Laura.

"Don't think we have a lot of choice. If you two can't come up with her name, I'll go over the list of names we collected from the people who went to the party at Roach and Bagger's place. Start hammering on doors and shaking people until we figure out who she is. Her voice is distinctive enough. I'll recognize her if I talk to her."

"That will heat everyone up," said Jack. "Satans Wrath will sever Cocktail's relationship with Sy and anyone else in his gang. Even if they don't, contacting her will make it extremely dangerous for Laura and me. Satans Wrath will suspect us no matter how you do it. I know Damien. The man isn't stupid."

"Which is why you can't continue the UC," said Connie. "It will be too dangerous."

Jack looked at Laura, who shrugged her shoulders in response.

"I'm sorry, but I don't really have a choice," said Connie. "We have to find this kid and talk to her parents."

"Okay," replied Jack, "but don't go hammering on doors yet. Give Laura and me a chance to review our undercover notes. As I said, her name is on the tip of my tongue."

"I really would have thought that between the two of you, one of you would know something to help identify her," said Connie suspiciously. She looked at Laura and asked, "Laura? Is there anything?"

Laura eyed Jack a little longer before turning to Connie and saying, "I can't think of anything at the moment. Let us review our notes. Maybe something will twig."

Connie stared a Laura without speaking.

Laura did her best to appear innocent, but saw the harsh look on Connie's face. *She knows I'm lying ...*

"I may have even written her name down," said Jack. He glanced at his watch and said, "It's six o'clock. Give us half-an-hour and I'll call you."

* * *

Connie waited until she was alone with Dallas and returning to their office, before saying, "Don't count on Jack or Laura finding something in their notes to identify the girl. I think they wanted time out to talk in private."

"Can you blame them?" asked Dallas. "You're asking them to save some kid who's trying to kill them. Christ, they were almost killed for the second time since starting this investigation. I wouldn't blame them if they do decide to pull out altogether."

"Is that how you read it?" asked Connie.

"What do you mean?"

Connie sighed and said, "Jack once told me that as an undercover operator you need to see the big picture. He said the scales of justice are different in that line of work."

"How so?"

"He says he includes the moral issues as a counter-balance to the legal issues."

"I don't get what you're saying," replied Dallas.

"I'd say Jack and Laura are weighing whether to terminate the operation or let a teenaged girl be murdered so they can find some guy who smashed the brains out of a priest with a cement block. I think they already know who she is and are stalling."

"Jesus ... I mean ... she's evil, but she's still just a kid."

"Yeah," sighed Connie, "a kid who likes to kill people."

"And who knows what else she has done."

Connie nodded.

"So what do we do about it?"

Connie shook her head and said, "We have to give them time to peruse their notes, it only makes sense. My guess is they will try to stall us for a day or two and continue the UC."

"A day or two isn't long."

"It is if the kid gets murdered. We can't afford to take that chance. We'll start pounding on doors tonight and talking to as many young women as we can. She better hope that we find her before its too late."

"For Jack and Laura ... how do you decide on something like this? To live with that ..."

"I don't know. Maybe in their work the instinct to survive precludes armchair morality, but I don't agree with it. Right is right and wrong is wrong." Connie looked at Dallas and pointed her finger at him and added, "And having a sixteen-year-old kid murdered is wrong."

"Did you say, *have* the kid murdered?"

Chapter Thirty-Seven

Jack and Laura sat at their desks for the next half-hour. Eventually Jack received a text message. He glanced at it and said, "It's done. The devil is in the hole."

Laura nodded.

Jack called Connie and said, "I've got her name."

"You're kidding," said Connie in surprise. "Are you positive?"

"Yes. I told you it was on the tip of my tongue. Her name is Lorraine Calder."

"Lorraine Calder? I know that name."

"She's the one involved in the suicide of Julie Goodwin, so you'll have her address in your file. She also set up another young girl by the name of Cassandra."

"Who's that?"

"Another kid at the party the night Lorraine made a pass at me. Consider it good news that you don't have Cassandra's name in your file."

"And you're just remembering Lorraine's name now? She's Brewski's girlfriend. You guys know her!"

"What can I say. It's been a hell of a day. You try to remember details and voices after the day we had."

"Yeah … okay. Sorry."

"What are you going to do?"

"Go over to her house and speak with her parents. Maybe say we heard from an undisclosed source that some gang is going to kill her because they don't trust her."

"Lorraine won't scare. She'll tell you to pound sand and it will still heat things up as far as Laura and I are concerned. Satans Wrath will pull Cocktail away from these guys."

"I don't have a choice. As far as you and Laura go, it's time for you to pull out."

"Let me know how it goes."

After hanging up, Connie looked at Dallas and said, "He gave me her name. Lorraine Calder. Her address is in our file. Somewhere in Surrey, as I recall."

"Guess you were wrong about Jack," replied Dallas.

Connie sat for a moment. "I wonder if I am," she said, reaching for the telephone.

"Who you calling?" asked Dallas.

"Surrey Detachment."

Moments later, Connie hung up the phone and said, "You can quit looking in the file. Lorraine's parents came home from work an hour ago and found her dead in the washroom."

"What?"

"It looks like an accidental overdose. When Lorraine's parents got home they found that their bathroom door was locked. They banged on it and eventually opened it to find Lorraine slumped over the toilet with an empty syringe beside her. She had old track marks on her arms. The case looks pretty open and shut."

"Man, what a coincidence," said Dallas.

"Gee, that's a word I've never heard before," said Connie, sarcastically.

"Aren't you going to phone Jack and Laura and let them know the investigation is still on?"

"You do it. Personally, I think they already know."

Jack hung up the telephone after a short conversation with Dallas.

Laura looked at him and said, "That sounded amiable. I thought Connie would have grilled you more."

"It wasn't Connie on the other end. It was Dallas. I have a feeling that Connie is too angry to talk to us at the moment."

"I understand that," replied Laura. "I feel sickened and angry myself."

"Are you in a hurry to get home?" asked Jack.

"Let's see. Almost got killed this morning. Set up a drug lab this afternoon ... not to mention what ... or I should say who we set up at the same time. I've missed supper with my husband who I've hardly seen enough to recognize. I'm exhausted ..."

Jack nodded his understanding.

Laura sighed and said, "With what happened today, I know I won't be able to sleep tonight. What did you have in mind? Double martinis?"

"Tea."

"Tea!"

"Gabriel called yesterday. She's having your typical adolescent problems with Noah and sounded stressed. Faith is at home, too. I thought a visit to let them know they haven't been forgotten would help."

"You're hoping that seeing Faith will convince our brains that what we did was the right thing? Finding Cocktail is more important than a young girl's life?"

Jack gave Laura a sideways glance and said, "Well … this particular girl, yes. Also a yes for my motive to see Gabriel tonight. You're getting to know me pretty well."

"The sad thing is I think it's a good idea. The emotional baggage I'm carrying is not something I want to bring home."

"Then let's see if we can shed some baggage."

Gabriel, grateful for the visitors, poured tea while Noah sat watching television in another room. Faith was asleep in her bedroom.

"How has he been doing?" asked Jack, with a nod of his head toward the living room.

"Not well," replied Gabriel, with a frown. "His grades are still slipping. I know he can do the work if he wants. A couple of years ago he was a top student. His personality has changed. Acts macho sometimes and listless other times. Gets angry with me all the time."

Jack and Laura exchanged a glance and Jack looked at Gabriel and asked, "Any money disappearing around the house?"

"No, I keep track of every dime. Why would you ask that?"

"Does he have any new friends? Phone conversations that he hangs up on or changes when you come in the room?"

"No, he's really a loner. Why ... you think he could be on drugs! Good Lord, no. He goes to church every Sunday. He would never take any alcohol or drugs."

"Have you talked to him about his behaviour?" asked Jack.

"I tried, but he walks away."

"Would you like me to talk him?" asked Jack.

"Thanks, but no. I asked him how it was going with the counsellor at school and he just blew up at me. Said he wanted to be left alone and didn't appreciate me interfering in his life. I think it best to leave him alone for now."

"Do his moods seem to change, in that sometimes he seems really happy or other times tense or jittery?" asked Laura.

"No, more often he is off in his own little dream world, staring blankly into space."

"Have you searched his room?" asked Jack.

"Why would I? I told you he would never use drugs. He is a good Christian."

"I'm sure he is, but Noah has been under a lot of stress. He probably feels he has to be the man of the house. There is also a lot of peer pressure at his age."

"What if he found out I searched his room? He would think I don't trust him."

"He would know that you care and that you love him," replied Jack.

Gabriel thought for a moment and said, "I'll think about it."

Jack arrived home as the CBC National news was starting. Natasha stood up from the television set and gave him a long kiss followed by an even longer hug.

"What's that for?" asked Jack.

"Can't a girl give her guy a hug and a kiss? Even if he does stink," she added. "You smell like your hair got scorched."

"I was near a fire," he said, plunking himself down to stare at the television set. "Let me catch the news, then I'll take a shower.

Natasha saw the distant look in Jack's eyes. She knew that there was something more to the fire than Jack wanted to talk about.

"Three days ago you said this assignment might be over in a week," said Natasha. "Do you still think that?"

She saw a brightness flicker in his eyes. "We're almost finished," he said. "I'm thinking it will be over in a couple of days now."

"Good."

"Yeah, good," he said, once more staring blankly at the news.

Natasha knew the ritual. She did the same thing after a day that was particularly tough. Jack needed to give his brain a rest. She had something she had been holding back from telling him. She decided she couldn't wait any longer.

As the news ended, Nastasha brought Jack a martini and sat beside him.

"Hey, this is unexpected," he said, "where's yours?"

"There is something I have to tell you," replied Natasha. "Something I've known for a little while. I was going to wait until your investigation was over, but I can't keep this from you any longer."

"Is everything okay?"

"How is your martini?" she asked.

Jack took a sip and said, "Fine. Aren't you going to have one?"

"No," replied Natasha, before smiling. "That's what I have to tell you. No drinking for me for a while. At least, not for another six months or so."

Chapter Thirty-Eight

It was eleven o'clock at night when Damien turned off the news and buzzed his electronic gate to let Pussy Paul inside. Moments later, the two men went for a walk outside.

"Our Horseman narc got a call this afternoon," said Pussy Paul. "He's being transferred back to uniform. They told him it was time to circulate some people out of some small detachment up north."

"Too bad, that's the trouble with the RCMP. They keep transferring people. Makes it hard to develop permanent rats. This guy's father is a Member of Parliament, I was hoping we could eventually get him to co-operate with us in exchange for saving his son."

"I know. Even more disturbing is our narc thinks the transfer is a bit sudden and premature. He says other guys have been in the unit longer than he has."

"Interesting," replied Damien. "Has he done anything for us recently?"

"Yeah, he checked out a couple of people for us. Some guy by the name of Jay, along with his girlfriend. Jay is rumoured to be part of the Irish mafia from back east. They moved here recently."

"Where do they fit in?" asked Damien.

"Jay's cousin is a cook who works under Sy and he introduced the two of them. Jay and Sy are doing business together. They were with Sy this morning when Fateh showed up. It was Jay who convinced Hamburger to send the text. Hamburger relayed to Whiskey Jake, who decided to put a stop to Fateh's plan."

"I haven't spoken to Whiskey Jake about that yet, but I'm glad he put a stop to it," replied Damien.

"Because we might be starting a war with the Irish?"

"Fuck the Irish. No, it's the heat I'm trying to avoid. The Brotherhood has the attention of the police now, but it would be nothing compared to what they would have if they opened up with a 50 calibre. The city would panic. There isn't a politician around who wouldn't jump on the bandwagon to demand more police and resources to keep the city safe."

"Gotcha. Well, maybe it's a coincidence about the narc being transferred, but I thought I should tell you," said Pussy Paul.

"I'm glad you did. I don't believe in coincidences. Hasn't Sy suffered some serious losses in the last couple of weeks? Some of his guys busted with guns?"

"Yeah, but Sy figured he took care of that. Two of his guys named Roach and Bagger."

"Maybe he took care of it and maybe he didn't," replied Damien.

"You think Jay is a rat?"

"Or a cop ... possible ..."

"Balvinder's guys tried to do them all last Saturday when they left a party. That was the deal on the news."

"I spoke to Lance and Whiskey Jake about it," said Damien.

"I know. Lance filled me in on your meeting. The thing is, there haven't been any arrests over the car chase and shootings. Also none today after Fateh showed up and donated the 50 calibre to us."

"You would think there would be if Jay was a cop. Still, who knows, it's possible he's a rat."

"Want him taken out?" asked Pussy Paul.

"I heard that Rashard is hooking up with Balvinder, Fateh, and Quang."

"Yeah, I think he heard about the 50 cal and figured he would go with whoever had access to the biggest guns. Of course, that was before we took it."

"Sy's gang has had some serious problems lately," noted Damien. "He, Mongo, and Munch will lose the war for sure. With all this bullshit that's taking place, it's not worth jeopardizing Cocktail to let it continue."

"Time to eliminate the weak?"

Damien looked thoughtfully at Pussy Paul and said, "Yes, time to protect our assets. Have the three losers taken care of. If Jay tags along with Sy, do him, too."

"When?"

"Tell Cocktail to arrange it before the week is over. Tell the losers we will broker a truce talk between all the bosses of both sides. Tell them everyone will be searched and that no guns or phones will be allowed and that they will be blindfolded. If Jay is a rat, it will make us sound like good guys for trying to stop the violence. Have Cocktail set up the ambush using Balvinder, Fateh, Quang, and Rashard to carry it out."

"You want them all involved?" asked Pussy Paul.

"Yes. Tell Cocktail we will supply him with a couple of guys to help with the initial search of Sy, Munch, and Mongo, but after that, the killing will be done by the new Brotherhood. Don't lend Cocktail any of our prospects for the search. I want our hands to look clean if something goes sideways. Use some wannabe bikers. Someone expendable."

"Why use four bosses to carry it out? I'm sure any one of the gangs are capable of looking after three or four unarmed guys."

"I want the remaining four bosses from The Brotherhood in on it together. Make sure all their hands are dirty. No loose ends to ever rat out. Once Sy and his buddies are taken care of, bury the bodies and tell everyone to keep mum about it."

Jack put his martini glass down on the table. "Are you sure?"

Natasha smiled. "If I'm not, I shouldn't be practising medicine."

"I'm going to be a dad!"

"I'm eleven weeks along. I'd like to wait another week or two before telling anyone."

Jack held both of Natasha's hands in his as he gazed at her, before his eyes watered and he wrapped his arms around her and kissed her.

Incredible, unbelievable ... I'm going to be a dad!

When he stopped kissing Natasha he leaned back as his BlackBerry vibrated. It was Gabriel. Jack answered automatically, but his thoughts were with Natasha.

"I did it," Gabriel whispered. "I searched his room tonight when he was watching television. You were right that I should have."

Jack felt his heart sink. Gabriel did not need the extra stress.

"Marijuana?" asked Jack.

"No. Smut. Filthy smut."

"Smut?"

"Magazines. They were under his mattress. *Playboy* ... something called *Hustler*."

Jack was glad that Gabriel couldn't see him smile.

"What should I do? Maybe confront him," said Gabriel as her initial shock turned to anger.

"Uh, I wouldn't get too upset," said Jack. "Your son has reached puberty. It is perfectly normal."

"Normal! These magazines are not normal. Where could he have gotten them from? They're lurid, un-Christian, disgusting —"

"Explains why he has been staring off into space," said Jack. "He's thinking about girls. It is a phase that most young men go through. Be happy that there was no sign of drugs. What Noah is going through is life.

His blank stares ... give him time. He'll mature and snap out of it."

"Do you think so?"

"Yes. I would leave him be for now."

Jack was wrong. Noah would *never* snap out of it for as long as he lived.

Chapter Thirty-Nine

Three days later, Cocktail rented a room at the Best Western in Richmond and waited as Satans Wrath prospects eventually delivered Balvinder, Fateh, Quang, and Rashard to his room.

"Gentlemen," said Cocktail. "I have some good news. As you all know, Satans Wrath are upset that the war is dragging out."

"Who needs them," said Fateh. "You're the guy with the chemicals. Deal straight to us."

"That isn't going to happen. What you are suggesting is that I become their competition. I think we all know what happens to their competition ... or were you hoping to take out a life insurance policy on me?"

A few in the room chuckled. Cocktail smiled and thought, *Sounds better than saying you four are a bunch of uneducated yahoos. I need Satans Wrath to protect me from degenerates like yourselves.*

"So what is the good news?" asked Rashard.

"The good news, especially for you," replied Cocktail, "is that Satans Wrath believe that the four of you should be the only ones in charge of The Brotherhood and they are willing to help. Which is where I come in."

"They're going to help us?" said Fateh. "Does this mean they're gonna give Big Bertha back to me? Or do they plan on killin' the fuckers for us?"

"There is one small test that the four of you have to complete. For you, I am sure it is not a big deal."

"And that is?" asked Balvinder.

"I will arrange for Sy, Mongo, and Munch to go to a place that I choose. None of them will be armed or have any contact with anyone. In fact, we might even blindfold them. When they arrive, they will be tied up and interviewed in regard to their personal assets, such as where they hide their money. The four of you are then to ensure that they are never found again."

"How will you get them to go along with this?" asked Quang.

"I will tell them that Satans Wrath is brokering a truce. That everyone will be taken to a secret location to start the negotiations. I will say that everyone will be searched and that guns and cellphones will not be allowed to ensure everyone's safety. I'll tell them that Satans Wrath will be doing extensive counter-surveillance to make sure nobody decides to try and follow."

"The bikers will do that for us?" asked Balvinder.

"No. As I said, this is a test of leadership for the four of you. The bikers want to see how you handle it. It should be relatively easy because Sy and his associates will believe the bikers are protecting them."

"They could still be there," said Balvinder. "It would be good to have them around for security in case someone tries to escape or somethin'."

"Quite frankly I believe it is because you have not proven yourself to them yet that they won't be there," replied Cocktail. "They don't trust you enough. This task will not only change that, but it will result in a lot more profit for you in the future."

"How do we know that we can trust the bikers … or you," said Quang. "Maybe you're telling the same bullshit to Sy and the rest of 'em."

Cocktail sighed and slowly shook his head like an adult about to admonish a child. "To start with, you will all be armed," said Cocktail. "As far as the location goes, I was thinking that the farm out in Mt. Lehman would be good. Your brother still has the lab there, does he not?"

Quang nodded and said, "It's my farm, too. I'm looking after the lab while my brother is away."

"It is only an hour drive out of the city," continued Cocktail, "yet isolated enough that we won't be bothered by anyone when we find out where they hide their money. As I recall, you have the equipment there to dig a deep hole."

"I have a backhoe."

"Good. I would suggest you get busy digging a pit. Today is Friday. I would like to be cracking the champagne open this Sunday night over their grave."

"Who gets their money?" asked Balvinder. "Us or the bikers?"

"The five of us get it. Consider it a reward for what we must do."

"Sounds perfect," said Quang. "Cut off the heads of the snakes and the rest of the bodies will wither and disappear."

The following day, Cocktail had a meeting with Sy, Mongo, and Munch. They were told that Satans Wrath wanted to broker a truce and that a meeting was being arranged for the next night.

"Only I will know the location," said Cocktail. "I'll give you a place to meet me first. After that, no guns and no phones. You'll be driven to a safe location to talk. Same thing for the guys on the other side. They'll be met, searched, and driven, as well. Everyone will be blindfolded. We don't expect the first meeting to resolve everything, but the negotiations will be conducted in a proper and civilized fashion. Anyone even thinking of causing violence will have to deal with Satans Wrath."

"The other side might not go for it," said Sy. "I heard Rashard has joined up with them. They may think they can get everything and us nothin'."

"The bikers won't put up with any more bullshit," said Cocktail. "They want the territory divided fairly. They're not going to sit back any longer and watch things shuffle back and forth as the bullets fly."

"But there are four of them and only three of us," said Mongo. "They'll still demand more of the action than they should get."

"I've got someone who could help all of us in that regard," said Sy. "My friend Jay."

"We don't need no more bosses to be making our share even smaller," said Mongo.

"You've met him," replied Sy. "Remember what he said in your office that night when I brought him and his girlfriend to your pizza place? He doesn't want to be a boss. The guy wants to be independent."

"If that is the case, why would he come to the negotiations?" asked Munch.

"Because he's in a business where the more contacts you have, the better. He could help us by strengthening what we say is our territory and we could help him unload some merchandise sometime."

Cocktail thought about it. *Four killers and four victims. Everyone will get a chance to prove themselves.* He smiled at Sy and said, "I don't see a problem. Bring him along. I look forward to meeting him."

Chapter Forty

Late Saturday afternoon, Jack listened intently as he walked down the apartment hallway with Sy and heard about Satans Wrath's plan to broker a truce.

"Cocktail told me about it an hour ago," continued Sy. "I trust him. He favours me over the others and nobody is gonna fuck with Satans Wrath, so safety isn't an issue."

"How long have you known Cocktail?" asked Jack.

"Met him a couple years back through the bikers. Don't even know where he lives, let along his real name, but I can tell ya, the dude is smart. We've come a long way since he came on the scene. We're making the best shit in Canada. Maybe even the world. The big problem is this fuckin' war. Once it is over, we sit back, relax, and rake in the dough."

"Hope it works out for you. Cocktail sounds like a guy I should meet sometime. Sammy should have his first batch done in a few days. He's using my contacts to ship some of it back east. Maybe we could get more people and expand operations there, as well."

"Fuck, am I glad to hear you say that."

"Why?"

"Tomorrow night you got your chance to meet him."

Jack could barely contain his excitement. "Oh?" he said, as casually as he could sound.

"At the truce meeting. I asked him and he said to bring you along. With your contacts, I figure you can help me, Mongo, and Munch when it comes to saying who has control of what territory. It will work out for the benefit of all of us."

"Maybe I could go with you," replied Jack, trying to sound like he wasn't sure whether or not he should. "I would like to talk to Cocktail about the possibility of starting other labs in other provinces. I don't want Mongo and Munch knowing the details as it doesn't concern them."

"I'm sure you can talk to him after the meeting. I told him a bit about you. He said he was looking forward to meeting you."

"Okay … sure, I'll go along with you."

"Good. Be here at eight o'clock tomorrow night. No guns and no phones. Satans Wrath will make us all dance through the ropes to make sure nobody is planning anything stupid."

* * *

It was early evening when Jack and Laura walked into Connie's office. Sammy and Dallas were waiting when they arrived.

"Sorry we're running late," said Jack. "Saturday shoppers. Traffic is bad."

"Your message said it was important," replied Connie, harshly.

"Yes. Everything okay, Connie?" asked Jack. "Haven't spoken to you since Tuesday."

"And you know damn well why!"

"I'm sorry, I don't. Have I offended you somehow?"

"Do you think I'm stupid?" replied Connie. "Last Tuesday was when Lorraine Calder *accidentally* overdosed.

"Yes?" replied Jack, furrowing his eyebrows.

"I was angry then. How do you think I felt later when I found out that Roach and Bagger *accidentally* died of carbon monoxide poisoning the morning before? That was the same morning I suggested we do surveillance of them and you said not to bother, that they were just low-level punks and that it would be a waste of time."

"Don't you think doing surveillance of dead bodies would be a waste of time?" replied Jack. "It's not like they would be doing much."

"Don't you get that tone with me! This … this … I've got nothing to say to you!" she said, folding her arms across her chest.

"Connie, I'm sorry," replied Jack glumly. "I was trying to be funny. Guess it didn't come across that way. It seems to me that every time a bad guy dies, you feel like I had something to do with it. You said yourself the deaths were accidental. Maybe it is time you had faith in the investigators that they know what they're doing."

Connie stared as Laura gave Jack a sympathy pat on his back while he looked mournfully around the room. *His big blue eyes ... he does look innocent. Am I wrong? Have I become that cynical and suspicious?*

"Let's get back to why I called this meeting," said Jack, with a sigh. "I met with Sy and he's arranged for me to meet Cocktail tomorrow night."

"You serious?" asked Dallas.

"Very."

"Yes!" said Sammy, and he and Dallas both clapped their hands.

Connie's frown dissolved. "Where? What time?"

Jack told them about the conversation he had with Sy.

"Any idea where the meeting will be?" asked Connie, becoming all business.

"No ... and don't even think of following. We're not blowing it after all this."

"Sy doesn't even know Cocktail's real name," noted Connie. "How do you expect to find out?"

"I'll figure something out. Seeing him is half the battle. Maybe I'll get a chance to scoop something with his fingerprints on it."

"That would work if he has a record," noted Dallas.

"I'll still need to prove it was him who killed Father Brown," said Connie.

"We've got the strand of hair found in the priest's smashed skull," said Dallas.

"Defence could claim the wind blew that in," replied Connie.

"I bet Gabriel or Noah will identify him," said Jack. "Coupled with renting under a false name, it should make him look pretty bad."

"Not to mention if you show a jury all the blood splatters up the back of the house," said Dallas. "They'll freak out when they see what a monster he really is."

"I know, I've thought of that, but I need to prove motive. How hard do you think it will be to prove he is directly involved with the labs?"

"There is no doubt that if you execute a search warrant on him you will come up with the chemical connection," said Jack.

"And the glassware," added Laura.

"And unexplained income," said Sammy.

"Hey, not to mention good old-fashioned police work," said Jack. "With what you have on him, I bet you get him to crack during interrogation."

Connie lifted the crucifix from her neck, kissed it, and smiled.

Jack and Laura spent late Sunday afternoon and early evening in Connie's office, reviewing her entire file. Every name, every address, and every detail were carefully examined. Jack knew that something considered trivial could have the utmost importance later.

At seven o'clock, Jack glanced at his watch and said, "Time to rock and roll."

Sammy, Dallas, and Connie wished him luck, but remained seated while Laura walked with him toward the exit.

"Wish I could come with you," said Laura.

"These guys are not enlightened when it comes to gender," replied Jack. "Strictly an old boys' club."

"It's dangerous going by yourself without backup. I've got an uneasy feeling about it."

"A meeting with no guns ... hell, it sounds safer than what we've been through so far."

"And no phones to call for help. Think you can trust the prospects to do their job?"

"You sound like you have trust issues."

"Maybe I do. You've been acting funny these last couple of days."

"Funny?"

"Not yourself. Everything okay at home with you and Natasha?"

"Is it ever," said Jack, grinning to himself. "It's great."

Laura saw the sparkle in Jack's eyes and smiled. She'd had a hunch and it would appear that she was right.

Jack drove to Sy's apartment complex and parked in the underground lot. He was about to take his BlackBerry off when a call came through. He hesitated when he saw that it was Gabriel and checked his watch. He still had ten minutes to spare.

"Hi, Gabriel."

"Hi," said Gabriel, sounding exasperated. "I wanted to talk about something. Did I catch you at a bad time?"

"I'm about to go into a meeting, but I have a couple of minutes."

"You're working on the Sabbath? Oh, but you're not —"

"Couldn't be helped. What's up?"

"Noah's been acting up again. He got in trouble with the police."

"What happened?"

"Stupid kid's stuff. He lit the neighbour's fence on fire this afternoon. They got it out before there was any real damage. Another neighbour who lives behind us saw him do it."

"Did he say why he did it?"

"I asked. He says he doesn't know why. It's plain silly. I don't know what to do with him. One minute he throws a temper tantrum and the next minute he's crying over nothing."

"I'm going to be busy for a day or two, but how about I drop by and talk to him later in the week?"

"I hate to bother you."

"No bother," said Jack. *No time like the present to practise being a dad …*

Minutes later, Jack met Sy and went with him in Sy's car to a multi-level public parking lot where Sy parked on the roof level.

"How long do we wait?" asked Jack, reaching into his jacket pocket.

"Cocktail didn't say. All I know is we are to wait. Mongo and Munch should be along, too." Sy paused when he saw what Jack had in his hand and said, "What the fuck you doing?"

"Rubik's Cube," replied Jack. "It's something I play with when I'm nervous. Helps me chill out."

"Don't worry," replied Sy. "Tonight ya got nothin' to be nervous about."

Two more cars arrived and Jack saw that it was Mongo and Munch. Jack, Sy, and Mongo got out and grouped around the open window to Munch's car.

Moments later a van arrived, followed by another car.

Jack saw Munch undo his jacket and wrap his hand around the butt of a pistol stuck in his pants.

"Put it away," said Sy. "It's Cocktail in the car. Got a biker with him."

The van and the car parked and Jack saw a man walk toward them. The man was taller than Jack, but had a thin build. He had a full, neatly cropped beard and a trimmed moustache. His hair was wavy and cut to collar length. He was wearing slacks, black dress shoes, and an open sports-jacket that showed a silk shirt underneath.

Jack glanced at Mongo and saw him slip the pistol under his seat.

"Good evening, gentlemen," said Cocktail. "Glad that you are all on time."

"Yeah," said Sy. "This is my buddy I was telling you about. Jay, this is Cocktail."

Jack stuck out his hand and Cocktail shook it and smiled. His smile disappeared when he saw there was something in Jack's other hand.

"What's in your hand?" he said, stepping back cautiously.

"Oh, sorry," replied Jack. "Something I twiddle with to pass the time. Never have solved it," he said, passing the cube to Cocktail.

Cocktail twirled the cube with his fingers and said, "I used to do these in under a minute. Not much challenge, really." He gave it back to Jack and said, "Keep working on it. You'll get there some day."

Jack put it back in his pocket.

Cocktail waved over the two men who'd arrived with him and said, "Okay, gentlemen, the four of you will be frisked by my associates and taken for a ride. No talking until we get there. I hope it goes well tonight and I wish you all good fortune."

Jack studied the faces of the two men who searched them. *Don't recognize them from any pictures of Satans Wrath. The club must be growing ...*

Jack, Sy, Mongo, and Munch were subsequently searched, placed in the van, and blindfolded. They were driven for an hour before Jack could tell by the sound of the tires that they had left a paved road and had entered a road that was gravelled and bumpy. Within seconds, the van came to a stop.

The side door on the van slid open and Cocktail said, "Okay, gentlemen, we have arrived. You may take off your blindfolds and get out."

Jack did as instructed. He saw that they were parked in front of a small barn. The stench of manure hung in the air.

He looked around and saw that behind them there was a farmhouse near the road. Lights were on inside the home, but no other people were visible.

"Where are the bikers?" he asked.

"The others haven't arrived yet, so I expect there are only a couple out at the road and maybe some in the barn. Which, incidentally, is where we are meeting," he added, while gesturing toward the barn with a leather attaché case he was holding.

"It stinks here," said Mongo, while stroking his goatee and looking around.

"Pig farm up the road," replied Cocktail. "Shall we continue, gentlemen? Time is wasting, although it would appear that we will have a short wait."

They entered the barn and Jack saw that it was divided in half, with a wall down the centre. A glimpse through a doorway revealed that the far side held a row of empty stalls and stanchions to hold cattle in place. The section of the barn they were in was open in the middle with empty pens on each side. A wooden ladder nailed to a wall led to a hayloft up above.

A room at the far end of the barn locked with a combination lock caught Jack's attention. It wasn't the lock that caused his adrenalin to surge. It was the picture of a hamster on the door that told him they were not on mutual territory.

Jack spun around as Balvinder, Fateh, Quang, and Rashard appeared behind them. Balvinder and Rashard each brandished sawed-off shotguns while Fateh and Quang held pistols.

"Cocktail! What —"

Cocktail's chortle interrupted Sy's panicked voice. "Sorry guys," he said, "you didn't make the honour roll."

Jack glanced around for a chance to escape. His glance did not go unnoticed. Cocktail's smile mutated to a sneer. "All of you," he barked, "lay down on your stomachs and put your hands behind your back!"

They slowly complied, laying face down in a row on the floor.

Jack could taste the dust and particles of hay in his mouth as he lay on the floor. More of it caused his eyes to water, but he hardly noticed as he waited for the inevitable sound of gunfire to announce their executions. *I wish I could write a note to Natasha and tell her how much I love her ... and to say I'm sorry. Sorry that she will be a mom all on her own. Sorry, too, to my child for not being there ...*

Quang stuck his pistol in his belt and tied each of the captive's hands behind their backs with zip ties.

Jack pondered on the use of the zip ties. *Why didn't they shoot us? This is the ideal spot ...*

Jack's thoughts were interrupted when Fateh kicked Sy in the face and said, "That is for what you cost me the other morning."

"Fateh! Wait," commanded Cocktail. "Stick to the itinerary. You'll get your chance. Let Quang finish."

Quang picked up a short length of heavy chain and weaved one end through the bound arms of each of the captives.

"Gentleman, stand up," ordered Cocktail.

They did as told and the chain was used to bind them shoulder to shoulder in a circle with their backs against a thick support beam that ran from the floor up to the ceiling. The ends of the chain were tightened and padlocked together.

"Listen carefully," said Cocktail, "you will all die, that is without question. For those of you who are slow to grasp concepts easily, I will give you a moment to accept your fate."

Jack saw Cocktail smile before whistling part of the tune to *The Bridge on the River Kwai. He's enjoying this*, he thought. He recalled the bloody splashes up the back of Gabriel's house and looked around the barn. *Cocktail can do anything to us here ... drag it out for days ... try not to focus on the pain. Focus on something else ... Natasha ... too painful ... focus on an object ... the picture of Harry the Hamster...*

"Okay, gentlemen, your time is up," said Cocktail, as he strutted around his captives with his hands clasped behind him. "The bad news is that you're going to die, but the good news is you can decide how. It is all a question of economics. The richer you make us before you die will decide whether your death is quick and painless ... or long and slow. You see, I have listened to most of you brag about how much you've made."

Cocktail stopped to stare at Sy and continued, "Brag about how you made a million dollars ..." Cocktail shook his head and added, "How very, very foolish you have been."

"Fuck you," seethed Mongo. "You're gonna kill us, anyway. I sure as fuck ain't payin' you to do it."

"Well, thank you, Mongo, for volunteering to go first," said Cocktail. He nodded to Quang who approached Mongo with a dirty rag to use as a gag.

"Okay, you're right. You win," said Mongo, gruffly. "Let me go and I'll give ya the money. I'm done with this stuff. I give up. Let me go and I'm out of here. Fuck, I'll even leave B.C. if ya want me to."

"Of course you would," said Cocktail, "but you weren't paying attention. None of you will leave here alive." A bemused smile crossed Cocktail's face and he said, "Open your mouth like a good boy. You'll get a chance to talk later."

Jack saw the look of rage on Mongo's face turn to panic as the gag was tied around his mouth. The reason was obvious. Rashard had set the shotgun down and approached with a pitchfork, which he jabbed in the air toward Mongo's face. At the same time Rashard was joined by Quang who held a barbecue lighter.

"The rest of you watch our first volunteer closely," said Cocktail, "and decide how best you can spend your money before you die." Cocktail gestured for Rashard to stand back and said, "Mister Quang, please demonstrate to our audience how painful death can become."

Quang clicked the lighter. On the third click the flame erupted out the end and he slowly moved the flame under Mongo's goatee.

Jack heard Mongo scream through the gag and saw the big man's muscles bulge as he twisted and turned in an effort to get away.

Jack turned away as the smell of burned hair and flesh invaded his nostrils. Beside him he could feel Mongo lurch and twist his body as his muffled cries turned to whimpers.

Without warning, Rashard stabbed Mongo through the arm with the pitchfork, effectively pinning him to the beam. "This will hold the fucker still!"

The action caused the chain to tighten, jerking Jack back as a spray of blood shot out from an artery in Mongo's arm, hitting Cocktail in the face.

"What have you done?" screamed Cocktail.

Chapter Forty-One

Laura checked her watch and realized only four minutes had passed since she last looked.

"I don't see what we can do except wait," replied Connie, watching her.

"You've been checking with OCTF? The monitors?"

"Everyone is up to speed. Nothing unusual on the wiretap. OCTF has a room bug someplace where Fateh's guys are partying. Everything seems normal."

"Do they normally party on a Sunday night?" asked Laura.

"I guess so. These guys don't need to show up for work Monday morning."

"Jack is right about one thing," said Laura. "Waiting is —"

Connie's phone rang and she grabbed it.

"Is it Jack?" asked Laura, hopefully, although reason told her that Jack would call her first.

"No, it's Nicole Purney, one of the monitors," replied Connie, putting her finger up to her mouth for Laura to be quiet.

Laura saw the blood drain from Connie's face and her hand trembled as she passed the phone over to Laura. "You better hear what came over the room bug."

"Play it back for me," Laura asked into the receiver.

"As I told Connie when she called earlier," said Nicole, "Fateh's top guys are partying hard tonight. This just came in. I live monitored it. Here you go."

Laura strained to hear every sound. She heard laughter and the sound of ice being dropped in glasses. A male voice said, "Our fuckin' profit margin is gonna go up like a rocket."

"Yeah, guess tonight we can consider all of the competition buried!" replied another male voice.

"Literally," said a third person, followed by the sound of laughter.

Laura gasped and said, "I'm coming down there, Nicole," and hung up.

Connie stared wide-eyed at Laura and said, "Do you think—"

"It was a trap," replied Laura, getting to her feet. "Jack walked into an ambush."

"What was said?" asked Sammy.

"Party talk," mumbled Laura. "Sounds like Jack may already be dead and buried someplace."

"Jesus, Laura!" replied Connie. "Don't say that. What can we do?"

"All we can do is wait and listen," she replied, making no effort to wipe the tears from her face.

* * *

"You damned imbecile," screamed Cocktail leaping back and grabbing a tissue from his pocket to wipe the blood off his face. "What if he has AIDS?" he yelled at Rashard. "You ever think of that?" he continued.

Jack watched as Cocktail rubbed the tissue hard on his face, pausing to inspect it before continuing to rub some more. When he was satisfied he had removed all the blood, he carefully examined his clothing to look for blood.

"I thought you wanted these guys to get good and bloody," said Rashard.

"Next time warn me so I can stand back," said Cocktail tersely. He looked at Quang and said, "Enough barbecuing for the moment. Take his gag off and see if he has come to his senses."

Quang ripped the gag from Mongo's mouth and stood back as Mongo slumped forward and vomited.

"Enough," said Jack. "I don't want to go through this. I bet I've got more money than these three guys put together. It's yours."

"Interesting," replied Cocktail. "Where is it?"

"It's hidden and protected. I'd have to show you."

"Bullshit! Tell us where it is!"

"It's in a storage locker."

"Where's the key?" asked Cocktail.

"My girlfriend has it. I could call her."

"That isn't going to happen. No calls. Tell us which storage locker. You will remain here until we break into it. If you're telling the truth, your death will be painless and quick. I will leave it to your imagination to figure out what will happen if you are lying."

"I copied your idea of using an incendiary bomb on a shelf like you do in your labs. I rigged a more complicated and hidden triggering mechanism, though. I would need to show you the carboy to point out exactly how I have incorporated the device that would set it off."

"He's lying," said Balvinder. "He would be afraid of burning his money."

"Fireproof safe," said Jack. "There are other documents ... names ... that I wanted destroyed rather than fall into the hands of certain enemies. The safe I could actually afford to lose, but not the names."

"Your carboy and layout mimics the setup in the labs?"

"Yes, except I used a mercury switch so that motion will set off a blasting cap to trigger the contents of the carboy. I also installed two tripwires."

"Mercury switch and two tripwires ... I'm impressed," replied Cocktail. "You are somewhat more sophisticated than your dysfunctional friends."

Jack shrugged in response.

"So tell me, where exactly are these tripwires?"

"My carboy is in the middle of a shelf above the safe. There are loose boards scattered about that have to be moved to get to either the safe or the cardboard file folder containing my documents. One board has a tripwire to the left of the carboy, no ... the right ... maybe the left. The one on the floor by the safe is the opposite."

"Which is it?" demanded Cocktail.

"He's lyin'," said Rashard.

"I'm not lying. I've seen what you would do to me if I was. Even worse if one of you got hurt getting it. The trouble is, I'm dyslexic. If I was in the room with the carboy I could describe it accurately, but to try and tell you by memory … I'm afraid I would make a mistake. Take me to the locker and I could tell you."

"You're not leaving here," said Cocktail. "Not alive, at least. You said the layout mimics our labs." He looked at Quang and said, "Take him over to your lab, but leave his hands tied behind his back." Cocktail looked at Jack and said, "You can verbalize or gesture to us exactly how you have supposedly done this."

Jack was released from the chain, but his hands remained tied behind his back with the zip-tie. Sy, Mongo, and Munch remained padlocked around the beam.

Quang headed for the locked room and Balvinder grabbed Jack by the arm as they followed.

Jack glanced behind him and saw Rashard aim a pistol at his head. Cocktail followed behind Rashard while Fateh remained with the other prisoners.

Jack stood quietly with his head slumped on his chest as Quang undid the lock and opened the door slightly, before reaching up to pull down the lever.

Jack reacted instantly by kicking Quang in the middle of his back, propelling him into the room, before tumbling to one side as a loud *whoosh*, accompanied by a huge fireball, engulfed the room.

Quang, a distorted image of a human fireball turned to run and slammed into Balvinder and Rashard.

Jack was already on his feet, running to the nearest doorway, which led to the other side of the barn.

"Shoot him! Shoot him!" screamed Cocktail through a fog of smoke and fire.

Jack glanced back and saw Quang and Rashard both rolling on the floor while Balvinder jumped around them yelling for them to roll faster.

Jack burst through the doorway and saw a large sliding door in front of him. It was closed and with his hands tied behind his back, he knew he couldn't open it in time. He looked at the empty stanchions and a gutter used to collect manure. At the far end of the barn, three planks nailed together made a ramp up to a door made of rough boards.

Jack raced up the ramp and kicked the door. It burst open immediately and he found himself on a ramp leading to a pile of manure. Beyond the pile was an open yard leading to a large hangar-styled building that was open on all sides. At one end of the building was a tractor and a hay baler. Outside the building stood a large, overhead gravity-fed tank of gas.

Jack glanced behind him. Screaming through the smoke and crackling fire told him that Quang was being dragged out the front entrance of the barn. Footsteps pounding through the barn said others were coming his way.

He looked back at the hangar and saw that the rest of building was filled with rows of bales of hay, stacked to roof level. *It will take about ten seconds to make it to the hangar. Maybe longer. Can I make it? The hangar has nothing but field around it. No place to run to …*

Balvinder and Rashard, with guns in hand, burst out onto the ramp, followed seconds later by Fateh and Cocktail.

"The fucker is hiding in the storage hangar," yelled Rashard.

Balvinder glanced back inside the barn and said, "What about our three prisoners?"

"Let them burn to death," replied Cocktail. "Murder will be hard to prove, besides, it was Jay who started the fire, not us."

"The fucking neighbours are bound to see the fire," continued Rashard. "We might never find him before the cops and fire department show up."

"Then torch the hangar, too," yelled Cocktail. "There's farm equipment in there, better yet, that's an overhead gas tank beside the hangar. Use it!"

Moments later, another large *whoosh* of flame erupted as the hangar, fuelled by gas, turned the building into an inferno.

Jack squirmed out from underneath the plank and peeked over the manure pile. Cocktail, Balvinder, and Rashard were watching different corners of the hangar. Within seconds, all the hay was burning. No living creature could survive inside.

Jack stumbled back into the barn and crouched low as he ran back through the barn. In the dense smoke and heat, he saw Sy, Mongo, and Munch. They had dropped to the ground, fighting and kicking in an unsuccessful attempt to free themselves. Their lungs choked and gasped for air while the roar of the fire sounded like a jet engine screaming around them.

Jack kicked a window and used his foot to hook a piece of shattered glass and pull it inside.

"Jay! Help us!" coughed Sy.

"I will," replied Jack. "Give me a minute to free myself," he said, plunking himself down on the floor. He picked up the broken glass with his fingers and feverishly sawed away at the zip tie. Precious seconds ticked past and his fingers became slippery with blood.

"Jay! Look out!" yelled Sy.

Jack saw Cocktail charging at him with a pitchfork as the zip tie broke. He didn't have time to get up. His eyes met Cocktail and he saw the blind rage.

"You're dead!" screamed Cocktail.

Jack was sitting cross-legged on the floor. He rested his elbow on his knee with his arm extended upward. Jack's face and open chest looked like an easy target and Cocktail lunged at it with the pitchfork.

A look of surprise crossed Cocktail's face when Jack used his arm to knock the pitchfork to one side, while grabbing the wooden shaft with his other hand and giving it a tug as if to pull it from Cocktail's grasp.

Cocktail responded as most people would. He yanked hard on the pitchfork. It was what Jack had been waiting for. The movement gave Jack the momentum to rise with the pitchfork and propel himself forward, knocking Cocktail to the floor, with himself on top.

Jack punched him viciously five times in the face. Cocktail let go of the pitchfork and Jack pressed the wooden handle across his throat and leaned on it with all his weight.

"Help us," pleaded Mongo behind him. "We're burning …"

Cocktail lost consciousness and Jack continued to press down.

"Jay! Come on!" said Sy, barely able to cough out the words.

Jack cursed and scrambled across the floor to the broken window. He grabbed two shards of glass and used one to free Sy. When he did, he said, "Grab the other piece and help me."

As Mongo and Munch got free, Jack heard Cocktail yell and saw him moving on all fours, like a crab, as he grabbed his attaché case and scurried away, disappearing into the smoke on the far side of the barn. His screams alerted Balvinder, Rashard, and Fateh.

Jack, Sy, Mongo, and Munch ran out the front door. Munch stumbled over Quang's smouldering body, got to his feet, and followed the others. Jack quickly checked the van they had arrived in … no keys in the ignition. A scream from Balvinder said they had been spotted.

"Run for it!" yelled Jack, while darting for the darkness away from the lights of the farm.

Chapter Forty-Two

Police and fire department crews were on the scene soon after a neighbour reported hearing an explosion and seeing the fire. The fire department soon realized there was nothing they could do to save the barn or the storage hangar behind it. They did discover a burned and unconscious figure lying in the barnyard. Despite third degree burns to half his body, he was still alive and an ambulance rushed him away.

A police officer saw a pickup truck drive into the yard and a man ran over to speak to him.

"I live over there," he yelled, pointing off to a neighbouring farm.

"You the fellow who reported this?"

"Nope. The sirens woke me up. Then someone stole my flatbed truck and took off in it. I got dressed and came over to tell you. Happened ten or fifteen minutes ago."

"Did you call it in?"

"No, I could see your flashing lights so I thought maybe you caught the guy."

"I didn't see it, but I'll radio it in." The officer paused and asked, "Had you left the keys in the ignition?"

"No, of course not. I leave them in the ashtray."

"Brilliant."

Laura answered her BlackBerry on the first ring.

"Hi, Princess. Calling to let you know I'm still above ground."

Laura burst out crying, but Jack continued, "Some bad shit came down tonight. Cocktail went in with Balvinder, Fateh, Rashard, and Quang and tried to set us up."

"Where are you?" she asked, as the release of tension brought more tears.

"At a gas station on the Number One highway near Clearbrook. I borrowed someone's truck, but decided to ditch it. I need a ride. Sy, Mongo, and Munch are with me, but they are contacting their own people."

After Jack gave Laura directions, he hung up and the four men walked a short distance from the gas station to a place they could stand in darkness and wait.

Jack saw the blood dripping from Mongo's hand and said, "Your arm is going to need medical attention."

"Fuckin' tell me about it. That fuckin' Rashard must have hit an artery. There's a hospital in Abbotsford. I'll get my guys to take me there."

"When the cops locate that flatbed and find your blood in it, they might check the local hospitals. Not to mention, they're liable to show up there with Quang. You should pick a hospital that's farther away."

Mongo nodded his head in agreement and said, "Good thinkin'. Thanks."

"Let me take a look at it," said Jack. "I may need to rip your shirt and use it to stop the bleeding."

Mongo agreed.

Jack tended to his arm and as he worked on it, he said, "It might be in everyone's best interests to find new places to sleep and lay low for awhile until we sort this out."

"Lay low!" replied Mongo. "Fuck that! Somehow I'm gonna find Cocktail. He's the one who set us up. Then I'm gonna take Rashard and —"

"Who is Cocktail?" asked Jack. "What's his real name?"

Sy, Mongo and Munch each looked at each other and shrugged their shoulders.

"Nobody knows who he really is," said Sy. "He came to us through Satans Wrath."

"Speaking of fucking Satans Wrath," said Munch, looking at Sy and Mongo, "looks like we're at war with them, too. Better tell our people to start spraying the shit out of those guys."

"Guess so," replied Mongo.

Jack swallowed. He knew that as things stood, the risk to every man, woman and child living in the lower mainland would equate to living in a war zone.

He also knew Damien and thought about how tonight's ambush had been planned. *Damien is too professional to get into an all out war with these bunch of losers if he can avoid it. Will attract too much heat ... which is why I didn't recognize the so-called prospects tonight. Damien made himself a buffer of deniability ...*

Jack thought over his next response. *As much as I'd like the bikers to take a few bullets, I can't risk the possibility of an innocent person getting hurt by mistake. No more thinking required ...I have to do what is right ...*

"Did any of you guys recognize the bikers who searched us tonight when we met Cocktail?" asked Jack.

Sy, Mongo, and Munch shook their heads.

"Before you start shooting up the streets, it might be a good idea to find out if Satans Wrath knew about it," suggested Jack. "Is it possible that Cocktail and these other guys set it up on their own, hoping to get a bigger slice of the action?"

"Possible," conceded Munch.

"How the hell do we find out?" asked Sy.

"Simply wait," replied Jack. "Satans Wrath will make their intentions known soon. They aren't the types who are known for doing drive-bys or spraying restaurants with bullets."

"What do you mean?" asked Sy.

"For the next couple of days I suggest you hide," replied Jack. "Satans Wrath won't let this sit. They'll do something soon. You've all got enough people working for you that if the bikers are at war with you, some of them will get whacked. If Cocktail did act on his own, Satans Wrath will deal with him."

"You sound like you know these guys pretty good," said Munch, suspiciously.

"Satans Wrath? Hell, yes. They're back east, as well. All over the globe. I know lots of gangs who have had encounters with them."

"Maybe Jay is right," said Sy. "Tonight is the first time that two bikers showed up where I didn't know either one of 'em."

"I would like to find Cocktail," said Jack. "After tonight, I owe him one."

"We all fuckin' owe him one," said Mongo.

"Something about Cocktail looked familiar," said Jack. "I could have seen him at a party someplace or perhaps a restaraunt. I'm not sure, but maybe I could help find out who he is or where he lives."

"That would be great," said Sy. "We definitely gotta put that fuckin' devil in the hole!"

"I get first dibs," said Mongo, pointing to his arm. "Gonna blow his balls off first and let him crawl around before I gut-shoot him. After that, I'll put one up his ass. Same for Rashard. You guys can do Balvinder and Fateh. Quang, too, if he ain't already gook food."

"Whatever," replied Jack. "But for now, find a safe place to hide out and we'll all text each other so the four of us are kept in the loop."

* * *

The Major Crime Unit, housed in Surrey, was normally a thirty-minute drive from where Jack was calling from. Laura arrived in seventeen minutes and drove Jack to Connie's office so he could give a complete account of what had happened. On the way back, Laura asked Jack for the details. He told her to wait so he wouldn't have to repeat everything a few minutes later.

As soon as they arrived at the Major Crime Unit, Jack retrieved a couple of bandages from a first aid kit and went to the washroom to attend to the minor cuts on his fingers and wash the manure off his clothes and body. It was Laura's next clue that something was amiss.

The blood on Jack's fingers had already started to dry. She was surprised that he even thought of his fingers over the urgency of giving everyone the details of what had occurred. *He is taking time to decide what to tell us ... and what not to tell us ...*

Jack had glimpsed the licence plate of the van that drove them to Quang's farm and Laura checked it while Jack was in the washroom. It turned out to be registered to Quang and she gave Jack the bad news when he returned.

Connie sat behind her desk while Jack, Laura, and Sammy pulled up chairs. Everyone listened quietly as Jack roughly outlined what had transpired. When he finished, he leaned forward and picked up a photo from Connie's file.

Laura saw that it was a photo of Amanda Flowers, taken in the hospital emergency room shortly after she had been attacked. Jack studied the photograph intently, before gazing off into space as if trying to figure something out ... *or perhaps make a decision.*

"Anything back on Quang's injuries?" asked Laura, hoping to give her partner more time.

"A member from MCU is at the hospital," said Connie. "The doctors think Quang will live, although they are worried about infection setting in. It will take years of surgery for him to recover fully. It will be a long, painful process and he'll still end up with a face that looks like a can of smashed worms."

"Too bad we couldn't slap him into a jail cell, too," said Sammy.

"Or the rest of them for attempted murder," added Connie. She looked at Jack and said, "Do you want to reconsider? If you could testify it —"

"No," replied Jack, sharply. "We can't charge anyone without burning the informant."

Connie nodded and said, "We still don't know who Cocktail is. Isn't there anything you heard or saw tonight to help?"

"I might have his prints," said Jack, carefully taking the Rubik's cube from his pocket and placing it on Connie's desk. "Cocktail handled it tonight."

"Good going," replied Connie, reaching for her brief case to find a plastic exhibit bag, "but is there anything else? Even if we get prints, who is to say he has a criminal record?"

Jack stared at the picture of Amanda. Her bloodshot, glassy eyes stared back at him from under a mutilated forehead. His mind went back to when he had last seen her, shortly after being criticized in court for not telling a drug dealer that he was an undercover police officer.

She begged me to keep her out of court. I promised her that justice would be served ... and that was before Ngọc Bích called to tell me the judge wouldn't accept her testimony because she had been a prostitute. Does being raped and enslaved in a brothel make you a prostitute? Personally, I would take the word of most prostitutes over the word of a judge ...

"Jack? Did you hear me?" asked Connie. "Is there anything else that would help?"

"I can't think clearly," said Jack. "I need time to clear my head. You may as well go home. It will take me another three or four hours to write my UC notes. When I'm finished that, I'd like to review your file again. Maybe something will trigger. If it does, I'll call you. Otherwise I'm going to go home and sleep."

"I have notes I need to make, as well," said Laura.

Connie sighed and pushed her chair back and stood up. She looked at Jack and said, "I want you to know something. You and I have had our differences, but you scared the crap out of me tonight. I was really worried about you. I'm glad you're okay."

"Thanks."

Connie gestured to her desk and said, "Be my guest. We can talk about it again tomorrow. Lock the door when you leave."

"Sounds like you might have averted an all-out war in the streets," said Sammy as he stood up to leave.

"Guess the next day or two will tell us that," replied Jack. He looked at Connie and said, "I bet we find out who he is by Tuesday."

Connie frowned and said, "That's only two days away. What makes you think that?"

"Because he screwed up with three major gangs tonight. Between Sy, Mongo, and Munch, surely someone will find him."

"Make that four gangs," said Sammy. "You forgot about us. We're the biggest gang."

Connie nodded and said, "Cocktail better hope we find him first."

"For sure," replied Jack.

As soon as Connie was gone, Jack started flipping through the pages of her file.

"What are you looking for?" asked Laura.

"Clue to a murderer," replied Jack.

"Think Cocktail's real name is in there?"

"I can find out who Cocktail is. That's not who I'm looking for."

"You're not looking for Cocktail?" asked Laura in surprise.

"Not at the moment. When we were ambushed tonight, Cocktail made a comment about us not being on his honour roll."

"He's a teacher!"

"With what happened to Amanda, I'm guessing he knows her. In the morning I'll go to the school when classes have started and look through their yearbooks. Bet I find his picture."

"Why didn't you tell Connie? You've even got her

looking for fingerprints. He likely won't have a record if he's a teacher."

Jack looked toward the ceiling as he took a deep breath and slowly exhaled. He turned to Laura and said, "I want to talk with Amanda Flowers first. She was adamant about not testifying again."

"We are talking about nailing Cocktail for the murder. That part doesn't need to involve Amanda."

"I don't think Cocktail is our murderer."

"You what? Not the murderer! He tried to kill you tonight!"

"I mean as far as the priest goes. Tonight, when Mongo got stabbed with the pitchfork, blood sprayed out. A little got on Cocktail and he freaked out. Started cleaning himself immediately. Gave Rashard hell and was worried about getting AIDS."

Laura thought for a moment and said, "Whoever killed the priest wasn't afraid of blood. They would have drenched themselves in it."

"Exactly. I don't think Cocktail did it. I think he only dragged the body inside to hide it from view while they cleaned out the lab."

"If it wasn't the lab rats, then who did it?" asked Laura. "It wasn't a robbery. He still had on his gold crucifix."

"Gabriel called me tonight before I met with Sy. You remember she said that Noah's grades have fallen in the last couple of years … fighting in school?"

Laura nodded.

"Gabriel called to say he lit a neighbour's fence on fire for no apparent reason. Said he has been throwing temper tantrums one minute and crying over nothing the next."

"What are you getting at?"

Jack pointed to the file and said, "Read the background that Connie dug up on Father Brown. He was at Kuper Island from 1971 to 1974. You familiar with the history of that place?"

Laura's face turned grim and she nodded. "Indian residential school where the children were taken from their families in a government project to try and force them into assimilation."

"You know what happened to those children?"

"Lots of sexual abuse by the priests.... Oh, man. You're thinking Noah was sexually abused by Father Brown?"

"It's possible. His behaviour falls in line with post-traumatic stress disorder. Classic symptoms."

"But he wouldn't have killed Father Brown. The amount of force ... the blood ... it would have been discovered in the house."

"Noah isn't responsible, but the rage exhibited in the murder makes me think it was someone who knew him. Many people who attended the residential schools never recovered. Drug addiction, suicide ... and alcoholism," said Jack, carefully enunciating the last word.

"One of the winos," said Laura.

Jack nodded and said, "Connie's list of winos is in here someplace. I read it before. Some she found by hanging out at the liquor store and talking to people. Others she got from fingerprints off of empty bottles in the area."

"Connie's pretty astute at interviewing," said Laura. "If she talked to the culprit I bet she would have her suspicions. She would have said something."

"She didn't find them all. Some were never — here it is," said Jack, pointing to a list of names, most of which had been stroked off. Two names remained.

"One looks Ukrainian and one aboriginal," noted Laura.

"She has an alphabetical index with notes on every name. Let's see what she has done to find them," said Jack, turning to the index. "Forget the Ukrainian. What does Connie say about the aboriginal ... criminal record three pages long ... mostly theft ... drunk driving ... a few assaults ... most of these started years ago and are out of Prince George. Last few are local. Connie has contacted social service agencies ... shelters ... Prince George ... this guy's locale doesn't fit."

"So much for that theory," said Laura.

Jack turned back to the list of names. He flipped the page over and saw one more name at the top of the next page. It was not stroked off. "Take a look," said Jack, jabbing at the name with his finger. "John-Wayne Charlie." Jack looked at Laura. He felt no elation at his discovery. If he had been asked to solve the murder of a pedophile he would have declined.

"Charlie is common to the Chemainus, Cowichan, Duncan area north of Victoria," said Laura. "Next door to Kuper Island."

"I know."

Jack checked the index and found that John-Wayne Charlie's criminal record consisted entirely of offences related to public intoxication. Many of the offences were committed in Duncan.

Jack read Connie's notes to see what action she had taken to locate John-Wayne. "Connie called Duncan Detachment and a note says someone went to his brother's place … a guy by the name of Gunnar Charlie. Gunnar said he hadn't seen his brother in five years."

"Any other clues as to where he hangs out?" asked Laura.

Jack checked the criminal record again and said, "The funny thing is, John-Wayne's last conviction for public intoxication in Duncan was only two years ago."

"His brother gave a flippant response to cover for him."

"Exactly," said Jack, grimly. "First thing in the morning I'll call Gunnar. Let's see if John-Wayne Charlie has returned home."

Jack started flipping through the file again and said, "Connie has a photo of Father Brown before he was murdered. I'm going to take it."

"What will you say to Gunnar when you phone him?"

"I'll tell him I'm with the Department of Indian and Northern Affairs and say that there is money owed to his brother."

"That might work."

Jack had a deeper feeling of depression. *One more lie a white man tells an Indian …*

Chapter Forty-Three

Jack and Laura waited at Queen Elizabeth Secondary School until the bell announced the start of the first class. Minutes later, they introduced themselves to the secretary who rounded up several copies of school yearbooks from recent years.

It only took Jack a couple of minutes to find a picture of Cocktail taken when he was addressing an assembly. Cocktail was clean shaven in the picture, but Jack had no doubt it was the right man. He nudged Laura and gave her the thumbs-up sign.

"Betty, excuse me," said Jack, with a smile at the secretary. "Could you tell me who this person is?"

Betty used her feet to propel the castors on her chair over to Jack and Laura. "That is Lyle Ryker," she said. "He's no longer with us."

"His name is familiar," replied Jack, flipping through his notebook. "I believe your principal,

Morris Bloomquist, mentioned him before. Someone popular with the students I understand. Taught math."

"Yes, he did. He's the nicest man," continued Betty. "He organized a humanitarian drive with the students for that big tsunami in Thailand. I was sorry to see him leave after last semester."

"Where did he go?" asked Jack, not looking up from his notebook as he found the notes he had made earlier.

"He started a humanitarian relief agency that provides medical equipment to hospitals and research facilities in third-world countries."

"Do you know the name of the company?" asked Jack.

"No, but it is in Vancouver someplace. Lyle is the dearest man. I can definitely assure you that he is not who you are looking for. As a matter of fact, he stopped in about a month ago and dropped off a box of chocolates for me."

And looked through Amanda's file ...

Whiskey Jake and Lance walked up to Damien's house as he opened the front door.

"This better be good," said Damien. "You interrupted my breakfast."

"There's something you need to hear," replied Lance.

Minutes later they strolled through the backyard. Damien's face darkened when he received the news about what had happened overnight.

"A complete fiasco," Lance muttered. "These guys aren't competent enough to tie their own fucking shoelaces."

"I can't believe it," said Damien. "You're telling me that they were armed and had four guys tied up and still couldn't kill them! They even let them burn the barn down!"

"And a shed behind," added Whiskey Jake.

"Fucking Christ!" yelled Damien.

"And let them escape," said Lance. "Which means they might be looking for revenge."

"Want to join up with Balvinder, Fateh, Rashard, and Quang and wipe the fuckers out?" asked Whiskey Jake.

"Are you stupid, too?" roared Damien. "There's no fuckin' way we're doin' business with any of these dumb fucks! I must have been out of my mind to have considered it in the first place."

"What are we gonna do?" asked Whiskey Jake.

"Grab either Sy, Mongo, or Munch. If you can't find them, grab someone in their gangs who has some clout. Tell them we found out that Cocktail tried to backstab us. Take whoever that is to see the two dumb shits we sent to help Cocktail. Blow the two dumb shits away as a sign of good faith and give their driver's licences to whoever you grabbed from The Brotherhood."

"So they'll have pictures to show we took care of the right guys," said Lance.

"Exactly. Mention we're still looking for Cocktail and let the guy go."

"What do we do about Cocktail?" asked Lance.

"He's too valuable to waste. We'll have to move him. Maybe back east. Tell him to lay low until we set up someone in his company to act as a replacement. After that, we'll start Cocktail off all over again some-place else."

Jack called Amanda's home in Victoria and her mother said that Amanda was doing volunteer work at a senior's lodge, but would be home by suppertime. "Perfect," said Jack.

He and Laura caught the eleven o'clock ferry departing from Tsawwassen to Swartz Bay on Vancouver Island. They arrived in the Victoria PD office after lunch and Jack called Connie.

"You just waking up?" asked Connie.

"No, I couldn't sleep. After talking with you last night, I remembered a comment Cocktail made when we were ambushed about how we weren't on the honour roll. I figured maybe he is, or was, a teacher."

"Get down to the school and check it out," replied Connie. "I'm sure it's the same school Amanda Flowers taught at."

"Already did it. Came up with some snapshots in school yearbooks from previous years. Some are of teachers who don't work there anymore. I've got a suspect, but he doesn't have a beard and the school pictures are grainy."

"Who's your suspect?"

"I don't want to say until I'm positive. If I did pick the wrong photo and sent you to scoop the wrong guy ... I mean, in court, that would blow everything ... I want to talk to Amanda Flowers first."

"Where are you?"

"At the Victoria PD office, having coffee with a friend. Laura and I are going to interview Amanda. I think when we do, I'll know for sure."

"Why didn't you call me sooner?" asked Connie suspiciously.

"If I give you his name and you make the arrest, defence may demand that I appear in court. I can't risk that because of our informant. It won't be me that tips you."

"Then who ... Christ ... Crime Stoppers? That's not really kosher."

"Neither is murdering someone or ordering a multiple rape and mutilation. Do you want to find out or not? I won't jeopardize the informant."

Connie sighed and said, "You know I want to find out."

"Good. As soon as we know you will know. I want to talk to Amanda. Cocktail's order to have the punks slash her face had to be personal. I think when we talk to her and ask her about her relationship with the suspect, it will come together."

"I should be the one to interview her."

"She trusts Laura and me. I know she will open up to us. She might not to you."

"So it's someone she dated? Maybe a married guy?"

Jack remained silent.

"All I want is for you to identify him, right? It will be me who makes the arrest."

"Oh, for sure. As I said, we have to stay out of it to protect our informant."

"Good, as long as we're clear on that."

"At that point, as far as I am concerned, Laura and I are finished. It will be up to you. Hope you have him in cuffs before we're back."

"Hope so," said Connie, feeling relieved that Jack was going to let her handle it. "Well quit talking to me and go see her."

"Unfortunately, we discovered she started a job at a senior's lodge and won't be home until suppertime. Her parents say she is still really distraught. I don't want to bother her at work and cause a scene. We're going to wait until she gets home. I want her as relaxed as possible. Her own home will help."

"Yeah, okay," sighed Connie. "Guess another three or four hours won't hurt."

"As long as we're killing time," suggested Jack, "I remember reading your file and there were three potential witnesses you never interviewed."

"What? Those three winos?"

"Yes. As I recall, one of them was originally from the Duncan area. That's less than an hour away. Want Laura and me to make a few inquiries? Maybe check with relatives and come up with an address or something?"

"I tried before but it wouldn't hurt to ask again. That would be appreciated. Then I can stroke it off."

Jack waited patiently as Connie gave him the

details about John-Wayne Charlie and said, "We'll see what we can find out."

"You'll let me know as soon as you talk to Amanda."

"That's a promise," said Jack.

"One more thing about Amanda. An hour ago I got a call from the prosecutor handling the case on the three punks who attacked her. Defence is willing to plead to a three-year sentence for each of them to be served in juvenile detention. Ask her what she thinks."

"Amanda doesn't want to testify. I know she will go for it, but I'll still ask."

An hour later, Jack and Laura parked their car and approached a man who was working under the hood of a car in his driveway. He looked up as they approached and asked, "You from the department? The guy who called me this morning?"

"Yes," said Jack.

"My brother is around back in a shed. He carves masks. They're nice. You should buy one."

"How long has he been doing that?" asked Laura.

"A few months, but he's good. So how come he is getting some money? I'm his brother, Gunnar. How come I don't get any?"

"Are you older or younger?" asked Jack.

"I'm two years younger. What's that got to do with it?"

Jack opened his briefcase and passed Gunnar a picture of Father Brown.

"Evil eye!" said Gunnar. "So that is what this is about."

"You know him?" asked Jack.

Gunnar nodded and quietly passed the picture back to Jack. "None of us will forget him. His name is Father Brown, but all us kids called him Evil Eye because of the mark on his forehead." Gunnar looked at Jack and nodded in understanding and said, "So that is why my brother is getting money. It's for what Evil Eye did to him on Kuper Island."

Jack took a deep breath and slowly exhaled. "I'm sorry, but I lied. We are both RCMP officers. I know you tried to protect your brother by lying to one of our members a couple of months ago, so I lied, too."

Gunnar stared blandly at Jack as he tried to contemplate the logic of the situation. When he spoke, his voice became a whisper. He pointed to the picture and said, "You finally arrested him. You want John-Wayne to testify … he won't. He won't talk about it to anyone. Not even me … and I was there."

Jack and Laura exchanged a glance. Gunnar thought Father Brown was still alive.

"Please, say you can't find him," pleaded Gunnar. "My brother has lots of problems. He can't sleep … he quit drinking four months ago. This will make him start again."

"Tell me about Evil Eye," replied Jack.

Gunnar leaned back against the front of the car. His eyes brimmed over and he wiped his face with his hand, leaving a black streak of grease down his cheek.

He breathed heavily for a moment and his eyes drifted off into space. Finally he spoke.

"All us kids had to play basketball in a gym. We all had numbers on our shirts. I was about seven and stayed close to John-Wayne because he was my big brother. All you could hear was the sound of the ball bouncing and kids' feet movin'. Every day Evil Eye would come out from the office above and stand on a balcony and watch us. He would call out a number and the kid with that number had to go up to his office. One day he called mine and John-Wayne traded shirts with me. I never did have to go up there, but we all knew what Evil Eye was doing."

"We need to talk to your brother alone," said Jack.

"He won't talk about it. He's too ashamed."

"That's too bad. I think he's a hero," replied Jack.

"He's my hero."

"Let us talk to him alone," replied Jack. "Maybe we can work something out."

"You know what was real bad?" said Gunnar as Jack and Laura turned to leave.

Jack and Laura shook their heads.

"After Evil Eye called a number, all the rest of us kids were real happy and laughed and played. That still bothers me."

"Because you knew you were safe for another day," said Jack.

Gunnar nodded.

* * *

Jack and Laura followed a path behind the house that was bordered by wildflowers. The sun was shining and it was a beautiful day. *Too beautiful*, thought Jack, *to be going to jail*. He stopped and placed a hand on Laura's shoulders.

"What is it?" she asked.

"We can't do this," he replied.

"You son of a bitch."

Jack's mouth gaped open. He could not remember the last time he ever heard Laura swear, let alone at him. "You're angry with me because —"

"Damn right I'm angry with you. Angry that you would even have to ask me."

They found John-Wayne alone in a shed. He was sitting on a wooden stool, carving a wooden mask that he held between his knees. He looked up when they came in and said, "You want to buy a mask ... or are you from the government?"

"We're with the RCMP," said Jack. "We're here because of this guy," he added, holding out the picture of Father Brown for John-Wayne to take.

John-Wayne refused to take the picture in his hand. Instead, he slowly put the mask and the carving tools on the ground and stood up. His face showed no emotion. "I wondered when you would come for me," he said, holding his wrists straight out in front of him so he could be handcuffed.

"We're not handcuffing you," said Jack. "Put your arms down."

John-Wayne slowly lowered his arms and said, "I don't care that I gotta go to jail. I'd smash his head again if I could."

Jack remembered that Connie had some hold-back evidence. He looked at John-Wayne and asked, "What else did you do to him?"

"I killed him."

"I know, but besides hitting him with a cement block, what else did you do?"

John-Wayne stood quietly for a moment and shook his head. "I used to drink. Hard to remember."

"You did something besides hit him on the head," said Jack. "Close your eyes. Try to remember. What sounds did you hear? Maybe a smell or the feel of something ..."

John-Wayne closed his eyes briefly and said, "I stomped him after."

"Stomped him?" asked Jack.

John-Wayne turned slightly so Laura couldn't see and pointed to his crotch. "Down there," he said. "I stomped him a bunch."

"Did you ever tell anyone about what Father Brown did to you?" asked Laura.

John-Wayne shook his head.

"Or what you did to Father Brown?" asked Jack.

"No. I don't want to talk about it with nobody."

Jack looked at Laura and she gave a slight nod of approval.

"There is something I need to tell you," said Jack. "Please listen carefully. There is no evidence to prove what you did. Possibly a hair, but that could have been blown into the yard or left there by you some other time."

"But I told you," said John-Wayne, sounding matter-of-fact. There was no anger or emotion in his voice. He looked at Jack, once more raised his wrists and said simply, "I know you will make me pay for what I have done."

Pay? You have suffered in silence all these years … you have already paid and will no doubt keep on paying. Jack cleared his throat and said, "I'm sorry, I haven't been able to hear a word you said so far. How about you, Laura?"

"What did you say?" she asked, cupping a hand to her ear. "I can't hear a thing. It must be the wind."

Jack looked at John-Wayne and in a loud voice said, "The person in the photograph we showed you was murdered near an alley that you used to frequent. We came to ask you if you saw or know anything that would help our investigation."

John-Wayne looked confused.

"Did you watch someone attack Father Brown?"

"No."

"Thank you."

"That I heard," added Laura, dutifully making an entry into her notebook.

John-Wayne slowly lowered his arms. Jack put a hand on his shoulders and said, "Good luck with your life. I think you're on the right path, but what the hell do I know, I'm white."

On the drive back to Victoria, Laura turned to Jack and said, "What are we going to do about Noah? He could end up like John-Wayne."

"I'm going to talk to Victim Services to start with. I don't need to say anything about John-Wayne. With Father Brown being at Kuper Island and the symptoms that Noah is exhibiting, I think it will be self-evident."

"Noah may clam up and deny everything."

"We can be pretty sure that the girly magazines that Gabriel found under his mattress were given to him by Father Brown. If Noah needs prompting, I will tell him that we found Father Brown's fingerprints all through the magazines. Noah is emotionally distraught. He will open up."

"And if Connie finds out? What then? She might piece it together like you did."

"I'll tell Connie that I suspect Father Brown of being a pedophile because of Noah's behaviour. It won't matter. She will still think Cocktail is the murderer, especially after my next phone call to her."

Jack and Laura went to Amanda's parents' house, arriving at the same time she did. She introduced them to her parents, after which Jack said, "Is there someplace we could talk in private?"

Moments later, Jack, Laura, and Amanda were alone in a spare bedroom that had been turned into an office.

"Where are you working?" asked Laura.

"I volunteer to read aloud at a senior's lodge," said Amanda.

"The opposite end of the spectrum from teaching childen," replied Laura.

Amanda pursed her lips and said, "Not really. A lot of the seniors behave like children." She looked at Jack and said, "You wanted to speak to me in private. What's up?"

"To start with, the defence lawyers for the three punks who attacked you have offered to have their clients plead guilty with a joint submission for a three-year sentence in juvenile detention. The prosecutor will leave the decision up to you."

"No decision there," replied Amanda, looking relieved. "I told you I don't want to testify. Three years is better than I expected."

Jack nodded.

"Did you come all the way over here to ask me that?"

"No," replied Jack. "What can you tell us about Lyle Ryker?"

"Lyle," said Amanda, sitting back in her chair with surprise. "Well ... I was told he used to be a nice guy. The year before I did my practicum at QE, he and his wife lost their first baby to SIDS. I know they went through a rough time and ended up getting divorced."

"You ever go out with him?"

"No, he's much older than me."

"So ... never anything between you?" asked Jack.

"Well ... he made several passes," admitted Amanda. "It was getting embarrassing. That was my first teaching job ... I wasn't sure how to handle it and not cause a stink."

"What did you do?" asked Laura.

"I finally threatened to go to Mr. Bloomquist and complain of sexual harassment. That put a stop to it. When the semester was over, he quit teaching. I think the sight of children bothered him. He never got over losing his baby. When he left, Mrs. Jenkins replaced him as a chemistry teacher."

"Chemistry?" replied Jack. "Bloomquist said he was replaced as a math teacher."

"He did that, as well. Many teachers handle more than one subject. Why all the questions about Lyle?"

"He is the person who goes by the name of Cocktail. The one pulling the strings with The Brotherhood. The one responsible for your attack."

"No!" said Amanda, putting her hand to her mouth. "Oh, no," she repeated and began to cry.

Jack put his arm around her shoulder to comfort her.

"Are you sure?" she sobbed.

"Positive," replied Jack. "This is highly confidential, but he set up an ambush and tried to kill four men last night over the war that The Brotherhood are having. The victims escaped, but I happened to be in a position to see Lyle myself. There is no doubt."

Amanda touched the scars under her bangs and said, "He told them to do this, didn't he?"

"Yes."

"My God," replied Amanda, slowly regaining her composure. "So he has been arrested ... you want me to testify about my past relationship with him? I told you ... I won't go through that again."

"He hasn't been arrested yet, but could be soon. The men he tried to kill last night are also looking for him."

"I hope they find him first."

Jack nodded and said, "I have to send a text message. Would you mind making us a cup of coffee? We need to talk to you about all the other teachers to ensure that Ryker did not have an accomplice."

It was several cups of coffee later when Jack received a text message back that read: 666-0. Jack excused himself to send a short message to Natasha.

Connie rolled her eyes when Crime Stoppers called to say they had been given a tip about a man named Lyle Ryker who had confided in the tipster that he had murdered Father Brown. The tipster gave enough details to sound credible.

Jack's BlackBerry rang immediately. He walked out into the hallway so he could talk in private before answering.

"Hi, Connie, I was about to call you."

"Really? What on earth for?"

"Uh, to let you know that Laura and I located that wino for you. John-Wayne Charlie."

"Is that a fact? That is why you were going to call me if I hadn't called you first?"

"Of course. I'm afraid it's not good news. John-Wayne doesn't know anything. Looks like we've hit another dead end."

"Yeah, thanks, I'll stroke him off my list. Well, goodbye …" Connie didn't hang up and could hear Jack's breathing on the other end of the line. She enjoyed making him wait for the news she knew he already possessed. Finally she said, "Oh, I almost forgot the reason I called. There is something I am sure you will be interested in."

"Oh?"

"Crime Stoppers got a tip that a Lyle Ryker killed Father Brown. Have you ever heard of him? Do you think the tip is genuine?"

"Lyle Ryker … well, I'll be damned. Did you know that he used to teach chemistry at Queen Elizabeth? Laura and I are having coffee with Amanda. She mentioned she had to threaten Ryker with sexual harassment once. Could explain her vicious attack. Cocktail also resembles the picture in the yearbook, except for the beard."

"Anything else that would support the, uh, tipster?"

"Ryker owns a company that supplies humanitarian aid."

"Humanitarian aid? I said, help my investigation, not hinder it."

"Let me finish. The aid is in the form of medical equipment to hospitals and research facilities in third-world countries."

"Chemicals and glassware!"

"You got it," replied Jack. "Do you have an address for him?"

"Yup."

"Be damned careful," cautioned Jack. "I saw first-hand how violent he was last night."

"If he comes to the door with a pitchfork, I'll double-tap two into his chest," replied Connie.

"Good. Watch yourself. The guy is a real psycho. Last night he said he was even going to stomp on my nuts after he killed me. Something about making sure I never spawned again."

"He what?"

"Sorry, I'm talking low. I said —"

"No, I heard you! ... Jack! That's the hold-back information. Cocktail ... I mean, Ryker, that's what he did to Father Brown. He stomped on his crotch after he killed him."

"Wow. Good going, Connie. You got your murderer. Go get the son of a bitch!"

"I'm on my way."

"Let me know, will you? Laura and I will stay with Amanda until you call. In fact, my battery is getting low in my cell. I'll give you Amanda's number."

An hour later, Connie called Jack back from the living room of Lyle Ryker's house.

"You got him?" asked Jack, sounding excited.

"Only pieces of him," replied Connie, suspiciously.

"What do you mean?"

"We're too late. Looks like his enemies in The Brotherhood found him first. Murdered about an hour ago. City Homicide were here when we arrived. Someone took off his balls with a 12-gauge. Whoever did it let him crawl across his rug and then took off the top of his head."

"Guess that's what happens when you botch the murder of a bunch of thugs. Saves going to court."

After Connie hung up, Dallas looked at her and said, "Well, at least Jack and Laura were in Victoria when the murder happened."

"Yeah ... hell of a good alibi, isn't it?"

Epilogue

1. *June 11, 2008 — The prime minister of Canada, the Right Honourable Stephen Harper, on behalf of the government of Canada, made a Statement of Apology to former students of Indian Residential Schools. Further details are available at:*
www.ainc-inac.gc.ca/ai/rqpi/apo/index-eng.asp.

2. *Faith's prognosis looks good and she has remained cancer-free for five years. Her brother, Noah, is progressing on an emotional level with continued support from a psychologist who specializes in cases of sexual abuse.*

3. *December 13 — Jack and Natasha made an announcement. It's a boy!*

More Jack Taggart Mysteries by Don Easton

Loose Ends
A Jack Taggart Mystery
978-1550025651
$11.99

Jack Taggart, an undercover Mountie, lives in a world where the good guys and the bad guys change places in a heartbeat. Taggart is very good at what he does. Too good to be playing by the rules. The brass decide to assign a new partner to spy on him. Taggart's new partner discovers a society dependent upon unwritten rules. To break these rules is to lose respect. To lose respect is to lose one's life. *Loose Ends* is terrifying. It is a tale of violence, corruption, and retribution, but it is also a story of honour and respect.

Above Ground
A Jack Taggart Mystery
978-1550026818
$11.99

For RCMP detective Jack Taggart, the consequences of his actions in *Loose Ends* linger. His deal with Damien, leader of the Satans Wrath motorcycle gang, has put him in a bind and has jeopardized an informant in the gang. Meanwhile, other members of the gang, led by a mysterious figure known only as "The Boss," have been working to eliminate Taggart by destroying the lives of anyone with connections to him. And if the bad guys aren't enough of an obstacle, there are problems to be found on the force itself. With Jack's life and career on the line, *Above Ground* is a tough and gritty follow-up that will more than satisfy readers who were pulled into the dark Vancouver underworld by *Loose Ends*.

Angel in the Full Moon
A Jack Taggart Mystery
978-1550028133
$11.99

In this sequel to *Loose Ends* and *Above Ground*, Jack Taggart continues as an undercover Mountie whose quest for justice takes him from the sunny, tourist-laden beaches of Cuba to the ghettos of Hanoi. His targets deal in human flesh, smuggling unwitting victims for the sex trade. Jack's personal vendetta for justice is questioned by his partner, until he reveals the secret behind his motivation, exposing the very essence of his soul. This is the world of the undercover operative: a world of lies, treachery, and deception. A world where violence erupts without warning, like a ticking time bomb on a crowded bus. It isn't a matter of if that bomb will go off — it is a matter of how close you are to it when it does.

Samurai Code
A Jack Taggart Mystery
978-1554886975
$11.99

In the fourth Jack Taggart Mystery, the implacable Mountie goes undercover to follow the trail of a cheap Saturday-night special found at the scene of a murder. He traces the gun until the trail leads him to a suspected heroin importer. Taggart poses as an Irish gangster and penetrates the criminal organization, only to discover that the real crime boss is a mysterious figure out of Asia. When Taggart and his partner find themselves alone and without backup in the lair of one of the largest yakuza organized crime families in Japan, the clash of culture explodes into violence when their real identities are discovered.

Available at your favourite bookseller.

DUNDURN
www.dundurn.com

What did you think of this book?
Visit *www.dundurn.com*
for reviews, videos, updates, and more!